A Frank O'Connor Reader

Richard Fallis, *Series Editor*

Frank O'Connor
Courtesy of Harriet Sheehy.

A
Frank
O'Connor
Reader

Edited by
Michael Steinman

SYRACUSE UNIVERSITY PRESS

Syracuse University Press Edition 1994
94 95 96 97 98 99   6 5 4 3 2 1

The paper used in this publication meets the minimum requirements of American National Standards for Information Sciences—Permanence of Paper for Printed Library Materials, ANSI Z39.48-1984. ∞™

Library of Congress Cataloging-in-Publication Data
O'Connor, Frank, 1903–1966.
A Frank O'Connor reader / edited by Michael Steinman.
p.   cm.—(Irish studies)
Includes bibliographical references (p.).
ISBN 0-8156-2614-2.—ISBN 0-8156-0278-2 (paper)
1. Ireland—Literary collections.   I. Steinman, Michael (Michael
A.)   II. Title.   III. Series: Irish studies (Syracuse, N.Y.)
PR6029.D58A6   1994
823'.912—dc20   93-26230

Manufactured in the United States of America

I prefer to write about Ireland and Irish people merely because I know to a syllable how everything in Ireland can be said: but that doesn't mean that the stories themselves were inspired by events in Ireland. Many of them should really have English backgrounds; a few should even have American ones. Only language and circumstance are local and national; all the rest is, or should be, part of the human condition, and as true for America and England as it is for Ireland. The nicest compliment I have ever received was from a student while the authorities of the university were considering the important question whether I was a resident or non-resident alien. "Mr. O'Connor, I find it hard to think of you as an alien at all."

Frank O'Connor,
October 1952

Michael Steinman is associate professor of English at Nassau Community College, Garden City, New York. He is the author of *Yeats's Heroic Figures: Wilde, Parnell, Swift, Casement* and *Frank O'Connor at Work* (Syracuse University Press, 1990).

Contents

Poetry—Translations

Self-Portraits

Essays and Portraits

Acknowledgments

This book would not have taken shape without the help and encouragement of Harriet O'Donovan Sheehy, who has generously granted permission to reprint all the Frank O'Connor materials it includes. Ruth Sherry's guidance and scholarship have been invaluable. Carmen Russell Hurff (University of Florida Libraries) and Marilyn Rosenthal (Nassau Community College Library) magically unearthed hidden treasures. I am grateful to Terence Walsh for allowing me to reprint his late father's translation of "Darcy in Tír na nÓg." Many thanks, as well, to Thomas Flanagan, William Maxwell, Joan Daves, Richard Fallis, John L. Fell, Maureen Murphy, Robert Rhodes, William McBrien, Cynthia Maude-Gembler, Charles Backus, and my colleagues at Nassau Community College. As always, my greatest debt is to my wife.

Introduction

A distinctive voice, ardor, and knowledge reverberate through Frank O'Connor's writings: stories, novels, biography and autobiography, poetry and translations, memoirs, plays, essays, journalism. The roster of his peers and colleagues who praised him fervently is impressive: W. B. Yeats, Sean O'Faoláin, George Russell, William Maxwell, V. S. Pritchett, Elizabeth Bowen, Thomas Flanagan. This collection presents a selection from his fiction, poetry, essays, and portraits—all memorable and almost all currently unavailable.

Not long ago, O'Connor's work was read enthusiastically in America, Ireland, Great Britain, Germany, Denmark, and Japan, yet he has been less celebrated than he deserves since his death in 1966 for reasons that have nothing to do with his achievement. He was an extraordinary short story writer, but that form seems an evanescent one, finding only brief fame before vanishing in a readers' Limbo between its first publication and the eventual collection or anthology. Most of O'Connor's fiction first appeared in weekly magazines, media noted for their disposable character, and loyal publishers seemed less so after his death.

His fame was also limited by the paradox of early renown, the result of "Guests of the Nation," and his later reputation, based on the affectionate, bittersweet "My Oedipus Complex," "Judas," "First Confession," stories that have buoyed many anthologies. Those who know only his most popular stories might be unaware that his vision was subtler, darker, and his range far broader than the occasional happy ending would suggest. In thirty years, he wrote more than two hundred stories, a great number of them notable, published in ten collections. They offer a close examination, amused, rueful, or angry, of a middle-class Irish world whose inhabitants seem quite familiar. Characters under immense emotional pressure are transfigured against recognizable backdrops with a few crucial props—a card game, a bottle of homemade liquor, a Sacred Heart lamp. He chronicles loss, loneliness, and estrangement, yearnings that cannot be spoken, exiles, solitary figures amid crowds and conversations. Emotionally complex and often painful, his stories depict people uprooted by forces they cannot control and do not wholly comprehend. Although the stories take place in kitchens, bedrooms, and living rooms, their results are startling disorientations as the familiar, comfortable reality cracks open to reveal abysses beneath. Passions are strong, whether expressed or suppressed. Events transform the participants irrevocably; O'Connor spoke of "an iron bar" that "must have been bent and been seen to be bent," (*The Lonely Voice,* 216) or, as Bonaparte says, ending "Guests of the Nation," "And anything that happened me afterwards, I never felt the same about again." A few stories end with conflicts resolved, but those endings seem well-deserved rewards for great labors.

Some have judged his fiction simple, unfashionable, even dated. (Such perceptions may have accounted for O'Connor's wariness of Joyce, whose example could trouble writers who chose to be forthright.) True, an O'Connor story is comprehensible on its first reading, but it reveals more each time because its simplicity is deceptive. He is surely old-fashioned but only to those who would find Austen hopelessly distant or to those put off by the book-jacket portrait of a silver-haired and bespectacled author. Superficially, his stories do not seem "contemporary"; they do not grapple with topical politics, and his portrayals of love are emotionally frank, not erotically graphic. His dear friend Richard Ellmann, introducing the 1981 *Collected Stories,* fondly but wrongly depicted O'Connor as a citizen of a departed world: "His stories preserve in ink like amber his perceptive, amused, and sometimes tender observations of the fabric of Irish customs, pieties, superstitions, loves, and hates. He wrote at that moment when that fabric was being slowly torn by modern conditions" (vii). I prefer William Maxwell's faith in O'Connor's lasting presence: "In speaking of him I cannot bring myself to use the past tense" (Sheehy, *Michael/Frank,* 147). Indeed, we feel kin to his blood-warm, surprising characters. If we have not ourselves experienced the events and emotions of his fiction, we easily feel that we might. If one grew up in Brooklyn, not Cork; if one was never a wild youth in a provincial town or an outraged woman bolting the door against her husband, what matter? We know the souls we meet on every page, and his work retains its power to move and to startle.

His moral sense is equally timeless for his writing is illumined by a deep intuitive feeling for life's complexity. In his risky universe, disillusionment and frustration are constants—he celebrates our propensity for making wrong choices while we tell ourselves that we are striving for happiness and order—but joy appears as well. Compassionate rather than cynical, he was always intrigued by the people he met and those he created (who borrowed from one another). Not given to sentimentality, he could say, "I can't imagine anything better in the world than people" and "I can't write about something I don't admire—it goes back to the old concept of the celebration: you celebrate the hero, an idea" (*Writers at Work*, 172, 181).

O'Connor was rooted in a tradition of storytelling, his narrators observing everyone in the smaller community, whether it be household, town, or city street, minutely aware of "what the neighbors think" as well as the larger world outside and the two often contradictory expectations. Every story bestows—as its gift to readers—his detailed scrutiny of the emotional currents of everyday life, the stresses and affections of lovers, parents, children, the tensions between the intimacies we seek and the forces that isolate us. He consciously chose a different path from his peers, perceiving himself a "nineteenth-century realist," who had grown up in a provincial world, influenced by French and Russian masters and their work "domestic and civic . . . concentrate[d] on the study of society and the place of the individual in it" (*The Mirror in the Roadway*, 12). What he made of his antecedents—Chekhov, Flaubert, and the native oral tradition, dramatic and improvisatory—remains vivid.

This traditional worldview is complemented by the clear structures of his fiction. For him, art required design, inspiration and passion had to be married to techniques that would convey them wholly, and his stories have shape and focus. Organic form, "the form of life itself . . . not imposed" but "inherent in the experience," which would "follow a man's life or character," was essential (Breit, *The Writer Observed*, 261). Even when depicting emotional chaos, his fiction had its own logic: "You have to have a theme, a story to tell. Here's a man at the other side of the table and I'm talking to him; I'm going to tell him something that will interest him. . . . The moment you grab somebody by the lapels and you've got something to tell, that's a real story. It means that you want to tell him and think the story is interesting in itself. If you start describing your own personal experiences, something that's only of interest to yourself, then you cannot express yourself, you cannot say, ultimately, what you think about human beings" (*Writers at Work*, 180–81).

Mozart, perhaps more than any single writer, seems his spiritual ancestor (see "For a Two-Hundredth Birthday") for the delights O'Connor cherished in Mozart are evident in his work: its intermingled sadness and exuberance, melancholy and wit; its consistent clarity; the way each distinctive voice sings its own resonant song. Those musical voices are all; for him, the ideal story "rang with a man's voice speaking," and his narrators were enthusiastically involved listeners, as he was: "If you're the sort of a person that meets a girl in the street and instantly notices the color of her eyes and of her hair and the sort of dress she's wearing, then you're not in the least like me. I just notice a feeling from people. I notice particularly the cadence of their voices, the sort of phrases they'll use, and that's what I'm all the time trying to hear in my head, how people word things—because everybody speaks an entirely different language, that's really what it amounts to" (*Writers at Work*, 169).

Approximately half of this collection is devoted to his short fiction; fifteen stories are currently unavailable, including "The Rebel," never before published, and "Darcy in Tír na nÓg," only recently translated into English. I begin with his 1930 masterpiece, "Guests of the Nation," in a superior later version and conclude with two little-known stories from his last decade. In between, a reader will encounter remarkable yet familiar individuals: a bride revolted by her husband's sexuality; an old countryman who has cracked his neighbor's skull in disagreement; a young woman who has poisoned her miserly spouse; precocious boys, adolescent voyeurs, self-styled saviors; lovers and spouses; policemen and priests. Their situations are equally varied from the most remote countryside to town, suburb, and city, from bedroom to office to church to pub, from the Troubles of British-Irish warfare to the troubles of love, marriage, and an often censorious community.

Not surprisingly, O'Connor's prose self-portraits are as perceptive and ingratiating; his memoirs and fiction draw strength from each other, and readers of his first autobiography, *An Only Child*, have never forgotten it. This collection includes comic and moving self-portraits, more than reminiscences, as O'Connor considers childhood from different angles, his year's internment in a prison camp, and his creative process. Although the two interviews I have included are not as evocative, they provide glimpses of O'Connor that few got.

He began as a lyric poet, yet his poetic achievements were his translations from the Irish, where he combined a scholar's accuracy with a poet's intuition. When an eighteenth-century original was bawdy and vigorous, (*The Midnight Court*) he reproduced its swagger faithfully; when tender ("I Am Stretched on Your Grave") or passionate ("The Lament for Art O'Leary"), his rendering was equally sensitive. The poet Patrick Kavanagh said, "Surely nobody has ever done such exciting translations as he has. What a lovely cadence he brings to his re-creation. . . . How warmly human, rooted in life." ("Coloured Balloons," 13). His friend Daniel Binchy knew O'Connor as a remarkable collaborator: "It was not merely his power to make you share his own excitement and enthusiasm. There was the fascination of watching him wrestle with a problem which had baffled the professionals, and after a number of wildly false starts, produce the right solution. 'Nonsense!' he would cry out against the received translation. 'No poet would ever have said a thing like that. It must be——' and he would propose something quite off the beam. 'Impossible, Michael, the grammar would be all wrong.' 'Well, what about this?' And so on until, suddenly, the lightning struck and you said to yourself half-incredulously: 'He's done it again.' " O'Connor's genius was not simple intuition: "He worked tirelessly at Old and Middle Irish, so much so that in fact professional scholars like myself were shamed by his wholly disinterested pursuit of the subject we were paid to study. His own copies of the texts were black with notes and cross-references; how on earth did he manage to cram so much research into the intervals between his own writing?" (Sheehy, *Michael/Frank*, 18–19).

Fiction, memoirs, and translations form only a portion of his work. In thirty-five years, in addition to stories, he wrote a biography, an autobiography, three travel books, two novels, six books of literary criticism, five plays, and nine books of poetry as well as more than two hundred and fifty essays and articles. Hugh Kenner whimsically titles him "penman" in *A Colder Eye,* praise rather than disparagement. When a story or translation proved recalcitrant, he would write with conviction and knowledge on Irish history, politics, archaeology, and culture, current fiction and theatre, dream interpretation, John F. Kennedy, Shakespeare, Roger Casement, Michael Collins, Mary Lavin, Proust, Woolf, Arthur Miller, Anouilh, Trollope, Shaw, Swift, Dickens, Hardy, Flaubert, Austen, Chekhov, Synge, O'Casey, AE, Yeats, and Joyce. His prose is always compelling even when one is sure that its eloquent statements are debatable. I have selected essays offering new perspectives on Yeats, Synge, Lady Gregory, Joyce, New York City, Mozart, Ireland, English and Irish bars, and a surprising religious experience. Sean O'Faoláin, who met O'Connor in 1918, sketched his impression of his friend's "intuitive processes": "He was like a man who takes a machine gun to a shooting gallery. Everybody falls flat on his face, the proprietor at once takes to the hills, and when it is all over, and cautiously peep up, you find that he has wrecked the place but got three perfect bull's-eyes" (*Vive Moi!* 369). Readers will find these essays less anarchic but no less illuminating.

.   .   .

Introducing *The Stories of Frank O'Connor* (1952), the first collection of his finest stories, he spoke of "the Perfect Book," which would sum up all he had ever wanted to do. Recalling his struggles, he noted ruefully that the Perfect Book began "to dwindle to the proportions of Just Another Book" (*Stories of Frank O'Connor,* "Author! Author!" v–vi). This *Reader* is no Perfect Book; if that eluded O'Connor, how should an editor presume? The Perfect Book of O'Connor's lifework might be that personal anthology, not restricted to a single collection, that anyone might compile after reading him deeply. I hope this selection inspires others to take more O'Connor volumes off the shelves and fix them indelibly in their minds and hearts.

For those who wish to know more of his life and work than I have offered here and in the notes that preface each selection, I recommend *Michael/Frank: Studies on Frank O'Connor,* edited by the late Maurice Sheehy, an unequalled collection of essays with the best bibliography now available.

Melville, New York   Michael Steinman
March 1993

A Frank O'Connor Reader

Stories

Guests of the Nation

Simultaneously a story of war's inhumanity and the friendships it de-stroys, "Guests of the Nation" moves inexorably from harmony to des-olation. Although O'Connor said modestly it was only an imitation of an Isaac Babel story in The Red Cavalry, *its singularity came from his experiences during the Troubles: "One day, when I was sitting on my bed in an Irish internment camp . . . I overheard a group of country boys talking about two English soldiers whom they had held as hostages and who soon got to know the countryside better than their guards. It was obvious from the conversation that the two English boys had won the affection and understanding of our own fellows, though it wasn't the understanding of soldiers who find they have much in common, but the understanding of two conflicting ways of life which must either fight or be friends" ("Interior Voices," 10).*

A first reading will leave one shaken by the cold cruelty of those who profess devotion to "duty," "principle," and ideology, ignoring human beings; deeper readings reveal that every detail is resonant from "foreign dances" and card games among "chums" to arguments about capitalism and life after death, Belcher's last comments about home and family. Appropriately, John Hildebidle has described it as a story of family, although its members are related to one another by circumstances and affection rather than blood (180). Bonaparte's famous last sentence, "And anything that happened me afterwards, I never felt the same about again," echoes Gogol's "The Overcoat" and is the introduction to any O'Connor short story—a transfiguring experience for its characters and the reader.

This 1954 version departs stylistically from the first text, written "with the mind of a young poet . . . in a fever, weeping, laughing, singing the dialogue to myself" (Voices, 201–2); the revision gains clarity from

*two decades of experience. Had O'Connor written no more after March
1930, we would still remember him for this story.*

At dusk the big Englishman, Belcher, would shift his long legs out of
the ashes and say "Well, chums, what about it?" and Noble or me would
say "All right, chum" (for we had picked up some of their curious
expressions), and the little Englishman, Hawkins, would light the lamp
and bring out the cards. Sometimes Jeremiah Donovan would come up
and supervise the game and get excited over Hawkins's cards, which he
always played badly, and shout at him as if he was one of our own "Ah,
you divil, you, why didn't you play the tray?"

But ordinarily Jeremiah was a sober and contented poor devil like the
big Englishman, Belcher, and was looked up to only because he was a
fair hand at documents, though he was slow enough even with them. He
wore a small cloth hat and big gaiters over his long pants, and you
seldom saw him with his hands out of his pockets. He reddened when
you talked to him, tilting from toe to heel and back, and looking down
all the time at his big farmer's feet. Noble and me used to make fun of
his broad accent, because we were from the town.

I couldn't at the time see the point of me and Noble guarding Belcher
and Hawkins at all, for it was my belief that you could have planted that
pair down anywhere from this to Claregalway and they'd have taken
root there like a native weed. I never in my short experience seen two
men to take to the country as they did.

They were handed on to us by the Second Battalion when the search
for them became too hot, and Noble and myself, being young, took over
with a natural feeling of responsibility, but Hawkins made us look like
fools when he showed that he knew the country better than we did.

"You're the bloke they calls Bonaparte," he says to me. "Mary Brigid
0'Connell told me to ask you what you done with the pair of her brother's socks you borrowed."

For it seemed, as they explained it, that the Second used to have little
evenings, and some of the girls of the neighbourhood turned in, and,
seeing they were such decent chaps, our fellows couldn't leave the two
Englishmen out of them. Hawkins learned to dance "The Walls of Limerick," "The Siege of Ennis," and "The Waves of Tory" as well as any
of them, though, naturally, he couldn't return the compliment, because
our lads at that time did not dance foreign dances on principle.

So whatever privileges Belcher and Hawkins had with the Second they just naturally took with us, and after the first day or two we gave up all pretence of keeping a close eye on them. Not that they could have got far, for they had accents you could cut with a knife and wore khaki tunics and overcoats with civilian pants and boots. But it's my belief that they never had any idea of escaping and were quite content to be where they were.

It was a treat to see how Belcher got off with the old woman of the house where we were staying. She was a great warrant to scold, and cranky even with us, but before ever she had a chance of giving our guests, as I may call them, a lick of her tongue, Belcher had made her his friend for life. She was breaking sticks, and Belcher, who hadn't been more than ten minutes in the house, jumped up from his seat and went over to her.

"Allow me, madam," he says, smiling his queer little smile, "please allow me"; and he takes the bloody hatchet. She was struck too paralytic to speak, and after that, Belcher would be at her heels, carrying a bucket, a basket, or a load of turf, as the case might be. As Noble said, he got into looking before she leapt, and hot water, or any little thing she wanted, Belcher would have it ready for her. For such a huge man (and though I am five foot ten myself I had to look up at him) he had an uncommon shortness—or should I say lack?—of speech. It took us some time to get used to him, walking in and out, like a ghost, without a word. Especially because Hawkins talked enough for a platoon, it was strange to hear big Belcher with his toes in the ashes come out with a solitary "Excuse me, chum," or "That's right, chum." His one and only passion was cards, and I will say for him that he was a good card-player. He could have fleeced myself and Noble, but whatever we lost to him Hawkins lost to us, and Hawkins played with the money Belcher gave him.

Hawkins lost to us because he had too much old gab, and we probably lost to Belcher for the same reason. Hawkins and Noble would spit at one another about religion into the early hours of the morning, and Hawkins worried the soul out of Noble, whose brother was a priest, with a string of questions that would puzzle a cardinal. To make it worse, even in treating of holy subjects, Hawkins had a deplorable tongue. I never in all my career met a man who could mix such a variety of cursing and bad language into an argument. He was a terrible man, and a fright to argue. He never did a stroke of work, and when he had no one else to talk to, he got stuck in the old woman.

He met his match in her, for one day when he tried to get her to complain profanely of the drought, she gave him a great comedown by blaming it entirely on Jupiter Pluvius (a deity neither Hawkins nor I had ever heard of, though Noble said that among the pagans it was believed that he had something to do with the rain). Another day he was swearing at the capitalists for starting the German war when the old lady laid down her iron, puckered up her little crab's mouth, and said: "Mr. Hawkins, you can say what you like about the war, and think you'll deceive me because I'm only a simple poor countrywoman, but I know what started the war. It was the Italian Count that stole the heathen divinity out of the temple in Japan. Believe me, Mr. Hawkins, nothing but sorrow and want can follow the people that disturb the hidden powers."

A queer old girl, all right.

. . .

We had our tea one evening, and Hawkins lit the lamp and we all sat into cards. Jeremiah Donovan came in too, and sat down and watched us for a while, and it suddenly struck me that he had no great love for the two Englishmen. It came as a great surprise to me, because I hadn't noticed anything about him before.

Late in the evening a really terrible argument blew up between Hawkins and Noble, about capitalists and priests and love of your country.

"The capitalists," says Hawkins with an angry gulp, "pays the priests to tell you about the next world so as you won't notice what the bastards are up to in this."

"Nonsense, man!" says Noble, losing his temper. "Before ever a capitalist was thought of, people believed in the next world."

Hawkins stood up as though he was preaching a sermon.

"Oh, they did, did they?" he says with a sneer. "They believed all the things you believe, isn't that what you mean? And you believe that God created Adam, and Adam created Shem, and Shem created Jehoshophat. You believe all that silly old fairytale about Eve and Eden and the apple. Well, listen to me, chum. If you're entitled to hold a silly belief like that, I'm entitled to hold my silly belief—which is that the first thing your God created was a bleeding capitalist, with morality and Rolls Royce complete. Am I right, chum?" he says to Belcher.

"You're right, chum," says Belcher with his amused smile, and got up

from the table to stretch his long legs into the fire and stroke his moustache. So, seeing that Jeremiah Donovan was going, and that there was
no knowing when the argument about religion would be over, I went
out with him. We strolled down to the village together, and then he
stopped and started blushing and mumbling and saying I ought to be
behind, keeping guard on the prisoners. I didn't like the tone he took
with me, and anyway I was bored with life in the cottage, so I replied by
asking him what the hell we wanted guarding them at all for. I told him
I'd talked it over with Noble, and that we'd both rather be out with a
fighting column.

"What use are those fellows to us?" says I.

He looked at me in surprise and said: "I thought you knew we were
keeping them as hostages."

"Hostages?" I said.

"The enemy have prisoners belonging to us," he says, "and now
they're talking of shooting them. If they shoot our prisoners, we'll shoot
theirs."

"Shoot them?" I said.

"What else did you think we were keeping them for?" he says.

"Wasn't it very unforeseen of you not to warn Noble and myself of
that in the beginning?" I said.

"How was it?" says he. "You might have known it."

"We couldn't know it, Jeremiah Donovan," says I. "How could we
when they were on our hands so long?"

"The enemy have our prisoners as long and longer," says he.

"That's not the same thing at all," says I.

"What difference is there?" says he.

I couldn't tell him, because I knew he wouldn't understand. If it was
only an old dog that was going to the vet's, you'd try and not get too
fond of him, but Jeremiah Donovan wasn't a man that would ever be in
danger of that.

"And when is this thing going to be decided?" says I.

"We might hear tonight," he says. "Or tomorrow or the next day at
latest. So if it's only hanging round here that's a trouble to you, you'll
be free soon enough."

It wasn't the hanging round that was a trouble to me at all by this
time. I had worse things to worry about. When I got back to the cottage
the argument was still on. Hawkins was holding forth in his best style,

maintaining that there was no next world, and Noble was maintaining that there was; but I could see that Hawkins had had the best of it.

"Do you know what, chum?" he was saying with a saucy smile. "I think you're just as big a bleeding unbeliever as I am. You say you believe in the next world, and you know just as much about the next world as I do, which is sweet damn-all. What's heaven? You don't know. Where's heaven? You don't know. You know sweet damn-all! I ask you again, do they wear wings?"

"Very well, then," says Noble, "they do. Is that enough for you? They do wear wings."

"Where do they get them, then? Who makes them? Have they a factory for wings? Have they a sort of store where you hands in your chit and takes your bleeding wings?"

"You're an impossible man to argue with," says Noble. "Now, listen to me——" And they were off again.

It was long after midnight when we locked up and went to bed. As I blew out the candle I told Noble what Jeremiah Donovan was after telling me. Noble took it very quietly. When we'd been in bed about an hour he asked me did I think we ought to tell the Englishmen. I didn't think we should, because it was more than likely that the English wouldn't shoot our men, and even if they did, the brigade officers, who were always up and down with the Second Battalion and knew the Englishmen well, wouldn't be likely to want them plugged. "I think so too," says Noble. "It would be great cruelty to put the wind up them now."

"It was very unforeseen of Jeremiah Donovan anyhow," says I.

It was next morning that we found it so hard to face Belcher and Hawkins. We went about the house all day scarcely saying a word. Belcher didn't seem to notice; he was stretched into the ashes as usual, with his usual look of waiting in quietness for something unforeseen to happen, but Hawkins noticed and put it down to Noble's being beaten in the argument of the night before.

"Why can't you take a discussion in the proper spirit?" he says severely. "You and your Adam and Eve! I'm a Communist, that's what I am. Communist or anarchist, it all comes to much the same thing." And for hours he went round the house, muttering when the fit took him. "Adam and Eve! Adam and Eve! Nothing better to do with their time than picking bleeding apples!"

.   .   .

I don't know how we got through that day, but I was very glad when it was over, the tea things were cleared away, and Belcher said in his peaceable way: "Well, chums, what about it?" We sat round the table and Hawkins took out the cards, and just then I heard Jeremiah Donovan's footstep on the path and a dark presentiment crossed my mind. I rose from the table and caught him before he reached the door.

"What do you want?" I asked.

"I want those two soldier friends of yours," he says, getting red.

"Is that the way, Jeremiah Donovan?" I asked.

"That's the way. There were four of our lads shot this morning, one of them a boy of sixteen."

"That's bad," I said.

At that moment Noble followed me out, and the three of us walked down the path together, talking in whispers. Feeney, the local intelligence officer, was standing by the gate.

"What are you going to do about it?" I asked Jeremiah Donovan.

"I want you and Noble to get them out; tell them they're being shifted again; that'll be the quietest way."

"Leave me out of that," says Noble under his breath.

Jeremiah Donovan looks at him hard.

"All right," he says. "You and Feeney get a few tools from the shed and dig a hole by the far end of the bog. Bonaparte and myself will be after you. Don't let anyone see you with the tools. I wouldn't like it to go beyond ourselves."

We saw Feeney and Noble go round to the shed and went in ourselves. I left Jeremiah Donovan to do the explanations. He told them that he had orders to send them back to the Second Battalion. Hawkins let out a mouthful of curses; and you could see that though Belcher didn't say anything, he was a bit upset too. The old woman was for having them stay in spite of us, and she didn't stop advising them until Jeremiah Donovan lost his temper and turned on her. He had a nasty temper, I noticed. It was pitch-dark in the cottage by this time, but no one thought of lighting the lamp, and in the darkness the two Englishmen fetched their topcoats and said good-bye to the old woman.

"Just as a man makes a home of a bleeding place, some bastard at headquarters thinks you're too cushy and shunts you off," says Hawkins, shaking her hand.

"A thousand thanks, madam," says Belcher. "A thousand thanks for everything"—as though he'd made it up.

We went round to the back of the house and down towards the bog. It was only then that Jeremiah Donovan told them. He was shaking with excitement.

"There were four of our fellows shot in Cork this morning and now you're to be shot as a reprisal."

"What are you talking about?" snaps Hawkins. "It's bad enough being mucked about as we are without having to put up with your funny jokes."

"It isn't a joke," says Donovan. "I'm sorry, Hawkins, but it's true," and begins on the usual rigmarole about duty and how unpleasant it is.

I never noticed that people who talk a lot about duty find it much of a trouble to them.

"Oh, cut it out!" says Hawkins.

"Ask Bonaparte," says Donovan, seeing that Hawkins isn't taking him seriously. "Isn't it true, Bonaparte?"

"It is," I say, and Hawkins stops.

"Ah, for Christ's sake, chum!"

"I mean it, chum," I say.

"You don't sound as if you meant it."

"If he doesn't mean it, I do," says Donovan, working himself up.

"What have you against me, Jeremiah Donovan?"

"I never said I had anything against you. But why did your people take out four of our prisoners and shoot them in cold blood?"

He took Hawkins by the arm and dragged him on, but it was impossible to make him understand that we were in earnest. I had the Smith and Wesson in my pocket and I kept fingering it and wondering what I'd do if they put up a fight for it or ran, and wishing to God they'd do one or the other. I knew if they did run for it, that I'd never fire on them. Hawkins wanted to know was Noble in it, and when we said yes, he asked us why Noble wanted to plug him. Why did any of us want to plug him? What had he done to us? Weren't we all chums? Didn't we understand him and didn't he understand us? Did we imagine for an instant that he'd shoot us for all the so-and-so officers in the so-and-so British Army?

By this time we'd reached the bog, and I was so sick I couldn't even answer him. We walked along the edge of it in the darkness, and every now and then Hawkins would call a halt and begin all over again, as if he was wound up, about our being chums, and I knew that nothing but the sight of the grave would convince him that we had to do it. And all

the time I was hoping that something would happen; that they'd run for
it or that Noble would take over the responsibility from me. I had the
feeling that it was worse on Noble than on me.

.   .

At last we saw the lantern in the distance and made towards it. Noble
was carrying it, and Feeney was standing somewhere in the darkness
behind him, and the picture of them so still and silent in the bogland
brought it home to me that we were in earnest, and banished the last bit
of hope I had.

Belcher, on recognizing Noble, said: "Hallo, chum," in his quiet way,
but Hawkins flew at him at once, and the argument began all over again,
only this time Noble had nothing to say for himself and stood with his
head down, holding the lantern between his legs.

It was Jeremiah Donovan who did the answering. For the twentieth
time, as though it was haunting his mind, Hawkins asked if anybody
thought he'd shoot Noble.

"Yes, you would," says Jeremiah Donovan.

"No, I wouldn't, damn you!"

"You would, because you'd know you'd be shot for not doing it."

"I wouldn't, not if I was to be shot twenty times over. I wouldn't
shoot a pal. And Belcher wouldn't—isn't that right, Belcher?"

"That's right, chum," Belcher said, but more by way of answering the
question than of joining in the argument. Belcher sounded as though
whatever unforeseen thing he'd always been waiting for had come at
last.

"Anyway, who says Noble would be shot if I wasn't? What do you
think I'd do if I was in his place, out in the middle of a blasted bog?"

"What would you do?" asks Donovan.

"I'd go with him wherever he was going, of course. Share my last bob
with him and stick by him through thick and thin. No one can ever say
of me that I let down a pal."

"We had enough of this," says Jeremiah Donovan, cocking his revolver. "Is there any message you want to send?"

"No, there isn't."

"Do you want to say your prayers?"

Hawkins came out with a cold-blooded remark that even shocked me
and turned on Noble again.

"Listen to me, Noble," he says. "You and me are chums. You can't come over to my side, so I'll come over to your side. That show you I mean what I say? Give me a rifle and I'll go along with you and the other lads."

Nobody answered him. We knew that was no way out.

"Hear what I'm saying?" he says. "I'm through with it. I'm a deserter or anything else you like. I don't believe in your stuff, but it's no worse than mine. That satisfy you?"

Noble raised his head, but Donovan began to speak and he lowered it again without replying.

"For the last time, have you any messages to send?" says Donovan in a cold, excited sort of voice.

"Shut up, Donovan! You don't understand me, but these lads do. They're not the sort to make a pal and kill a pal. They're not the tools of any capitalist."

I alone of the crowd saw Donovan raise his Webley to the back of Hawkins's neck, and as he did so I shut my eyes and tried to pray. Hawkins had begun to say something else when Donovan fired, and as I opened my eyes at the bang, I saw Hawkins stagger at the knees and lie out flat at Noble's feet, slowly and as quiet as a kid falling asleep, with the lantern-light on his lean legs and bright farmer's boots. We all stood very still, watching him settle out in the last agony.

Then Belcher took out a handkerchief and began to tie it about his own eyes (in our excitement we'd forgotten to do the same for Hawkins), and, seeing it wasn't big enough, turned and asked for the loan of mine. I gave it to him and he knotted the two together and pointed with his foot at Hawkins.

"He's not quite dead," he says. "Better give him another."

Sure enough, Hawkins's left knee is beginning to rise. I bend down and put my gun to his head; then, recollecting myself, I get up again. Belcher understands what's in my mind.

"Give him his first," he says. "I don't mind. Poor bastard, we don't know what's happening to him now."

I knelt and fired. By this time I didn't seem to know what I was doing. Belcher, who was fumbling a bit awkwardly with the handkerchiefs, came out with a laugh as he heard the shot. It was the first time I heard him laugh and it sent a shudder down my back; it sounded so unnatural.

"Poor bugger!" he said quietly. "And last night he was so curious about it all. It's very queer, chums, I always think. Now he knows as much about it as they'll ever let him know, and last night he was all in the dark."

Donovan helped him to tie the handkerchiefs about his eyes. "Thanks, chum," he said. Donovan asked if there were any messages he wanted sent.

"No, chum," he says. "Not for me. If any of you would like to write to Hawkins's mother, you'll find a letter from her in his pocket. He and his mother were great chums. But my missus left me eight years ago. Went away with another fellow and took the kid with her. I like the feeling of a home, as you may have noticed, but I couldn't start again after that."

It was an extraordinary thing, but in those few minutes Belcher said more than in all the weeks before. It was just as if the sound of the shot had started a flood of talk in him and he could go on the whole night like that, quite happily, talking about himself. We stood round like fools now that he couldn't see us any longer. Donovan looked at Noble, and Noble shook his head. Then Donovan raised his Webley, and at that moment Belcher gives his queer laugh again. He may have thought we were talking about him, or perhaps he noticed the same thing I'd noticed and couldn't understand it.

"Excuse me, chums," he says. "I feel I'm talking the hell of a lot, and so silly, about my being so handy about a house and things like that. But this thing came on me suddenly. You'll forgive me, I'm sure."

"You don't want to say a prayer?" asks Donovan.

"No, chum," he says. "I don't think it would help. I'm ready, and you boys want to get it over."

"You understand that we're only doing our duty?" says Donovan.

Belcher's head was raised like a blind man's, so that you could only see his chin and the tip of his nose in the lantern-light.

"I never could make out what duty was myself," he said. "I think you're all good lads, if that's what you mean. I'm not complaining."

Noble, just as if he couldn't bear any more of it, raised his fist at Donovan, and in a flash Donovan raised his gun and fired. The big man went over like a sack of meal, and this time there was no need of a second shot.

I don't remember much about the burying, but that it was worse than all the rest because we had to carry them to the grave. It was all mad lonely with nothing but a patch of lantern-light between ourselves and the dark, and birds hooting and screeching all round, disturbed by the guns. Noble went through Hawkins's belongings to find the letter from his mother, and then joined his hands together. He did the same with Belcher. Then, when we'd filled in the grave, we separated from Jeremiah Donovan and Feeney and took our tools back to the shed. All the way we didn't speak a word. The kitchen was dark and cold as we'd left it, and the old woman was sitting over the hearth, saying her beads. We walked past her into the room, and Noble struck a match to light the lamp. She rose quietly and came to the doorway with all her cantankerousness gone.

"What did ye do with them?" she asked in a whisper, and Noble started so that the match went out in his hand.

"What's that?" he asked without turning round.

"I heard ye," she said.

"What did you hear?" asked Noble.

"I heard ye. Do ye think I didn't hear ye, putting the spade back in the houseen?"

Noble struck another match and this time the lamp lit for him.

"Was that what ye did to them?" she asked.

Then, by God, in the very doorway, she fell on her knees and began praying, and after looking at her for a minute or two Noble did the same by the fireplace. I pushed my way out past her and left them at it. I stood at the door, watching the stars and listening to the shrieking of the birds dying out over the bogs. It is so strange what you feel at times like that that you can't describe it. Noble says he saw everything ten times the size, as though there were nothing in the whole world but that little patch of bog with the two Englishmen stiffening into it, but with me it was as if the patch of bog where the Englishmen were was a million miles away, and even Noble and the old woman, mumbling behind me, and the birds and the bloody stars were all far away, and I was somehow very small and very lost and lonely like a child astray in the snow. And anything that happened me afterwards, I never felt the same about again.

In the Train

Dermot Foley, O'Connor's friend for thirty-five years, was the catalyst for this 1935 story: "One day he looked so distressed that I dragged him out, and for want of somewhere better to go, headed for the Central Criminal Court. The galleries were jammed with onlookers, but no one appeared to have any interest in the little woman with the shawl in the dock, charged with poisoning her husband. A barrister whom Michael knew came across to us at the adjournment, and with cheerful detachment tried to soothe Michael's compassionate questions with the remark: 'Oh, she'll get off. Poisoners usually do, you know.' In a café downtown we talked for an hour about the life that lay before her if she were acquitted, as we hoped she would be, and . . . within a week I was sitting with him again, listening to that wonderful story." (Sheehy, Michael/Frank, 61).

More than just a trial and acquittal, "In the Train" focuses on the provincial town, its traditions and code in relation to the fascinating yet alien modern world. The journey from Farranchreesht to the city and back covers cultural distances not measurable in miles, but O'Connor refuses to value one culture over the other. Apparently minor characters and incidents exemplify both worlds: the drunken man, searching for Michael O'Leary (a last-minute inspiration, according to O'Connor), the sergeant's restless wife, who calls him "Jonathon" when his fellows know him as "plain John"; even the ghoulish story of the cats tells more than one might think.

Sean O'Faoláin praised O'Connor's mastery of technique: "He takes the story long after its obvious climax; he shows us the acquitted woman, the Guards, and the witnesses, all coming back in the train to their home. But within that general setting with what subtlety the camera approaches, one might almost say coyly approaches, the central figure. We

15

get glimpses of her through the minds of almost everybody else before at last the camera slews full face on to the woman the story is about." (The Short Story, 205).

There!' said the sergeant's wife. 'You would hurry me.'

'I always like to be in time for a train,' replied the sergeant with the equability of one who has many times before explained the guiding principle of his existence.

'I'd have had heaps of time to buy the hat,' added his wife.

The sergeant sighed and opened his evening paper. His wife looked out on the dark platform, pitted with pale lights under which faces and faces passed, lit up and dimmed again. A uniformed lad strode up and down with a tray of periodicals and chocolates. Farther up the platform a drunken man was being seen off by his friends.

'I'm very fond of Michael O'Leary,' he shouted. 'He is the most sincere man I know.'

'I have no life,' sighed the sergeant's wife. 'No life at all! There isn't a soul to speak to, nothing to look at all day but bogs and mountains and rain—always rain! And the people! Well, we've had a fine sample of them, haven't we?'

The sergeant continued to read.

'Just for the few days it's been like heaven. Such interesting people! Oh, I thought Mr. Boyle had a glorious face! And his voice—it went through me.'

The sergeant lowered his paper, took off his peaked cap, laid it on the seat beside him, and lit his pipe. He lit it in the old-fashioned way, ceremoniously, his eyes blinking pleasurably like a sleepy cat's in the match-flame. His wife scrutinised each face that passed, and it was plain that for her life meant faces and people and things and nothing more.

'Oh dear!' she said again. 'I simply have no existence. I was educated in a convent and play the piano; my father was a literary man, and yet I am compelled to associate with the lowest types of humanity. If it was even a decent town, but a village!'

'Ah,' said the sergeant, gapping his reply with anxious puffs, 'maybe with God's help we'll get a shift one of these days.' But he said it without conviction, and it was also plain that he was well pleased with himself, with the prospect of returning home, with his pipe and with his paper.

'Here are Magner and the others,' said his wife as four other police-men passed the barrier. 'I hope they'll have sense enough to let us alone. . . . How do you do? How do you do? Had a nice time, boys?' she called with sudden animation, and her pale, sullen face became warm and vivacious. The policemen smiled and touched their caps but did not halt.

'They might have stopped to say good evening,' she added sharply, and her face sank into its old expression of boredom and dissatisfaction. 'I don't think I'll ask Delancey to tea again. The others make an attempt, but really, Delancey is hopeless. When I smile and say "Guard Delancey, wouldn't you like to use the butter-knife?" he just scowls at me from under his shaggy brows and says, without a moment's hesitation "I would not.' "

'Ah, Delancey is a poor slob,' said the sergeant affectionately.

'Oh yes, but that's not enough, Jonathon. Slob or no slob, he should make an attempt. He's a young man; he should have a dinner-jacket at least. What sort of wife will he get if he won't even wear a dinner-jacket?'

'He's easy, I'd say. He's after a farm in Waterford!'

'Oh, a farm! A farm! The wife is only an incidental, I suppose?'

'Well, now from all I hear she's a damn nice little incidental.'

'Yes, I suppose many a nice little incidental came from a farm,' an-swered his wife, raising her pale brows. But the irony was lost on him.

'Indeed, yes; indeed, yes,' he said fervently.

'And here,' she added in biting tones, 'come our charming neigh-bours.'

Into the pale lamplight stepped a group of peasants. Not such as one sees in the environs of a capital but in the mountains and along the coasts. Gnarled, wild, with turbulent faces, their ill-cut clothes full of character, the women in pale brown shawls, the men wearing black sombreros and carrying big sticks, they swept in, ill at ease, laughing and shouting defiantly. And, so much part of their natural environment were they, that for a moment they seemed to create about themselves rocks and bushes, tarns, turf-ricks and sea.

With a prim smile the sergeant's wife bowed to them through the open window.

'How do you do? How do you do?' she called. 'Had a nice time?'

At the same moment the train gave a jolt and there was a rush in which the excited peasants were carried away. Some minutes passed; the influx of passengers almost ceased, and a porter began to slam the doors. The drunken man's voice rose in a cry of exultation.

'You can't possibly beat O'Leary!' he declared. 'I'd lay down my life for Michael O'Leary.'

Then, just as the train was about to start, a young woman in a brown shawl rushed through the barrier. The shawl, which came low enough to hide her eyes, she held firmly across her mouth, leaving visible only a long thin nose with a hint of pale flesh at either side. Beneath the shawl she was carrying a large parcel.

She looked hastily around, a porter shouted to her and pushed her towards the nearest compartment which happened to be that occupied by the sergeant and his wife. He had actually seized the handle of the door when the sergeant's wife sat up and screamed.

'Quick! Quick!' she cried. 'Look who it is! She's coming in! Jonathon! Jonathon!'

The sergeant rose with a look of alarm on his broad red face. The porter threw open the door, with his free hand grasping the woman's elbow. But when she laid eyes on the sergeant's startled countenance, she stepped back, tore herself free, and ran crazily up the platform. The engine shrieked, the porter slammed the door with a curse, somewhere another door opened and shut, and the row of watchers, frozen into effigies of farewell, now dark now bright, began to glide gently past the window, and the stale, smoky air was charged with the breath of open fields.

·   ·   ·

The four policemen spread themselves out in a separate compartment and lit cigarettes.

'Ah, poor old Delancey!' said Magner with his reckless laugh. 'He's cracked on her all right.'

'Cracked on her,' agreed Fox. 'Did ye see the eye he gave her?'

Delancey smiled sheepishly. He was a tall, handsome, black-haired young man with the thick eyebrows described by the sergeant's wife. He was new to the force and suffered from a mixture of natural gentleness and country awkwardness.

'I am,' he said in his husky voice, 'cracked on her. The devil admire me, I never hated anyone yet, but I think I hate the living sight of her.'

'Oh, now! Oh, now!' protested Magner.

'I do. I think the Almighty God must have put that one in the world with the one main object of persecuting me.'

'Well, indeed,' said Foley, 'I don't know how the sergeant puts up with the same damsel. If any woman up and called me by an outlandish name like Jonathon when all knew my name was plain John, I'd do fourteen days for her—by God, I would, and a calendar month!'

The four men were now launched on a favourite topic that held them for more than an hour. None of them liked the sergeant's wife, and all had stories to tell against her. From these there emerged the fact that she was an incurable scandal-monger and mischief-maker, who couldn't keep quiet about her own business, much less that of her neighbours. And while they talked the train dragged across a dark plain, the heart of Ireland, and in the moonless night tiny cottage windows blew past like sparks from a fire, and a pale simulacrum of the lighted carriages leaped and frolicked over hedges and fields. Magner shut the window, and the compartment began to fill with smoke.

'She'll never rest till she's out of Farranchreesht,' he said.

'That she mightn't!' groaned Delancey.

'How would you like the city yourself, Dan?' asked Magner.

'Man, dear,' exclaimed Delancey with sudden brightness, 'I'd like it fine. There's great life in a city.'

'You can have it and welcome,' said Foley, folding his hands across his paunch.

'Why so?'

'I'm well content where I am.'

'But the life!'

'Ah, life be damned! What sort of life is it when you're always under someone's eye? Look at the poor devils in court!'

'True enough, true enough,' said Fox.

'Ah, yes, yes,' said Delancey, 'but the adventures they have!'

'What adventures!'

'Look now, there was a sergeant in court only yesterday telling me about a miser, an old maid without a soul in the world that died in an ould loft on the quays. Well, this sergeant I'm talking about put a new man on duty outside the door while he went back to report, and all this fellow had to do was to kick the door and frighten off the rats.'

'That's enough, that's enough!' cried Foley.

'Yes, yes, but listen now, listen, can't you? He was there about ten

minutes with a bit of candle in his hand and all at once the door at the
foot of the stairs began to open. "Who's there?" says he, giving a start.
"Who's there I say?" There was no answer and still the door kept opening quietly. Then he gave a laugh. What was it but a cat? "Puss, puss,"
says he, "come on up, puss!" Thinking, you know, the ould cat would
be company. Up comes the cat, pitter-patter on the stairs, and then
whatever look he gave the door the hair stood up on his head. What
was coming in but another cat? "Coosh!" says he, stamping his foot
and kicking the door to frighten them. "Coosh away to hell out of
that!" And then another cat came in and then another, and in his fright
he dropped the candle and kicked out right and left. The cats began
to hiss and bawl, and that robbed him of the last stitch of sense. He
bolted down the stairs, and as he did he trod on one of the brutes,
and before he knew where he was he slipped and fell head over heels,
and when he put out his hand to grip something 'twas a cat he gripped,
and he felt the claws tearing his hands and face. He had strength enough
to pull himself up and run, but when he reached the barrack gate
down he dropped in a fit. He was a raving lunatic for three weeks
after.'

'And that,' said Foley with bitter restraint, 'is what you call adven-
ture!'

'Dear knows,' added Magner, drawing himself up with a shiver, ' 'tis
a great consolation to be able to put on your cap and go out for a drink
any hour of the night you like.'

' 'Tis of course,' drawled Foley scornfully. 'And to know the worst
case you'll have in ten years is a bit of a scrap about politics.'

'I dunno,' sighed Delancey dreamily. 'I'm telling you there's great
charm about the Criminal Courts.'

'Damn the much charm they had for you when you were in the box,'
growled Foley.

'I know, sure, I know,' admitted Delancey, crestfallen.

'Shutting his eyes,' said Magner with a laugh, 'like a kid afraid he was
going to get a box across the ears.'

'And still,' said Delancey, 'this sergeant fellow I'm talking about, he
said, after a while you wouldn't mind it no more than if 'twas a card
party, but talk up to the judge himself.'

'I suppose you would,' agreed Magner pensively.

There was silence in the smoky compartment that jolted and rocked on its way across Ireland, and the four occupants, each touched with that morning wit which afflicts no one so much as state witnesses, thought of how they would speak to the judge if only they had him before them now. They looked up to see a fat red face behind the door, and a moment later it was dragged back.

'Is thish my carriage, gentlemen?' asked a meek and boozy voice.

'No, 'tisn't. Go on with you!' snapped Magner.

'I had as nice a carriage as ever was put on a railway thrain,' said the drunk, leaning in, 'a handsome carriage, and 'tis losht.'

'Try farther on,' suggested Delancey.

'Excuse me interrupting yeer conversation, gentlemen.'

'That's all right, that's all right.'

'I'm very melancholic. Me besht friend, I parted him thish very night, and 'tish known to no wan, only the Almighty and Merciful God (here the drunk reverently raised his bowler hat and let it slide down the back of his neck to the floor), if I'll ever lay eyes on him agin in thish world. Good night, gentlemen, and thanks, thanks for all yeer kindness.'

As the drunk slithered away up the corridor Delancey laughed. Fox resumed the conversation where it had left off.

'I'll admit,' he said, 'Delancey wasn't the only one.'

'He was not,' agreed Foley. 'Even the sergeant was shook. When he caught up the mug he was trembling all over, and before he could let it down it danced a jig on the table.'

'Ah, dear God! Dear God!' sighed Delancey, 'what killed me most entirely was the bloody ould model of the house. I didn't mind anything else but the house. There it was, a living likeness, with the bit of grass in front and the shutter hanging loose, and every time I looked down I was in the back lane in Farranchreesht, hooshing the hens and smelling the turf, and then I'd look up and see the lean fellow in the wig pointing his finger at me.'

'Well, thank God,' said Foley with simple devotion, 'this time tomorrow I'll be sitting in Ned Ivers' back with a pint in my fist.'

Delancey shook his head, a dreamy smile playing upon his dark face.

'I dunno,' he said. ' 'Tis a small place, Farranchreesht, a small, mangy ould *fothrach* of a place with no interest or advancement in it.'

'There's something to be said on both sides,' added Magner judicially. 'I wouldn't say you're wrong, Foley, but I wouldn't say Delancey was wrong either.'

'Here's the sergeant now,' said Delancey, drawing himself up with a smile of welcome. 'Ask him.'

'He wasn't long getting tired of Julietta,' whispered Magner maliciously.

The door was pushed back and the sergeant entered, loosening the collar of his tunic. He fell into a corner seat, crossed his legs and accepted the cigarette which Delancey proffered.

'Well, lads,' he exclaimed. 'What about a jorum!'

'By Gor,' said Foley, 'isn't it remarkable? I was only talking about it!'

'I have noted before now, Peter,' said the sergeant, 'that you and me have what might be called a simultaneous thirst.'

.   .   .

The country folk were silent and exhausted. Kendillon drowsed now and again, but he suffered from blood-pressure, and after a while his breathing grew thicker and stronger until at last it exploded in a snort, and then he started up, broad awake and angry. In the silence rain spluttered and tapped along the roof, and the dark window-panes streamed with shining runnels of water that trickled on to the floor. Moll Mor scowled, her lower lip thrust out. She was a great flop of a woman with a big coarse powerful face. The other two women, who kept their eyes closed, had their brown shawls drawn tight about their heads, but Moll's was round her shoulders and the gap above her breasts was filled by a blaze of scarlet.

'Where are we?' asked Kendillon crossly, starting awake after one of his drowsing fits.

Moll Mor glowered at him.

'Aren't we home yet?' he asked again.

'No,' she answered. 'Nor won't be. What scour is on you?'

'Me little house,' moaned Kendillon.

'Me little house,' mimicked Moll. ' 'Twasn't enough for you to board the windows and put barbed wire on the ould bit of a gate!'

' 'Tis all dom well for you,' he snarled, 'that have someone to mind yours for you.'

One of the women laughed softly and turned a haggard virginal face within the cowl of her shawl.

' 'Tis that same have me laughing,' she explained apologetically. 'Tim Dwyer this week past at the stirabout pot!'

'And making the beds!' chimed in the third woman.

'And washing the children's faces! Glory be to God, he'll blast creation!'

'Ay,' snorted Moll, 'and his chickens running off with Thade Kendillon's roof.'

'My roof, is it?'

'Ay, your roof.'

' 'Tis a good roof. 'Tis a better roof than ever was seen over your head since the day you married.'

'Oh, Mary Mother!' sighed Moll, ' 'tis a great pity of me this three hours and I looking at the likes of you instead of me own fine bouncing man.'

' 'Tis a new thing to hear you praising your man, then,' said a woman.

'I wronged him,' said Moll contritely. 'I did so. I wronged him before the world.'

At this moment the drunken man pulled back the door of the compartment and looked from face to face with an expression of deepening melancholy.

'She'sh not here,' he said in disappointment.

'Who's not here, mister?' asked Moll with a wink at the others.

'I'm looking for me own carriage, ma'am,' said the drunk with melancholy dignity, 'and, whatever the bloody hell they done with it, 'tish losht. The railways in thish counthry are gone to hell.'

'Wisha, if 'tis nothing else is worrying you wouldn't you sit here with me?' asked Moll.

'I would with very great pleasure,' replied the drunk, 'but 'tishn't on'y the carriage, 'tish me thravelling companion. . . . I'm a lonely man, I parted me besht friend this very night, I found wan to console me, and then when I turned me back—God took her!'

And with a dramatic gesture the drunk closed the door and continued on his way. The country folk sat up, blinking. The smoke of the men's pipes filled the compartment, and the heavy air was laden with the smell of homespun and turf smoke, the sweet pungent odour of which had penetrated every fibre of their garments.

'Listen to the rain, leave ye!' said one of the women. 'We'll have a wet walk home.'

' 'Twill be midnight before we're there,' said another.

'Ah, sure, the whole country will be up.'

' 'Twill be like daylight with collogueing.'

'There'll be no sleep in Farranchreesht tonight.'

'Oh, Farranchreesht! Farranchreesht!' cried the young woman with the haggard face, the ravished lineaments of which were suddenly trans-figured. 'Farranchreesht and the sky over you, I wouldn't change places with the Queen of England this night!'

And suddenly Farranchreesht, the bare boglands with the hump-backed mountain behind, the little white houses and the dark fortifica-tions of turf that made it seem the flame-blackened ruin of some mighty city, all was lit up within their minds. An old man sitting in a corner, smoking a broken clay pipe, thumped his stick upon the floor.

'Well, now,' said Kendillon darkly, 'wasn't it great impudence in her to come back?'

'Wasn't it now?' answered a woman.

'She won't be there long,' he added.

'You'll give her the hunt, I suppose?' asked Moll Mor politely, too politely.

'If no one else do, I'll give her the hunt myself.'

'Oh, the hunt, the hunt,' agreed a woman. 'No one could ever darken her door again.'

'And still, Thade Kendillon,' pursued Moll with her teeth on edge to be at him, 'you swore black was white to save her neck.'

'I did of course. What else would I do?'

'What else? What else, indeed?' agreed the others.

'There was never an informer in my family.'

'I'm surprised to hear it,' replied Moll vindictively, but the old man thumped his stick three or four times on the floor requesting silence.

'We told our story, the lot of us,' he said, 'and we told it well.'

'We did, indeed.'

'And no one told it better than Moll Mor. You'd think to hear her she believed it herself.'

'God knows,' answered Moll with a wild laugh, 'I nearly did.'

'And still I seen great changes in my time, and maybe the day will come when Moll Mor or her likes will have a different story.'

A silence followed his words. There was profound respect in all their eyes. The old man coughed and spat.

'Did any of ye ever think the day would come when a woman in our parish would do the like of that?'

'Never, never, ambasa!'

'But she might do it for land?'

'She might then.'

'Or for money?'

'She might so.'

'She might, indeed. When the hunger is money people kill for money, when the hunger is land people kill for land. There's a great change coming, a great change. In the ease of the world people are asking more. When I was a growing boy in the barony if you killed a beast you made six pieces of it, one for yourself and the rest for the neighbours. The same if you made a catch of fish, and that's how it was with us from the beginning of time. And now look at the change! The people aren't as poor as they were, nor as good as they were, nor as generous as they were, nor as strong as they were.'

'Nor as wild as they were,' added Moll Mor with a vicious glare at Kendillon. 'Oh, glory be to You, God, isn't the world a wonderful place!'

The door opened and Magner, Delancey and the sergeant entered. Magner was drunk.

'Moll,' he said, 'I was lonely without you. You're the biggest and brazenest and cleverest liar of the lot and you lost me my sergeant's stripes, but I'll forgive you everything if you'll give us one bar of the "Colleen Dhas Roo".'

.   .   .

'I'm a lonely man,' said the drunk. 'And now I'm going back to my lonely habitation.'

'Me besht friend,' he continued, 'I left behind me—Michael O'Leary. 'Tis a great pity you don't know Michael, and a great pity Michael don't know you. But look now at the misfortunate way a thing will happen. I was looking for someone to console me, and the moment I turned me back you were gone.'

Solemnly he placed his hand under the woman's chin and raised her face to the light. Then with the other hand he stroked her cheeks.

'You have a beauful face,' he said, 'a beauful face. But whass more important, you have a beauful soul. I look into your eyes and I see the beauty of your nature. Allow me wan favour. Only wan favour before we part.'

He bent and kissed her. Then he picked up his bowler which had fallen once more, put it on back to front, took his dispatch case and got out.

.   .   .

The woman sat on alone. Her shawl was thrown open and beneath it she wore a bright blue blouse. The carriage was cold, the night outside black and cheerless, and within her something had begun to contract that threatened to crush the very spark of life. She could no longer fight it off, even when for the hundredth time she went over the scenes of the previous day; the endless hours in the dock; the wearisome speeches and questions she couldn't understand and the long wait in the cells till the jury returned. She felt it again, the shiver of mortal anguish that went through her when the chief warder beckoned angrily from the stairs, and the wardress, glancing hastily into a handmirror, pushed her forward. She saw the jury with their expressionless faces. She was standing there alone, in nervous twitches jerking back the shawl from her face to give herself air. She was trying to say a prayer, but the words were being drowned within her mind by the thunder of nerves, crashing and bursting. She could feel one that had escaped dancing madly at the side of her mouth but she was powerless to recapture it.

'The verdict of the jury is that Helena Maguire is not guilty.' Which was it? Death or life? She couldn't say. 'Silence! Silence!' shouted the usher, though no one had tried to say anything. 'Any other charge?' asked a weary voice. 'Release the prisoner.' 'Silence!' shouted the crier again. The chief warder opened the door of the dock and she began to run. When she reached the steps she stopped and looked back to see if she were being followed. A policeman held open a door and she found herself in an ill-lit, draughty, stone corridor. She stood there, the old shawl about her face. The crowd began to emerge. The first was a tall girl with a rapt expression as though she were walking on air. When she saw the woman she halted suddenly, her hands went up in an instinctive gesture, as though she wished to feel her, to caress her. It was that look of hers, that gait as of a sleepwalker that brought the woman to her senses . . . .

But now the memory had no warmth in her mind, and the something within her continued to contract, smothering her with loneliness and shame and fear. She began to mutter crazily to herself. The train, now almost empty, was stopping at every little wayside station. Now and again a blast of wind from the Atlantic pushed at it as though trying to capsize it.

She looked up as the door was slammed open and Moll Mor came in, swinging her shawl behind her.

'They're all up the train. Wouldn't you come?'

'No, no, no, I couldn't.'

'Why couldn't you? Who are you minding? Is it Thade Kendillon?'

'No, no, I'll stop as I am.'

'Here! Take a sup of this and 'twill put new heart in you.' Moll fumbled in her shawl and produced a bottle of liquor as pale as water. 'Wait till I tell you what Magner said! That fellow's a limb of the divil. "Have you e'er a drop, Moll?" says he. "Maybe I have then," says I. "What is it?" says he. "What do you think?" says I. "For God's sake," says he, "baptize it quick and call it whiskey".'

The woman took the bottle and put it to her lips. She shivered as she drank.

' 'Tis powerful stuff entirely,' said Moll with respect.

Next moment there were loud voices in the corridor. Moll grabbed the bottle and hid it under her shawl. The door opened and in strode Magner, and behind him the sergeant and Delancey, looking rather foolish. After them again came the two country women, giggling. Magner held out his hand.

'Helena,' he said, 'accept my congratulations.'

The woman took his hand, smiling awkwardly.

'We'll get you the next time though,' he added.

'Musha, what are you saying, mister?' she asked.

'Not a word, not a word. You're a clever woman, a remarkable woman, and I give you full credit for it. You threw dust in all our eyes.'

'Poison,' said the sergeant by way of no harm, 'is hard to come by and easy to trace, but it beat me to trace it.'

'Well, well, there's things they're saying about me!'

The woman laughed nervously, looking first at Moll Mor and then at the sergeant.

'Oh, you're safe now,' said Magner, 'as safe as the judge on the bench. Last night when the jury came out with the verdict you could have stood there in the dock and said "Ye're wrong, ye're wrong, I did it. I got the stuff in such and such a place. I gave it to him because he was old and dirty and cantankerous and a miser. I did it and I'm proud of it!" You

could have said every word of that and no one would have dared to lay
a finger on you.'

'Indeed! What a thing I'd say!'

'Well, you could.'

'The law is truly a remarkable phenomenon,' said the sergeant, who
was also rather squiffy. 'Here you are, sitting at your ease at the expense
of the State, and for one word, one simple word of a couple of letters,
you could be lying in the body of the gaol, waiting for the rope and the
morning jaunt.'

The woman shuddered. The young woman with the ravished face
looked up.

' 'Twas the holy will of God,' she said simply.

' 'Twas all the bloody lies Moll Mor told,' replied Magner.

' 'Twas the will of God,' she repeated.

'There was many hanged in the wrong,' said the sergeant.

'Even so, even so! 'Twas God's will.'

'You have a new blouse,' said the other woman in an envious tone.

'I seen it last night in a shop on the quay,' replied the woman with
sudden brightness. 'A shop on the way down from the court. Is it nice?'

'How much did it cost you?'

'Honour of God!' exclaimed Magner, looking at them in stupefaction.
'Is that all you were thinking of? You should have been on your bended
knees before the altar.'

'I was too,' she answered indignantly.

'Women!' exclaimed Magner with a gesture of despair. He winked at
Moll Mor and the pair of them retired to the next compartment. But the
interior was reflected clearly in the corridor window and they could see
the pale, quivering image of the policeman lift Moll Mor's bottle to his
lips and blow a long silent blast on it as on a trumpet. Delancey laughed.

'There'll be one good day's work done on the head of the trial,' said
the young woman, laughing.

'How so?' asked the sergeant.

'Dan Canty will make a great brew of poteen while he have yeer backs
turned.'

'I'll get Dan Canty yet,' replied the sergeant stiffly.

'You will, as you got Helena.'

'I'll get him yet.'

He consulted his watch.

'We'll be in in another quarter of an hour,' he said. ' 'Tis time we were all getting back to our respective compartments.'

Magner entered and the other policemen rose. The sergeant fastened his collar and buckled his belt. Magner swayed, holding the door frame, a mawkish smile on his thin, handsome, dissipated face.

'Well, good night to you now, ma'am,' said the sergeant primly. 'I'm as glad for all our sakes things ended up as they did.'

'Good night, Helena,' said Magner, bowing low and promptly tottering. 'There'll be one happy man in Farranchreesht to-night.'

'Come! Come, Joe!' protested the sergeant.

'One happy man,' repeated Magner obstinately. ' 'Tis his turn now.'

'Come on back, man,' said Delancey. 'You're drunk.'

'You wanted him,' said Magner heavily. 'Your people wouldn't let you have him, but you have him at last in spite of them all.'

'Do you mean Cady Driscoll?' hissed the woman with sudden anger, leaning towards Magner, the shawl drawn tight about her head.

'Never mind who I mean. You have him.'

'He's no more to me now than the salt sea!'

The policeman went out first, the women followed, Moll Mor laughing boisterously. The woman was left alone. Through the window she could see little cottages stepping down through wet and naked rocks to the water's edge. The flame of life had narrowed in her to a pin-point, and she could only wonder at the force that had caught her up, mastered her and thrown her aside.

'No more to me,' she repeated dully to her own image in the window, 'no more to me than the salt sea!'

The Majesty of the Law

O'Connor said that both "In the Train" and this story came from "a phase in which I was fumbling for a new style" (Stories by, vii). We should not take "fumbling" literally because "The Majesty of the Law" is assured throughout from the quiet opening description of Dan at home to the discussion of conflicting codes of honor and duty. Echoing "Guests of the Nation" and "In the Train," traditional obligations to oneself, town, or family oppose rigid, formalized statutes. Readers may take pleasure in watching Dan, surprisingly surefooted in a world whose character is eroding, maintain his integrity.

As in "Guests of the Nation," O'Connor is a master of dramatic irony, for the sergeant and Dan know that the visit has another purpose that is hidden from the reader until the story is almost over. Note especially the delicacy with which Dan explains the offense that requires his imprisonment; our sympathies do not change. The irony is complete, as Vivian Mercier points out, because Dan is going to prison "instead of paying a fine, solely to humiliate his accuser. . . . The ends of impersonal modern justice are frustrated by an older code, which reverses the role of punisher and punished" (241). When the story concludes, with Dan "alone along the road to prison," we admire rather than condemn him, and the title is resonant: what we might have seen as the "majesty" of an inflexible law, punishing evildoers, is the "majesty" of Dan's noble refusal to lose his principles.

Old Dan Bride was breaking brosna for the fire when he heard a step up the path. He paused, a bundle of saplings on his knee.

Dan had looked after his mother while the spark of life was in her, and after her death no other woman had crossed the threshold. Signs on

30

it, his house had that look. Almost everything in it he had made with his own hands in his own way. The seats of the chairs were only slices of log, rough and round and thick as the saw had left them, and with the rings still plainly visible through the grime and polish that coarse trouser bottoms had in the course of long years imparted. Into these Dan had rammed stout knotted ash boughs which served alike for legs and back. The deal table, bought in a shop, was an inheritance from his mother, and a great pride and joy to him, though it rocked forward and back whenever he touched it. On the wall, unglazed and flyspotted, hung in mysterious isolation a Marcus Stone print and beside the door was a calendar representing a racehorse. Over the door hung a gun, old but good and in excellent condition, and before the fire was stretched an old setter who raised his head expectantly whenever Dan rose or even stirred.

He raised it now as the steps came nearer, and when Dan, laying down the bundle of saplings, cleaned his hands thoughtfully in the seat of his trousers, he gave a loud bark, but this expressed no more than a desire to display his own watchfulness. He was half human and knew that people thought he was old and past his prime.

A man's shadow fell across the oblong of dusty light thrown over the half door before Dan looked round.

'Are you alone, Dan?' asked an apologetic voice.

'Oh, come in, come in, sergeant, come in and welcome,' exclaimed the old man, hurrying on rather uncertain feet to the door, which the tall policeman opened and pushed in. He stood there, half in sunlight, half in shadow, and seeing him so, you would have realised how dark was the interior of Dan's house. One side of his red face was turned so as to catch the lights and behind it an ash tree raised its boughs of airy green against the sky. Green fields, broken here and there by clumps of red-brown rock, flowed downhill, and beyond them, stretched all across the horizon was the sea, flooded and almost transparent with light. The sergeant's face was fat and fresh, the old man's face, emerging from the twilight of the kitchen, had the colour of wind and sun, while the features had been so shaped by the struggle with time and the elements that they might as easily have been found impressed upon the surface of a rock.

'Begor, Dan,' said the sergeant, ' 'tis younger you're getting.'

'Middling I am, sergeant, middling,' agreed the old man in a voice which seemed to accept the remark as a compliment of which politeness would not allow him to take too much advantage. 'No complaints.'

'Faix, and 'tis as well. No wan but a born idiot would believe them. And th' ould dog don't look a day older.'

The dog gave a low growl as though to show the sergeant that he would remember this unmannerly reference to his age, but indeed he growled every time he was mentioned, under the impression that people could have nothing but ill to say of him.

'And how's yourself, sergeant?'

'Well, now, like that in the story, Dan, neither on the pig's back or at the horse's tail. We have our own little worries, but, thanks be to God, we have our compensations.'

'And the wife and care?'

'Good, glory and praise be to God, good. They were away from me with a month, the lot of them, at the mother-in-law's place in Clare.'

'Ah, do you tell me so?'

'I had a fine, quiet time.'

The old man looked about him, and then retired to the near-by bed-room from which he emerged a moment later with an old shirt. With this he solemnly wiped the seat and back of the log-chair nearest the fire.

'Take your ease, now, take your ease. 'Tis tired you must be after the journey. How did you come?'

'Teigue Leary it was that gave me a lift. Wisha, now Dan, don't you be putting yourself about. I won't be stopping. I promised them I'd be back inside an hour.'

'What hurry is on you?' asked the old man. 'Look now, your foot was on the path when I rose from putting kindling on the fire.'

'Now! Now! You're not making tea for me.'

'I am not then, but for myself, and very bad I'll take it if you won't join me.'

'Dan, Dan, that I mightn't stir, but 'tisn't an hour since I had a cup at the barracks.'

'Ah, *Dhe,* whisht, now! Whisht, will you! I have something that'll put an appetite on you.'

The old man swung the heavy kettle on to the chain over the open fire, and the dog sat up, shaking his ears with an expression of the deepest interest. The policeman unbuttoned his tunic, opened his belt, took a pipe and a plug of tobacco from his breast-pocket, and crossing his legs in easy posture, began to cut the tobacco slowly and carefully with his pocket-knife. The old man went to the dresser, and took down two handsomely decorated cups, the only cups he had, which, though chipped and handleless, were used at all only on very rare occasions: for himself, he preferred tea from a basin. Happening to glance into them, he noticed that they bore the trace of disuse and had collected a substantial share of the fine white dust which was constantly circulating within the little smoky cottage. Again he thought of the shirt, and, rolling up his sleeves with a stately gesture, he wiped them inside and out till they shone. Then he bent and opened the cupboard. Inside was a quart bottle of pale liquid, obviously untouched. He removed the cork and smelt the contents, pausing for a moment in the act as though to recollect where exactly he had noticed that particular smoky odour before. Then, reassured, he rose and poured out with a liberal hand.

'Try that now, sergeant,' he said.

The sergeant, concealing whatever qualms he might have felt at the thought of imbibing illegal whiskey, looked carefully into the cup, sniffed, and glanced up at old Dan.

'It looks good,' he commented.

'It should be.'

'It tastes good, too,' he added.

'Ah, sha,' said Dan, clearly not wishing to praise his own hospitality in his own house, ' 'tis of no great excellence.'

'You're a good judge, I'd say,' said the sergeant without irony.

'Ever since things became what they are,' said Dan, carefully guarding himself from a too direct reference to the peculiarities of the law administered by his guest, 'liquor is not what it used to be.'

'I have heard that remark made before now,' said the sergeant thoughtfully. 'I have often heard it said by men of wide experience that liquor used to be better in the old days.'

'Liquor,' said the old man, 'is a thing that takes time. There was never a good job done in a hurry.'

' 'Tis an art in itself.'

'Just so.'

'And an art takes time.'

'And knowledge,' added Dan with emphasis. 'Every art has its secrets, and the secrets of distilling are being lost the way the old songs were lost. When I was a boy there wasn't a man in the barony but had a hundred songs in his head, but with people running here, there and everywhere, the songs were lost. . . . Ever since things became what they are,' he repeated on the same guarded note, 'there's so much running about the secrets are lost.'

'There must have been a power of them.'

'There was. Ask any man to-day that makes liquor do he know how to make it of heather.'

'And was it made of heather?' asked the policeman.

'It was.'

'Did you ever drink it yourself?'

'I did not; but I knew men that drank it. And a purer, sweeter, wholesomer drink never tickled a man's gullet. Babies they used to give it to and growing children.'

'Musha, Dan, I think sometimes 'twas a great mistake of the law to set its hand against it.'

Dan shook his head. His eyes answered for him, but it was not in nature that in his own house a man should criticise the occupation of his guest.

'Maybe so, maybe not,' he said in a noncommittal tone.

'But sure, what else have the poor people?'

'Them that makes the laws have their own good reasons.'

'All the same, Dan, all the same, 'tis a hard law.'

The sergeant would not be outdone in generosity. Politeness required him not to yield to the old man's defence of his superiors and their mysterious ways.

'It is the secrets I would be sorry for,' said Dan, summing up. 'Men die, and men are born, and where one man drained another will plough, but a secret lost is lost for ever.'

'True,' said the sergeant mournfully. 'Lost forever.'

Dan took the policeman's cup, rinsed it in a bucket of clear water beside the door and cleaned it anew with the aid of the shirt. Then he placed it carefully at the sergeant's elbow. From the dresser he took a jug of milk and a blue bag containing sugar: this he followed up with a slab of country butter and—a sign that his visitor was not altogether unexpected—a round cake of home-made bread, fresh and uncut. The kettle sang and spat, and the dog, shaking his ears, barked at it angrily.

'Go 'way, you brute!' growled Dan, kicking him out of his way.

He made the tea and filled the two cups. The sergeant cut himself a large slice of bread and buttered it thickly.

'It is just like medicines,' said the old man, resuming his theme with the imperturbability of age. 'Every secret there was is lost. And leave no one tell me a doctor is the measure of one that has secrets from old times.'

'How could he?' asked the sergeant with his mouth full.

'The proof of that was seen when there were doctors and wise people there together.'

'It wasn't to the doctors the people went, I'll engage.'

'It was not. And why?' . . . With a sweeping gesture the old man took in the whole world outside his cabin. 'Out there on the hillsides is the sure cure for every disease. Because it is written'—he tapped the table. with his thumb—'it is written by the poets "*an galar'san leigheas go bhfaghair le ceile*" ("wherever you find the disease you will find the cure"). But people walk up the hills and down the hills and all they see is flowers. Flowers! As if God Almighty—honour and praise to Him—had nothing better to do with His time than be making ould flowers!'

'Things no doctor could cure the wise people cured.'

'Ah musha, 'tis I know it,' said Dan bitterly, ' 'tis I know it, not in my mind but in my own four bones.'

'Do you tell me the rheumatics do be at you always?'

'They do. . . . Ah, if you were living, Kitty O'Hara, or you, Nora Malley of the Glen, 'tisn't I would be dreading the mountain wind or the sea wind; 'tisn't I'd be creeping down with me misfortunate red ticket for the blue and pink and yellow dribble-drabble of their ignorant dispensary!'

'Why then, indeed,' said the sergeant with sudden determination, 'I'll get you a bottle for that.'

'Ah, there's no bottle ever made will cure me!'

'There is, there is. Don't talk now till you try it. My own mother's brother, it cured him when he was that bad he wanted the carpenter to cut the two legs off him with a hand-saw.'

'I'd give fifty pounds to be rid of it,' said Dan. 'I would and five hundred!'

The sergeant finished his tea in a gulp, blessed himself and struck a match which he then allowed to go out as he answered some question of the old man's. He did the same with a second and third, as though titillating his appetite with delay. At last he succeeded in getting it alight, and then the two men pulled round their chairs, placed their toes side by side in the ashes, and in deep puffs, lively bursts of conversation and long long silences, enjoyed their pipes.

'I hope I'm not keeping you,' said the sergeant, as though struck by the length of his visit.

'Erra, what keep?'

'Tell me if I am. The last thing I'd like to do is to waste a man's time.'

'Och, I'd ask nothing better than to have you here all night.'

'I like a little talk myself,' admitted the policeman.

And again they became lost in conversation. The light grew thick and coloured, and wheeling about the kitchen before it disappeared became tinged with gold; the kitchen itself sank into a cool greyness with cold light upon the cups and the basins and plates upon the dresser. From the ash tree a thrush began to sing. The open hearth gathered brightness till its light was a warm, even splash of crimson in the twilight.

Twilight was also descending without when the sergeant rose to go. He fastened his belt and tunic and carefully brushed his clothes. Then he put on his cap, tilted a little to side and back.

'Well,' he said, 'that was a great talk.'

'It's a pleasure,' said Dan, 'a real pleasure, that's what it is.'

'And I won't forget the bottle.'

'Heavy handling from God to you!'

'Good-bye now, Dan.'

'Good-bye and good luck.'

Dan did not offer to accompany the sergeant beyond the door. Then he sat down in his old place by the fire. He took out his pipe once more, blew through it thoughtfully, and just as he leaned forward for a twig to kindle it he heard steps returning to the house. It was the sergeant. He put his head a little way over the half door.

'Oh, Dan,' he called softly.

'Ay, sergeant,' replied Dan, looking round, but with one hand still reaching for the twig. He could not see the sergeant's face, only hear his voice.

'I suppose you're not thinking of paying that little fine, Dan?'

There was a brief silence. Dan pulled out the lighted twig, rose slowly and shambled towards the door, stuffing it down into the almost empty bowl of the pipe. He leaned over the half door, while the sergeant with hands in the pockets of his trousers gazed rather in the direction of the laneway, yet taking in a considerable portion of the sea-line.

'The way it is with me, sergeant,' replied Dan unemotionally, 'I am not.'

'I was thinking that, Dan. I was thinking you wouldn't.'

There was a long silence during which the voice of the thrush grew shriller and merrier. The sunken sun lit up islands of purple cloud moored high above the wind.

'In a way,' said the sergeant, 'that was what brought me.'

'I was just thinking so, sergeant, it struck me and you going out the door.'

'If 'twas only the money, I'm sure there's many would be glad to oblige you.'

'I know that, sergeant. No, 'tisn't the money so much as giving that fellow the satisfaction of paying. Because he angered me, sergeant.'

The sergeant made no comment upon this and another long silence ensued.

'They gave me the warrant,' he said at last in a tone which dissociated him from all connection with the document.

'Ay, begod!' said Dan, without interest.

'So whenever 'twould be convenient to you———.'

'Well, now you mention it,' said Dan, by way of throwing out a suggestion for debate, 'I could go with you now.'

'Oh, tut, tut!' protested the sergeant with a wave of his hand, dismissing the idea as the tone required.

'Or I could go tomorrow,' added Dan, warming up to the issue.

'Just as you like now,' replied the sergeant, scaling up his voice accordingly.

'But as a matter of fact,' said the old man emphatically, 'the day that would be most convenient to me would be Friday after dinner, seeing that I have some messages to do in town, and I wouldn't have me jaunt for nothing.'

'Friday will do grand,' said the sergeant with relief that this delicate matter was now practically disposed of. 'You could just walk in yourself and tell them I told you.'

'I'd rather have yourself, if 'twould be no inconvenience, sergeant. As it is, I'd feel a bit shy.'

'You needn't then. There's a man from my own parish there, a warder; one Whelan. You could say you wanted him, and I'll guarantee when he knows you're a friend of mine he'll make you as comfortable as if you were at home by your own fire.'

'I'd like that fine,' said Dan with satisfaction.

'Well, good-bye again now, Dan. I'll have to hurry.'

'Wait now, wait, till I see you to the road!'

Together the two men strolled down the laneway while Dan explained how it was that he, a respectable old man, had had the grave misfortune to open the head of another old man in such a way as to necessitate his being removed to hospital, and why it was that he could not give the old man in question the satisfaction of paying in cash for an injury brought about through the victim's own unmannerly method of argument.

'You see, sergeant,' he said, 'the way it is, he's there now, and he's looking at us as sure as there's a glimmer of sight in his wake, wandering, wathery eyes, and nothing would give him more gratification than for me to pay. But I'll punish him. I'll lie on bare boards for him. I'll suffer for him, sergeant, till he won't be able to rise his head, nor any of his children after him, for the suffering he put on me.'

On the following Friday he made ready his donkey and butt and set out. On his way he collected a number of neighbours who wished to bid him farewell. At the top of the hill he stopped to send them back. An old man, sitting in the sunlight, hastily made his way within doors, and a moment later the door of his cottage was quietly closed.

Having shaken all his friends by the hand, Dan lashed the old donkey, shouted 'hup, there!' and set out alone along the road to prison.

Michael's Wife

The genesis of this 1935 story—full of unanswered questions that resist logical inquiry—is best described by O'Connor himself: "We had climbed a hill overlooking the sea, and on the horizon . . . was an American liner on its way into Cobh. A farmer working in a field joined us; he too had been watching the liner and it had reminded him of his son who had emigrated to America when he was quite young. After a few years the boy had married an Irish-American girl whose family had come from Donegal, and soon after ceased to write home, though his wife continued to write. Then she fell ill and her doctor suggested a holiday in Ireland. She had arrived one day on a liner like the one we were watching, and her father-in-law had met her at the station with his horse and cart. She had stayed with them for weeks, regained her health, and gradually won the affection of the family. After that she had set off to visit her parents' family in Donegal, and it was only then that the old Cork couple learned from a letter to a neighbour that their son was dead before ever she left America.

Up there on the hill in the evening with the little whitewashed farmhouse beside us and the liner disappearing in the distance, it was an extraordinarily moving story, all the more so because the farmer was obviously still bewildered and upset by it.

'Why would she do a thing like that to us?' he asked. 'It wasn't that we weren't fond of her. We liked her, and we thought she liked us.'

Clearly he suspected that some motive of self-interest was involved, and I was afraid to tell him my own romantic notion that the girl might have liked them all too well and kept her husband alive in their minds as long as she could and—who knows?—perhaps kept him alive in her own.

I knew that some time I should have to write that story." (My Father's Son, 47–48).

The station—it is really only a siding with a shed—was empty but for the station-master and himself. When he saw the station-master change his cap he rose. From far away along the water's edge came the shrill whistle of the train before it puffed into view with its leisurely air that suggested a trot.

Half a dozen people alighted and quickly dispersed. In a young woman wearing a dark-blue coat who lingered and looked up and down the platform he recognised Michael's wife. At the same moment she saw him but her face bore no smile of greeting. It was the face of a sick woman.

'Welcome, child,' he said, and held out his hand. Instead of taking it, she threw her arms about him and kissed him. His first impulse was to discover if anyone had noticed, but almost immediately he felt ashamed of the thought. He was a warm-hearted man and the kiss silenced an initial doubt. He lurched out before her with the trunk while she carried the two smaller bags.

' 'Tis a long walk,' he said with embarrassment.

'Why?' she asked wearily. 'Can't I drive with you?'

'You'd rather have McCarthy's car but 'tisn't back from Cork yet.'

'I would not. I'd rather drive with you.'

' 'Tis no conveyance,' he said angrily, referring to the old cart. Nevertheless he was pleased. She mounted from behind and sat on her black trunk. He lifted himself in after her, and they jolted down the village with the bay on their left. Beyond the village the road climbed a steep hill. Through a hedge of trees the bay grew upon the sight with a wonderful brightness because of the dark canopy of leaves. On and up, now to right, now to left, till the trees ceased, the bay disappeared over the brow of a hill, and they drove along a sunlit upland road with sunken fences. Hills like mattresses rose to their right, a brilliant green except where they were broken by cultivated patches or clumps of golden furze; a bog, all brown with bright pools and tall grey reeds, flanked the road.

'Ye were in about eight, I'd say,' he commented, breaking the silence.

'Oh yes. About that.'

'I seen ye.'

'You did?'

'I was on the look out. When she rounded the head I ran in and told the wife "Your daughter-in-law's coming." She nearly had me life when she seen 'twas only the ould liner.'

The girl smiled.

'Ah, now,' he added proudly, a moment later, 'there's a sight for you!'

She half raised herself on the edge of the cart and looked in the direction his head indicated. The land dropped suddenly away from beneath their feet, and the open sea, speckled white with waves and seagulls' wings, stretched out before them. The hills, their smooth flanks patterned with the varying colours of the fields, flowed down to it in great unbroken curves, and the rocks looked very dark between their windflawed brightness and the brightness of the water. In little hollows nestled houses and cottages, diminutive and quaint and mostly of a cold, startling whiteness that was keyed up here and there by the spring-like colour of fresh thatch. In the clear air the sea was spread out like a great hall with all its folding doors thrown wide; a dancing floor, room beyond room, each narrower and paler than the last, till on the farthest reaches steamers that were scarcely more than dots jerked to and fro as on a wire.

Something in the fixity of the girl's pose made Tom Shea shout the mare to a standstill.

' 'Tis the house beyond,' he said, brandishing his stick. 'The one with the slate roof on the hill.'

With sudden tenderness he looked quizzically down at her from under his black hat. This stranger girl with her American clothes and faintly American accent was his son's wife and would some day be the mother of his grandchildren. Her hands were gripping the front of the cart. She was weeping. She made no effort to restrain herself or conceal her tears, nor did she turn her eyes from the sea. He remembered a far-away evening when he had returned like this, having seen off his son.

'Yes,' he said after a moment's silence. ' 'Tis so, 'tis so.'

.   .   .

A woman with a stern and handsome face stood in the doorway. As everything in Tom seemed to revolve about a fixed point of softness; his huge frame, his comfortable paunch, his stride, his round face with the shrewd, brown, twinkling eyes and the big grey moustache, so everything in her seemed to obey a central reserve. Hers was a nature refined to the point of hardness, and while her husband took colour from everything about him, circumstances or acquaintance would, you felt, leave no trace on her.

One glance was enough to show her that he had already surrendered. She, her look said, would not give in so easily. But sooner than he she recognised the signals of fatigue.

'You're tired out, girl!' she exclaimed.

'I am,' replied the younger woman, resting her forehead in her hands as though to counteract a sudden giddiness. In the kitchen she removed her hat and coat and sat at the head of the table where the westering light caught her. She wore a pale-blue frock with a darker collar. She was very dark, but the pallor of illness had bleached the dusk from her skin. Her cheekbones were high so that they formed transparencies beneath her eyes. It was a very Irish face, long and spiritual, with an inherent melancholy that might dissolve into sudden anger or equally sudden gaiety.

'You were a long time sick,' said Maire Shea, tossing a handful of brosna on the fire.

'I was.'

'Maybe 'twas too soon for you to travel?'

'If I didn't, I'd have missed the summer at home.'

'So Michael said, so Michael said.'

'Ah,' declared Tom with burning optimism, 'you won't be long pulling round now, with God's help. There's great air here, powerful air.'

'You'll be finding us rough, simple poor people,' added his wife with dignity, taking from him a parcel that contained a cheap glass sugarbowl to replace the flowered mug without a handle that had served them till now. 'We're not used to your ways nor you to ours but we have a great will to please you.'

'We have,' agreed Tom heartily. 'We have indeed.'

The young woman ate nothing, only sipped her tea that smelled of burnt wood, and it was clear, as when she tried to pour milk from the large jug, that she was completely astray in her new surroundings. And that acute sense of her discomfort put a strain on the two old people, on Tom especially, whose desire to make a good impression was general and strong.

After tea she went upstairs to rest. Maire came with her.

' 'Tis Michael's room,' she said. 'And that's Michael's bed.'

It was a bare, green-washed room with a low window looking on to the front of the house, an iron bed and an oleograph of the Holy Family. For a moment an old familiar feeling of wild jealousy stole over Maire

Shea, but when the girl, in undressing, exposed the scar across her stomach, she felt guilty.

'You'll sleep, now,' she said softly.

'I ought to.'

Maire stole down the straight stair. Tom was standing in the doorway, his black hat over his eyes, his hands clasped behind his back.

'Well?' he asked in a whisper.

'Whist!' she replied irritably. 'She shouldn't be travelling at all. I don't know what come over Michael, and to leave her and he knowing well we have no facility. The cut in her stomach————'tis the length of your arm.'

'Would I run up and tell Kate not to come? Herself and Joan will be in soon.'

' 'Twould be no use. All the neighbours will be in.'

'So they will, so they will,' he admitted in a depressed tone.

He was very restless. After a while he stole upstairs and down again on tiptoe.

'She's asleep. But whisper, Moll, she must have been crying.'

' 'Tis weakness.'

'Maybe she'd be lonely.'

' 'Tis weakness, 'tis weakness. She should never be travelling.'

.   .   .

Later Kate and Joan arrived and after them three or four other women. Twilight fell within the long white-washed kitchen; and still they talked in subdued voices. Suddenly the door on the stair opened and Michael's wife appeared. She seemed to have grown calmer, though she still retained something of the air of a sleep-walker, and in the half-light with her jet-black eyes and hair, her long pale face had a curious ethereal beauty.

The sense of strain was very noticeable. Tom fussed about her in a helpless fidgety way till the women, made nervous by it, began to mock and scold him. Even then a question put at random caused him to fret.

'Can't ye leave her alone now, can't ye? Can't ye see she's tired? Go on with yeer ould talk, leave ye, and don't be bothering her any more.'

'No, no,' she said. 'I'm not so tired now.' Her voice retained a memory of her native Donegal in a certain dry sweetness.

'Have a sup of this,' urged Tom. 'A weeshy sup—'twill do you no harm.'

She refused the drink, but two of the other women took it, and Tom, having first toasted 'her lovely black eyes,' drank a glass without pausing for breath. He gave a deep sigh of content.

> 'The curate was drunk and the midwife was tipsy
> And I was baptized in a basin of whiskey,'

he hummed. He refilled his glass before sitting down beside the open door. The sky turned deep and deeper blue above the crown of a tree that looked in the low doorway and a star winked at the window-pane. Maire rose and lit the wall-lamp with its tin reflector. From far away in a lag between two headlands a voice was calling and calling on a falling cadence 'Taaaamie! Taaaamie!' and in the distance the call had a remote and penetrating sweetness. When it ceased there came to their ears the noise of the sea, and suddenly it was night. The young woman drew herself up. All were silent. One of the women sighed. The girl looked up, throwing back her head.

'I'm sorry, neighbours,' she said. 'I was only a child when I left Ireland and it's all strange to me now.'

' 'Tis surely,' replied Kate heartily. ' 'Tis lonely for you. You're every bit as strange as we'd be in the heart of New York.'

'Just so, just so,' exclaimed Tom with approval.

'Never mind,' continued Kate. 'You have me to take your part.'

'You be damned!' retorted Tom in mock indignation. 'No one is going to look after that girl but meself.'

'A deal she have to expect from either of ye!' added Maire coldly. 'It wouldn't occur to ye she should be in bed.'

She dipped a candle in the fire and held it above her head. The girl followed her. The others sat on and talked; then all took their leave together. Maire, busy about the house and yard for a long time, heard voices and footsteps coming back to her on the light land wind.

She was thinking in her dispassionate way of Michael's wife. She had thought of her often before, but now she found herself at sea. It wasn't only that the girl was a stranger and a sick one at that, but—and this Maire had never allowed for—she was the child of a strange world, the atmosphere of which had come with her, disturbing judgment. Less clearly than Kate or Tom, yet clearly enough, she realised that the girl was as strange amongst them as they would be in New York. In the bright starlight a cluster of white-washed cottages stood out against the hillside like a frame of snow about its orange window-squares. For the first time Maire looked at it, and with a strange feeling of alienation wondered what it was like to one unused to it.

A heavy step startled her. She turned in to see that Tom had disappeared. Heated with drink and emotion he had tiptoed up the stairs and opened the girl's door. He was surprised to find her sitting on the low window-ledge in her dressing-gown. From the darkness she was looking out with strange eyes on the same scene Maire had been watching with eyes grown too familiar, hills, white-washed cottages and sea.

'Are 'oo awake?' he asked—a stupid question.

'Wisha, for goodness' sake will you come down and leave the girl sleep?' came Maire's voice in irritation from the foot of the stairs.

'No, no, no,' he whispered nervously.

'What is it?' asked the girl.

'Are 'oo all right?'

'Quite, thanks.'

'We didn't disturb 'oo?'

'Not at all.'

'Come down out of that, you ould fool!' cried Maire in an exasperated tone.

'I'm coming, I'm coming—Jasus, can't you give us a chance?' he added angrily. 'Tell me,' this in a whisper, 'the ould operation, 'twon't come again you?'

He bent over her, hot and excited, his breath smelling of whiskey.

'I don't understand you.'

'Ah,' he said in the same low tone, 'wouldn't it be a terrible misfortune? A terrible misfortune entirely! 'Tis great life in a house, a child is.'

'Oh, no,' she answered hastily, nervously, as though she were growing afraid.

'Are 'oo sure? What did the doctors say?'

'It won't, it won't.'

'Ah, glory be to the hand of God!' he said turning away, ' 'tis a great ease to my mind to know that. A great ease! A great ease! I'm destroyed thinking of it.'

He stumbled downstairs to face his wife's anger that continued long after he had shut up the house for the night. She had a bitter tongue when she chose to use it, and she chose now. For weeks they had been screwing themselves up, to make a good impression on Michael's wife, and now it was spoiled by a drunken fool of a man.

He turned and tossed, unable to sleep at the injustice of it. As though a man wouldn't want to know a thing like that, as though he mightn't ask his own daughter-in-law a civil question, without being told he was worse than a black, a heathen savage from Africa, without niceness or consideration except for his own dirty gut!

He, Tom Shea, who tried to leave a good impression on every hog, dog and devil that came the road!

.   .   .

In the morning Michael's wife was somewhat better. The sun appeared only at intervals, but for the greater part of the day she was able to sit by the gable where she had a view of the sea in shelter from the wind. A stream ran just beneath her, and a hedge of fuchsia beside it bordered a narrow stony laneway leading to the strand. The chickens raced about her with a noise like distant piping and from the back of the house came the complaining voice of a hen saying without pause, 'Oh, God! God! God! God!'

Occasionally Maire came and sat beside her on a low stool. Maire asked no questions—her pride again—and the conversation was strained, almost hostile, until the girl became aware of what ailed her: curiosity for the minute trifles of their life in America, hers and Michael's; the details that had become so much part of her that she found it difficult to remember them. How much the maid was paid, how the milk was delivered, the apartment house with its central heating, the negro lift-hop, the streetcars and the rest of it. At last her mind seemed to embrace the old woman's vivid and unlettered mind trying to construct a picture of the world in which her son lived, and she continued to talk for the sake of talking, as though the impersonality of it was a relief.

It was different when at dinner-time Tom came in from the strand in a dirty old shirt and pants, his black hat well forward on his eyes.

'Listen, girleen,' he said in a gruff voice, very different from that of the previous night, as with legs crossed and hands joined behind his back he leaned against the wall. 'Tell that husband of yours he should write oftener to his mother. Women are like that. If 'twas your own son now, you'd understand.'

'I know, I know,' she said hastily.

'Of course you do. You're a fine big-hearted girl, and don't think we're not thankful to you. The wife now, she's a fine decent woman but she have queer ways. She wouldn't thank God Almighty if she thought He was listening, and she'll never say it to you but she said it to others, how good you are to us.'

'Don't blame Michael,' she replied in a low voice. 'It isn't his fault.'

'I know, sure, I know.'

'He never has time.'

'Mention it to him though, you! Mention it to him. The letter to say you were coming, 'twas the first we had from himself for months. Tell him 'tis his mother, not me at all.'

'If you only knew how he wanted to come!' she exclaimed with a troubled glance.

'Yes, yes, yes; but 'twill be two years more before he can. Two years to one at his hour of life 'tis only like to-morrow, but for old people that never know the time or the place . . .! And that same, it may be the last he'll see of one or the other of us. And we've no one but him, girleen, more's the pity.'

It was certainly different with Tom, who had but one approach to any situation.

.   .   .

In a few days she had regained something of her strength. Tom cut her a stout ashplant and she went for short walks, to the strand, to the little harbour or to the post office which was kept by Tom's sisters. Mostly she went alone. To his delight the weather turned showery, but it never completely broke.

All day long the horizon was peopled by a million copper-coloured cloudlets, rounded and tiny and packed back to the very limits of the sky like cherubs in a picture of the Madonna. Then they began to swell, bubble on bubble, expanding, changing colour; one broke away from the mass and then another; it grew into a race; they gathered, sending out dark streamers that blackened the day and broke the patina of the water with dark-green stormy paths; lastly, a shrill whistle of wind and wild driving rain enveloped everything in mist. She took shelter under a rock or at the lee-side of a fence, and watched the shower dissolve in golden points of light that grew into a sunlit landscape beyond, as the clouds like children in frolic terror scampered back pell-mell to the horizon, the blue strip of sky they left broadening, the rain thinning, the fields and sea stripping off their scum of shadow till everything was sparkling and steaming again.

What it meant to her they could only guess when she returned. Whenever she remained too long in the house the shadow came on her again. Kate bade them take no notice.

She seemed to be very drawn towards Kate. Her walks often took her to the post office, and there she sat for hours with the two sisters, frequently sharing their meals, and listening to Kate's tales of old times in the parish, about her parents and her brother Tom, but most frequently about Michael's youth.

Kate was tall and bony with a long nose, long protruding chin and wire spectacles. Her teeth, like her sister's, were all rotten. She was the sort country people describe as having a great heart, a masterful woman, always busy, noisy and goodhumoured. Tom, who was very proud of her, told how she had gone off for a major operation carrying a basket of eggs to sell so that she wouldn't have her journey for nothing. Her sister Joan was a nun-like creature who had spent some time in an asylum. She had a wonderfully soft, round, gentle face with traces of a girlish complexion, a voice that seldom rose above a whisper and the most lovely eyes; but when the cloud came on her she was perverse and obstinate. On the wall of the living-room, cluttered thick with pictures, was a framed sampler in ungainly lettering, 'Eleanor Joan Shea, March 1881.' She was nominally postmistress but it was Kate who did the work.

As much as Michael's wife took to them, they took to her. Joan would have wept her eyes out for a homeless dog, but Kate's sympathy was marked by a certain shrewdness.

'You had small luck in your marriage,' she said once.

'How?' The young woman looked at her blankly.

'For all you're only married a year you had your share of trouble. No honeymoon, then the sickness and now the separation.'

'You're right. It's nothing but separations.'

'Ye had only seven months together?'

'Only seven.'

'Ah, God help you, I never saw a lonelier creature than you were the night you came. But that's how we grow.'

'Is it, I wonder?'

' 'Tis, 'tis. Don't I know it?'

'That's what Father Coveney says,' wailed Joan, 'but I could never understand it myself. All the good people having all the misfortunes that don't deserve them, and the bad ones getting off.'

'You'll be happier for it in the latter end, and you've a good boy in Michael. . . . Musha, listen to me talking about Michael again. One'd think I was his mother.'

'You might be.'

'How so?'

'He has a lot of your ways.'

'Ah, now, I always said it! Didn't I, Joan? And why wouldn't he? When his mother leathered him 'twas up to me he came for comfort.'

'He often said it—you made a man of him.'

'I did,' said Kate proudly. 'I did so. Musha, he was a wild boy and there was no one to understand him when he was wild. His mother— not judging her—was born heavy with the weight of sense.'

Kate rarely lost the chance of a jeer at Maire.

'You're getting to like us, I think?' she said at last.

'I am,' admitted the girl. 'When I came first I was afraid.'

'You won't be so glad to get back to the States.'

'I wish I never saw the States again.'

'Och, aye!'

'It's true.'

'Ah, well. Two years more and ye'll be back together. And what's a couple of years to one of your age?'

'More than you think.'

'True, true, years are only as you feel them.'

'And I'll never come back here again.'

'Ach, bad cess to you, you're giving into it again! And now, listen to me. 'Tis a thing I often said to Tom Shea, why wouldn't ye come back? What's stopping ye? Never mind that ould fool telling you Michael wouldn't get a job! Why wouldn't he? And only Tom was such a gligin he'd never have left the boy go away.'

.   .   .

To Tom's disgust the weather cleared without heavy rain, though there was little sun, and that wandering, bursting out here and there on the hills or in mirror-like patches on the water and then fading into the same grey sultry light. Now, early and late, Michael's wife was out, sitting on the rocks or striding off to the village. She became a familiar figure on the roads in her blue dress with her ashplant. At first she stood far off, watching the men at the nets or sitting at the crossroads; as time went on she drew nearer, and one day a fisherman hailed her and spoke to her.

After that she went everywhere, into their houses, on to the quay and out in the boats when they went fishing: Maire Shea didn't like it, but all the men had known Michael as a boy and had tales of him and his knowledge of boats and fishing, and after a few days it was as though she too had grown up with them. It may be also that she gathered something from those hours on the water, in silent coves on grey days when the wind shook out a shoal of lights, or in the bay when the thunderous light moved swiftly, starting sudden hares of brightness from every hollow, blue from the hills, violet from the rocks, primrose from the fields, and here and there a mysterious milky glow that might be rock or field or tree. It may be these things deepened her knowledge so that she no longer felt a stranger when she walked in the morning along the strand, listening to the tide expand the great nets of weed with a crisp, gentle, pervasive sound like rain, or from her window saw the moon plunge its silver drill into the water.

But there was a decided change in her appearance and in her manner. She had filled out, her face had tanned and the gloomy, distraught air had left it.

'There,' said Tom, 'didn't I tell ye we'd make a new woman of her? Would anyone know her for the girl she was the night she came? Would they? I declare to me God, the time she opened the door and walked down the stairs I thought her own were calling.'

Kate and Joan, too, were pleased. They liked her for her own sake and Michael's sake, but they had come to love her for the sake of her youth and freshness. Only Maire held her peace. Nothing had ever quite bridged the gap between the two women; in every word and glance of hers there was an implicit question. It was some time before she succeeded in infecting Tom. But one day he came for comfort to Kate. He was downcast, and his shrewd brown eyes had a troubled look.

'Kate,' he said, going to the heart of things as his way was, ' 'tis about Michael's wife.'

'Och, aye! What about her?' asked Kate, pulling a wry face. ' 'Tisn't complaining you are?'

'No, but tell me what you think of her.'

'What I think?'

' 'Tis Maire.'

'Well?'

'She's uneasy.'

'Uneasy about what, aru?'

'She thinks the girl have something on her mind.'

'Tom Shea, I tell you now as I told you many a time before your wife is a suspicious woman.'

'Wisha, wisha, can't you forget all that? I never seen such a tribe for spite. We know ye never got on. But now, Kate, you can't deny she's a clever woman.'

'And what do the clever woman think?'

'She thinks the pair of them had a row; that's what she thinks now plain and straight, and I won't put a tooth in it.'

'I doubt it.'

'Well now, it might be some little thing a few words would put right.'

'And I'm to say the few words?'

'Now Kate, 'twas my suggestion, my suggestion entirely. The way 'tis with Moll, she'd say too much or say too little.'

'She would,' agreed Kate with grim amusement. Maire Shea had the reputation for doing both.

Next day she reported that the idea was absurd. He had to be content, for Kate too was no fool. But the question in Maire's manner never ceased to be a drag on him, and for this he did not know whether to blame her or the girl. Three weeks had passed and he began to find it intolerable. As usual he came to Kate.

'The worst of it is,' he said gloomily, 'she's making me as bad as herself. You know the sort I am. If I like a man, I don't want to be picking at what he says like an ould hen, asking "What did he mean by this?" or "What's he trying to get out of me now?" And 'tisn't that Moll says anything, but she have me so bothered I can hardly talk to the girl. Bad luck to it, I can't even sleep. . . . And last night———'

'What happened last night?'

He looked at her gloomily from under his brows.

'Are you making fun of me again?'

'I am not. What happened last night?'

'I heard her talking in her shleep.'

'Michael's wife?'

'Yes.'

'And what harm if she do in itself?'

'No harm at all!' howled Tom in a sudden rage, stamping up and down the kitchen and shaking his arms. 'No harm in the bloody world, but, Chrisht, woman, I tell you it upsot me.'

Kate looked at him over her wire spectacles with scorn and pity.

'Me mother's hood cloak that wasn't worn since the day she died, I must get it out for you. You'll never be a proper ould woman without it.'

.   .   .

'Moll,' said Tom that night, as they were going to bed, 'you're dreaming.'

'How so?'

'About Michael's wife.'

'Maybe I am,' she admitted grudgingly, yet surprising him by any admission at all.

'You are,' he said to clinch it.

'I had my reasons. But this while past she's different. Likely Kate said something to her.'

'She did.'

'That explains it so,' said Maire complacently.

Two nights later he was wakened suddenly. It happened now that he did waken like that at any strange noise. He heard Michael's wife again speaking in her sleep. She spoke in a low tone that dwindled drowsily away into long silences. With these intervals the voice went on and on, very low, sometimes expressing—or so it seemed to him—a great joy, sometimes as it were pleading. But the impression it left most upon him was one of intimacy and tenderness. Next morning she came down late, her eyes red. That same day a letter came from Donegal. When she had read it she announced in a halting way that her aunt was expecting her.

'You won't be sorry to go,' said Maire, searching her with her eyes.

'I will,' replied the girl simply.

'If a letter comes for you!'

' 'Tisn't likely. Any letters there are will be at home. I never expected to stay so long.'

Maire gave her another long look. For the first time the girl gave it back, and for a moment they looked into one another's eyes, mother and wife.

'At first,' said Maire, turning her gaze to the fire, 'I didn't trust you. I'm a straight woman and I'll tell you that. I didn't trust you.'

'And now?'

'Right or wrong, whatever anyone may say, I think my son chose well for himself.'

'I hope you'll always think it,' replied the girl in the same serious tone. She looked at Maire, but the older woman's air repelled sentiment. Then she rose and went to the door. She stood there for a long time. The day was black and heavy, and at intervals a squall swept its shining net over the surface of the water.

·　　·　　·

And now the positions of Tom and his wife were reversed as frequently happens with two such extremes of temperament. Before dusk rain began to fall in torrents. He went out late to the post office and sat between his two sisters, arguing.

'There's a woman all out,' he said bitterly. 'She upsets me and then sits down on me troubles. What's on the girl's mind? There's something queer about her, something I can't make out. I've a good mind to send word to Michael.'

'And what would you say?' asked Kate. 'Disturbing him without cause! Can't you be sensible!'

'I can't be sensible,' he replied angrily. 'She's here in my charge and if anything happened her———'

'Nothing will happen her.'

'But if it did?'

'She's all right. She got back her health that none of us thought she would. Besides, she's going away.'

'That's what's worrying me,' he confessed. 'She'll leave me with the trouble on me, and I haven't the words to walk back and have it out with her.'

He returned late through the driving rain. The women had gone to bed. He turned in but could not sleep. The wind rose gradually from the squalls that shook the house and set the window-panes rattling.

All at once he caught it again, the damned talking. He lay perfectly still in order not to wake Maire. Long intervals of silence and then the voice again. In a sudden agony of fear he determined to get up and ask what was on her mind. Anything was better than the fear that was beginning to take hold of him. He lifted himself in the bed, hoping to crawl out over Maire's feet without waking her. She stirred, and he crouched there listening to the wind and the voice above his head, waiting till his wife should settle out again. And then, suddenly in a moment when wind and sea seemed to have died down to a murmur, the voice above him rose in three anguished mounting breaths that ended in a suppressed scream. 'Michael! Michael! Michael!'

With a groan he sank back and covered his eyes with his hands. He felt another hand coldly touching his forehead and his heart. For one wild, bewildering moment it was as though Michael had really entered the room above his head, had passed in his living body across all those hundreds of miles of waves and storm and blackness; as though all the inexpressible longing of his young wife had incarnated him beside her. He made the sign of the cross as if against some evil power. And after that there was silence but for the thunder of the rising storm.

.   .   .

Next morning he would have avoided her eyes, but there was something about her that made him look and look in spite of himself. A nervous exaltation had crystallised in her, making her seem ethereal, remote and lovely. Because of the rain that still continued to pour Maire would have had her remain, but she insisted.

She went out in heavy boots and raincoat to say good-bye to Kate and Joan. Joan wept. 'Two years,' said Kate in her hearty way, ' 'twill be no time passing, no time at all.' When she left it was as if a light had gone out in the childless house.

Maire's good-bye was sober but generous too.

'I know Michael is in good hands,' she said.

'Yes,' replied the girl with a radiant smile, 'he is.'

And they drove off through the rain. The sea on which she looked back was blinded by it, all but a leaden strip beside the rocks. She crouched over her black trunk with averted head. Tom, an old potato bag over his shoulders, drove into it, head down. The fear had not left him. He looked down at her once or twice, but her face was hidden in the collar of her raincoat.

They left the seemingly endless, wind-swept upland road and plunged down among the trees that creaked and roared above their heads, spilling great handfuls of water into the cart. His fear became a terror.

When he stood before the carriage door he looked at her appealingly. He could not frame the question he looked; it was a folly he felt must pass from him unspoken; so he asked it only with his eyes, and with her eyes she answered him—a look of ecstatic fulfillment.

The whistle went. She leaned out of the carriage window as the train lurched forward, but he was no longer looking. He raised his hands to his eyes and swayed to and fro, moaning softly to himself. For a long time he remained like that, a ridiculous figure with the old potato bag and the little pool of water that gradually gathered on the platform about his feet.

Orpheus and His Lute

This vivid tale grew out of O'Connor's memories of his father, Mick Donovan, who played "the big drum" in the Blackpool Brass and Reed Band—which provided opportunities for political brawling and brotherly drinking as well as music (An Only Child, 6–11). "Orpheus and his Lute" seems a larger-than-life depiction of a mythical band's descent, brief triumph, and dissolution, narrated by a speaker immersed in folk tradition. Yet the closing scene—where the belligerents are transformed by music—testifies to the power of art, even when it is half-stifled by an unsympathetic community of merchants and priests, who value stability and "temperance" above all. What is lost when the "Saint Patrick's Temperance Sodality" buys the band's instruments—which they cannot play well—is lost forever. Appropriately, the epigraph, "Thou holy art," is from Schubert's "An die Musik."

O'Connor, rarely satisfied with his own work, often rewrote stories he had successfully published two decades earlier as they came to seem inauthentic in their "colour and extravagance" (Stories by, viii). His changing relationship to the Irish cultural landscape is evident in the differences between this 1935 version and his 1954 revision (More Stories by Frank O'Connor); the latter has no affectionate tolerance of provincialism. In it, beauty is crushed by the ignorant. For another chapter in his saga of Cork brass bands, see "The Cornet Player Who Betrayed Ireland," where music and politics are predictably at odds, each demanding complete loyalty.

Du holde kunst . . .

The changes in this city——!' said the old man, and then paused as though overcome.

'What changes?' I enquired.

'Ah, well,' he concluded in a shocking anticlimax, ' 'tis God's holy will.'

'But what are the changes,' I persisted.

'What are the changes? Isn't it change enough for anyone that the two things the people were fondest of under the sun, the two things they'd give body and soul for, are after falling into disrespect?'

'And what are they?'

'What else but porter and music?—Sometimes it was the music got the upper hand and sometimes the porter, but the one and the other were in every bit of sport and mischief there was. Did I ever tell you the story of the Irishtown band?'

'You did not.'

'Well, now 'tis a little story worth telling, just to show you the sort of windfalls that pass for musicians nowadays. In those days—I'm speaking of fifty years ago—every parish had a band, and some had two bands and even three bands, but the Irishtown band was the best of the lot. There wasn't a man in it that wasn't born and reared as you might say between bar lines, and every one of them would drink Lough Erne dry. That was a well-known fact: a man wouldn't have a chance of being taken in that band unless he could do something remarkable in the way of drinking, and it used to be said of a certain notorious cadger—one, Dazza—that after a band promenade or a procession, with respects to you, he could get blind drunk on the emptying of the instruments.

'They were grand musicians—'twas given up to them— but everyone was beginning to get sick of their begging. They were forever collecting at the chapel gates for new this and new that, and of a cold winter's night you'd hear a knock at the door, and when you went out you'd see a couple of them outside with a collecting-box, and they not able to stop it rattling with the shivering and the lust for drink, and one of them would up and say "Sorry for troubling you, old flower, but 'tis the way we're collecting for new uniforms for the band." Uniforms! No one ever saw tale or tidings of anything new on them, and the old rags they had, there wasn't a vestige of a seat in them.

'You wouldn't remember it, but in those days it was the fashion for bands to serenade supporters of their own—Aldermen or M.P.'s or big butter merchants—more particularly when they were giving dinner-parties, and when dinner was over the man of the house would come out and slip the bandmaster ten shillings or a pound to get drinks for the men. But in the latter end no one would open his doors to the Irishtown band, for as sure as they got any sort of an innings, they'd be up week after week and night after night, puffing and blowing outside, and midnight wouldn't see a sign of staggering or giving out in them till they got the price of a wet. And that was the rock they perished on, for one by one they lost their backers, and towards the end even the dirtiest old ward politician wouldn't have the nerve to give them a show.

'Well, one cold wet night in February they all gathered in for a practice. Practice, my eye! Damn the bit of practice they were fit for, any of them! They sat down round the fire, the whole lot, in the jim-jams, and 'twas two fellows called Butty Bowman and Ned Hegarty that weren't as bad as the rest that were lighting the pipes for them. That much they couldn't do for the jigs in their hands, and whenever the door opened or a cinder fell out of the fire, the whole lot would give one loud shriek and rise three feet in the air, chairs and all.

' "Boys, boys," says the bandmaster, trembling and rubbing his hands, "what in the name of the sweet and suffering God are we going to do this night?"

' "Send out the conjuring-box quick!" says Shinkwin, the big drummer.

' "But who will we send it to?"

' "Send it to the pubs. Crowley's at the bridge ought to be good for a bob."

' "Here, Hegarty," says the bandmaster, "take a turn at it you now, yourself and Butty Bowman. And to make the one errand of it, ye might as well take the jug as well."

'So off went Hegarty with the collecting-box, and little Butty Bowman behind with the jug; and there were the rest of them, some walking up and down, clenching their fists and grinding their teeth; some, too bad to move, stretched out on the benches, and the whole lot shivering and moaning like men in their last agony, "Oh, Mother of God, have pity on me! I'm dying, I'm dying! Oh, will this night ever be over me?" And every few minutes, like Sister Anne in the story, the bandmaster would hop to the window looking across the bridge, and all the poor penitents would cry together "Joe, Joe, are they coming yet?"

'After three-quarters of an hour back comes me two buckos. The bandmaster made one wild dive for the jug, and when he looked into it he gave a holy oath and covered his face with his hands. Butty Bowman held out his palm and there were three coppers in it. All at once the whole band began to shriek and shiver again.

' "Boys!" says the bandmaster.

' "What is it, Joe?" says a few of them.

' "Ye know me a long time, boys," says he, "don't ye?"

' "We do so, Joe," says they.

' "And ye'll bear witness," says he in the voice of a man that was inviting them all to his funeral, "ye'll bear witness before the world that I'm a musician to the eyelets of me boots."

' "You are, Joe," says they, "you are, of course, but how's that going to help us?"

' "Well," says he, standing to attention and thumping his chest, "I don't care who hears me say it but I was a man before I was a musician. . . . Butty, run down to Coveney's and tell them to send up the donkey and butt."

' "Erra, what's up with you, Joe?" says Butty, thinking, you know, the bandmaster was after going dotty.

' "Do what you're told," says Joe, with the teeth chattering in his head, "do what you're told and do it quick, for be the Lord above me, I'm not responsible for me actions at this present instant."

'Well, Joe being twice his height, away with Butty, and no sooner was he out of the room than the bandmaster broke down. They didn't like the look of him at all, and no one went near him till Butty Bowman came back and tapped him on the shoulder. He got up without looking at anyone, took the keys from his side pocket and opened the instrument cupboard.

'At the sight of this they all brightened up like one man, because though only a few of them guessed what he was about, they knew there was hope in sight.

' "One minute," says Ned Hegarty, "can we do this without a comity meeting?"

' "I'm the meeting," says the bandmaster.

' "But shouldn't we have a resolution or something?" says Ned.

' "I'm proposing it," says Shinkwin.

' "I'm seconding it," says another.

' "Any objections?" asks the bandmaster.

' "Anyone that have," says Shinkwin, "just leave him take off his coat and I won't be long dealing with them."

' "Passed unanimously," says the bandmaster. "Hurry up, boys, or ould Moon's will be shut."

'With that, out with them all in a scramble, every fellow carrying his own instrument, and Shinkwin cursing, trying to get the big drum downstairs. They put the instruments into the old donkey-butt and covered them with bags and tarpaulins, and off with them, beside the butt, in the pouring rain.

'Old Moon, the pawnbroker, thought they were mad when they came in, one by one, each of them with his own contraption. He didn't want to take the things at all, but they wouldn't listen to objections.

' "How much so?" says he.

' "Ten quid," says the bandmaster like a shot.

' "Erra, what ten quid?" says old Moon.

' "Ten bob a man?" bawls the bandmaster, doing the morse code on the counter. ' " 'Twill only quieten the drouth in us."

' "Five," says the pawnbroker.

' "What, five?" says the bandmaster. "The drum alone is worth more than that."

' "And a lot of use a drum will be to me if ye don't release it!" says Moon.

' "On the sacred work of a musician," says the bandmaster, "we'll release the lot on Saturday night. . . . Take pity on us, Mr. Moon! For the sake of your dead mother, Mr. Moon, or your dead father, or whoever is dearest to you of all that's dead and gone, take pity on us this night."

' "Seven-ten," says the pawnbroker, and not a ha'penny more would he give them if they lay down on the floor and breathed their last on him. Well, when they got the money out with them in one mad rush like a lot of demented creatures, seeing who'd be first to reach the pub, when all at once Butty Bowman gives a yell. They stopped, and the eyes hopping out of their heads.

' "Jasus," says he in a disgusted voice, "are ye going to spoil it all, are ye? Are ye going into that pub with our sorrowful seven pound ten to blow it on the shawlies and cadgers of Irishtown? How long will it last ye? Be said by me, and in God's holy name, have grace about ye and leave the bandmaster order the porter, and we'll bring it back in the donkey-butt."

'They saw the sense in that, and, holding up their stomachs the way they wouldn't drop out of them with the drouth, they went round to a quiet little pub, and by the back way they brought out four half-tierces. Then back with them the way they came, and when they got inside the bandroom, Butty Bowman turned the key in the door and went upstairs to the window.

' "What are you up to?" says Shinkwin.

'Butty said nothing but threw the key clean over the bridge into the river. They all applauded him for this, and well they might, because it wasn't long before one woman and two women and three women began to hammer on the door below.

' "Leave them hammer away to hell now!" says Butty.

'Then they set to it and they didn't leave much of the liquor behind. What made it worse was the mob that was after gathering outside. The women were dancing and shouting and screaming for drink, and when they wouldn't get it they drove in the window with stones, and when that didn't serve them they took a ladder to it. Butty Bowman and the bandmaster had rare fun knocking them off it again.

.   .   .

'The following night there wasn't a shilling left of the seven-ten.

' "Boys," says the bandmaster, "we'll have to steady up now and try to realise the old instruments. And as we're about it, I'll start taking the subscriptions from ye." And what he collected was the sum of fourpence ha'penny.

' "This won't do, boys," says he, "this won't do at all at all. Seven and six a man is what I want from ye, and I want it in a hurry."

'He might as well have been asking a slice of the sky as asking seven and six from that crowd. Weeks passed and a month passed, and three days before Patrick's Day they had five and ninepence collected between them.

' "Oh, boys, boys," says the bandmaster, "this is shocking. On Sunday morning I want every man jack of ye at the chapel gates and if that money isn't collected there'll be bad work." And to make it more solemn he got special labels for the old collecting-boxes printed "Great National Appeal."

'That was the sorrowful national appeal for them. The people went in and out without as much as good-morrow to the boxes or the men that were rattling them. One gentleman they stopped put the whole thing in a couple of words. "After yeer last escapade," says he, "no decent man will ever put his hand in his pocket for ye again." At the end of that day they had twenty-seven and six. The bandmaster was crazy.

' "'Tis the end of the band, boys," says he.

' "Erra," says Shinkwin, "we won't go down as easy as that. We'll make a house-to-house."

' "Take an oath first then," says the bandmaster. . . . "Not a drop of drink till the instruments are back. . . . Right hand up, everyone!. . . . So help me, God!"

' "So help me, God!" says they all.

' "That I might be killed stone dead!"

' "That I might be killed stone dead!"

' "Well, for Christ's sake will ye remember it?" says Joe.

.   .   .

'And they did. They stuck to that as they never stuck to a pledge before. And much use it was to them. They made another pound out of the house-to-house. "My God," says the bandmaster, beating his head, "we'll be the laughingstock of Ireland if we don't turn out o' Patrick's Day." They all had the scour on them now. Every hour or two one of them would be racing round to the bandmaster with a shilling or sixpence or even a couple of coppers he was after collecting somewhere. The bandmaster's hair was turning grey with anxiety.

'On Patrick's Eve up with him to the pawn.

' "This and that, Mr. Moon," says he, "we'd be eternally obliged to you if you'd give us the loan of the instruments for the one day."

' "What a fool I'd be!" says old Moon, laughing in his face.

' "For the love of God and the souls of the faithful departed!"

' "No," says old Moon, being a Lutheran by persuasion.

' "Then," says the bandmaster, "hire 'em out to us."

' "No," says old Moon again.

' "For a quid."

' "No."

' "For two quid."

' "No."

' "For three quid then, and that's every ha'penny we have and more, and may the shining angels make a bed in glory for your soul this night."

' "No, I tell you," bawled old Moon.

' "You dirty little Protestant scut!" says the bandmaster. "Hell is too good for the likes of you."

.   .   .

'After that Shinkwin went in and by main persuasion got the pawn-broker to agree to put the instruments on separate tickets. The first thing he released was his own big drum, and that walked away with one pound ten; then he took out a trombone, a cornet, a euphonium and two B flat clarinets. That left them without a penny in the world, and there was Shinkwin with tears in his eyes begging old Moon for the sake of the souls in Purgatory to throw in one of the side-drums, and he wouldn't, he was that black.

'They put what they had on the donkey and butt, and, 'twould break your heart to see them, one by one, running in distracted, crying out, "Mr. Moon, Mr. Moon, throw in the old piccolo and I'll pay you o' Sathurday!" or "Mr. Moon, Mr. Moon, take pity on us and give us the little drum!" They were bad for drink but they were worse for music, and after the pawn shut they were still there, decorating the wall outside, and every now and then one of them would give a tap on the window and if old Moon looked out they'd be all winking and crying and pointing with their thumbs, and saying, "Mr. Moon, Mr. Moon, for the love of God and his Blessed Mother!"

'In the latter end they got desperate entirely and up with a couple of them to Father Dennehy at the presbytery, begging him to intercede for them, but all the satisfaction he gave them was to say he'd be glad if the instruments were at the bottom of the sea, for all the scandal they were after causing in the parish.

'That finished them. Next morning, down with them to the bandroom and in the cold light of day there wasn't one that could face the thought of a turn-out with their couple of mangy instruments, and Melancholy Lane band appearing for the first time in their new uniforms. So off with them behind the bandmaster to get what little satisfaction they could out of jeering the other bands. They took up their stance at the end of a lane where there was a flight of steps, and no one that saw them but was sorry for them.

'Well, you know the sort of turn-outs there used to be in the old times: bands and banners and floats and drays with living pictures of Brian Boru and St. Patrick and Mother Erin playing her harp and National Foresters with their horses and big feathers out of their hats, and the devil knows what else. A procession like that would take two hours to pass, and there were the bandmaster, Shinkwin, Butty Bowman, Ned Hegarty and the others, with their tongues hanging out, and anyone that wouldn't jeer them, be God, they'd jeer him, but you could see the music was after going to their heads, by the way they were hopping and screaming.

'However, that was nothing till the Melancholy Lane Brass and Reed came by in their new uniforms playing—of all the tunes they could find —"Defiance," a march the Irishtown fellows were very fond of. Now, some to this day maintain that Melancholy Lane were to blame, and some say Irishtown; some say the bandmaster of the Melancholy Lane gave the order "Eyes Right" and some say 'twas pure curiosity made his buckos turn their instruments on the Irishtown contingent. But, whatever it was, there was a roar, and the next minute the two bands were at one another's throats, and the new uniforms that Melancholy Lane took such pride in were wiping the mud from the streets so clean you could nearly eat your dinner off it after.

'Well, as God done it, Butty Bowman happened to have a bit of a heavy stick with him and with one lucky swipe he opened the head of a flute player and grabbed his flute. Then he made a run after the procession, and, falling into step as if nothing had happened, he struck up "Brian Boru's March" on his own. And whether 'twas the warlike sound of that or the way they were after being starved for music for a month past till they were more like hungry lions and tigers than men, the Irishtown fellows whipped off their belts and laid out all round them, and one by one they were racing after Bowman with cornets, clarinets, piccolos and trombones; and, if they were, their supporters were springing up from every quarter and falling in two deep at each side. And still the band kept running up with bleeding noses and broken heads and faces that were after being painted and decorated with mud. The last out were the bandmaster and Shinkwin, fighting a rear-guard action with the big drum.

'Within five minutes of the first blow being struck Shinkwin gave the three taps, and if that band didn't play "Brian Boru's March" it'll never be played in this world. Every time they had to drop the instruments and shout they shouted in a way that would deafen you, and the people cheered them to the echo.

.　　.　　.

'But every good thing comes to an end, and so did the procession. The band returned by the Stream Road, and by that time they had a force three hundred strong behind them ready to shed blood or tear iron. Just at the bottle-neck bend they saw a cordon of police stretched across the road. The inspector stepped out and signalled them to stop. The crowd began to wave their sticks, and the bandmaster paid no heed to the signal. The police drew their batons but still Joe marched on. Then, about six yards from the cordon, he suddenly swung round, marking time. And as if they had it all planned, the band began to fall into concert formation in front of him. Before the march they were playing stopped, he snapped out "Auld Lang Syne, boys!"

'A dead silence fell in the road as they struck up "Auld Lang Syne." They played it so that no one who heard them ever forgot it, they played it as if they were too full of music and couldn't get it out of their systems. On the last bar the bandmaster snapped out *"Piano!"* The people knew then they were in for a treat. The Irishtown fellows were famous for their *piano;* they could make those instruments sing like choir boys and never blur a note. The tears began to come to the people's eyes, and just when they thought they couldn't stand any more the bandmaster yelled so that he could be heard at the farthest corner of the crowd *"Pianissimo!"*

'At that word everyone held his breath. They knew now the band was out to beat itself. For about six bars Shinkwin tapped out the time softly on the big drum. All the other instruments except the clarinets and flutes came in on a whisper, playing staccato, but the six clarinets took up the tune, and I never heard fiddles to compare with the Irishtown clarinets for sweetness. Then Hegarty, the champion piccolo player of Ireland, began to improvise a very melancholy ornamental passage above the clarinets—a thing he never did in his life before and that might have spoiled it all, but that day not a man in the Irishtown band could have made a mistake if you paid him for it. They were inspired, and Hegarty was inspired, and that one voice, playing trills and shakes over the clarinets, gave the last touch to it. After the first bar the inspector of the police took off his little round cap and every man there followed him.

'When the tune was over there was silence as if everyone was coming back to earth by a slow train, and then the inspector laid his hand on the bandmaster's shoulder.

' "I have to arrest you and your men, Mr. Dorgan," says he, "and I assure you no arrest I ever made caused me more regret, because in my opinion you're a genius."

' "You needn't arrest us, inspector," says the bandmaster, and some say there were tears in his eyes. "We'll go to the Bridewell ourselves. The holy spirits are round us, and we must treat them gently."

'And there and then they walked back to the Bridewell and surrendered without striking a blow.'

.   .   .

'And did they get back their instruments?' I asked.

'They did not,' said the old man. 'They never played again. The Saint Patrick's Temperance Sodality bought the tickets for a couple of pounds, and the band had one terrible night before they broke up for good.

'But sure The Temperance Sodality couldn't play for toffee. Temperance and music don't seem to go together somehow.'

What's Wrong with the Country

"What's Wrong with the Country" is superficially a series of playfully interconnected commentaries on the title with each new conversation growing increasingly vehement, denouncing earlier positions and assertions. Energetic and pointless, these discussions are hilarious, and, as Harriet Sheehy has noted, "though there are odd bits that would not be true now, this same sort of conversation goes on endlessly in Ireland— either in pubs or in the correspondence columns of the newspapers." What is wrong with the country is plain: too much talk about the subject. Ironically, all the participants but one are unaware of this as they argue into the night. Like "Orpheus and his Lute," national stagnation is the issue as if Joyce's "Ivy Day in the Committee Room" were revisited thirty years later, still with no solution found. O'Connor's perspective is rueful and satiric; rivers of words make redemptive action impossible, but he is still fascinated by the national addiction to talk, the vehement personalities and their often dubious arguments.

This Christmas, said Desmond, as you know, I went home on vacation. I fell in with a group of old friends; many of them I hadn't seen for ten years; some had risen in the world since then; some had gone downhill. You know, the usual way, and in the usual way you ponder upon the significance of time and feel damnably reverential and rather frightened and then forget all about it.

One wet evening three of us were drinking in Dolan's back, Ferguson the solicitor, Joyce the stockbroker and myself. Young Dolan too was there. There was a great change in Dolan's since the old man's death. On the walls were portraits of actresses, actors and lecturers, the sort of visiting celebrities you find in a small town. And young Dolan was very different to his father. He is a slim, dark, serious lad; his greatest grief that he got no education. The old man had been barely able to write his name, and that same, he used to say, had involved him in more trouble than anything else in his life.

Ferguson had spent a week's holiday in some seaside place in Kerry and was complaining bitterly about the food. With Ferguson it's always a feast or a famine; either everything, at home and abroad, is marvellous, superb, magnificent, or else it's going to the devil, and for a week he had been moaning that all through Kerry he could get nothing but bottled coffee and that the natives were savages.

'What's wrong with the country,' he said—I'm hardly likely ever to forget the exact words he used—'is that we're so damned lazy and dirty that we never take the trouble to do anything properly.'

'I'm afraid I don't agree with you,' said Joyce. Joyce is a small, stocky, obstinate fellow with a precise and cynical mind.

'Oh, my dear man,' said Ferguson, growing worried, 'don't mind the hotels. Just take anything you like. Take the trains—they don't run up to time. They're old and dirty and draughty. The buses break down and dump you twenty miles from anywhere without an apology. We put up a bridge and it falls to pieces. Our electrical undertakings produce everything except electricity. It's no use hiding our weakness. Let us be honest with ourselves. We're the most backward, ignorant race in Europe.'

'I'm not trying to hide anything,' replied Joyce. 'I know our faults. I'm as ready to admit them as you are. But I say that what you call a cause is only an effect. You get bad food? I say the fault is your own. Your train is late? I don't blame the guard or the engine driver. It's none of their business. I blame no one but the passengers.'

'But really, Joyce, old man, really—consider what you're saying,' continued Ferguson, who, having no perfect joints in his mind, is easily upset. 'Do you expect me to run the train? Do you expect me to cook the dinner? For instance, only last week in one of the best hotels in Galway, I asked for cold lamb and ham and instead I got cold beef and mutton. I told the waiter to take it back, and what do you think he brought the second time? Now what do you think?'

'I don't give tuppence what he brought,' said Joyce with his cold smile. 'It doesn't really matter a hang if he brought cold octopus and cabbage. The fault is not the waiter's but yours. . . . I don't mean that in a personal sense, naturally. It isn't you alone. It's the whole people.' Joyce was getting hotter. 'It's this damned moral cowardice of ours. What's wrong with the country is that the people as a whole suffer from a fundamental weakness of character. Examine your conscience, Ferguson, and you, Desmond, examine yours. How many times have you tolerated this state of affairs rather than make a scene? How many times have you put up with negligence, extortion, lying and impertinence, simply because you couldn't be bothered seeing the thing through? How many times have you been told to address your complaints to So-and-so? And how many times have you complained?'

'You don't want much,' grumbled Ferguson. 'That's a whole-time job, and what the devil do we have inspectors for if not to see that things are done right?'

'It isn't a whole-time job, Ferguson. If you did it once a day, it would be more than you'd ever need to do. And these things are infectious. When other people see you do it they'll do it too. It's only the general atmosphere of moral cowardice that needs to be broken up.'

Before any of us knew where we were we were engaged in a violent argument that went on until closing time, and would have gone on longer but that Ferguson had had an appointment a half-hour previously.

.   .   .

I found myself thinking a good deal of what Joyce had said. I did really examine my conscience and discovered that a good deal of it was true enough. Like many of my contemporaries I had been abominably weak, characterless and afraid to square up to situations. I could not in honesty deny that if there was anything wrong with the country (and everyone seemed to agree that there was) it was almost certainly the moral cowardice he spoke of.

But one day, walking into town, I bumped into Monahan. Monahan is a man with a country accent, an expert on business methods and manager of one of our new factories. As usual he was in a hurry and asked me to stroll along with him.

'I believe,' he said in his quick, sarcastic way, 'ye had a great post-mortem on the old country the other night?'

'We had,' I agreed.

'And Ferguson was there?'

'He was.'

'And left half an hour late for an appointment?'

'So he did. How did you know?'

'I was the man he had the appointment with,' said Monahan, chuckling.

'Oh, I see.'

'So ye settled it?'

'More or less.'

'Joyce spoke well, I believe?'

'I never heard him speak better.'

'And I'll guarantee the humour of it didn't strike any of ye?'

'The humour of what?'

'It didn't strike ye as funny to see Fergie diagnosing what was wrong with the country and then going off half an hour late for an appointment?'

'I don't quite see what you mean,' I said.

'Sorry I haven't more time to explain. But, me dear good man, don't you realise yet that Fergie—and no wan likes Fergie more than I do: I put dozens of jobs in his way—Fergie is simply the typical Irishman. Brilliant, charming, kind, loved by everyone and—absolutely unreliable! From his heart out he's yours for as long as you have him, but once out of your sight—bah, a black man would do more for you! You meet him at the theatre. He's falling over you, he's so delighted to see you. "You must come home with me and have a drink," says he. "Just one moment till I say good night to this idiot." After that you never see him again! He's off to the other fellow's house, the fellow he called an idiot. . . . Desmond, old boy, surely, surely, as an intelligent man, you realise that what's wrong with the country is simply that we're hopelessly unbusinesslike. You write a letter and get no reply. You call. Oh yes, that'll be all right in a day or two. The moment your back is turned, forgotten, absolutely forgotten! . . . Excuse me, me dear fellow,' he continued feverishly, 'I have an appointment at three-thirty and it's wan minute to. But, of course, Downes won't be there. Downes probably won't turn up at all. He'll waste my evening as well as his own. Think of that in terms of hard cash, Desmond; then multiply it by all the unpunctual people in Ireland, and I'll eat my hat if it doesn't cost us twenty million a year. And yet people ask what's wrong with the country!'

That evening I arrived in Dolan's back to find a crowd before me. The Professor was in the chair. The Professor is a fat man with a considerable capacity for whiskey. Dolan began to speak of our previous discussion and I could see that the Professor did not like at all the idea of anybody discussing anything in his absence. I could see he was preparing to launch out on a disquisition when he was anticipated by a young man sitting on a barrel. The speaker had a thin pale face, rather bloated, with curious hanging jaws and ears pressed close to his head.

'Now isn't that amusing?' he said with a giggle, looking straight at me. (I had just told them of Monahan's summing-up.) 'Isn't that typical of Monahan? By God, there's a man, and if energy could be converted into cash, he'd be worth a fortune.'

'I don't see what that has to do with the question,' said the Professor, clearing his throat.

'I do,' said the young man arrogantly. 'Monahan is a shining example of the type that's ruining this country, the type that's always in a hurry, always pulling up the flowers to see how they're going on. Fellows like that start an industry and expect to get their capital back in six months, and if they don't, they're off on a deputation to the Government to say they're ruined. Not that they're ever any other way: we all know Monahan is living on charity.'

'Give him a chance,' growled the Professor. 'He's only beginning.'

'Beginning? That fellow has twenty years of disasters behind him from the day he started the poultry farm and killed the hens in mistake for the cocks. And look at the mess he made of the Fun City. A week ago I was in Kilkenny and found the African Village trying to work its way back to Africa. The Tyrolese Restaurant is probably in the wilds of Donegal and the Waxworks in Kenmare. . . . But do you think it deters Monahan? Do you think he's worried? Not at all. His latest is a daily aeroplane service to Paris.'

'There,' said the Professor firmly (he had been listening with growing disgust), 'I entirely disagree with you. I'm not saying anything in favour of Monahan. In fact, I consider Monahan a charlatan, a bumptious cheapjack, but all the same he's the exception. I'm not defending his Fun City either. But all the same it was ridiculed, not for that reason but because it was a new idea. It was unprecedented, that's why. There's the real weakness of our people, their slavish respect for tradition and precedent.'

'I question that,' said the young man.

'It's obvious,' replied the Professor coolly.

'I question it.'

'It's none the less true for that,' said the Professor, opening another button of his trousers. 'It's a fact recognised by all historians. We refused to adopt armour, we wouldn't live in walled cities, we wouldn't go to sea, we wouldn't take up printing; we wouldn't do any damn thing except what they did in the year One. And we won't do it now. Monahan wants aeroplanes! Aeroplanes in a country that hasn't as much as an old ferry-boat of its own!'

'There you are. We won't bother to build the boats because we keep dreaming about aeroplanes.'

'But you don't see the point,' said the Professor, hammering his glass on the counter. 'Wake up, man, and use your critical faculty! It's the difference between black and white. You say the people make a mess of things because they look forward. I tell you it's because they look back. Think of kilts! And bagpipes! And Irish! And now they want laws to prevent us waltzing, and doing Swedish drill, and some of them would like to revive the Brehon laws! Good God Almighty, 'tis as plain as the nose on your face what's wrong with the country.'

'Now, don't try to browbeat me,' said the young man, rising.

'I'm not trying to browbeat you. I'm trying to knock sense into you.'

'You may be a Professor, but the only intelligence this country produced came from outside the universities.'

'From outside the universities?'

'Yes.'

'Are you trying to pick a quarrel about the universities now?'

At this point Dolan signalled to some friends of the young man. It was some time before they got him out, but in that time he was able to tell the Professor pretty well all he thought of him. He said the Professor's mind had stopped developing twenty years before, and that whoever had wangled him into the university must have had a taste for archaeology.

'Now,' said a teacher called Linehan, as the young man's parting shot died on our ears, 'we can talk. Nobody could open his mouth while that fellow was here. . . . Professor, take him as my contribution to the discussion.'

'Explain yourself, Linehan,' cried Dolan.

'He's my contribution.'

'You think he's what's wrong with the country?'

'I know it, to my sorrow. . . . Mind you, I agree with the Professor about the tradition. He's right, dead right, but it springs from nothing more or less than vanity. Vanity—there's the national vice.'

'And a very interesting contribution too,' said the Professor. 'Is somebody going to stand me a drink?'

'I will,' replied Linehan.

'Good man! So you think it's vanity?'

'I'm certain of it.'

'Well, mind you, I'm not. And I'll tell you why. It's because vanity is a normal human weakness. The French have it; the Germans think they made the bloody world, and the English aren't exactly what you'd call retiring. On the other hand, the worship of tradition is abnormal.'

'But vanity can become abnormal.'

'Yes, but history———'

'Oh, you can read history how you like. But even, taking history; why do you think the English laws forbade an Irishman to strut and swagger through an English town? Why did they say *strut* and *swagger?*'

'Propaganda,' said Dolan firmly. 'The English were always trying to give us a bad name.'

'Propaganda, my bloody eye!' howled Linehan. ''Twas because they had young pups like Foley in their minds. . . . Think of our history in the past twenty years. It's been dictated by personal vanity, nothing else. Look at the Treaty. You're not going to pretend there was a single principle involved in the Civil War?'

'Except what someone said in 1798.'

'Window dressing!'

'No, it wasn't. Those fellows really believe that what some idiot said a hundred and fifty years ago is God's truth. And if they were conceited they wouldn't be falling back on precedents.'

'That's where you're wrong,' put in a tall ugly man with a stormy head of white hair, a straggling moustache and a stutter. 'The vain man is always a traditionalist. Look at the priests.'

'None of your anti-clericalism here, O'Leary!' said Dolan.

'Who's anti-clerical?'

'You are.'

'One minute, O'Leary,' said Linehan testily. 'I want to finish what I was saying.'

'But the pair of ye are saying the same thing,' spluttered O'Leary. 'He says tradition, you say vanity. It's only a question of which came first, the chicken or the egg. And anyway, in my opinion ye're both wrong.'

' 'Twouldn't be like you if you hadn't some queer notion.'

'Queer notion, is it? Maybe I didn't tell ye twenty times before what was wrong with the country?'

'Go on, Jock, go on and never mind him,' said Dolan.

'Dolan, I told you.'

'You did, you did, acushla, but never mind. Go on.'

'Twenty times over!'

'For God's sake, go on,' said the Professor. 'I'm getting mental paralysis, waiting.'

'What's wrong with this country is that the people haven't learned how to live.'

'How do you make that out?'

'How do I make it out?'

'Almighty God, don't start again!'

'Look round you, man, look round you. We have no arts and crafts; the only people that went to America and didn't know how to do a single thing with their hands. That's why we're detested there.'

'But history———!'

'Are you back to history again? I suppose history prevents them cooking a dinner or singing a song. . . . My dear man, I thought all this out twenty years ago. Now, take a man we were speaking about, Joyce. I don't deny that Joyce is a clever fellow in his way, but go into his house! Look at his furniture. Awful gilt-framed pictures of swans—'twould give you the horrors. And Joyce is typical of hundreds of thousands of people in Ireland who live in an atmosphere that would drive a Frenchman mad in a week. And what's the result? They're all eaten up with dissatisfaction, vanity and envy; they don't know what's wrong themselves, but they hate their lives; they don't believe in anything; they're restless, and at last they bust out in some crazy bloody racket like the Civil War. Anything to let off steam! The censorship is the sort of thing they do. They simply don't understand that people need comfort, luxury, spaciousness, and excuse the word—sensuality. Old maids, damned old maids, by Christ.'

'Now, Jock, now Jock!' said Dolan.

'It's true.'

'It isn't true.'

'A race of old maids,' repeated O'Leary angrily. 'Petticoats they should be wearing, instead of trousers. Did I ever tell you the story of Lightning?'

'Lightning? Who's Lightning?'

'Lightning is one of my foremen. And we call him Lightning because he's the slowest bloody animal the Lord God created. Well, one day Lightning was in Folkestone on a holiday and the notion took him to have a look at the sinful country where they invented the Continental Sunday he was after hearing such a lot about. Off with him on a one-day trip to Boulogne, and no sooner was he out of the boat than a bloke comes up with picture postcards—you know the sort. And what does my bold Lightning do? He drew himself up like a man and *Monsieur,* says he politely, *monsieur, je suis Irlandais!'*

.　　.　　.

When one of the bar hands came to tell Dolan it was time to close he was making a speech and gave the bar hand such a push that he tumbled him over a barrel. At midnight I left half a dozen of them in a little ice-cream shop on the quays, eating fish and chips and still arguing.

Maybe I hadn't a bad head next morning? Because damn the wink of sleep did I get; turning the thing over and over in my mind; at one moment agreeing with Fergie, at the next with Joyce, then with the Professor, Linehan, O'Leary and Foley in turn: and I ended up by evolving theories of my own; theories that seemed so plausible while I was thinking of them that I wanted to get up and find someone to air them to.

.　　.　　.

The same night the confounded thing popped up again. To escape Dolan's I went to a party at Ferguson's. I had scarcely been there ten minutes when someone began to attack the Professor. For the life of him, said Cusack, he couldn't understand people listening to the Professor—a contemptible type. In spite of his name he wasn't Irish at all. His father was a Liverpool man, who had to clear back to his native land as a result of some shady business transaction. The Professor himself had been barred from a card school for cheating, and was supposed to have played some particularly shabby trick upon an old maiden aunt, who had brought him up.

As for tradition, what was really wrong, according to Cusack, was that there was no tradition at all! Take the Professor himself, doubtfully Irish, knowing nothing of Irish language or literature, and depending for

his opinion of it on the work of foreigners. What sort of professor of
history was that? Could a country be normal with such an intelligentsia?
What was wrong was that we were all living from hand to mouth, our
bookshops full of foreign books, and nothing to be seen in theatres and
cinemas but foreign plays and pictures.

'I suppose you'd like us to go back to kilts?' asked Ferguson.

'Well, what's wrong with kilts?' asked the patriot belligerently.

'If you think I'm going to let my husband go to the office in kilts
———!' interrupted Mary Ferguson.

'And anyway,' added a fair-haired young man in the corner, 'tradition
is all rot.'

This was a young fellow called Sullivan, who had been educated for
the priesthood but had to give it up as the result of a succession of
nervous breakdowns. His favourite subject was Thomistic philosophy,
and it was said that he couldn't even put on his hat without satisfying
himself of its subsistent reality.

'Well?' asked Ferguson. 'What do *you* think is wrong with the country?'

'No established principle of order,' replied Sullivan promptly.

'One minute,' said the traditionalist. 'I want to sing an Irish song—
just to show you what Irish culture is like.'

'Irish songs,' snapped Sullivan, to the relief of everyone, 'may be very
nice—when they're properly sung, I mean—but they're no alternative to
philosophy, and there's no evidence that at any time the people of this
country bothered their heads with philosophy. And look at the result.
Irish history is simply a record of chaos, of defeat after defeat, all because
of the lack of one unifying formula, one simple principle of order. Somebody talked about the Civil War a moment ago. Well, consider the Civil
War! What was it about? One party declared that the State could not
abrogate its sovereignty, that if every soul in Ireland were wiped out it
would still continue to exist—an untenable hypothesis that any man
with a logical mind could have wiped the floor with in ten minutes cost
the country millions of pounds!'

'The Civil War was the result of foreign notions,' growled Cusack.

'That's entirely irrelevant,' snapped Sullivan. 'There's not a tittle of
evidence that the idea of order ever established itself. Take the public life
of the country. You all know it's rotten with intrigue, corruption, graft
and intellectual dishonesty. Men who imagine they're good Christians

lic, cheat and bribe in every position. Why? Because the idea of justice isn't known to them, that's why. And we brought our corruption to America with us, and founded Tammany Hall. That's why our people are detested there.'

'O'Leary says it's because we have no arts and crafts,' I suggested mildly.

'Well, you can tell O'Leary from me that he's wrong.'

'Does anyone want tea?' asked Mrs. Ferguson; but by this time everyone was so excited that she was not heard. Ferguson's young sister and I held an impassioned conversation about the theatre. In a lull, when it seemed that we must have said everything that could be said, my heart sank as a new voice broke in.

'Surely,' I heard, 'the thing goes deeper than that. We don't pay much attention to ideas; unfortunately that's true, but isn't it because of the extraordinary imagination of the people? The real trouble, as I see it, is that the whole country exists in a sort of daydream.'

'A daydream, Nagle?' asked Sullivan politely.

'Yes, I mean it.'

'You call our Tammany Halls a daydream?'

'No, but———'

'Secret societies, public dishonesty, pilfering, lying, murder, a daydream?'

'But, damn it, the people aren't aware of it!'

'They come up against it every other day and yet they're not aware of it?'

'They don't come up against it—that's the point. They evade it, if you like. They're not aware of it. They're still in the twilight of the primitive world. . . . And how can you expect them to be interested in abstractions when they're not even interested in realities? For example, over the August Bank Holiday, I was in a long queue, waiting for a bus. Well, people stepped in just when and where they liked. One bus came, two, three; they filled up and went off and we were just where we began. I started remonstrating, but I saw that no one would back me up. Then I called a policeman, but he only added a few remonstrances of his own and walked away.'

'Go on,' said Sullivan, 'you're making out a nice case for me.'

'Listen, can't you? Just at that moment I heard a man behind me speaking. "If I won the Sweep," said he, " 'tisn't here I'd be, but driving home in my own car." And at that moment it became perfectly plain to me that everyone else in the queue was thinking something of the sort, and that if they had to stand there till morning they'd still be comforting themselves with dreams of what they'd do if only someone left them a legacy.'

I rose. I had had one sleepless night.

'By the way,' I said to Ferguson, 'I'm giving a bachelor party to-morrow evening. Will you come?'

'Delighted,' he answered. 'Who else is coming?'

'Just a few of the boys. Anderson, the Professor, Joyce—you know them all.'

'Oh,' he said, his face falling, 'I'm afraid I'll be———'

'Who is it?' I asked. 'Not the Professor?'

'No.'

'Oh, Joyce? Well, I'm sorry, old man, but it's too late to make altera-tions.'

I left with a meek-looking man who hadn't opened his mouth all the evening. It was he who told me what had occurred to estrange two old friends like Joyce and Ferguson. It appeared that as a result of their argument Joyce had reported that Ferguson was intellectually dishonest.

'And you know,' added my meek neighbour, 'personally, what I think is wrong with the country———'

I looked at him in fury. What was wrong with the country according to him was sheer stagnation. Everyone was too provincial. Joyce, Fer-guson, the whole lot; it was ten years since any of them had been out of Ireland, and their brains were spoiling for want of fresh contacts. I tried not to listen. I started counting my steps. I counted the stars. At last I stopped dead and begged him for the sake of his dead mother to shut up. He looked staggered. And then, as we were standing under a street lamp, there sailed into view the Professor and Dolan.

'Where are you two off at this hour of night?' I asked.

'He's looking for a fight,' said Dolan in a disgusted tone.

'I am,' agreed the Professor, who was rather oiled.

'Who is it now?' I enquired.

'O'Leary,' replied the Professor, 'that son of a so-and-so, O'Leary. By God, I'll break his bloody neck when I lay hold of him.'

'Get it over before to-morrow night,' I said. 'He's coming to my party too.'

'Party!' he shouted. 'I'll go to no party with that would-be gentleman with his posing and his arts and crafts. Because I wouldn't agree with his preposterous notions about what was wrong with the country.... Christ!' he shouted, throwing down his bowler and resting his heel on it, 'I never said that what was really wrong with the country was that no one had sense enough to cut O'Leary's throat in the cradle.'

'Yes, yes, yes,' said Dolan. 'Come on home!'

'Desmond, did you hear him? The people didn't know how to live. Did you hear him?'

'Of course he heard him,' said Dolan. 'Come on now, like a good chap!'

'A lot he knew about living and his mother an apple-woman at the foot of Bindon Street.... And 'tisn't that at all—oh, Christ, 'tisn't that, but the airs he puts on, carrying round a bloody Greek play that he can't read a word of, and stuttering about people not knowing how to behave like gentlemen.'

'Yes, yes,' I said, 'Dolan's right. You'd better go home.'

'And Liebfraumilch, Desmond. Liebfraumilch!'

'Of course, of course!'

'Pretending he can't stomach porter!'

'For God Almighty's sake,' said Dolan imploringly, 'take his arm. I'm trailing round after him for two solid hours.'

'Be Jases,' said the Professor, driving his heel through his bowler hat, 'if there's one thing I can't stand 'tis anti-clericals. I'd crucify every bloody man that opened his mouth against religion. I would, be God, I'd crucify him!'

I helped to take the Professor home. And do you know? all the way back, every five minutes or so, I found myself saying 'What's wrong with the country?' and an abyss opened in my mind and I had the sort of sick feeling you get sometimes after a heavy feed. I kicked my toe against a flagstone and my first thought was 'What's wrong with the country?' I bashed my face against a gas-lamp and asked 'What's wrong with the country?' I lost my way in a network of dark alleys and muttered 'What's wrong with the country?' Then as I was getting into bed I thought of Sullivan, the Thomist, and how he couldn't put on his shoes without wondering about their subsistent reality, and felt I was on the point of a nervous breakdown myself.

Next evening while I was waiting for my guests I prepared a little speech. This time I wasn't going to allow myself to be upset. I made that speech to the wall fifty times if I made it once, and each time it grew more and more impassioned. Then I looked at the clock. I realised suddenly that I might go on making it; no one was coming. But by this time the theme was flaming in my mind, and I put on my hat and rushed down to Dolan's. Though it was within ten minutes of closing time there was no one in the back but a coal-heaver.

'Well?' I asked Dolan.

'Well?' he replied, rather unpleasantly, I thought.

'I was supposed to be giving a party———' I began.

'And no one turned up!'

'Exactly.'

'Well, it's much the same here.'

'Oh!' I exclaimed.

'And it all hinges about what Linehan really said Nagle's sister was doing with the soldier.'

'Oh!' I repeated.

'And furthermore, Desmond, for your information, this time it's for good, so far as I'm concerned. . . . This decent man,' pointing to the coal-heaver, 'is taking over possession of the back, and the first man that tries to start an intellectual conversation is going to get swiped. . . . I tell you, Desmond, one time I used to think it was a fine thing to have brains and be gassing away about Suetonius and Sybarius, and the divil knows what else, and I used to read all the books them goms gave me till I had me misfortunate head moidhered, but I'm after coming to the conclusion that me father was right, and that what's really wrong with this country is that there's too much brains in it, and it have the country as moidhered as meself. Isn't that right, Packey?'

Packey showed his teeth in a sinister smile and raised his glass.

'Ah, 'tis yourself have the language, Mr. Dolan.'

And that (added Desmond) was my experience, and this year I'm taking my holidays in Paris. Because what's really wrong with this country is that there's too much old talk in it.

.   .   .

'Yes,' I said when Desmond had spun his yarn (more or less as I have set it out in my own words), 'that rather describes an experience of my own. But do you really think we talk so much? Now, I should have said that what was wrong with the country———'

I hesitated when I saw the curious look that came into Desmond's eyes.

'What's wrong with the country,' I repeated weakly, but I could not continue. 'What's wrong with the country———'

Old Fellows

Like other O'Connor stories of precocious, vulnerable young boys, this 1940 tale is rooted in autobiography, with O'Connor as the child, Mick Donovan as his father, and the woolly dog playing himself, although the facts (as described in An Only Child, *9–11) are more frightening than their recreation. What evokes the central "terror and despair" is the fear of being physically and emotionally abandoned by one's parent, a situation the young O'Connor knew well; because of this experience, this story transcends the cliché of a child waiting outside the pub for a drunken father. Although "Old Fellows" ends more favorably than we might expect, its conclusion compensates neither protagonist nor readers for the loss and emptiness stirred here. As in "My Oedipus Complex," we miss the point if we see Towser as a consoling* canis ex machina *who solves all; he is another object, like the model railway, that attempts— and fails—to fill the void where parental love should be.*

If there was one thing I could not stand as a kid it was being taken out for the day by Father. My mature view is that he couldn't stand it either but did it to keep Mother quiet. Mother did it to keep him out of harm's way; I was supposed to act as a brake on him.

He always took me to the same place—Crosshaven—on the paddle-boat. He raved about Cork Harbour, its wonderful scenery and sea-air. I was never one for scenery myself, and as for air, a little went a long way with me. With a man as unobservant as Father, buttons like mine, and strange boats and public-houses which I couldn't find my way about, I lived in mortal fear of an accident.

One day in particular is always in my memory; a Sunday morning with the bells ringing for Mass and the usual scramble on to get Father out of the house. He was standing before the mirror which hung over the mantelpiece, dragging madly at his dickey, and Mother on a low stool in front of him, trying to fasten the studs.

"Ah, go easy!" she said impatiently. "Go easy, can't you?"

Father couldn't go easy. He lowered his head all right, but he shivered and reared like a bucking bronco.

"God Almighty give me patience!" he hissed between his teeth. "Give me patience, sweet God, before I tear the bloody house down!"

It was never what you'd call a good beginning to the day. And to see him later, going down to Pope's Quay to Mass, you'd swear butter wouldn't melt in the old devil's mouth.

After Mass, as we were standing on the quay, J. J. came along. J. J. and father were lifelong friends. He was a melancholy, reedy man with a long sallow face and big hollows under his cheeks. Whenever he was thinking deeply he sucked in the cheeks till his face caved in suddenly like a sandpit. We sauntered down a side street from the quay. I knew well where we were bound for, but with the incurable optimism of childhood I hoped again that this time we might be going somewhere else. We weren't. J. J. stopped by a door at a streetcorner and knocked softly. He had one ear cocked at the door and the other eye cocked at Father. A voice spoke within, a soft voice as in a confessional, and J. J. bowed his head reverently to the keyhole and whispered something back. Father raised his head with a smile and held up two fingers.

"Two minutes now!" he said, and then took a penny from his trousers pocket.

"There's a penny for you," he said benignly. "Mind now and be a good boy."

The door opened and shut almost silently behind Father and J. J. I stood and looked round. The streets were almost deserted, and so silent you could hear the footsteps of people you couldn't see in the laneways high up the hill. The only thing near me was a girl standing a little up from the streetcorner. She was wearing a frilly white hat and a white satiny dress. As it happened, I was wearing a sailor suit for the first time that day. It gave me a slightly raffish feeling. I went up to where she was standing, partly to see what she was looking at, partly to study her closer. She was a beautiful child—upon my word, a beautiful child! And, whatever way it happened, I smiled at her. Mind you, I didn't mean any harm. It was pure good-nature. To this day, that is the sort I am, wanting to be friends with everybody.

The little girl looked at me. She looked at me for a long time; long enough at any rate for the smile to wither off me, and then drew herself up with her head in the air and walked past me down the pavement. Looking back on it, I suppose she was upset because her own father was inside the pub, and a thing like that would mean more to a girl than a boy. But it wasn't only that. By nature she was haughty and cold. It was the first time I had come face to face with the heartlessness of real beauty, and her contemptuous stare knocked me flat. I was a sensitive child. I didn't know where to look, and I wished myself back at home with my mother.

After about ten minutes Father came out with his face all shiny and I ran up to him and took his hand. Unobservant and all as he was, he must have noticed I was upset, because he was suddenly full of palaver about the grand day we were going to have by the seaside. Of course it was all propaganda, because before we reached the boat at all, he had another call.

"Two minutes now!" he said with his two fingers raised and a roguish grin on his face. "Definitely not more than two minutes! Be a good boy!"

At last we did get aboard the paddle-steamer, and, as we moved off down the river, people stood and waved from the road at Tivoli and from under the trees on the Marina walk, while the band played on deck. It was quite exciting, really. And then, all of a sudden, I saw coming up the deck towards us the little girl who had snubbed me outside the public-house. Her father was along with her, a small, fat, red-faced man with a big black beard and a bowler hat. He walked with a sort of roll, and under his arm he carried a model ship with masts and sails—a really superior-looking ship which took my eye at once.

When my father saw him he gave a loud triumphant crow.

"We'll meet in heaven," he said.

"I'd be surprised," said the fat man none too pleasantly.

"Back to the old ship, I see?" said Father, giving J. J. a wink to show he could now expect some sport.

"What exactly do you mean by that?" asked the fat man, giving his moustache a twirl.

"My goodness," said Father, letting on to be surprised, "didn't you tell me 'twas aboard the paddle-boat in Cork Harbour you did your sailoring? Didn't you tell me yourself about the terrible storm that nearly wrecked ye between Aghada and Queenstown?"

"If I mentioned such a thing," said the fat man, "it was only in dread you mightn't have heard of any other place. You were never in Odessa, I suppose?"

"I had a cousin there," said Father gravely. "Cold, I believe. He was telling me they had to chop off the drinks with a hatchet."

"You hadn't a cousin in Valparaiso, by any chance?"

"Well, now, no," said Father regretfully, "that cousin died young of a Maltese fever he contracted while he was with Nansen at the North Pole."

"Maltese fever!" snorted the fat man. "I suppose you couldn't even tell me where Malta is."

By this time there was no holding the pair of them. The fat man was a sailor, and whatever the reason was, my father couldn't see a sailor without wanting to be at his throat. They went into the saloon, and all the way down the river they never as much as stuck their noses out. When I looked in, half the bar had already joined in the argument, some in favour of going to sea and some, like Father, dead against it.

"It broadens the mind, I tell you," said the sailor. "Sailors see the world."

"Do they, indeed?" said Father sarcastically.

"Malta," said the sailor. "You were talking about Malta. Now, there's a beautiful place. The heat of the day drives off the cold of the night."

"Do it?" asked Father in a far-away voice, gazing out the door as though he expected someone to walk in. "Anything else?"

"San Francisco," said the sailor dreamily, "and the scent of the orange blossoms in the moonlight."

"Anything else?" Father asked remorselessly. He was like a priest in the confessional.

"As much more as you fancy," said the sailor.

"But do they see what's under their very noses?" asked Father, rising with his eyes aglow. "Do they see their own country? Do they see that river outside that people come thousands of miles to see? What old nonsense you have!"

I looked round and saw the little girl at my elbow.

"They're at it still," I said.

" 'Tis all your fault," she said coldly.

"How is it my fault?"

"You and your old fellow," she said contemptuously. "Ye have my day ruined on me."

And away she walked again with her head in the air.

I didn't see her again until we landed, and by that time her father and mine had to be separated. They were on to politics, and J. J. thought it safer to get Father away. Father was all for William O'Brien, and he got very savage when he was contradicted. I watched the sailor and the little girl go off along the sea-road while we went in the opposite direction. Father was still simmering about things the sailor had said in favour of John Redmond, a politician he couldn't like. He suddenly stopped and raised his fists in the air.

"I declare to my God if there's one class of men I can't stand, 'tis sailors," he said.

"They're all old blow," agreed J. J. peaceably.

"I wouldn't mind the blooming blow," Father said venomously. " 'Tis all the lies they tell you. San Francisco? That fellow was never near San Francisco. Now, I'm going back," he went on, beginning to stamp from one foot to the other, "and *I'm* going to tell *him* a few lies for a change."

"I wouldn't be bothered," said J. J., and, leaning his head over Father's shoulder, he began to whisper in his ear the way you'd whisper to a restive young horse, and with the same sort of result, for Father gradually ceased his stamping and rearing and looked doubtfully at J. J. out of the corner of his eye. A moment later up went the two fingers.

"Two minutes," he said with a smile that was only put on. "Not more. Be a good boy now."

He slipped me another copper and I sat on the sea-wall, watching the crowds and wondering if we'd ever get out of the village that day. Beyond the villages were the cliffs, and pathways wound over them, in and out of groups of thatched cottages. The band would be playing up there, and people would be dancing. There would be stalls for lemonade and sweets. If only I could get up there I should at least have something to look at. My heart gave a jump and then sank. I saw, coming through the crowd, the sailor and the little girl. She was swinging out of his arm, and in her own free arm she carried the model ship. They stopped before the pub.

"Daddy," I heard her say in that precise, ladylike little voice of hers, "You promised to sail my boat for me."

"In one second now," said her father. "I have a certain thing to say to a man in here."

Then in with him to the pub. The little girl had tears in her eyes. I was sorry for her—that's the sort I am, very soft-hearted.

"All right," I said. "I'll go in and try to get my da out."

But when I went in I saw it was no good. Her father was sitting on the windowsill, and behind him the blue bay and the white yachts showed like a newspaper photo through the mesh of the window screen. Father was walking up and down, his head bent, like a caged tiger.

"Capwell?" I heard him say in a low voice.

"Capwell I said," replied the sailor.

"Evergreen?" said Father.

"Evergreen," nodded the sailor.

"The oldest stock in Cork, you said?" whispered Father.

"Fifteenth century," said the sailor.

Father looked at him with a gathering smile as though he thought it was one of the sailor's jokes. Then he shook his head good-humouredly, and walked to the other side of the bar as though to say it was too much for him. Madness had out-ranged itself.

"The north side of the city," said the sailor, growing heated at such disbelief, "what is it only foreigners? People that came in from beyond the lamps a generation ago. Tramps and fiddlers and pipers."

"They had the intellect," Father said quietly.

"Intellect?" exclaimed the sailor. "The north side?"

" 'Twas always given up to them," said Father firmly.

"That's the first I heard of it," said the sailor.

Father began to scribble with a couple of fingers on the palm of his left hand.

"Now," he said gravely, "I'll give you odds. I'll go back a hundred years with you. Tell me the name of a single outstanding man—now I said an *outstanding* man, mind you—that was born on the south side of the city in that time."

"Daddy," I said, pulling him by the coattails, "you promised to take me up the cliffs."

"In two minutes now," he replied with a brief laugh, and, almost by second nature, handed me another penny.

That was four I had. J. J., a thoughtful poor soul, followed me out with two bottles of lemonade and a couple of packets of biscuits. The little girl and I ate and drank, sitting on the low wall outside the pub. Then we went down to the water's edge and tried to sail the boat, but, whatever was wrong with it, it would only float on its side; its sails got wringing wet, and we left them to dry while we listened to the organ of the merry-go-rounds from the other side of the bay.

It wasn't until late afternoon that the sailor and Father came out, and by this time there seemed to be no more than the breath of life between them. It was astonishing to me how friendly they were. Father had the sailor by the lapel of his jacket and was begging him to wait for the boat, but the sailor explained that he had given his solemn word to his wife to have the little girl home in time for bed and insisted that he'd have to go by the train. After he had departed, my father threw a long, lingering look at the sky, and seeing it was so late, slipped me another penny and retired to the bar till the siren went for the boat. They were hauling up the gangway when J. J. got him down.

It was late when we landed, and the full moon was riding over the river; a lovely, nippy September night; but I was tired and hungry and blown up with wind. We went up the hill in the moonlight and every few yards Father stopped to lay down the law. By this time he was ready to argue with anyone about anything. We came to the cathedral, and there were three old women sitting on the steps gossiping, their black shawls trailing like shadows on the pavement. It made me sick for home, a cup of hot cocoa, and my own warm bed.

Then suddenly under a gas lamp at the streetcorner I saw a small figure in white. It was like an apparition. I was struck with terror and despair. I don't know if J. J. saw the same thing, but all at once he began to direct Father's attention to the cathedral and away from the figure in white.

"That's a beautiful tower," he said in a husky voice.

Father stopped and screwed up his eyes to study it.

"What's beautiful about it?" he asked. "I don't see anything very remarkable about that."

"Ah, 'tis, man," said J. J. reverently. "That's a great tower."

"Now, I'm not much in favour of towers," said Father, tossing his head cantankerously. "I don't see what use are towers. I'd sooner a nice plain limestone front with pillars like the Sand Quay."

At the time I wasn't very concerned about the merits of Gothic and Renaissance, so I tried to help J. J. by tugging Father's hand. It was no good. One glance round and his eye took in the white figure at the other side of the road. He chuckled ominously and put his hand over his eyes, like a sailor on deck.

"Hard aport, mate!" he said. "What do I see on my starboard bow?"

"Ah, nothing," said J. J.

"Nothing?" echoed Father joyously. "What sort of lookout man are you? . . . Ahoy, shipmate!" he bawled across the road. "Didn't your old skipper go home yet?"

"He did not," cried the little girl—it was she of course—"and let you leave him alone!"

"The thundering ruffian!" said my father in delight, and away he went across the road. "What do he mean? A sailorman from the south side, drinking in my diocese! I'll have him ejected."

"Daddy," I wailed, with my heart in my boots. "Come home, can't you?"

"Two minutes," he said with a chuckle, and handed me another copper, the sixth.

The little girl was frantic. She scrawled and beat him about the legs with her fist, but he only laughed at her, and when the door opened he forced his way in with a shout: "Anyone here from Valparaiso?"

J. J. sucked in his cheeks till he looked like a skeleton in the moonlight, and then nodded sadly and followed Father in. The door was bolted behind them and the little girl and I were left together on the pavement. The three old women on the cathedral steps got up and shuffled off down a cobbled laneway. The pair of us sat on the curb and snivelled.

"What bad luck was on me this morning to meet you?" said the little girl.

" 'Twas on me the bad luck was," I said, "and your old fellow keeping my old fellow out."

"Your old fellow is only a common labouring man," said the little girl contemptuously, "and my daddy says he's ignorant and conceited."

"And your old fellow is only a sailor," I retorted indignantly, "and my father says all sailors are liars."

"How dare you!" she said. "My daddy is not a liar, and I hope he keeps your old fellow inside all night, just to piece you out for your impudence."

"I don't care," I said with mock bravado, "I can go home when I like and you can't—bah!"

"You'll have to wait till your father comes out."

"I needn't. I can go home myself."

"I dare you! You and your sailor suit!"

I could have let it pass but for her gibe at my suit; but that insult had to be avenged. I got up and took a few steps, just to show her. I thought she'd be afraid to stay behind alone, but she wasn't. She was too bitter. Of course, I had no intention of going home by myself at that hour of night. I stopped.

"Coward!" she said venomously. "You're afraid."

"I'll show you whether I'm afraid or not," I said sulkily, and went off down Shandon Street—I who had never before been out alone after dark. I was terrified. It's no use swanking about it. I was simply terrified. I stopped every few yards, hoping she'd call out or that Father would come running after me. Neither happened, and at each dark laneway I shut my eyes. There was no sound but feet climbing this flight of steps or descending that. When I reached the foot of Shandon Street by the old graveyard, and saw the long, dark, winding hill before me, my courage gave out. I was afraid to go on and afraid to turn back.

Then I saw a friendly sign; a little huxter shop with a long flight of steps to the door, flanked by iron railings. High over the basement I could see the narrow window decorated in crinkly red paper, with sweet bottles and a few toys on view. Then I saw one toy that raised my courage. I counted my coppers again. There were six. I climbed the steps, went in the dark hallway, and turned right into the front room, which was used as the shop. A little old Mother Hubbard of a woman came out, rubbing her hands in her apron.

"Well, little boy?" she asked briskly.

"I want a dog, ma'am."

"Sixpence apiece the dogs," she said doubtfully. "Have you sixpence?"

"I have, ma'am," said I, and I counted out my coppers. She gave me the dog, a black, woolly dog with two beads for eyes. I ran down the steps and up the road with my head high, whistling. I only wished that the little girl could see me now; she wouldn't say I was a coward. To show my contempt for the terrors of night I stood at the mouth of each laneway and looked down. I stroked the dog's fur, and when some shadow loomed up more frightening than the others I turned his head at it.

"Ssss!" I said. "At him, boy! At him!"

When Mother opened the door I caught him and held him back.

"Down, Towser, down!" I said commandingly. "It's only Mummy."

The Holy Door

One of O'Connor's favorite stories, "The Holy Door" examines the tensions between individuals and the community, husbands and wives, even between parents and their adult children. As in "The Little Mother" and "The Luceys," the world is defined by intertwined expectations and the complications they provoke. The musical theme underlying all the characters' actions is in the minor key of sexual repression, as emotional and physical needs are thwarted by piety, respectability, and prudery.

This, his longest story, like its counterparts above, resembles a novella: it contained too much—events and reverberations—for his usual contained form. Completing the story to his satisfaction was difficult—he began it in 1943 and wrote more than twenty versions before its 1947 publication. Both he and Sean O'Faoláin knew the story of a Cork wife who could tolerate intercourse only when imagining her husband a movie star. O'Faoláin's version is "The Woman Who Married Clark Gable"; typically, it is pungently specific (the wife is enraptured only by the Gable of the movie San Francisco, which she sees over and over; her husband attempts a mustache, which makes the fantasy more tangible). "The Holy Door" is more troubling as it characterizes a nation's obsession, not simply one skewed relationship.

Polly Donegan and Nora Lawlor met every morning after eight o'clock Mass. They were both good-living girls; indeed, they were among the best girls in town. Nora had a round soft face and great round wondering eyes. She was inquisitive, shy, and a dreamer—an awkward combination. Her father, a builder called Jerry Lawlor, had been vice-commandant of the Volunteers during the Troubles.

Polly was tall, with coal-black hair, a long, proud, striking face, and

91

an air of great calm and resolution. As they went down the hill from the church she saluted everyone with an open pleasant smile and accepted whatever invitations she got. Nora went through the torments of the damned whenever anyone invited her anywhere; curiosity and timidity combined made her visualize every consequence of accepting or not accepting, down to the last detail.

Now Nora, with that peculiar trait in her make-up, had a knack which Polly found very disconcerting of bringing the conversation round to the facts of life. To Nora the facts of life were the ultimate invitation; acceptance meant never-ending embarrassment, refusal a curiosity unsatisfied until death. While she struggled to put her complex in words Polly adopted a blank and polite air and without the least effort retreated into her own thoughts of what they should have for dinner.

"You're not listening to a word I say," Nora said on a note of complaint.

"Oh, I am, Nora, I am," Polly said impatiently. "But I'll have to be rushing or I'll be late for breakfast."

Nora could see that Polly wasn't even interested in the facts of life. She wondered a lot about that. Was Polly natural? Was it possible not to be curious? Was she only acting sly like all the Donegans? Nora had thought so long about God's inscrutable purpose in creating mankind in two sexes that she could hardly see the statue of a saint without wondering what he'd be like without his clothes. That was no joke in our church, where there are statues inside the door and in each of the sidechapels and along the columns of the arcade. It makes the church quite gay, but it was a terrible temptation to Nora, who found it hard not to see them all like Greek statues, and whatever it was about their faces and gestures they seemed worse like that than any Greek divinities. To the truly pious mind there is something appalling in the idea of St. Aloysius Gonzaga without his clothes.

That particular notion struck Polly as the height of nonsense.

"Wisha, Nora," she said with suppressed fury, "what things you think about!"

"But after all," retorted Nora with a touch of fire, "they must have had bodies like the rest of us."

"Why then indeed, Nora, they'd be very queer without them," said Polly serenely, and it was clear to Nora that she hadn't a glimmer. "Anyway, what has it to do with us?"

"You might find it has a lot to do with you when you get married," said Nora darkly.

"Ah, well, it'll never worry me so," said Polly confidently.

"Why, Polly? Won't you ever get married?"

"What a thing I'd do!" said Polly.

"But why, Polly?" asked Nora eagerly, hoping that at last she might discover some point where Polly's fastidiousness met her own.

"Ah," Polly sighed, "I could never imagine myself married. No matters how fond of them you'd be. Like Susie. I always hated sharing a room with Susie. She was never done talking."

"Oh, if talking was all that was in it!" exclaimed Nora with a dark brightness like a smile.

"I think talking is the worst of all, Nora," Polly said firmly. "I can't imagine anything worse."

"There's a shock in store for you if you do marry," said Nora darkly.

"What sort of shock, Nora?" asked Polly.

"Oh, of course, you can't even describe it," said Nora fretfully. "No one will even tell you. People you knew all your life go on as if you were only a child and couldn't be told."

"Do they really, Nora?" Polly said with a giggle, inspired less by thought of what the mystery could be than by that of Nora's inquisitiveness brought to a full stop for once.

"If you get married before me will you tell me?" Nora asked.

"Oh, I will to be sure, girl," said Polly in the tone of one promising to let her know when the coal man came.

"But I mean everything, Polly," said Nora earnestly.

"Oh, why wouldn't I, Nora?" cried Polly impatiently, showing that Nora's preoccupation with the facts struck her as being uncalled-for. "Anyway, you're more likely to be married than I am. Somehow I never had any inclination for it."

It was clear that her sister's garrulity had blighted some man's chance of Polly.

.   .   .

Charlie Cashman was a great friend of Nora's father and a regular visitor to her home. He had been her father's Commandant during the Troubles. He owned the big hardware store in town and this he owed entirely to his good national record. He and his mother had never got on, for she hated the Volunteers as she hated the books he read; she looked on him as a flighty fellow and had determined early in life that the shop would go to her second son, John Joe. As Mrs. Cashman was a woman who had never known what it was not to have her own way, Charlie had resigned himself to this, and after the Troubles, cleared out and worked as a shop assistant in Asragh. But then old John Cashman died, having never in his lifetime contradicted his wife, and his will was found to be nothing but a contradiction. It seemed that he had always been a violent nationalist and admired culture and hated John Joe, and Charlie, as in the novels, got every damn thing, even his mother being left in the house only on sufferance.

Charlie was a good catch and there was no doubt of his liking for Nora, but somehow Nora couldn't bear him. He was an airy, excitable man with a plump, sallow, wrinkled face that always looked as if it needed shaving, a pair of keen grey eyes in slits under bushy brows; hair on his cheekbones, hair in his ears, hair even in his nose. He wore a dirty old tweed suit and a cap. Nora couldn't stand him—even with his clothes on. She told herself that it was the cleft in his chin, which someone had once told her betokened a sensual nature, but it was really the thought of all that hair. It made him look so animal!

Besides, there was something sly and double-meaning about him. He was, by town standards, a very well-read man. Once he'd found Nora reading St. Francis de Sales and asked her if she'd ever read *Romeo and Juliet* with such a knowing air that he roused her dislike even further. She gave him a cold and penetrating look which should have crushed him but didn't—he was so thick.

"As a matter of fact I have," she said steadily, just to show him that true piety did not exclude a study of the grosser aspects of life.

"What did you think of it?" he asked.

"I thought it contained a striking moral lesson," said Nora.

"Go on!" Charlie exclaimed with a grin. "What was that, Nora?"

"It showed where unrestrained passion can carry people," she said.

"Ah, I wouldn't notice that," said Charlie. "Your father and myself were a bit wild too, in our time."

Her father, a big, pop-eyed, open-gobbed man, looked at them both and said nothing, but he knew from their tone that they were sparring across him and he wanted to know more about it. That night after Charlie had gone he looked at Nora with a terrible air.

"What's that book Charlie Cashman was talking about?" he asked. "Did I read that?"

"*Romeo and Juliet?*" she said with a start. "It's there on the shelf behind you. In the big Shakespeare."

Jerry took down the book and looked even more astonished.

"That's a funny way to write a book," he said. "What is it about?"

She told him the story as well as she could, with a slight tendency to make Friar Laurence the hero, and her father looked more pop-eyed than ever. He had a proper respect for culture.

"But they were married all right?" he asked at last.

"They were," said Nora. "Why?"

"Ah, that was a funny way to take him up so," her father said cantankerously. " 'Tisn't as if there was anything wrong in it." He went to the foot of the stairs with his hands in his trouser pockets while Nora watched him with a hypnotised air. She knew what he was thinking of. "Mind," he said, "I'm not trying to force him on you, but there's plenty of girls in this town would be glad of your chance."

That was all he said but Nora wanted no chances. She would have preferred to die in the arena like a Christian martyr sooner than marry a man with so much hair. She never even gave Charlie the opportunity of proposing, though she knew her father and he had discussed it between themselves.

And then, to her utter disgust, Charlie transferred his attentions to Polly, whom he had met at her house. Of course, her disgust had nothing to do with jealousy of Polly. Mainly it was inspired by the revelation it afforded of masculine character, particularly of Charlie's. Sensual, flighty, he had not the decency to remain a celibate the rest of his life; he hadn't threatened suicide, hadn't even to be taken away for a long holiday by his friends. He merely cut his losses as though she were a type of car he couldn't afford and took the next cheapest.

It left her depressed about human nature in general. Only too well had her father gauged the situation. Not only did the Donegans go all-out to capture Charlie but Polly herself seemed quite pleased. After all she had said against marriage, this struck Nora as sly. In more judicious moments she knew she was not being quite fair to Polly. The truth was probably that Polly, being a good-natured, dutiful girl, felt if she were to marry at all, she should do so in such a way as to oblige her family. She did not mind the hair and had a genuine liking for Charlie. She was a modest girl who made no claim to brains; she never even knew which of the two parties was the government of the moment, and Charlie could explain it all to her in the most interesting way. To her he seemed a man of really gigantic intellect, and listening to him was like listening to a great preacher.

Yet, even admitting all this, Nora thought her conduct pretty strange. The Donegans were all sly. It caused a certain coldness between the two girls, but Polly was self-centered and hard-hearted and Nora got the worst of that.

.   .   .

Like all young brides-to-be, Polly was full of plans. When Charlie asked where they should go on their honeymoon she looked troubled.

"Ah, 'twould cost too much," she said in her tangential way.

"What would cost too much, girl?" Charlie replied recklessly. "Never mind what it costs. Where do you want to go?"

"Lourdes," Polly asked, half as a question. "Is that far, Charlie?"

"Lourdes," repeated Charlie in bewilderment. "What do you want to go to Lourdes for?"

"Oh, only for the sake of the pilgrimage," said Polly. "You never read *The Life of Bernadette,* Charlie?"

"Never," said Charlie promptly, in dread he was going to be compelled to read it. "We'll go to Lourdes."

It was all arranged when one day Polly and Nora met in the street. Nora was self-conscious; she was thinking of all the things she had said of Charlie to Polly and certain they had got back (they hadn't, but Nora judged by herself).

"Where are ye going for the honeymoon?" she asked.

"You'd never guess," replied Polly joyously.

"Where?" Nora asked, her eyes beginning to pop.

"Lourdes, imagine!"

"Lourdes?" cried Nora aghast. "But didn't you know?"

"Know what, Nora?" Polly asked, alarmed in her turn. "Don't tell me 'tis forbidden."

" 'Tisn't that at all but 'tis unlucky," said Nora breathlessly. "I only knew one girl that did it and she died inside a year."

"Oh, Law, Nora," Polly cried with bitter disappointment, "how is it nobody told me that, or what sort of people do they have in those travel agencies?"

"I suppose they took it for granted you'd know," said Nora.

"How *could* I know, Nora?" Polly cried despairingly. "Even Charlie doesn't know, and he's supposed to be an educated man."

Away she rushed to challenge Charlie and they had their first big row. Charlie was now reconciled to Lourdes by the prospect of a few days in Paris, and he stamped and fumed about Nora Lawlor and her blasted pishrogues, but you did not catch a prudent girl like Polly risking fortune and happiness by defying the will of God, and a few days before the wedding everything was cancelled. They went to Connemara instead.

They arrived there on a wet evening and Polly said dismally that it wasn't in the least like what she expected. This was not the only thing that failed to come up to her expectations, nor was hers the only disappointment. She had brought a little statue of the Blessed Virgin and put it on the table by her bed. Then she said her night prayers and undressed. She was rather surprised at the way Charlie looked at her but not really upset. She was exhausted after the journey and remarked to Charlie on the comfort of the bed. "Oh," she said with a yawn, "I don't think there's anything in the world like bed." At this Charlie gave her a wolfish grin, not like any grin she'd ever seen before, and it filled her with alarm. "Oh, Charlie, what did I say?" she asked. Charlie didn't reply, which was still more alarming; he got into bed beside her and she gave a loud gasp that could be heard right through the hotel.

For the rest of the night, her brain, not usually retentive of ideas, had room only for one. "Can it be? Is it possible? Why did nobody tell me?" She kept herself from flying out of the room in hysterics only by repeating aspirations like "Jesus, mercy! Mary, help!" She thought of all the married women she had known from her mother on—fat, pious, good-natured women you saw every morning at Mass—and wondered if they had lived all those years with such a secret in their hearts. Now she knew exactly what Nora had been trying to find out and why no one had ever told her. It was something that couldn't be told, only endured. One faint hope remained; that after years she might get used to it as the others seemed to have done. But then it all began again and she muttered aspirations to herself loud enough for Charlie to hear, and knew she could never, never get used to it; and when it was over a bitter anger smouldered in her against all the old nonsense that had been written about it by old gasbags like Shakespeare, "Oh, what liars they are!" she thought, wishing she could just lay hands on one of them for five minutes. "What liars!"

The day after they returned from the honeymoon Nora called. She had managed to bottle her curiosity just so far. Charlie was in the shop and she smiled shyly at him. Polly and herself sat in the best room overlooking the Main Street and had their tea. Nora noticed with satisfaction that she looked a bit haggard. Then Nora lit a cigarette and sat back.

"And what does it feel like to be married?" she asked with a smile.

"Oh, all right, Nora," Polly replied, though for a moment her face looked more haggard than before.

"And how do you find Charlie?"

"Oh, much like anyone else, I suppose," Polly said doubtfully, and her eyes strayed in the direction of the window.

"And is that all you're going to tell us?" Nora went on with a nervous laugh.

"Oh, whatever do you mean, Nora?" Polly asked indignantly.

"I thought you were going to advise me," Nora said lightly, though with a growing feeling that there was nothing to be got out of Polly.

"Oh, Law, Nora," Polly said with a distraught air, "I don't think it can ever be right to talk about things like that."

Nora knew she would never get anything out of Polly. She would never get anything out of anybody. They were all the same. They went inside and the door closed behind them forever. She felt like crying.

"Was it as bad as that?" she asked with chagrin.

"I think I'd sooner not talk about it at all, Nora," Polly said firmly. She bowed her head; her smooth forehead became fenced with wrinkles and a second chin began to peep from beneath the first.

. . .

Charlie's shop was on Main Street; a store like a cave, with buckets and spades hanging and stacked at either side of the opening. When you went in there was hardware on your right and the general store on the left. Charlie looked after the hardware and Polly and a girl assistant after the rest. Charlie's end of it was really well run; there wasn't a bit of agricultural machinery for miles around that he didn't know the workings of and for which, at a pinch, he couldn't produce at least the substitute for a spare part.

Polly wasn't brilliant in that way, but she was conscientious and polite. In every way she was all a wife should be; obliging, sweet-tempered, good-humoured, and so modest that she wouldn't even allow

Charlie to put on the light while she dressed for Mass on a winter morning. Mrs. Cashman had always had a great selection of holy pictures but Polly had brought a whole gallery with her. There was also a Lourdes clock which played the Lourdes hymn at the Angelus hours—very soothing and devotional—but at the same time Charlie was just the least bit disappointed.

He was disappointed and he couldn't say why. "Romeo, Romeo, wherefore art thou, Romeo?" he would suddenly find himself declaiming about nothing at all. Italian women were probably different. No doubt it was the sun! He was a restless man and he had hoped marriage would settle him. It hadn't settled him. When he had closed the shop for the night and should have been sitting upstairs with his book and his pipe, the longing would suddenly seize him to go out to Johnny Desmond's pub instead. He would walk in and out the hall and peer up and down the street till the restlessness became too much for him. It was all very disconcerting. Sometimes for consolation he went back to the shop, switched on the lamp over his desk, and took out the copy of his father's will. This was the will from which he had expected nothing and which gave him everything. He read it through again with a reverent expression. He had always liked the will; admired its massive style; the way it carefully excluded all possibility of misunderstanding; it had given him a new respect for lawyers; indeed, in its own way it was as powerful as Shakespeare.

One murky, gloomy afternoon when business had stopped his mother came in and found him at it. He gave her a sly grin. She was a cranky, crafty, monotonous old woman, twisted with rheumatics and malice.

"I was just saying my office," he said.

"Oh, I see what you're at," she said with resignation. "I saw it long ago."

"Fine, devotional reading!" said Charlie, slapping a hairy paw on the will.

"Go on, you blasphemous bosthoon!" she said without rancour. "You were always too smart for your poor slob of a brother. But take care you wouldn't be keeping the bed warm for him yet!"

"What's that you say?" asked Charlie, startled.

"God spoke first," intoned his mother. "Many a better cake didn't rise."

She went out, banging the door behind her, and left Charlie gasping, naked to the cruel day. The will had lost its magical power. There was one clause in it to which he had never paid attention—there never had been any reason why he should do so—entailing the shop on his children and, failing those, on John Joe's. And John Joe had four with another coming while Charlie still had none.

Another man only a year married wouldn't have given it a thought, but Charlie wasn't that kind. The man was a born worrier. With his hands in his pockets he paced moodily to the shop door and stood there, leaning against the jamb, his legs crossed and his cap pulled down over his eyes.

His mother read him like a book. The least thing was enough to set him off. At the first stroke of the Angelus he put up the shutters and ate his supper. Then he lit his pipe and strolled to the hall door for a look up and down the Main Street on the off chance of seeing somebody or something. He never did, but it was as well to make sure. Then he returned to the kitchen, his feet beginning to drag as they usually did before he set out to Johnny Desmond's. It was their way of indicating that they weren't moving in the right direction. His mother had gone to the chapel and Polly was sitting by the table under the window. Charlie took a deep breath, removed his hands from his pockets, raised his head, and squared his shoulders.

"Well," he said briskly, "I might as well take a little turn."

"Wisha, you might as well, Charlie," Polly replied without resentment.

It was only what she always said, but in Charlie's state of depression it sounded like a dead key on the piano. He felt it was a hard thing that a married man of a year's standing had no inclination to stop at home and that his wife had no inclination to make him. Not that she could have made him even if she had tried but he felt that a little persuasion wouldn't have been out of place.

"The mother wasn't talking to you?" he asked keenly.

"No, Charlie," Polly said in surprise. "What would she talk to me about?"

"Oh, nothing in particular. . . . Only she was remarking that you were a long time about having a family," he added with a touch of reproach.

"Oh, Law, Charlie," Polly cried, "wasn't that a very queer thing for her to say?"

"Was it, I wonder?" Charlie said as though to himself but giving her a sideway glance.

"But Charlie, you don't think I won't have children, do you?" she exclaimed.

"Oh, no, no, no," Charlie replied hastily, in dread he might have said too much. "But 'twould suit her fine if you hadn't. Then she'd have the place for John Joe's children."

"But how would John Joe's children get it?" asked Polly. "Didn't your father leave it to you?"

"To me and my children," said Charlie. "If I hadn't children 'twould go to John Joe's."

"Oh, Law, Charlie, isn't that a great worry to you?"

"Well, it is, a bit," Charlie conceded, scratching his poll. "I put a lot of work into the place. No one likes working for another man's family. You wouldn't see a doctor?"

"I'd have to ask Father Ring first."

That upset Charlie again. He nearly told her it was Father Ring she should have married, but remembered in time that she'd be bound to confess it. There's nothing a good-living woman likes as much as confessing her husband's sins.

.   .   .

Charlie's remarks brought Polly for the first time up against the facts of life. This made her very thoughtful, but it was a week before she could even bring herself to discuss it with Nora. It was a subject you could only discuss with a woman, and an intellectual woman at that, and Nora was the only intellectual woman Polly knew.

Nora was not inclined to treat it as seriously as Charlie had done. According to her there was a lot of chance in it. Some people went on for years before they had a child; others didn't even wait for their time to be up. It was quite shocking when you came to think of it, but somehow Polly never did get round to thinking of it. If you were really in trouble, there was always the Holy Door. Johnny Fleming the barrister and his wife had been married ten years without having children, and they had made the pilgrimage to the Holy Door, and now people were beginning to say it was about time they made another to shut off the power.

"I suppose I could go next year if I had to," said Polly doubtfully.

"You'll have to go this year if you're going at all," said Nora. "It's only opened once in seven years."

"Seven years!" cried Polly. "Oh, I could never wait as long as that."

"It would be too dangerous anyway," said Nora. "There was a woman up our road waited till she was thirty-eight to have a child, and she died."

"Oh, Law!" cried Polly, a little peeved. "I suppose 'tis wrong to be criticizing, but really, the Lord's ways are very peculiar."

So back she went to Charlie with her story. Charlie screwed up his face as though he were hard of hearing, a favourite trick of his whenever he wanted to gain time. He wanted to gain it now.

"Where did you say?" he asked searchingly.

"Rome," repeated Polly.

"Rome?" echoed Charlie with a mystified air. "And what did you say you wanted to go to Rome for?"

"It's the pilgrimage to the Holy Door," said Polly. "You wouldn't know about that?" she asked in the trustful tone she used to indicate the respect she had for his learning.

"No," replied Charlie doubtfully, playing up to the part of the well-informed husband. "What sort of door?"

"A holy door."

"A holy door?"

" 'Tis only opened once in seven years, and 'tis good for people that want families," prompted Polly hopefully.

"Is that so?" asked Charlie gravely. "Who told you about that?"

"Nora Lawlor."

"Tut, tut, tut," clucked Charlie impatiently, "ah, I wouldn't say there would be any truth in that, Polly."

"Oh, Law, Charlie," she cried in ringing tones, outraged at his lack of faith, "you surely don't think the Flemings would go all that way unless there was something in it?"

"Oh, no, no, no, I dare say not," Charlie said hastily, seeing that any further objections he made were likely to be reported back to Father Ring. "I'm afraid I couldn't get away, though."

"Well, I'll have to get away, Charlie," Polly said with quiet decision. "It might be too late if I left it for another seven years. Nora says 'tis very dangerous."

"And a hell of a lot of danger that one will ever be in!" snapped Charlie fierily.

His bad temper did not last long. This was an excuse for an outing, and Charlie loved an outing. He had never been farther than London before; Paris staggered him; he experimented with green drinks, pink drinks, and yellow drinks with the satisfied expression of a child in a pantry; and while the train passed through the Alps in the late evening he wedged himself in the corridor with his elbows on the rail, humming "Home to Our Mountains," while tears of excitement poured down his hairy cheeks. He couldn't forget that he was going to the homeland of Romeo and Juliet.

He quickly made friends with the other two occupants of the carriage, a fat Dutchman in shirtsleeves who ate sausages and embraced the woman beside him who he said was his wife. The sight was too gross for Polly and she went and stood in the corridor but not to look at the scenery.

"Isn't she beautiful?" said the Dutchman, stroking his companion affectionately under the chin.

"Grand! grand!" agreed Charlie enthusiastically, nodding and smiling encouragement to the woman, who couldn't speak English and to all appearances didn't know much of any other language either.

"That's a nice-looking girl with you," said the Dutchman. "Who is she?"

"Polly?" said Charlie, looking at the gloomy figure in the corridor. "Oh, that's the wife."

"Whose wife?" asked the Dutchman.

"Mine," said Charlie.

"And don't you love her?"

"Love her?" echoed Charlie, giving another peep out. "I'm cracked on her, of course."

"Then why don't you make love to her?" asked the Dutchman in surprise. "Women can't have enough of it. Look at this!"

"Ah, mine wouldn't like it," said Charlie in alarm. "In Ireland we don't go in much for that sort of thing."

"And what do you go in for?"

"Well," said Charlie doubtfully, seeing that he didn't quite know, himself—apart from politics, which didn't sound right—"we're more in the sporting line; horses and dogs, you know."

"Ah," said the Dutchman earnestly, "you can't beat women."

Charlie went out to Polly, who was leaning with her back to the compartment and with a brooding look on her face.

"Charlie, how do they do it?" she asked in a troubled voice. "Wouldn't you think the woman would drop dead with shame? I suppose they're Protestants, are they, Charlie?"

"I dare say, I dare say," said Charlie, thinking it was better not to try and explain.

.   .   .

It was a great outing and it lasted Charlie in small talk for a month. The grapes like gooseberries, and from nightfall on every little café with soprano or tenor or baritone bawling away about love—*amore, mio cuore, traditore*—you could see where Juliet got it. But they weren't there long enough for Polly to be infected, and all the wonders she brought back was her astonishment at the way the men in St. Peter's pinched her bottom. "Your what, Polly?" the neighbours asked in surprise. "My bottom," repeated Polly, incredulously. "Would you believe it?"

After that, Morgan, the wit of Johnny Desmond's pub, began dropping nasty remarks about doors of one sort and another, while old Mrs. Cashman, getting over her alarm at the possibility of divine intervention, declared loudly that it would be a poor lookout for a woman like her to be relying on a son who had to take his wife to Rome. It didn't take a miracle to start John Joe's wife off, for the poor wretch had only to look at her.

But Polly, to give her her due, was every bit as upset as Charlie. Sixty pounds odd the pilgrimage had cost, and they had absolutely nothing to show for it. If the Holy Door couldn't do a thing like that it couldn't be so holy after all. She scolded Nora Lawlor a lot over her bad advice.

"But after all, Polly," Nora said reasonably, "you mustn't expect too much. It might be something mental."

"Oh, how could it, Nora?" Polly cried in a fury. "What a thing to say!"

"But why not?" asked Nora with a touch of asperity. "If you didn't feel attracted to Charlie———"

"Oh," said Polly vaguely and guardedly but with a dim comprehension dawning in her eyes, "would that make a difference?"

"It might make all the difference in the world, Polly," Nora said severely. "After all, there was Kitty Daly. She was married eight years without having a family, and one night she pretended to herself that her husband was Rudolph Valentino, and everything was all right."

"Rudolph Valentino?" said Polly. "Who's he?"

"He was a film actor," said Nora.

"But why would she do that?"

"Well, I suppose he was a nice-looking man, and you know what sort Jerome Daly is."

"Would there be a picture of that fellow that I could see?" asked Polly.

"I wouldn't say so," replied Nora. "Anyway, he's dead now, so I suppose it wouldn't be right. But, of course, there are plenty of others just as nice-looking."

"Oh, I don't think it could ever be right," cried Polly with a petulant toss of her head. She was feeling very sorry for herself. She knew quite well that that sly thing, Nora, was trying to worm out of her what Charlie really did to her and she was torn asunder between the need for revealing something and the desire not to reveal anything at all. "I'm sure Father Ring would say it was wrong."

"I don't see why he would," Nora said coolly. "After all, it was done with a good purpose."

Polly had no reply for that, for she knew the importance of doing things with a good purpose, but at the same time the temptation lingered. The following Saturday evening she went to confession to Father Ring. Her sins didn't take long to tell. They were never what you'd call major ones.

"Father," she said when she had done, "I want to ask your advice."

"What about, my child?" asked Father Ring.

"It's my husband, father," said Polly. "You see, we have no children, and I know it's a terrible worry to him, so I went on the pilgrimage to the Holy Door but it didn't do me any good."

"Go on," said Father Ring.

"So a friend of mine was telling me about another woman that was in the same position. It seems she imagined her husband was Rudolph Valentino."

"Who was he?"

"Some sort of fellow in the pictures."

"But what made her think he was her husband?" asked Father Ring with a puzzled frown.

"Oh, she didn't think it," said Polly in distress. "She only pretended. It seems he was a very nice-looking fellow and her husband is an insignificant little man. . . . Of course, I could understand that," she added candidly. "My husband is a very good fellow, but somehow it doesn't look right."

"Is it Charlie?" exclaimed Father Ring, so astonished that he broke the tone of decent anonymity in which the discussion was being conducted. "Sure, Charlie is a grand-looking man."

"Oh, would you think so?" asked Polly with real interest. "Of course I might be wrong. But anyway, this woman had a child after."

"What did she call him?" asked Father Ring.

"I don't know, Father. Does it make any difference?"

"No. I was just wondering."

"But tell me, father, would that ever be right?" asked Polly.

"Ah, I don't say there would be anything wrong about it," said Father Ring, pulling aside the curtain before the confessional and peeping out into the darkened church. "Of course she did it with a good object."

"That's what my friend said," said Polly, amazed at the intellect of that little gligeen of a girl.

"Provided, of course, she didn't get any pleasure from it," Father Ring added hastily. "If she got carnal pleasure out of it that would be a different thing."

"Oh!" exclaimed Polly, aghast. "You don't think she'd do that?"

"What I mean," the priest explained patiently, "is more than the natural pleasure."

"The natural pleasure?" repeated Polly with a stunned air.

"However," said Father Ring hastily, "I don't think you're in much danger of that."

It was shortly after this that Charlie began to notice a change in the atmosphere in Johnny Desmond's. Charlie was very sensitive to atmosphere. First Morgan passed a remark about Polly and the new teacher, Carmody. Now, Carmody was a relative of Father Ring's, as has been said, a good-looking plausible Kerryman who put on great airs with the women. Charlie greeted the remark with a sniff and a laugh and was almost on the point of telling how Polly wouldn't let him switch on the light while she dressed for Mass. Then he began to wonder. The remark had stuck. The next time Polly's name was mentioned in connection with Carmody he scowled. It was clear that something was going on and that he was the victim. He couldn't bear the thought of that. It might be that in her innocence Polly was being indiscreet. On the other hand, it might well be that like many another woman before her, she was only letting on to be innocent to get the chance of being indiscreet. A man could never tell. He went home feeling very upset.

He strode in the hall and snapped a command to Polly, who was sitting in the darkness over the range. She rose in surprise and followed him meekly up the stairs. In the sitting-room he lit the gas and stooped to look up under the mantel as though to see if the burner was broken. Like all worriers Charlie considered nothing beneath him.

"Sit down," he said curtly over his shoulder.

"Oh, Law, what is it at all, Charlie?" Polly said nervously.

Charlie turned and stood on the hearthrug, his legs apart like buttresses, his cap drawn over his eyes, and seemed as if he were studying her through his hairy cheekbones. It was a matter that required study. He had no precedent for inquiring whether or not Polly had been unfaithful to him.

"Tell me, Polly," he said at last in a reasonable tone which seemed to suit the part, "did I do anything to you?"

"Oh, whatever do you mean, Charlie?" she asked in bewilderment. "What could you do to me?"

"That's just what I'd like to know," said Charlie, nodding sagaciously. "What I did out of the way."

"Oh, Charlie," she exclaimed in alarm, "what a thing to say to me! I never said you did anything out of the way."

"I'm glad to hear it," said Charlie, nodding again and looking away across the room at the picture of a sailing-ship in distress. "I suppose you don't know the new teacher in the school?" he added with the innocent air of a cross-examining lawyer.

"Is it Mr. Carmody?" she asked, giving herself away at once by the suspicion of a blush.

"Aha, I see you do," said Charlie.

"I met him a couple of times with Mrs. MacCann," Polly explained patiently. "What about him?"

"Now is that all?" Charlie asked accusingly. "You might as well tell me the truth now and not have me drag it out of you."

"Oh, what do you mean?" cried Polly, sitting erect with indignation. "What would you drag out of me? I don't know what's coming over you at all, Charlie."

"Hold on now, hold on!" Charlie said commandingly, raising one hand for silence. "Just sit where you are for a minute." He put his hands behind his back, tilted forward on his toes and studied his feet for a moment. "Do you know," he added gravely, barely raising his head to fix her with his eyes, "that 'tis all over the town that you and Carmody are carrying on behind my back? Isn't that a nice thing to have said about your wife?" he added, raising his voice.

Up to that moment he had only partly believed in her guilt, but he no longer had any doubt when he saw how she changed colour. It was partly anger, partly shame.

"Oh," she cried in a fury, tossing her handsome black head, "the badness of people! This is all Nora Lawlor's fault. Father Ring would never repeat a thing like that."

"Father Ring?" exclaimed Charlie with a start, seeing that, whatever her crime was, it was already public property. "What has he to do with it?"

"I see it all now," Polly cried dramatically with a large wave of her arm. "I should never have trusted her. I might have known she'd bell it all over the town."

"What would she bell?" snapped Charlie impatiently. At the very best of times Polly was not what you'd call lucid, but whenever anything happened to upset her, every joint in her mind flew asunder.

"She said," explained Polly earnestly, wagging a long arm at him, "that Kitty Daly had a child after imagining her husband was Rudolph Valentino."

"Rudolph who?" asked Charlie with a strained air.

"You wouldn't know him," replied Polly impatiently. "He's an old fellow on the pictures. He's dead now."

"And what has he to do with Carmody?" Charlie asked anxiously.

"He has nothing to do with Carmody," shouted Polly, enraged at his stupidity.

"Well, go on, woman, go on!" said Charlie, his face screwed up in a black knot as he tried to disentangle the confusion she had plunged him in.

"Oh, I know it couldn't be wrong, Charlie," Polly said positively, flying off at another tangent. "I asked Father Ring myself was it wrong for her."

"Wrong for who?" snarled Charlie, beside himself.

"Kitty Daly, of course," shouted Polly.

"Christ Almighty!" groaned Charlie. "Do you want to drive me mad?"

"But when you won't listen to me!" Polly cried passionately. "And Father Ring said there was no harm in it so long as she was doing it for a good purpose and didn't get any pleasure out of it. . . . Though indeed," she added candidly, "I'm sure I have no idea what pleasure she could get out of it."

"Ah, botheration!" shouted Charlie, shaking his fists at her. "What goings-on you have about Rudolph Valentino! Don't you see I'm demented with all this hugger-mugger? What did you do then, woman?"

"I went to the pictures," replied Polly with an aggrieved air.

"You went to the pictures with Carmody?" asked Charlie encouragingly, only too willing to compound for an infidelity with an indiscretion.

"Oh, what a thing I'd do!" cried Polly in a perfect tempest of indignation. "Who said I went to the pictures with Mr. Carmody? This town is full of liars. I went with Nora, of course."

"Well?" asked Charlie.

"Well," Polly continued in a more reasonable tone, "I thought all the old men in the pictures were terrible, Charlie. How people can bear the sight of them night after night I do not know. And as we were coming out Nora asked me wasn't there any man at all I thought was good-looking, and I said: 'Nora,' I said, 'I always liked Mr. Carmody's appearance.' 'Oh, did you?' said Nora. 'I did, Nora,' said I. Now that," said Polly flatly, bringing her palm down on her knee, "was all that either of us said; and, of course, I might be wrong about his appearance, though I always thought he kept himself very nicely; but anyone that says I went to the pictures with him, Charlie, all I can say is that they have no conscience. Absolutely no conscience."

Charlie stared at her for a moment in stupefaction. For that one moment he wondered at his own folly in ever thinking that Polly would have it in her to carry on with a man and in thinking that any man would try to carry on with her. *Amore, mio cuore, traditore,* he thought despairingly. Quite clearly Italian women must be different. And then the whole thing began to dawn on him and he felt himself suffocating with rage.

"And do you mean to tell me," he asked incredulously, "that you went to Father Ring and asked him could you pretend that I was Charlie Carmody?"

"Rudolph Valentino, Charlie," corrected Polly. "It was Nora Lawlor who suggested Mr. Carmody. . . . You don't think it makes any difference?" she added hastily, terrified that she might unwittingly have drifted into mortal sin.

"You asked Father Ring could you pretend that I was Rudolph Valentino?" repeated Charlie frantically.

"Oh, surely Charlie," Polly said, brushing this aside as mere trifling, "you don't think I'd do it without finding out whether 'twas a sin or not?"

"God Almighty!" cried Charlie, turning to the door. "I'm the laughing-stock of the town!"

"Oh, you think too much about what people say of you," Polly said impatiently. "What need you care what they say so long as 'tis for a good object?"

"Good object!" cried Charlie bitterly. "I know the object I'd like to lay my hands on this minute. It's that Nora Lawlor with her cesspool of a mind. By God, I'd wring her bloody neck!"

. . .

That was nothing to what Nora did later. Somebody, Charlie discovered, had put round the story that it was really his fault and not Polly's that they had no children. Of course, that might well have been a misconception of Polly's own, because he learned from a few words she dropped that she thought his mother was a witch and was putting spells on her. A girl who would believe that was quite capable of blaming it on the butcher's boy. But the obvious malice identified the story as Nora's. The Carmody business was only a flea-bite to it, because it lowered him in the estimation of everybody. Morgan made great play with it. And it was clever because Charlie was in no position to prove it a lie. Worst of all, he doubted himself. He was a nervous man; the least thing set him off; and for weeks and weeks he worried till he almost convinced himself that Nora was right, that he wasn't like other men. God had heaped so many burdens on him that this was all he could expect.

Now, the Cashmans had a maid called Molly O'Regan, a country girl with a rosy, laughing, good-natured face and a shrill penetrating voice. She was one of the few people Charlie knew who were not afraid of his mother, and in his bachelor days when she brought him his shaving-water of a morning, she had always leaned in the door and shown him just enough of herself to interest a half-wakened man. "Come in, girl," he would whisper, "come in and shut the door." "What would I come in for?" Molly would ask with a great air of surprise. " 'Pon my soul," Charlie would say admiringly, "you're most captivating." "Captivating?" Molly would shriek. "Listen to him, you sweet God! There's capers for you!" "You're like a rose," Charlie would say and then give one wild bound out of the bed that landed him within a few feet of her, while Molly, shrieking with laughter, banged the door behind her.

It was undoubtedly the slander on his manhood which interested Charlie in Molly, though it would be going too far to say that he had no other object than to disprove it. He liked Molly, and more than ever with Polly and his mother round the house she seemed like a rose. Sometimes when they were out he followed her upstairs and skirmished with her. She let on to be very shocked. "Sweet Jesus!" she cried, "What would I do if one of them walked in on me? And all the holy pictures!" She flashed a wondering look at all the coloured pictures, the statues, and the Lourdes clock. "Isn't it true for me?" she cried. "A wonder you wouldn't have a bit of shame in you!"

"As a matter of fact," said Charlie gravely, "that's the idea. You knew I was starting a religious order of my own here, didn't you?"

"A religious order?" echoed Molly. "I did not."

"Oh, yes, yes," said Charlie importantly. "I'm only waiting on the authority from Rome."

"What sort of religious order?" asked Molly suspiciously—she was not too bright in the head and, as she said herself, with that thundering blackguard, Charlie Cashman, you'd never know where you were.

"An order of Christian married couples," replied Charlie. "The old sort of marriage is a washout. Purity is what we're going in for."

"Purity?" shrieked Molly in a gale of laughter. "And you in it!"

Secretly she was delighted to see Charlie among all "them old holy ones," as she called them, showing such spunk, and couldn't bear to deprive him of his little pleasure. She didn't deprive him of it long.

And then one autumn evening she whispered to him that she was going to have a baby. She wept and said her old fellow would have her sacred life, which was likely enough, seeing that her father preferred to correct his large family with a razor. Charlie shed a few tears as well and told her not to mind her old fellow; while he had a pound in the bank he'd never see her short of anything. He meant it too, because he was a warm-hearted man and had always kept a soft spot for Molly. But what really moved and thrilled him was that in spite of everybody he was at last going to be a father. His doubts about his manhood were set at rest. In the dusk he went up to Johnny Desmond's overflowing with delight and good humour. He cracked half a dozen jokes at Morgan in quick succession and made them all wonder what he had up his sleeve. From this out they could pass what dirty remarks they liked, but these would be nothing compared with his secret laugh at them. It didn't matter if it took twenty years before they knew. He was in the wildest spirits, drinking and joking and making up rhymes.

Next morning, coming on to dawn, he woke with a very bad taste in his mouth. He glanced round and there, in the light of the colza-oil lamp that burned before the statue of the Sacred Heart, saw Polly beside him in the bed. She looked determined even in sleep. The Lourdes clock, which was suffering from hallucinations and imagining it was an alarm clock, was kicking up merry hell on the mantelpiece. He knew it was really playing "The bell of the Angelus calleth to pray," which is a nice, soothing, poetic thought, but what it said in his mind was: "You're caught, Charlie Cashman, you can't get away." He realized that, instead of escaping, he had only wedged himself more firmly in the trap, that if ever the truth about Molly became known, Polly would leave him, the Donegans would hound him down, Father Ring would denounce him from the altar, and his little business would go to pot. And in spite of it all he would not be able to leave the business to his son. "You're caught, Charlie Cashman, you can't get away," sang the clock with a sort of childish malice.

The skill with which he manœuvred Molly out of the house would have done credit to an international statesman. He found her lodgings in Asragh and put some money to her name in the bank without anyone being the wiser. But in crises it is never the difficulties you can calculate on that really upset you. How could anyone have guessed that Molly, without a job to do, would find her time a burden and spend hours in the Redemptorist church? After a couple of months Charlie started to receive the most alarming letters. Molly talked of telling Polly, of telling her father, of spending the rest of her days in a home doing penance. Charlie was getting thoroughly fed up with religion. When he saw her one night in a back street in Asragh—the only place where they could meet in comparative safety—he was shocked at the change in her. She was plumper and better-looking but her eyes were shadowy and her voice had dropped to a sort of whine.

"Oh, Charlie," she sighed with a lingering, come-to-Christ air, "what luck or grace could we have and the life of sin and deception we're leading?"

"A lot of deception and damn little sin," Charlie said bitterly. "What the hell do you want?"

"Oh, Charlie, I want you to put an end to the deception as well as the sin. Be said by me and confess it to your wife."

"What a thing I'd do!" Charlie said, scowling and stamping. "Do you know what she'd do?"

"What would any woman do and she finding you truly repentant?" asked Molly ecstatically.

"She'd take bloody good care I had cause," said Charlie.

He persuaded her out of that particular mood but all the same he wasn't sure of her. It was a nerve-racking business. In the evenings after his supper he lit his pipe and took his usual prowl to the door but he couldn't bring himself to leave the house. Nora Lawlor might drop in while he was away and tell the whole thing to Polly. He had a trick of making up little rhymes to amuse himself, and one that he made at this time ran:

> Brass, boys, brass. and not only buttons,
> The older we gets, the more we toughens.

Charlie didn't toughen at all, unfortunately.

"Wisha, wouldn't you go for a little stroll?" Polly would ask considerately.

"Ah, I don't feel like it," Charlie would say with a sigh.

"Oh, Law!" she would cry in gentle surprise. "Isn't that a great change for you, Charlie?"

Once or twice he nearly snapped at her and asked whose fault it was. Sometimes he went to the house door and stood there for a full half-hour with his shoulder against the jamb, drinking in the misery of the view in the winter dusk: the one mean main street where everyone knew him and no one wished him well. It was all very fine for Romeo, but Romeo hadn't to live in an Irish country town. Each morning he prowled about in wait for Christy Flynn, the postman, to intercept any anonymous letter there might be for Polly. As he didn't know which of them were anonymous, he intercepted them all.

Then one morning the blow fell. It was a solicitor's letter. He left the shop in charge of Polly and went down to Curwen Street to see his own solicitor, Timsy Harrington. Curwen Street is a nice quiet Georgian street, rosy and warm even on a winter's day, and signs on it; the cheapest call you could pay there would cost you a pound. Charlie knew his call would cost him more than that, but he smoked his pipe and tried to put a brave face on it, as though he thought actions for seduction the best sport in the world. That didn't go down with Timsy Harrington, though.

"Mr. Cashman," he said in his shrill, scolding, old woman's voice, "I'm surprised at you. I'm astonished at you. An educated man like you! You had the whole country to choose from and no one would do you but a daughter of Jim Regan, that stopped in bed with his son for eight months, hoping to get a couple of pounds out of the insurance company."

Charlie went back along the main street feeling as though he were bleeding from twenty gashes. He swore that if ever he got out of this scrape he'd live a celibate for the rest of his days. People said the woman always paid, but the particular occasion when she did was apparently forgotten. Outside the shop he was accosted by an old countryman with a long innocent face.

"Good morrow, Charlie," he said confidentially, giving Charlie a glimpse of a plug in the palm of his hand. "I wonder would you have the comrade of this?"

"I'll try, Tom," said Charlie with a sigh, taking it from him and turning it over in his hand. "Leave me this and I'll see what I can do. I'm very busy at the moment."

He opened the shop door, and knew at once that there was trouble in the wind. There was no one in the shop. He stood at the door with his ear cocked. He heard Polly moving with stallion strides about the bedroom and his heart misgave him. He knew well the Lawlor one had profited by his absence. Already the solicitor's letter was public property. He went up the stairs and opened the bedroom door a few inches. Polly was throwing clothes, shoes, and statues all together in a couple of suitcases with positive frenzy. Charlie pushed in the door a little further, looked at the suitcases, then at her, and finally managed to work up what he thought of as an insinuating smile.

"What's up, little girl?" he asked with a decent show of innocent gaiety.

He saw from her look that this particular line was a complete wash-out, so he entered cautiously, closing the door behind him for fear of being overheard from the shop.

"Aren't I in trouble enough?" he asked bitterly. "Do you know what the O'Regans want out of me?"

"Oh," cried Polly with the air of a tragedy queen, "if there was a man among them he'd shoot you!"

"Two hundred pounds!" hissed Charlie, his high hairy cheekbones twitching. "Isn't that a nice how-d'-ye-do?"

"Oh," she cried distractedly, "you're worse than the wild beasts. The wild beasts have some modesty but you have none. It was my own fault. Nora Lawlor warned me."

"Nora Lawlor will be the ruination of you," Charlie said severely. "She was in here again this morning—you needn't tell me. I can see the signs of her."

"Don't attempt to criticize her to me!" stormed Polly. "Get out of my sight or I won't be responsible. The servant!"

"Whisht, woman, whisht, whisht, whisht!" hissed Charlie, dancing in a fury of apprehension. "You'll be heard from the shop."

"Oh, I'll take care to be heard," said Polly, giving her rich voice full play. "I'll let them know the sort of man they're dealing with. I'll soho you well."

"So this is married life!" muttered Charlie in a wounded voice, turning away. Then he paused and looked at her over his shoulder as if he couldn't believe it. "Merciful God," he said, "what sort of woman are you at all? How well I didn't go on like this about the schoolmaster!"

"What schoolmaster?" Polly asked in bewilderment, her whole face taking on a ravaged air.

"Carmody," said Charlie reproachfully. "You thought it was my fault and I thought it was yours—what more was in it? We both acted with a good purpose. Surely to God," he added anxiously, "you don't think I did it for pleasure?"

"Oh," she cried, beside herself, "wait till I tell Father Ring! Wait till he knows the sort of comparisons you're making! With a good purpose! Oh, you blasphemer! How the earth doesn't open and swallow you!"

She pushed him out and slammed the door behind him. Charlie stood on the landing and gave a brokenhearted sigh. "So this is married life!" he repeated despairingly. He returned to the shop and stood far back at the rear, leaning against the stovepipe. It was a sunny morning and the sunlight streamed through the windows and glinted on the bright buckets hanging outside the door. He saw Nora Lawlor, wearing a scarlet coat, come out of the butcher's and give a furtive glance across the street. If he had had a gun with him he would have shot her dead.

He heard Polly come downstairs and open the hall door. Slowly and on tiptoe he went to the door of the shop, leaned his shoulder against the jamb and looked up the street after Nora. He saw her red coat disappear round the corner by the chapel. The old farmer who was waiting outside the Post Office thought that Charlie was hailing him, but Charlie frowned and shook his head. From the hall he heard Polly address a small boy in that clear voice of hers which he knew could be heard all along the street.

"Dinny," she said, "I want you to run down to Hennessey's and ask them to send up a car."

Charlie was so overcome that he retreated to the back of the shop again. Polly was leaving him. It would be all round the town in five minutes. Yet he knew he wasn't a bad man; there were plenty worse and their wives didn't leave them. For one wild moment he thought of making a last appeal to her love, but one glance into the hall at Polly sitting bolt-upright in her blue serge costume, her cases beside her and her gloves and prayer-book on the hall stand, and he knew that love wasn't even in the running. He went to the shop door and beckoned to another small boy.

"I want you to find Father Ring and bring him here quick," he whispered fiercely, pressing a coin into the child's palm. "Mr. Cashman sent you, say. And tell him hurry!"

"Is it someone sick, Mr. Cashman?" asked the little boy eagerly.

"Yes," hissed Charlie. "Dying. Hurry now!"

After that he paced up and down the shop like a caged tiger till he saw Father Ring rounding the corner by the chapel. He went up to meet him.

"What is it at all, Charlie?" the priest asked anxiously. "Is it the mother?"

"No, father," Charlie said desperately, seeing the twitching of curtains in top rooms. "I only wish to God it was," he ground out in a frenzy.

"Is it as bad as that, Charlie?" Father Ring asked in concern as they entered the shop.

"Ah, I'm in great trouble, father," Charlie said, tossing his head like a wounded animal. Then he fixed his gaze on a spot of light at the back of the shop and addressed himself to it. "I don't know did you hear any stories about me," he inquired guardedly.

"Stories, Charlie?" exclaimed Father Ring, who, being a Kerryman, could fight a better delaying-action than Charlie himself. "What sort of stories?"

"Well, now, father, not the sort you'd like to hear," replied Charlie with what for him was almost candour.

"Well, now you mention it, Charlie," said Father Ring with equal frankness, "I fancy I did hear something. . . . Not, of course, that I believed it," he added hastily, for fear he might be committing himself too far.

"I'm sorry to say you can, father," said Charlie, bowing his head and joining his hands before him as he did at Mass on Sunday.

"Oh, my, my, Charlie," said Father Ring, giving him a look out of the corner of his eye, "that's bad."

Charlie looked at the floor and nodded glumly a couple of times to show he shared the priest's view of it.

"And tell me, Charlie," whispered Father Ring, pivoting on his umbrella as he leaned closer, "what way did herself take it?"

"Badly, father," replied Charlie severely. "Very badly. I must say I'm disappointed in Polly."

This time it was he who looked out of the corner of his eye and somehow it struck him that Father Ring was not as shocked-looking as he might have been.

"I'd expect that, mind you," Father Ring said thoughtfully.

"By God, he isn't shocked!" thought Charlie. There was something that almost resembled fellow-feeling in his air.

"But heavens above, father," Charlie said explosively, "the woman is out of her mind. And as for that Lawlor girl, I don't know what to say to her." Father Ring nodded again, as though to say that he didn't know either. "Of course, she's a good-living girl and all the rest of it," Charlie went on cantankerously, "but girls with no experience of life have no business interfering between married couples. It was bad enough without her—I needn't tell you that. And there she is now," he added, cocking his thumb in the direction of the hall, "with her bags packed and after ordering a car up from Hennessey's. Sure that's never right."

"Well, now, Charlie," Father Ring whispered consolingly, "women are contrairy; they are contrairy, there's no denying that. I'll have a word with her myself."

He opened the house door gently, peeped in, and then went into the hall on tiptoe, as if he were entering a room where someone was asleep. Charlie held the door slightly open behind him to hear what went on. Unfortunately, the sight of the priest going in had given the old farmer the notion of business as usual. Charlie looked round and saw his long mournful face in the doorway.

"Charlie," he began, "if I'm not disturbing you————"

Charlie, raising his clenched fists in the air, did a silent war dance. The old farmer staggered back, cut to the heart, and then sat on the sill of the window with his stick between his legs. When another farmer came by the old man began to tell him his troubles with long, accusing glances back at Charlie, who was glued to the door with an agonized look on his face.

"My poor child!" he heard Father Ring say in a shocked whisper. "You were in the wars. I can see you were."

"Well, I'm going home now, father," Polly replied listlessly.

"Sure, where better could you go?" exclaimed Father Ring as if trying to disabuse her of any idea she might have of staying on. " 'Tis that husband of yours, I suppose? 'Tis to be sure. I need hardly ask."

"I'd rather not talk about it, father," Polly said politely but firmly. "I dare say you'll hear all about it soon enough."

"I dare say I will," he agreed. "People in this town don't seem to have much better to do. 'Pon my word, I believe I saw a few curtains stirring on my way down. You'll have an audience."

"I never minded much what they saw," said Polly wearily.

"Sure, you never had anything to conceal," said Father Ring, overwhelming her with agreement, as his way was. "I suppose you remember the case of that little girl from Parnell Street a few weeks ago?"

"No, father, I'm afraid I don't," replied Polly without interest.

"Sure, you couldn't be bothered. Ah, 'twas a sad business, though. Married at ten and the baby born at one."

"Oh, my, father," said Polly politely, "wasn't that very quick?"

"Well, now you mention it, Polly, it was. But that wasn't what I was going to say. The poor child came home at four in the morning to avoid attracting attention, and would you believe me, Polly, not a soul in Parnell Street went to bed that night! Sure, that's never natural! I say that's not natural. Where's that blackguard of a husband of yours till I give him a bit of my mind? Charlie Cashman! Charlie Cashman! Where are you, you scoundrel?"

"I'm here, father," said Charlie meekly, taking two steps forward till he stood between the crimson curtains with a blaze of silver from the fanlight falling on his bowed head.

"Aren't you ashamed of yourself?" shouted the priest, raising the umbrella to him.

"I am, father, I am, I am," replied Charlie in a broken voice without looking up.

"Oh, that's only all old connoisseuring, father," Polly cried distractedly, jumping to her feet and grabbing gloves and prayer-book. "No one knows what I went through with that man." She opened the hall door; the hall was flooded with silver light, and she turned to them, drawing a deep breath through her nose, as beautiful and menacing as a sibyl. "I'm going home to my father now," she continued in a firm voice. "I left my keys on the dressing-table and you can give Hennessey's boy the bags."

"Polly," Father Ring said sternly, leaning on his umbrella, "what way is this for a Child of Mary to behave?"

"Ah, 'tis all very fine for you to talk, father," Polly cried scoldingly. "You don't have to live with him. I'd sooner live with a wild beast than with that man," she added dramatically.

"Polly," Father Ring said mildly, "what you do in your own house is your business. What you do in the public view is mine. Polly, you're in the public view."

For the first time in Charlie's life he found himself admiring Father Ring. There was a clash and a grating of wills like the bending of steel girders, and suddenly Polly's girders buckled. She came in and closed the door. "Now, Polly," Father Ring said affectionately, "inside that door I don't want to interfere between ye, good or bad. Make what arrangements you like. Live with him or don't live with him; sleep in the loft or sleep in the stable, but don't let me have any more scandal like we had this morning."

"I wouldn't be safe from him in the stable," Polly said rebelliously. She felt that for the first time in her life she had been met and mastered by a man, and it rankled. There was more than a joke in Charlie's suggestion that it was Father Ring she should have married. If only she

could have gone to bed with him then and there she would probably
have risen a normal woman. But deprived of this consolation she was
ready to turn nasty, and Father Ring saw it. Charlie only noticed the
falsehood about himself.

"You wouldn't be what?" he cried indignantly. "When did I ever
raise a finger or say a cross word to you?"

"Now, Charlie, now!" Father Ring said shortly, raising his hand for
silence. "And woman alive," he asked good-humouredly, "can't you bolt
your door?"

"How can I," stormed Polly, as sulky as a spoiled child, "when there's
no bolt on it?"

"That's easily remedied."

"Then tell him send out for a carpenter and have it done now," she
said vindictively.

"Send out for a what?" shouted Charlie, cocking his head as if he
couldn't believe what he heard. "Is it mad you are? What a thing I'd
do!"

"Very well," she said, opening the hall door again. "I'll go home to
my father."

"Hold on now, hold on!" Charlie cried frantically, dragging her back
and closing the door behind her. "I'll do it myself."

"Then do it now!" she cried.

"Do what she says, Charlie," the priest said quietly. He saw that the
danger wasn't over yet. Charlie gave her a murderous glare and went
out to the shop. A crowd had gathered outside on the pavement, discussing the wrongs of the poor farmer, who was an object of the most intense
sympathy. Charlie returned with a brass bolt, a screwdriver, and a couple of screws.

"Show me that bolt!" said Polly menacingly. The devil was up in her
now. The priest might have bested her but she still saw a way of getting
her own back. Charlie knew that next day she and Nora Lawlor would
be splitting their sides over it; women were like that, and he vowed a
holy war against the whole boiling of them to the day of his death. "I'm
going home to my father's," she said, clamping her long lips. "That bolt
is too light."

"Get a heavier one, Charlie," Father Ring said quietly. "Don't argue,
there's a good man!"

Argument was about the last thing in Charlie's mind at that moment.

Murder would have been nearer the mark. He flung the bolt at Polly's feet but she didn't even glance at him. When he returned to the shop the crowd was surging round the door.

"Bad luck and end to ye!" he snarled, taking out his spleen on them. "Have ye no business of yeer own to mind without nosing round here?"

"Mr. Cashman," said a young man whom Charlie recognized as the old farmer's son, "you have a plug belonging to my father."

"Then take it and to hell with ye!" snarled Charlie, taking the plug from his pocket and throwing it into the midst of them.

"Oh, begor, we won't trouble you much from this day forth," the young man said fierily. "Nor more along with us."

That was the trouble in a quarrel with a country man. There always were more along with him. Charlie, aware that he might have seriously injured his business, returned to the hall with an iron bolt. "That's a stable bolt," he said, addressing no one in particular.

"Put it on," said Polly.

Charlie went upstairs. Father Ring followed him. The priest stood in awe, looking at all the holy pictures. Then he held the bolt while Charlie used the screwdriver. Charlie was so mad that he used it anyhow.

"You're putting that screw in crooked, Charlie," said the priest. "Wait now till I put on my specs and I'll do it for you."

"Let her go! Let her go!" said Charlie on the point of a breakdown. "It doesn't matter to me whether she goes or stays. I'm nothing only a laughing-stock."

"Now, Charlie, Charlie," said the priest good-naturedly, "you have your little business to mind."

"For my nephews to walk into," said Charlie bitterly.

"God spoke first, Charlie," the priest said gravely. "You're a young man yet. Begor," he added, giving Charlie a quizzical look over the specs, "I did a few queer jobs in my time but this is the queerest yet." He saw that Charlie was in no state to appreciate the humour of it, and gave him a professional look through the spectacles. "Ah, well, Charlie," he said, "we all have our burdens. You have only one, but I have a dozen, not to mention the nuns, and they reckon two on a count."

As they came down the stairs Charlie's mother appeared out of the kitchen as if from nowhere, drying her hands in her apron; a little bundle of rags, bones and malice, with a few wisps of white hair blowing about her.

"Aha," she cackled as if she were speaking to herself, "I hear the Holy Door is shut for the next seven years."

.   .   .

But, as she was so fond of saying herself, "God spoke first." It seemed as if Polly never had another day's luck. She fell into a slow decline and made herself worse instead of better by drinking the stuff Mrs. Cashman brought her from the Wise Woman, and by changing from the Nine Fridays to the Nine Tuesdays and from the Nine Tuesdays to the Nine Mondays on the advice of Nora Lawlor, who had tried them all.

A scandal of that sort is never good for a man's business. The Donegans and their friends paid their accounts and went elsewhere. The shop began to go down and Charlie went with it. He paid less attention to his appearance, served the counter unshaven and without collar and tie; grew steadily shabbier and more irritable and neglected-looking. He spent most of his evenings in Johnny Desmond's, but even there people fought shy of him. The professional men and civil servants treated him as a sort of town character, a humorous, unreliable fellow without much balance. To Charlie, who felt they were only cashing in on the sacrifices of men like himself, this was the bitterest blow, and in his anxiety to keep his end up before them he boasted, quarrelled, and generally played the fool.

But the funny thing was that from the time she fell ill Polly herself softened towards him. Her family were the first to notice it. Like everything else in Polly it went to extremes, and indeed it occurred to her mother that if the Almighty God in His infinite mercy didn't release her soon, she'd have no religion left.

"I don't know is he much worse than anyone else," she said broodingly. "I had some very queer temptations myself that no one knew about. Father Ring said once that I was very unforgiving. I think now he was right. Our family were always vindictive."

After that she began to complain about being nervous alone and Mrs. Cashman offered to sleep with her.

"Oh, I could never bear another woman in the room with me," Polly said impatiently. "What I want is a man. I think I'll ask Charlie to make it up."

"Is it that fellow?" cried Charlie's mother, aghast. "That scut—that —I have no words for him. Oh, my! A man that would shame his poor wife the way that ruffian did!"

"Ah, the way ye talk one'd think he never stopped," Polly said frac-
tiously. "Ye have as much old goings-on about one five minutes!"

At this Mrs. Cashman decided she was going soft in the head. When
a married woman begins to reckon her husband's infidelities in terms of
hours and minutes she is in a bad state. Polly asked Charlie meekly
enough to come back and keep her company. Charlie would have been
as well pleased to stay as he was, where he could come and go as he
liked, but he saw it was some sort of change before death.

It was cold comfort for Polly. Too much mischief had been made
between them for Charlie to feel about her as a man should feel for his
wife. They would lie awake in the grey, flickering light of the colza-oil
lamp, with all the holy pictures round them and the Lourdes clock on
the mantelpiece ticking away whenever it remembered it and making
wild dashes to catch up on lost time, and Charlie's thoughts would
wander and he would think that if Polly were once out of the way he
would have another chance of a woman who would fling herself into his
arms without asking Father Ring's permission, like the Yeoman Captain's daughter in the old song:

> A thousand pardons I'll give thee
> And fly from home with thee;
> I'll dress myself in men's attire
> And fight for Liberty.

Charlie was a romantic, and he couldn't get over his boyish notion
that there must be women like the Captain's Daughter, if only you could
meet them. And while he was making violent love to her, Polly, lying
beside him, thought of how her poor bare bones would soon be scattered
in the stony little patch above Kilmurray while another woman would
be lying in her bed. It made her very bitter.

"I suppose you're only waiting till the sod is over me?" she said one
night in a low voice when Charlie was just fancying that she must have
dropped off.

"What's that?" he asked in astonishment and exasperation, looking
at her with one arm under her head, staring into the shadows.

"You're only waiting till I'm well rotten to get another woman in my
place," she went on accusingly.

"What a thing I'd think of!" Charlie snapped, as cross as a man jolted
out of his sleep, for her words had caught the skirts of the Captain's

Daughter as she slipped out of the room, and Charlie felt it was shameful for him in his health and strength to be contriving like that against a sick woman.

"Nothing matters to you now only to best John Joe and have a son that'll come in for the shop," said Polly with the terrible insight of the last loneliness. "Only for the shop you might have some nature for me."

"And when the hell had I anything but nature for you?" he shouted indignantly, sitting up. "What do you think I married you for? Money?"

"If you had any nature for me you wouldn't disrespect me," Polly went on stubbornly, clinging to her grievance.

"And what about you?" said Charlie. "You had to think I was some old devil on the pictures before you could put up with me. There's nature for you!"

"I did it with a good object," said Polly.

"Good object!" snorted Charlie. He almost told her that Juliet and the Captain's Daughter didn't do it with a good object or any object at all only getting the man they wanted, but he knew she wouldn't understand. Polly lay for a long time drawing deep breaths through her nose.

"Don't think or imagine I'll rest quiet and see you married to another woman," she added in a very determined voice. "You may think you'll be rid of me but I'll make full sure you won't. All our family would go to hell's gates to be revenged."

"Christ Almighty," snarled Charlie, giving one wild leap out of the bed, "leave me out of this! This is my thanks for coming back here! Leave me out!"

"Mind what I say now," said Polly in an awe-inspiring voice, pointing a bony arm at him from the shadows. She knew she had him on a sore spot. Herself or Mrs. Cashman would have made no more fuss about meeting a ghost than about meeting the postman, but Charlie had enough of the rationalist in him to be terrified. His mother had brought him up on them. "Our family was ever full of ghosts," she added solemnly. "You won't have much comfort with her."

"My trousers!" cried Charlie, beside himself with rage and terror. "Where the hell is my trousers?"

"I'm giving you fair warning," Polly cried in bloodcurdling tones as he poked his way out of the room in his nightshirt. "I'll soho ye well, the pair of ye!"

.   .   .

She died very peacefully one evening when no one was in the room but old Mrs. Cashman. Even in death she made trouble for Charlie. Her last wish was to be buried in Closty, the Donegan graveyard. It wasn't that she bore any malice to Charlie, but the thought of the two wives in one grave upset her. She said it wouldn't be nice, and Nora agreed with her. Of course, when it got out it made things worse for Charlie, for it suggested that, at the very least, he had some hand in her death.

Nora felt rather like that too, but then a strange thing happened. She was coming down from the bedroom when she heard a noise from the shop. The door was closed, all but an inch or two, but Nora was of a very inquisitive disposition. She pushed it in. The shop was dark, several of the outside shutters being up, but in the dim light she saw the figure of a man and realized that the noise she had heard was weeping. It gave her a shock, for it had never once occurred to her that Charlie was that sort of man. She was a warm-hearted girl. She went up and touched his arm.

"I'm sorry, Charlie," she said timidly.

"I know that, Nora," he muttered without looking round. "I know you are."

"She'll be a terrible loss," she added, more from want of something to say than the feeling that she was speaking the truth.

"Ah, she was unfortunate, Nora," Charlie said with a sob. "She was a fine woman, a lovely woman. I don't know what bad luck was on us."

"What better luck could ye have and the poor orphan cheated?" cried a harsh, inexpressive voice from the hall. Nora started. Mrs. Cashman was standing in the doorway with her hands on her hips. Her voice and appearance were like those of an apparition, and for the first time Nora wondered if there wasn't something in Polly's fancy that she was really a witch. "She's better off, Nora girl."

"I suppose so," Nora agreed doubtfully, resenting her intrusion just at the moment when Charlie was ready for confidences. People with tears in their eyes will tell you things they'd never tell you at other times.

"She was a good girl and a just girl and she loved her God," hissed Mrs. Cashman, aiming every word at Charlie under Nora's guard. "It would be a bad man that would go against her dying wishes."

"Who talked of going against them?" snarled Charlie with the savagery of a goaded beast, and lunging past them went out and banged the hall door behind him.

"Poor Charlie is very upset," said Nora.

"Upset?" cackled Mrs. Cashman. "How upset he is! She's not in her grave yet, and already he's planning who he'll get instead of her. That's how upset he is! But he's not done with me yet, the blackguard!"

For the first time it occurred to Nora that perhaps Charlie had been misjudged—if men could ever be misjudged. From all accounts of what they did to poor women when they had them stripped, they could not, but something about Mrs. Cashman made her suspicious.

She went to the funeral in Mrs. Cashman's carriage. The moment she got out of it at the graveyard she knew there was trouble in store. The Donegans were there, a half dozen different families, and on their own ground they had taken complete command. Charlie was only an outsider. He stood by the hearse with his hands crossed before him, holding his hat, and a look of desperation on his dark face. Others besides herself had noticed the signs, and a group of men was standing in a semicircle a hundred yards down the road, where they wouldn't get involved. Her father was between them and the hearse, but sufficiently far away to keep out of it as well. He was scowling, his lips pouted, his eyes were half shut while he noticed everything that went on.

The procession into the graveyard would be the signal. Charlie would be shouldered away from the cemetery gate, and he knew it, and knew he was no match for half a dozen men younger than himself. He'd fight, of course; everyone who knew Charlie knew that, but he could be very quickly dragged down the lane and no one much the wiser. Just at the moment when the coffin was eased out of the hearse and four Donegans got under it Nora left Mrs. Cashman's side and stood by Charlie.

It was exactly as though she had blown a policeman's whistle. Her father raised his head and beckoned to the semicircle of men behind and then, pulling the lapels of his coat together, placed himself at the other side of her. One by one half a dozen middle-aged men came up and joined Charlie's party. They were all old Volunteers and could not stand aside and let their commandant and vice-commandant be hustled about by the seed of land-grabbers and policemen. Not a word was spoken, not a cross look exchanged, but everyone knew that sides had been taken and that Charlie could now enter the graveyard unmolested. As he and Nora emerged at the grave Father Ring looked up at them from under his bushy brows. He had missed none of the drama. There was very little that foxy little man missed.

"Thanks, Nora, thanks," said Charlie in a low voice as the service ended. "You were always a good friend."

Even Nora at her most complacent wouldn't have described herself as a friend of Charlie's, but the fact that he had understood what she had done proved him to have better feelings than she had given him credit for. She was embarrassed by the feelings she had roused. The old volunteers all came up and shook her formally by the hand. Her father was the most surprising of all. He stood aside sniffing, with tears in his eyes, too overcome even to tell her what he felt.

After that, everyone noticed the change in Charlie. His clothes were brushed, his boots were polished, his face was shaved, and no matter what hour of the morning you went in he had collar and tie on. He spent more time in the shop and less in Johnny Desmond's. He even gave up going to Johnny's altogether. That could only mean that he was looking for someone to take Polly's place. But who would have him? A respectable woman would be lowering herself. The general impression was that he'd marry Molly O'Regan, and Nora supposed that this would only be right, but somehow she couldn't help feeling it would be a pity. Mrs. Cashman, who saw all her beautiful plans for her grandchildren go up in smoke, felt the same. For the first time Nora included Charlie in her prayers, and asked the Holy Ghost to help him in making the right choice.

One night a few weeks later on her way back from the church she looked in on him. She was astonished at Mrs. Cashman's sourness.

"You'll have a cup of tea?" said Charlie.

"I won't Charlie, honest," she said hastily, alarmed at the puss the old woman had on her. "I'm rushing home."

"I'll see you home," he said at once, giving himself a glance in the mirror.

"If you're back before me, the key will be in the window," Mrs. Cashman said sourly.

"You're not going out again?" he asked.

"I'm not going to stop in this house alone," she bawled.

"Really, Charlie, there's no reason for you to come," said Nora in distress.

"Nonsense!" he snapped crossly. "Herself and her ghosts!"

It was a moonlit night and the street was split with silver light. The abbey tower was silhouetted against it, and the light broke through the deeply splayed chancel lancets, making deep shadows among the foundered tombstones.

"I only came to know how you were getting on," she said.

"Ah, I'm all right," said Charlie. "Only a bit lonesome, of course."

"Ah," she said with a half-smile, "I suppose you won't be long that way."

She could have dropped dead with shame as soon as she had said it. Nora was never one to make any bones about her inquisitiveness, but this sounded positively vulgar. It wasn't in line at all with her behaviour at the funeral. Charlie didn't seem to notice. He gave her a long look through screwed-up eyes, and then crossed the road to lean his back against the bridge.

"Tell me, Nora," he asked, folding his arms and looking keenly at her from under the peak of his cap, "what would you do in my position?"

"Oh, I don't know, Charlie," she replied in alarm, wondering how she could extricate herself from the consequences of her own curiosity. "What's to prevent you?"

"You know the sort of things Polly said?" he said with a sigh.

"I don't think I'd mind that at all," she replied. "After all, Polly was a very sick woman."

"She was," agreed Charlie. "Do you think 'twould be right to go against her wishes like that?"

"Well, of course, that would depend, Charlie," said Nora with sudden gravity, for like many of her race she combined a strong grasp of the truths of religion with a hazy notion of the facts of life.

"You mean on whether 'twas done with a good object or not?" Charlie asked keenly. All he had learned from years with Polly was the importance of doing things with a good object.

"And whether the wishes were reasonable or not," she added, surprised to find him so well-versed in religious matters.

"And you don't think they were?"

"I wouldn't say so. Father Ring could tell you that better than I could."

"I dare say, I dare say. Tell me, Nora, do you believe in things like that?"

"Like what, Charlie?" she asked in surprise.

"Ghosts, and things of that sort," he said with a nervous glance in the direction of the abbey, whose slender tapering tower soared from the rubbish-tip of ruined gables, with its tall irregular battlements that looked like cockades in the moonlight.

"We're taught to believe in them," she replied with a little shudder.

"I know we are," sighed Charlie. "But you never saw one yourself?"

"I didn't."

"Nor I."

They resumed their walk home. Nora saw now what was fretting him. Polly had said she'd haunt him and Polly was a woman of her word. Anything she had ever said she'd do she had done, and there was no saying that as a pure spirit she'd have changed much. Charlie himself had lost a lot of the cocksure rationalism of his fighting days. He had lived so long with women that he was becoming almost as credulous as they. He was reckoning up his chances in case Polly's ghost got out of hand. Nora couldn't give him much comfort, for her own belief in ghosts was determined by the time of day, and at ten o'clock of a moonlight night it was always particularly strong.

When they parted she blamed herself a lot. It was most unmaidenly of her first to call at all and, secondly, to ask point blank what his intentions were, for that was what it amounted to, and for a terrible few minutes she had dreaded that he might think it mattered to her. Of course it didn't, except for his own sake, because though she had begun to like him better, she knew there was no possibility of a Child of Mary like herself marrying him—even if Polly had been an unobtrusive ghost.

She would have been surprised and upset to know that her views were not shared by others. When Charlie got home he stood in the hall in surprise. There was something queer about the house. The hall was in darkness; there was light in the kitchen but it was very feeble. With all the talk of ghosts it upset him. "Are you there, mother?" he called nervously, but there was no reply, only the echo of his own voice. He went to the kitchen door and his heart almost stopped beating. The fire was out, the greater part of the room in shadow, but two candles in two brass candlesticks were burning on the mantelpiece, and between them, smiling down at him, a large, silver-framed photo of Polly.

Next moment, seeing how he was being baited, he went mad with rage. His mother, the picture of aged innocence, was kneeling by her bed when he went in, and she looked round at him in surprise.

"Was it you left that in the kitchen?" he shouted.

"What is it?" she asked in mock ignorance, rising and screwing up her eyes as she reached for the picture. "Oh, isn't it pretty?" she asked. "I found it today in one of her drawers."

"Put it back where you found it," he stormed.

"Oye, why?" she asked with a pretence of concern. "Wouldn't anyone like it—his poor, dead wife? Unless he'd have something on his conscience."

"Never mind my conscience," shouted Charlie. "Fitter for you to look after your own."

"Aha," she bawled triumphantly, throwing off the mask, "my conscience have nothing to trouble it."

"You have it too well seasoned."

"And don't think but she sees it all, wherever she is," the old woman cried, raising her skinny paw in the direction in which Polly might be supposed to exist. "Take care she wouldn't rise from the grave and haunt you, you and that little whipster you were out gallivanting with!"

"What gallivanting?" snarled Charlie. "You don't know what you're talking about."

"Maybe I'm blind!" bawled his mother. "Walking into the graveyard alongside you, as if she had you caught already! Aha, the sly-boots, the pussycat, with her novenas and her Nine Fridays! She thinks we don't know what she's up to, but God sees ye, and the dead woman sees ye, and what's more, I see ye. And mark my words, Charlie Cashman, that's the hand that'll never rock a cradle for you!"

.   .   .

Two days later Charlie happened to be serving behind the counter when he saw Father Ring busily admiring the goods in the shop window. The priest smiled and nodded, but when Charlie made to come out to him he shook his head warningly. Then he raised one finger and pointed in the direction of the house door. Charlie nodded gloomily. Father Ring made another sign with his thumb to indicate the direction he was going in and Charlie nodded again. He knew Father Ring wanted to talk to him somewhere his mother wouldn't know.

He found Father Ring letting on to be studying the plant life in the river. When Charlie appeared he indicated surprise and pleasure at such an unexpected meeting.

"Whisper, Charlie," he said at last, putting his left hand on Charlie's shoulder and bending his head discreetly across the other one, "I had a visit from your mother."

"My mother?"

"Your mother," the priest said gravely, studying his face again before making another little excursion over his shoulder. "She's afraid you're going to get married again," he whispered in amusement.

"She's easy frightened."

"That's what I told her. I know you'll keep this to yourself. She seems to think there's some special commandment to stop you. Of course," added the priest with a shocked air, "I told her I wouldn't dream of interfering."

"You did to be sure," said Charlie watchfully, knowing that this was the one thing in the world that no one could prevent Father Ring from doing.

"You know the girl I mean?"

"I do."

"A nice girl."

"A fine girl."

"And a courageous girl," said Father Ring. "Mind you, 'tisn't every girl would do what she did the day of the funeral. Of course," he admitted, "she should have been married ten years ago. They get very contrairy." Then he pounced. "Tell me, Charlie, you wouldn't be thinking about her, would you? I'm not being inquisitive?"

"You're not, to be sure."

"Because it struck me that if you were, I might be able to do you a good turn. Of course, she hasn't much experience. You know what I mean?"

"I do, father," said Charlie who realized as well as the priest did that it would be no easy job to coax a pious girl like Nora into marriage with a public sinner like himself. But at the same time he was not going to be bounced into anything. He had made a fool of himself once before. "Well now," he added with a great air of candour, turning towards the river as though for recollection, "I'll tell you exactly the way I'm situated, father. You know the old saying: 'Once bitten, twice shy.'"

"I do, I do," said Father Ring, turning in the same direction as if his thought and Charlie's might meet and mingle over the river. Then he started and gave Charlie a look of astonishment. "Ah, I wouldn't say that, Charlie."

"Well, maybe I'm putting it a bit strongly, father."

"I think so, Charlie, I think you are," Father Ring said eagerly. "I'd say she was a different class altogether. More feminine, more clinging—that's under the skin, of course."

"You might be right, father," Charlie said but he stuck to his point all the same. "But there's one thing you might notice about me," he went on, looking at the priest out of the corner of his eye. "You mightn't think it but I'm a highly strung man."

"You are, you are," said Father Ring with great anxiety. "I noticed that myself. I wonder would it be blood pressure, Charlie?"

"I was never the same since the Troubles," said Charlie. "But whatever it is, I want something to steady me."

"You do, you do," said the priest, trying to follow his drift.

"If I had a family I'd be different."

"You would," said Father Ring with a crucified air. "I can see you're a domesticated sort of man."

"And," added Charlie with a wealth of meaning in his tone, "if the same thing happened me again I might as well throw myself in there." He pointed at the river, scowling, and then took a deep breath and stepped back from the priest.

"But you don't think it would, Charlie?"

"But you see, father, I don't know."

"You don't, you don't, to be sure you don't," said Father Ring in a glow of understanding. "I see it now. And, of course, having doubts like that, they might come against you."

"You put your finger on it."

"And, of course, if you were to marry the other girl—what's that her name is?—Peggy or Kitty or Joan, you'd have no doubts, and, as well as that, you'd have the little fellow. You could look after him."

"That's the very thing, father," Charlie said savagely. "That's what has me demented."

"It has, it has, of course," said Father Ring, smiling at the sheer simplicity of it. "Of course, Nora is a nicer girl in every way but a bird in the hand is worth two in the bush. I know exactly how you feel. I'd be the same myself."

So Charlie returned to the shop, feeling worse than ever. Nora, as Father Ring said, was a nice girl, but a bird in the hand was worth two in the bush and Charlie felt he never really had a bird of any breed; nothing but a few tailfeathers out of Molly before she flew into the bush after the others. And even Father Ring didn't know how badly he felt about Molly's son. He was a warm-hearted man; how else could he feel? Once he had got out the car and driven to the village where the boy had been nursed, watched him come home from school, and then followed him to slip a half crown into his hand. If only he could bring the little fellow home and see him go to a good school like a Christian, Charlie felt he could put up with a lot from Molly. And he knew that he wouldn't really have to put up with much from her. Under normal circumstances, there was no moral or intellectual strain that Molly could be subjected to which could not be cured by a hearty smack on the backside.

But then his mind would slip a cog and he would think of the scene outside the graveyard, and Nora, grave and pale, stepping over to his side. "In comes the Captain's Daughter, the Captain of the Yeos"; "Romeo, Romeo, wherefore art thou Romeo?"—a couple of lines like those and Charlie would feel himself seventeen again, ready to risk his life for Ireland or anything else that came handy. Whatever misfortune was on him, he knew his mother was right all the time; that he could never be like any other sensible man but would keep on to the day he died, pining for something a bit larger than life.

That night the temptation to go to the pub was almost irresistible. He went as far as the door and then walked on. That was where people went only when their problems had grown too much for them. Instead he went for a lonesome stroll in the country, and as he returned his feet, as if by magic, led him past Nora's door. He passed that too, and then turned back.

"God bless all here," he said pushing in the door. She was sitting in the dusk and rose to meet him, flushed and eager.

"Come in, Charlie," she said with real pleasure in her tone. "You'll have a cup?"

"I'll have a bucket," said Charlie. "Since I gave up the booze I have a throat like a lime-kiln."

"And did you give it up entirely?" she asked with awe.

"Entirely," said Charlie. "There's no other way of giving it up."

"Aren't you great?" she said, but Charlie didn't know whether he was or not. Like all worriers he had at last created a situation for himself that he could really worry about. As she rose to light the gas he stopped her, resting his big paws on her shoulder.

"Sit down," he said shortly. "I want to have a word with you."

Her face grew pale and her big brown eyes took on a wide, unwinking stare as she did what he told her. If Charlie could only have forgotten his own problem for a moment he would have realized that Nora had also hers. Her problem was what she would say if he asked her to marry him.

"I'm in great trouble," he said.

"Oh, Law!" she exclaimed. "What is it?"

"I had a talk with Father Ring today."

"I heard about that." (There was very little she didn't hear about.)

"He wanted me to get married."

" 'Tisn't much when you say it quick," said Nora with rising colour. From Charlie's announcement that he was in trouble she had naturally concluded that Father Ring wanted him to marry Molly and, now that it had come to the point, she didn't really want him to marry Molly. "I wonder how people can have the audacity to interfere in other people's business like that."

"Ah, well," said Charlie, surprised at her warmth, "he intended it as a kindness."

"It mightn't turn out to be such a kindness," said Nora.

"That's the very thing," said Charlie. "It might not turn out to be a kindness. That's what I wanted to ask your advice about. You know the way I'm situated. I'm lonely down there with no one only the mother. I know it would probably be the makings of me, but 'tis the risk that has me damned. 'Twould be different if I knew I was going to have a family, someone to come in for the business when I'm gone."

"You mean the same thing as happened with Polly might happen with her?" Nora exclaimed in surprise.

"I mean I broke my heart once before," snapped Charlie, "and I don't want to do it again."

"But you don't think the same thing would happen again?" she asked with a hypnotised air.

"But I don't know, girl, I don't know," Charlie cried desperately. "You might think I'm being unreasonable, but if you went through the same thing with a man that I went through with Polly you'd feel the same. Did Polly ever tell you she thought the mother was putting spells on her?" he added sharply.

"She did."

"And what do you think of it?"

"I don't know what to think, Charlie," said Nora, the dusk having produced its periodical change in her views of the supernatural.

"When I married Polly first," Charlie went on reflectively, "she said: 'Many a better cake didn't rise.' The other night she said 'That's the hand that'll never rock a cradle for you.' " He looked at Nora to see if she was impressed, but seeing that Nora in her innocent way applied his mother's prophecy to Molly O'Regan she wasn't as impressed as she might have been if she had known it referred to herself. Charlie felt the scene wasn't going right, but he couldn't see where the error lay. "What knowledge would a woman like that have?" he asked.

"I couldn't imagine, Charlie," replied Nora with nothing like the awe he expected.

"So you see the way I am," he went on after a moment. "If I don't marry her—always assuming she'd have me, of course," he interjected tactfully—"I'm cutting my own throat. If I do marry her and the same thing happens again, I'm cutting her throat as well as my own. What can I do?"

"I'm sure I couldn't advise you, Charlie," replied Nora steadily, almost as though she was enjoying his troubles, which in a manner of speaking—seeing that her premises were wrong—she was. "What do you think yourself?"

Charlie didn't quite know what to think. He had come there expecting at least as much sympathy and understanding as he had received from Father Ring. He had felt that even a few tears and kisses wouldn't be out of place.

"If she was a different sort of girl," he said with an infinity of caution, "I'd say to her what I said to Father Ring and ask her to come to Dublin with me for a couple of days."

"But for what, Charlie?" asked Nora with real interest.

"For what?" repeated Charlie in surprise. Charlie was under the illusion most common among his countrymen that his meaning was always crystal-clear. "Nora," he went on with a touch of pathos, "I'll be frank with you. You're the only one I can be frank with. You're the only friend I have in the world. My position is hopeless. Hopeless! Father Ring said it himself. 'Marrying a girl with doubts like that, what can you expect, Charlie?' There's only one thing that would break the spell—have the honeymoon first and the marriage after."

It was dark, but he watched her closely from under the peak of his cap and saw that he had knocked her flat. No one had ever discussed such a subject with Nora before.

"But wouldn't it be a terrible sin, Charlie?" she asked with a quaver in her voice.

"Not if 'twas done with a good object," Charlie said firmly, answering her out of her own mouth.

"I'm sure she'd do it even without that, Charlie," Nora said with sudden bitterness.

"If she loved me she would," said Charlie hopefully.

"Love?" cried Nora scornfully, springing from her chair, all her maiden airs dropping from her and leaving her a mature, raging, jealous woman. "Don't be deceiving yourself like that, my dear man. That one doesn't love you."

"What? Who? Who doesn't love me?" asked Charlie in stupefaction.

It was her turn then.

"Weren't you talking about Molly O'Regan?" she asked in alarm.

"Molly O'Regan?" Charlie cried, raising his face to the ceiling like a dog about to bay. "What the hell put Molly O'Regan into your head, woman? Sure, I could have Molly O'Regan in the morning and the child along with her. Isn't that what I was saying to you?"

"Oh," said Nora, drawing back from him with a look of horror, "don't say any more!"

"But my God, girl," moaned Charlie, thinking of his beautiful scene absolutely wasted and impossible to begin on again, "sure you must know I don't give a snap of my fingers for Molly O'Regan! You were the first woman I ever gave a damn about, only you wouldn't have me. I only married Polly because she was your shadow. Even Father Ring knew that."

"Oh," she cried as if she were just ready to go into hysterics, "I couldn't do it! I couldn't!"

"No, no, no, no," said Charlie in alarm as though such an idea had never crossed his mind. "You're taking me up wrong. Whisht, now, whisht, or you'll be heard!"

"You must never, never say such a thing to me again," she said, looking at him as though he were a devil in human shape.

"But my God, woman," he cried indignantly, "I didn't. You're missing the whole point. I never asked you. I said if you were a different sort of woman I might ask you. I was only putting the case the way I put it to Father Ring. Surely you can understand that?"

It seemed she couldn't, not altogether anyhow, and Charlie strode to the door, his hands clasped behind his back and a gloomy look on his face.

"I'm sorry if I upset you," he snapped over his shoulder. " 'Tis your own fault didn't marry me first. You're the only woman I ever cared about and I wanted to explain."

She was staring at him incredulously, brushing back the loose black hair from her forehead with an uncertain hand. She looked childish and beautiful. If Charlie had only known, she was thinking what a very queer way the Holy Ghost had answered her prayer. As Polly had once said the Lord's ways were very peculiar. Charlie waited for some sign of relenting in her but saw none and, heaving a deep sigh, he left. Crossing the bridge when the abbey tower was all black and spiky against the sky and the lights in the back of the little shops were reflected in the river, he was like a man demented. He had done it again! This time he'd done it for good. It would soon be in everyone's mouth that he had tried to seduce a second girl. He knew how it would be interpreted. He saw it already like headlines in a newspaper: WELL-KNOWN SHOPKEEPER'S SHOCKING PROPOSAL OUTRAGED FATHER'S INDIGNATION. The girl who had stood by him when no one else would do it—this was her thanks! And it all came of Romeo and Juliet, the Captain's Daughter and the rest of the nonsense. There was a curse on him. Nora would tell her father and Father Ring; between them they would raise up a host of new enemies against him; no one would do business with him—a foolish, idle, dreamy, impractical man!

.   .   .

He let a week go by before he did anything. In that time he realized the full horror of the scrape he had got himself into, and avoided every contact with people he knew. He spent most of his time in the sitting-room, and only went down to the shop when the girl came up for him and he knew that the visitor was a genuine customer and not an angel of vengeance. Finally, he asked Jim O'Regan in for a drink.

Jim was an ex-soldier, small, gaunt, and asthmatic, dressed in a blue serge suit that was no bluer than his face and with a muffler high about his throat. Johnny Desmond gave them a queer look as they entered, but Charlie, seemingly in the highest spirits, rattled away about everything till it dawned on them both that he had opened negotiations for Molly and the child. Charlie could have gone further but one glance at Jim's mean poker face and he remembered the scene outside the graveyard, and then it was as if Holy Ireland, Romeo and Juliet, and all the romantic dreams of his youth started with a cry from their slumber. It was terrible, but he couldn't help it; he was an unfortunate dreamy man.

Later that morning he had to go to the bank. The whole week he had been putting it off, but he could put it off no longer. He gave a quick glance up the street to see that the coast was clear and then strode briskly out. He hadn't gone a hundred yards when he saw Jerry Lawlor coming down the same pavement. Charlie looked round frantically for some lane or shop he could take refuge in but there was none. "Brass, boys, brass!" he groaned. But to his great surprise Jerry showed no signs of anger, only a slight surprise at Charlie's slinking air.

"Good morrow, Charlie," he said, sticking his thumbs in the arm-holes of his vest, "as you won't say it yourself," he added.

"Oh, good morrow, good morrow, Jerry," cried Charlie with false heartiness, trying to read the signs on Jerry's battered countenance. "Up to the bank I'm rushing," he said confidentially.

"The bank?" Jerry said slyly. "Not the presbytery?"

"What the hell would I be doing at the presbytery?" Charlie exclaimed with a watchful smile.

"Oh, headquarters, headquarters," replied Jerry. "Who was it was telling me you were thinking of taking the field again? I believe your patrols were out."

"Patrols, Jerry?" Charlie echoed in surprise. "Ah, I'm too old for soldiering."

"I hope not, Charlie," said Jerry. "Begor," he added, squaring his shoulders, "I don't know that I'd mind shouldering the old shotgun again in a good cause. Well, be good!" he ended with a wink and a nod.

He left Charlie open-mouthed on the pavement, looking after him. What the blazes did Jerry Lawlor mean? he wondered, scratching his poll. "Be good"—was that the sort of advice you'd expect from a man whose daughter you had just been trying to seduce? "Be good"—was the man mad or something? He couldn't understand why Jerry, who had the devil's own temper, took his advances to Nora in that spirit. Was it possible that Nora had censored them so much that he hadn't understood? Was it—a wild hope—that she hadn't told him at all? His face fell again. No woman could keep a thing like that to herself. If she hadn't told her father, she'd told someone else, and sooner or later it would get back to him. He heaved a bitter sigh. The sooner he could fix up things with the O'Regans the sooner he would be armed to face the attack.

He went on, but his luck seemed to be dead out that morning. As he went in the door Father Ring came out. Charlie gave him a terrified look, but before he could even think of escape, Father Ring was shaking his hand.

"You're looking well, Charlie."

"I'm not feeling too good, father," said Charlie, thinking how far from the truth it was.

"Tell me," said Father Ring confidentially, "you didn't do any more about that little matter we were discussing?"

"To tell you the truth, father," Charlie said with apparent candour, "I didn't."

"Take your time," Father Ring said with a knowing look. "There's no hurry. I wouldn't be surprised if something could be done about that kid of yours. Mind! I'm not making any promises, but there's a soft corner there for you all right, and the father wouldn't let her go empty-handed. You know what I mean?"

"I do, father," groaned Charlie, meaning that he hadn't a notion, and as Father Ring went round the corner towards the church he stood on the bank steps with his head in a whirl. It was a spring day, a sunshiny day which made even the main street look cheerful, but Charlie was too confused for external impressions. For a week he had skulked like an assassin from Jerry Lawlor and Father Ring, yet here they treated him like lovers. And Nora went to confession to Father Ring! Admitting that he wouldn't let on what she did tell him, he couldn't conceal what she didn't, and it was quite plain that she hadn't told either of them about Charlie. Now what purpose would a girl have in concealing a thing like that? Modesty? But modesty in Charlie's mind was associated with nothing but hullabaloo. There was another flash of hope like a firework in his head, and then again darkness. "Christ!" he thought despairingly. "I'm going dotty! 'Tis giving up the drink in such a hurry."

"Morra, Charlie," said a farmer going in, but Charlie didn't even acknowledge the salute. His face was screwed up like that of a man who has forgotten what he came for. Then he drew a deep breath, pulled himself erect, and set off at a brisk pace for the Lawlors'.

Nora came out when she heard him banging on the door and gaped at him with horror-stricken eyes. He pushed her rudely back into the kitchen before him.

"Sit down, sit down!" he said shortly.

"What would I sit down for?" she asked in a low voice, and then her knees seemed to give way and she flopped.

"When can you marry me?" asked Charlie, standing over her like a boxer, ready to knock her flat if she rose again.

"Why?" she asked in a dead voice. "Wouldn't Molly O'Regan have you?"

"Ha, ha," laughed Charlie bitterly. "I see the tomtoms were working this morning."

"I suppose you think we don't know that 'tis all arranged?" she asked, throwing back her head to toss aside the stray curl that fell across her face.

"The trouble with you," Charlie said vindictively, "is that you always know other people's business and never know your own. When you met the one man that cared for you you let him slip. That's how much you knew. You're trying to do the same thing now."

"If you cared for me you wouldn't ask me to disrespect myself," she said with mournful accusation.

"If I didn't, I wouldn't ask you at all," snapped Charlie. "Now, I'm asking you properly. Once and for all, will you marry me?"

"But why should you?" she asked in a vague hysterical tone, rising with her hands thrown out and her head well back. "You know now the sort of woman I am. You need never respect me any more."

"What the hell is up with you?" shouted Charlie, almost dancing with fury. Whatever he said to this girl seemed to be wrong.

"There's nothing up with me," she answered in a reasonable tone which was as close to lunacy as anything Charlie had ever heard. "I know what I am now—that's all."

"And what are you?" asked Charlie in alarm.

"You ought to know," she said triumphantly. "I didn't slap your face, did I?"

"You didn't what?" cried Charlie with an agonized look.

"Oh," she cried in a rapture of self-abasement, "I deceived myself nicely all the years. I thought I was a good-living woman but you knew better. You knew what I was; a cheap, vulgar, sensual woman that you could say what you liked to. Or do what you liked to. I suppose it's the just punishment for my pride. Why would you marry me when you can get me for nothing?"

Charlie had another flash of inspiration, this time inspiration mixed with pity and shame. He suddenly saw the girl was fond of him and would do anything for him. Jessica, Juliet, the Captain's Daughter, the whole blooming issue. This was the real thing, the thing he had always been looking for and never found. He nearly swept her off her feet as he grabbed her.

"God forgive me!" he said thickly. "The finest woman in Ireland and I tormenting you like that! Your father and the priest have more sense than me. Put on your things and we'll go down and see them."

"No, no, no," she cried hysterically like a Christian martyr offering herself to the lions. "Your mother said I'd never rock a cradle for you."

"My mother, my mother—she has me as bad as herself. Never mind what she says."

"But what'll you do if she puts spells on me?" she asked in a dazed tone, putting her hand to her forehead.

"Roast her over a slow fire," snapped Charlie. He was himself again, aged seventeen, a roaring revolutionary and rationalist, ready to take on the British Empire, the Catholic Church, and the Wise Woman all together. "Now listen to me, girl," he said, taking her hands. "No one is going to put spells on you. And no one is going to haunt you, either. That's only all old women's talk and we had enough of it to last us our lives. We're a match for anyone and anything. Now, what are you doing?"

"Making the dinner," said Nora, blinking and smiling at anything so prosaic.

"We'll have dinner in town, the four of us," said Charlie. "Now come on!"

He stood behind her grinning as she put on her hat. She put it on crooked and her face was blotched beyond anything a powder-puff could repair, but Charlie didn't mind. He felt grand. At last he had got what he had always wanted, and he knew the rest would come. (It did too, and all Mrs. Cashman's spells didn't delay it an hour.) As for Nora, she had no notion what she had got, but she had an alarming suspicion that it was the very opposite of what she had always desired.

(Which, for a woman, is usually more or less the same thing.)

Darcy in Tír na nÓg

This 1950 story is unusual for its brevity, its reliance on narrative, and its original language, Irish. (It did not appear in English—in Richard B. Walsh's lyrical translation—until 1990.) Perhaps Irish seemed appropriate to the story itself, or writing fiction in it was O'Connor's way of remaining fluent. He had, however, a commitment to the original language, as David Greene has noted, stronger than either motive: "He had worked and fought for the Irish language in his youth, knowing that in it lay the key to all but two or three centuries of the history of this nation; in later years he had come to accept reluctantly the decision of the Irish people to reject by their own free will what their fathers had had wrenched from them by famine and oppression. . . . his zeal for the Irish language remained unabated; if the people had rejected the language itself, he was determined that they should at least be given some notion . . . of what had existed in it" (Michael/Frank, 137–38). What is characteristic is the story's melancholy emphasis on the essential mystery of human relations and a return to the theme of abandonment.

[In 1949, O'Connor had written "Darcy in the Land of Youth," which shares only its title; it is cheerfully romantic, dealing with the experiences of an Irishman who finds surprising love in wartime England.]

I went out into the garden. It was a fine Spring day. A slight coloured haze was filtering in from the sea, a blue heat-haze which would make the apple trees grow. The child was sleeping in the pram and the river was playing sleep-music for her. The sleep-music of the river and the sound of the wind in the oak tree at the bottom of the garden, and the heat-haze stretching from branch to branch—what was in my mind was something altogether different, but suddenly it slipped away from me. The story I wanted should have the joy of a Spring day in it, and then I began thinking and thinking about everything that came into my mind as I looked at the beauty of the day—the Mardyke in Cork and the sunlight filtering through the waving of the leaves, and the child playing with the watch-chain of the old man sitting on the bench—sweet, gentle thoughts like these set me laughing and sighing until Darcy came into my head and drove out every other thought.

Darcy was the youngest son. A small house and a big family; a mother who was half blind, half deaf and half crippled, a flock of grown lads and a flock of unmarried girls, and he and little Bridget at the bottom of the bag, the two best. And you certainly wouldn't find in the city of Cork a nicer nor a gentler girl than the girl he married. We all thought he did very well for himself, for she and her mother had a shop on the south side of the city. I have only to close my eyes to see her again: a tall, dark girl, with jet black hair like a Spanish girl; long features, big red lips and big dark eyes with the shadow of the eyelashes across them. Maybe I'm only dreaming but I always used to think because of her stiff way of moving and because of those big eyes that she was threatened with bad health. The picture is changed now; she's leaning across the counter with a rose in her hair talking to Bridget Darcy. Bridget was lame but she had been the most lovable child you ever saw in your life; a little fierce pale face and more cheek in her than in any ten street urchins. But she was forced to take on the housekeeping for that garrulous, squabbling family, and all the fire and the merriment and the fun in her gradually left her until her voice could be heard above every voice in the house and she had a laugh which had lost all its melody. But that's another story. She and Nora O'Leary had been great friends since they were children and it is said that it was she made the match between her brother and Nora. That may well be true. She had the nerve for it.

Another thing certain is that Nora and her mother were not the same kind of people. Not that there was any harm in that poor woman. She was a little, fat, rosy woman who was very satisfied with herself and was always reading pious papers; she never did much harm to anybody in her life, and many a help and many an alms the poor women in the lanes got from her. The only thing I would say against her is that she was a little too satisfied with herself and she had far too low an opinion of Darcy and his family, and that she had been spoiled a bit by Nora. She liked comfort and respect, and she liked people to be always asking her advice, and she wanted Nora to be helping her every second minute. If she only had a headache you could see the tears in Nora's eyes. She was that kind of a girl. But her mother was as jealous as a child and Nora had to be constantly on her guard against her, for if she and Darcy were too affectionate with one another, if she gave the impression that Darcy was the one she liked better, the old woman would get into a huff and mightn't talk to either of them for the whole day, or she might accuse them of wishing for nothing so much as her death, and keep saying that she wouldn't be long a trouble to them, and so on.

It was a small thing, something that any other man but Darcy could make a joke of—but Darcy was never like that. He was a solitary kind of man, a man you'd often see walking alone in the country, a man who wouldn't have a drink with the other clerks. Bridget thought that everything would be right when they had a family; but a son was born, and the old woman claimed Nora more than ever and also the child. You'd see Bridget Darcy going oftener to the shop, and sometimes if you went into the shop you'd see the traces of tears on Nora's face.

One day Darcy left. It makes no difference now what kind of trouble was going on between them: probably some little thing, something Darcy said to the little boy, or the like; this was not the reason why he went, it was something much deeper than that. Nora astonished us: she heard somehow that Darcy had gone to England, and she followed him. She was such a mild person, you wouldn't think she'd do anything like that, but she spent six months there searching every place where the Irish might have news of one another, without getting tale or tidings of him. In the end she came home, and once more we'd see her as we went by, looking out the window as she used to do before. And we pitied her; a young woman, a generous-hearted woman, now a laughing-stock for the neighbours.

Bridget was the only friend she had, and you'd see them on a summer evening out in the country walking slowly together, and the little boy, Dinny, running and jumping away ahead of them. They'd be talking about Darcy. Nora thought he wouldn't come back; she went on like that, quiet and dejected, but Bridget wouldn't let her believe it, and she'd get angry.

"But wouldn't you think he'd send us some news, even if it was only a postcard?"

"And let us know where he is, is that it? Tell me, how long would it be before you'd be off after him? The same evening!"

"I suppose so."

"You can be sure of it, and he knows that, and we'll get no news from him until he comes himself. How do we know what may be troubling him? Let him be, girl; whatever jigamareel he's going on with he'll come home when he gets tired of it."

And she was right, though even she had lost all hope by the time he came, eight years later. By this time the old woman was dead. Nora herself was in the kitchen when she thought she heard a footstep that came as far as the shop but didn't come any farther. It's amazing how people hear things like that in Cork; you'd hear a footstep and you'd say to yourself, "that's the old peeler from number two coming home, wherever he was"; or you'd hear a door being closed and you'd say, "aren't the McCarthys going to bed early?" She got up and went to the door of the shop. She heard the young lad's voice, playing with the other boys down the road. It was getting dark and she couldn't see the other side of the road, because of the street lamp which was in front of the door. She went across the road. "Is there anybody there?" she said, frightened. "Is it you Dinny?" and then, as if she was talking to herself, "Is it you, Ned?" It is not that she believed it was him, but the terror and the passion that were inside her, she released them into the darkness of the night. That whisper was something quite different from the sigh she released when she knew who was there. "Thank God you're home again. Come in. Thanks be to God." Full of joy, she brought him in; out she went again to call Dinny to send him for Bridget, under strict orders not to tell the secret to anybody else. What a happy little huddle they had that night, lightheartedly chatting and gossiping. Darcy told them very little about his travels and they didn't ask him many questions. It should have been a stark, bitter story like every other story, but it was the very opposite. He was as slippery as an inn-keeper's cat. He was well dressed. He had a sort of air of authority that he usedn't to have long ago. They knew that it was not hardship nor want that had made him come home at last.

But Nora didn't care what it was that brought him home, so long as he was there and she could look at him, and talk to him, and be kind to him, without fear of anybody. If you saw her in the street, you'd think from her laugh that what she wanted was to clasp you in her arms and tell you that Ned was home again. She was like a schoolgirl. She said nothing about all she had suffered without him. It was Bridget who told him that with tears in her eyes. "I often prayed to God that you'd die, Ned." He didn't answer her, but she knew that he understood well what she was trying to say. He got a new job. The wonder was dissipating and Nora was getting used to him again when a dreadful thing happened. She dreamt that she was in a certain place, but she couldn't remember the name of the place, only that she had read about it long ago in one of Ned's books. To put the finishing touch to the whole thing, she couldn't sleep and finally got up and went downstairs. She knew where the book was. She opened it, and as she did a postcard fell out of it. A little postcard with only two lines written on it but that was enough, and she understood clearly what an awful thing Darcy had done and why he seemed sometimes like a stranger in the house.

She didn't tell him what she had found out. She told nobody but Bridget. Bridget said nothing, but she burst into tears.

"I knew," said Nora quietly, "the night he came back that he had no intention of coming in, that he didn't want us to see him at all. It was God told me who was there. Only for that he would be gone in the morning and we'd never know that he had been there at all."

"Oh have sense, girl," said Bridget.

"But it's true for me. Why did he change his name when he left Cork, only to make himself believe that Ned Darcy was dead?"

"But why did Ned Darcy come back then?" said Bridget angrily.

"Maybe he couldn't help it, any more than a ghost whose lot it is that he has to come back to the place where he suffered the most hardship. Maybe I shouldn't have brought him in, and that it would be better if I had let him go again."

"Oh shut up, girl, shut up," said Bridget. "There's no knowing which of you is the worse."

"But what about the other woman he married?" said Nora, quaking. "She'll never know what happened to him any more than I do myself."

"It doesn't matter about her," said Bridget fiercely. "He should be ashamed of himself. Oh God," she wept bitterly, "to think how well off some people are in this world, and still they're not satisfied."

Nora never told him she knew he was married a second time. She knew that if she did she'd lose whatever grip she had on him; that she could never again be gentle with him when his heart was troubled and he couldn't sleep. She could help him only as long as he didn't know that she understood what was troubling him; the wonderful life he imagined for himself when he went and cut himself clean away from his home; when he changed his name as a sign that Ned Darcy no longer existed; all the pleasant days he spent with another woman and other children in a strange land—all being swallowed up in the years, being scattered like a heat-haze; Oisín dreaming of Tír na nÓg.

Maybe that's what the old story means: that nobody should go back in search of youth. If it is, it is a true story as far as Darcy was concerned. He wouldn't let go his grip on the old life. On Bridget, for instance. He saw as we all did what her family were making of her—a poor servant girl; he saw that the bitterness of the old maid had got into her in spite of herself, but when he attempted to do something for her the whole household rose up against him like a flock of geese. "What's this? A man like him who deserted his wife and family telling them what they should do! The cheek of him! And how would they manage without Bridget?" In the end he saw from what she said herself as she was weeping by the fire that it was better to let her be and not make her more unhappy than she was. "I'm too old, Ned," she said. "The best part of my life is spent and it's not worth my while trying to save the candle-butt. Maybe some day with the help of God when mother is no longer there and the boys are married Nora will give me a corner at her fireside. I wouldn't ask more than that of God now."

I don't know if there's any place on earth as lonely as Cork City, or if every place in the world seems lonely to those who were born and raised there. Should we all go away from the place where we spent our youth? Certainly it was not long until Darcy lost all appearance of happiness and was the same as the old Darcy. You'd see him from time to time out in the country alone. One Spring day like this he went away again and he has never been seen in Cork since. Where did he go? I don't know. I know he didn't go back to Tír na nÓg, for we're all destined to have only one Tír na nÓg, and that was swallowed up in years and in loneliness.

The wind was getting cold. I brought in the pram and closed the door. It's surprising how quickly the wind gets cold on a Spring evening when the sun goes down.

The Rebel

"The Rebel" calls to mind the opening lines of a contemporaneous story (1952), "Unapproved Route": "Between men and women, as between neighbouring states, there are approved routes which visitors must take. Others they take at their peril, no matter how high-minded their intentions may be" (Collection Three, 151). It is a mysterious story, unfinished and never published. Given O'Connor's conviction that no story was satisfactory without extensive revision, surely he would have "tinkered" with this one, perhaps developing and explaining what might seem stark in this version.

Yet this story can surprise with moving variations on an adulterous triangle and the painful revelations that result. Even the title is not simple; of Don, Carrie, and Jim, who is really rebelling, and against what? Eventually, Don rebels not against his morals but against the expectations (private and public) that he will rebel. What O'Connor calls "the ambiguities of daily life" are not easily sorted out, and the events of the story are less plain than they appear.

Almost from the first evening Don MacNamara dropped into the little pub he found himself accepted there. And that in itself was unusual for the English don't cotton on to strangers. It wasn't much of a pub; just a plain red-brick building in the village street with a parlour on the left where the ladies drank gin and a bar-room on the right where the men drank beer and played darts. The bar itself was in the hall-way, and behind it was a dark kitchen with a cellar beneath it where the beer was kept. Jim Wright, the publican, was a local man who worked in the factory by day; a thin, melancholy, obliging man with spectacles.

His wife, Carrie, was a townie from Lancashire, a tremendous worker

148

in the way of North Country women. In the morning when you passed the pub you saw her scrubbing with the wireless going full blast, and when she saw you she went full blast too. She was a shy girl who at first seemed plain and stupid, and was always nervous that she might be saying the wrong thing or giving the wrong change. But she didn't look plain or stupid when Don was around. He would come in, scarcely lifting his feet, an insignificant-looking man with a ravaged dyspeptic face and a tubercular complexion, a thin bitter mouth and long, limp hair, and all at once she was in a glow, putting on a turn as a fast piece of goods from the factory or making insulting remarks to the men till she had the place in a roar.

It wasn't that Don said or did anything very unusual. It was just a feeling of quiet enjoyment that seemed to emanate from him and made people feel good. He liked the country and he liked the people. The locals responded by confiding their troubles to him, like Eddie, an old friend of the publican's, who waited for Don like the souls in Purgatory just to tell him a bit more of his tragic life-story.

'I don't know how the hell it is,' Don would say with his dead-pan humour. 'I don't know whether it's the way the English suffer more than anyone else, or whether they can't find anyone that will listen to them, but the whole population seems to have been waiting for me to tell me the horrible agonies their mothers died in or how their wives ran away with someone else. I think I must have some sort of charm on me.'

The other customers agreed that Don did have a hard time with Eddie's hard life, but it was held greatly in his favour that he never hurt poor Eddie's feelings. 'The Irish are like that,' they said approvingly. 'Very kind.'

'They are like hell,' Don said mockingly. 'Is it people that come here by the hundred thousand just to get away from one another? Kind, how are you?' He never had a good word to say for Ireland himself, which they accepted as another form of his Irishness. 'Don's like all the Irish,' they said. 'A bit of a rebel.'

'Rebels, how are you?' added Don malevolently. 'Is it people that are afraid to eat meat on Friday for fear someone would turn them into a goat. Mind, I'm not saying they're not smart with a certain class of a weapon. Anonymous letters, for instance. With an anonymous letter an Irishman is out on his own. He can get his man at a hundred miles.' 'But you fought us, Don!' they protested. 'We did not fight ye,' said Don, the poison dropping from the side of his thin mouth. 'We sent anonymous letters all over the world about ye, and we shamed ye.' And then, with his battered face wrinkled up, he went into a melancholy caw of laughter.

They knew, of course, that he was exaggerating. Don always exaggerated things like that. You had only to look at himself if you wanted to see a born rebel. He was opposed on principle to every form of authority from the police to the Communist shop-stewards; he had only one answer to every order—'Why?'—and it was remarkable how rarely anyone could produce a satisfactory answer. Sometimes a fellow called Claude, who had risen to be an officer during the War, felt it his duty to defend discipline and stood up for the shooting of deserters, but Don overwhelmed him with scorn, pacing round him in tiny strides, his fists clenched, his face distorted with passion. 'My bold hero!' he snarled. 'What else would ye do with them? Sure, 'tis only the miracles of God that keeps ye fighting at all. 'Tis a wonder ye don't shoot their wives and children as well. That would teach them to be frightened.' He flared up at the least hint of injustice, and it was not the professional humanitarianism of the shop-stewards. He would see poor old Willy Wagtail, as they called him, hanging round the pub with what Don called 'a mouth' on him, and bring him in for a drink. He didn't like Willy any more than the others did, but as he said in his mocking way: 'If there's one thing in this world I can't stand, 'tis the image and likeness of God in want of a pint.'

Within a week everyone except her husband saw that Carrie was head and ears in love with him. It was only natural, of course. The girl wasn't really happy there. She was a superior sort of girl, with the North Country passion for self-improvement which is almost like an instinct in its violence, and Jim was a village boy who never wanted to leave his village, and had no interest but his car which he took to pieces every second week. One day when Don came to the pub she was alone, and began to talk of her troubles with Jim, and Don put his arms about her and kissed her. Don was like that. He would almost have done the same with Willy Wagtail, but while Carrie clung to him he realised that she was a different proposition from Willy Wagtail—an intelligent, passionate woman who was in love with him and would stick at nothing to get him. In a way it was a pleasant change from his own wife whose one conception of the duties of marriage was to make sure he didn't eat meat on Friday. And he, after all, had mocked at marriage and fidelity as just another of those regulations to ensure that no one eats meat on Friday or takes a drink after ten, not a ha'porth more reasonable and a good deal less practical.

After that, everything was different, for him and for her. He encouraged her to do things on her own; to see places she had always longed to see, to read and study and listen to the sort of music she liked. Carrie began to see life opening up in every direction about her. Of course, Don, with his embarrassing straightforwardness, could no more have carried on a love-affair than he could have flown, but Carrie surprised him by her qualities of calculation and determination, and planned the whole thing as if it were a military campaign. And it was not, as he knew, that she was accustomed to that sort of thing, for, according to herself, he was her first, and she was not the sort of girl to lie to a man she loved. Again, it was the North Country grit. Every few weeks she went off to spend a couple of days with her old parents who still lived in Burnley. Usually, she took Jim's car. Don would set off on his bicycle, supposedly to visit friends of his who lived near London; drop it at a station, and take the train to some spot where Carrie picked him up and they could go off together to places she wanted to see like Oxford or Stratford on Avon. It always came as something of a shock to him to find her waiting for him on the platform. He remembered her as he had seen her first, energetic, tight-lipped and a little bit grim, and was moved to see her looking for him, her face all smoothed out, eager, light-hearted and mawkish as a young girl. They stayed in some pleasant old inn whose name she had looked up; went to the theatre or visited some museum. It didn't much matter what they did. He could see her expanding under his eyes, becoming more confident of herself and her judgment of things. She discovered quite a taste for antiques, and they spent hours in some old shop from which she emerged clutching a pair of brass candlesticks apparently made by the village smith in a shape which was unconventional but nice. And anyway, for thirty bob they were a gift.

These were days that Don knew he would not forget, but apart from them he was not altogether happy. With a character like his he could not be at his ease in the pub, talking to Jim or the customers. He knew the customers guessed at the real state of affairs from the way Eddie ceased to tell him about his troubles and switched to a peculiar romance he had had with a 'certain lady in Cairo' for whom he had felt 'a deep veneration.' As Jim's friend as well as Don's, Eddie felt sympathetic but sad.

Don hated to give an imaginary account of how he had spent the week-end, and suffered from extraordinary waking night-mares in which he forgot himself and in his old straightforward way told the literal truth about what had really happened. Not only did Carrie not seem to mind, but Don sometimes felt she enjoyed it. As she washed glasses, she entered enthusiastically into conversations about her parents and their state of health and mind which merged into confidences about the peculiarities of elderly people; and Don, twisting his mouth into a wry smile, realised that the girl didn't even know she was telling lies.

It was worse when Jim had to go to the North of England on a special job, for a pub is one of those places where thieves know there is always a certain amount of money, and Don realised that it was taken for granted that he should keep Carrie company. It should have been a heaven-sent honeymoon for them both, but for Don it was anything but that. Of course, there were odd hours when he forgot himself and let himself go; when he came in from work to find Carrie waiting for him so that they could have a drink together before supper and the opening of the pub, or when he woke in the morning to see her bringing in a cup of tea while outside the window there was a green hill with a thatched Elizabethan cottage perched on top of it against the sky like the Ark come to rest, and they seemed like an old married couple. But there were longer and worse spells when he remembered what they really were. Carrie loved to play that they were married and lay out Jim's pyjamas, dressing gown and slippers, and she was hurt when he insisted on wear-ing his own old night shirt and coat.

'But why, Don?' she asked anxiously. 'You don't mind if they're Jim's, do you?' and all he could say was 'Ah, I like my own things, girl.'

It was the same with food. Much as he liked eating at home with her, he stayed out several evenings in town rather than come back to a meal, and face the gentle look of Eddie in the bar, a look that wished him every happiness but wished too that the happiness should not hurt Jim.

'Ah, don't mind me, Carrie,' he said miserably. 'I suppose I'm a cranky bastard, but I don't like eating another man's food.'

'But the house is as much mine as Jim's, Don,' she said despairingly. 'Don't you think I work as hard as Jim does?'

'You do, and harder,' he said. 'Ah, don't you see I'm not criticizing you at all. But what I'm looking forward to is a couple of days by ourselves in Brighton . . . I only wish to God I was there now!'

'Yes, Don,' she said, meek but misunderstanding. 'I know what you mean. We've had wonderful times together. But I don't really like hotels or boarding houses. I mean, they're not like home, are they?'

'No, of course they're not, but you're not beholden to anybody for them either.'

'Still, it's never like being married, Don, is it? I mean, you can't help feeling that you're doing wrong.'

'How the blazes do you make that out?'

'I don't know, Don, but it seems that way. I suppose it's different for a woman. A woman doesn't really feel the same, not without her own things.'

And Don couldn't help feeling that there must be something queer about women, to think less of deceiving their husbands at home than of doing so in a hotel bedroom, while Carrie felt that there must be something wrong with Don to see more guilt in a thing done at home than in a hotel room, and began to wonder if he really cared for her as much as he said. That showed how little she understood him because the only thing in his mind was how soon he could get them both out of the situation they were in. It wasn't easy. He hated to do something to his poor decent wife that she wouldn't even understand, and beside that, there was the question of keeping two homes. Carrie pointed out that she had a little money of her own, but he refused to consider letting her spend this. Then she pointed out that she was quite capable of supporting herself, but he wouldn't consider that either. She thought it hard of him, as she thought it hard of him to slight her little attempts at domesticity, and she could not understand that he didn't want either because he felt he hadn't earned it, and got more of the real feeling of home from a shabby hotel bedroom on which he felt he had some claim. There are certain things no woman ever understands in love, and one is the determination of a man like Don to pay for his girl as he would pay for anything else he regarded as his own. The idea of ownership is fixed more firmly in a man's mind than in a woman's, and ownership is as much a matter of duties as of rights. Don's way of love-making was to look for another job where he could earn overtime.

It was almost a relief to him when Jim got back from the North and he didn't need to stay in the pub any longer. It was no pleasure to Carrie because Jim came back too ill to work. He was self-conscious about his sickly looks and sat in the kitchen behind, listening to the wireless, absorbed in some dream of his own misfortunes. Don had to go and talk to him there, and found it doubly uncomfortable because Jim kept his eyes averted in a way that suggested hostility.

'Doctor says I ought to get out more,' he muttered to the stove. 'It's not so easy.'

'Why don't you go with Carrie, so?' asked Don.

'Carrie's got other things to do,' Jim said hopelessly.

'Well, why don't you come walking with me?' asked Don. 'I'm fond of walking, not like the rest of ye.'

'Could I, Don?' Jim cried with sudden eagerness. 'Could I really?' And he called out to Carrie who was working in the bar: 'Carrie! Don here says he'll walk with me.'

'That's right,' she said, standing in the doorway with her hands on her hips. 'That's what you need, you lazy old devil!'

Carrie was genuinely pleased. She felt it was just what her husband needed, and besides it would put an end to a lot of casual talk. Besides, she had something of a woman's pleasure in bringing together husband and lover. But Don, who could not have understood this even if she had been able to explain it to him, was miserable. He was the sort of man who had to do a kindness even if it killed him, but kindness to a man he felt he had wronged was no better than treachery.

Jim was in too bad a shape to notice what he was feeling. They set off for a long walk across the fields, up the hill as far as the church and manorhouse and back by country lanes. Don found Jim a better companion than he had expected. He was a country boy, and he knew every house in the neighbourhood and every grave in the churchyard. From the top of the hill he showed Don three counties and also some of their biggest houses. On these and on the families who occupied them he was positively entertaining, all the more because he did not understand why Don should be so entertained. He was only telling facts. After they returned he already declared he was feeling better and insisted on drinks all round.

'I don't want any blooming doctor,' he declared from the bar. 'Don's the doctor for me.'

It was Willy Wagtail all over again. Jim discovered a new interest in life, planning walks they could take together and places about which he felt he could talk interestingly to Don. A lot of the time they were of no interest to anybody, but Jim was beginning to see himself as quite a deep fellow who hadn't appreciated his own talents. His health really did improve, though not, Don suspected, so much from exercise as from having a new interest. He was a creature of habit, and it had made an old man of him before his time.

'You saved my life, Don,' he said one day they were walking up the hill from a church where Jim had taken him to see what he described as a real curiosity—a church bell hung in a tree. 'I know I'm not much company. I never had conversation like Eddie or the others. Didn't have their experience, I suppose. I brood too much, I know.'

'You and Carrie ought to get away more together,' Don said flatly.

'Too hard with the pub, Don,' said Jim.

'Then get rid of the bloody pub.'

'I like it, Don,' Jim replied simply. 'Anyhow, Carrie wouldn't care for me to be away with. Fact is, in my job I've got to have a wife, but I never was much at my ease with women. I'm happier in a pub with a lot of men. Can you understand that, Don?'

'I suppose so,' said Don, who could understand it only too well. Ireland was full of people like Jim, which was probably what had the country the way it was.

'Now, Carrie likes you, Don. Carrie likes people with conversation. Next time she goes to Lancashire, you should go with her. You'd like it there. It's different.'

And next time Carrie was going to her parents, Jim insisted that she should take Don as well. He even worked out an itinerary and leaned in the front of the car explaining it to Carrie. She listened to him with a slight smile. Even in matters of life and death no woman gets over her amusement at the ambiguities of daily life. But when she asked Don if they should spend the night in the old inn outside Lichfield he shook his head.

'I can't, Carrie,' he said despairingly.

She stopped the car and put her hands on her lap.

'You mean you don't want me any more, Don?' she asked in a dead voice.

'I mean nothing of the sort. It's that poor devil.'

'He's not the only one to be pitied, Don.'

'I never thought he was.'

'Oh, yes, Don, you did. Ever since you got so friendly to Jim, you've changed to me. I don't blame you. I suppose there's two sides to every story. You think I'm not being fair to him.'

'It's not that, Carrie, it's not that. It's only that I see now the man belongs to the place and he doesn't want to leave it.'

'And I don't belong to it and I do want to leave it,' she said dully. 'I suppose that's my bad luck. But I don't want to press you. I don't suppose I'd care so much except you're the sort that has to be pressed.'

'All right, all right,' said Don. 'Why don't you say it? You think I'm a mean, cowardly, guilt-ridden bastard.'

'No, Don,' she said, shaking her head. 'It's not that.'

'What else is it?'

'It's just that you're a different sort of man from what you thought you were,' she said, and gave him a long, curious look.

'Exactly,' he said bitterly. 'I thought I was a great fellow and I could do anything I liked, and it was only the sort of miserable life I led that made me close and cautious. And now when I go back to Ireland, I won't even have that satisfaction. I'll know 'tis all in myself. Come on and we'll stay here.'

'No, Don,' she said firmly. 'Not if you think it's wrong.'

'What does it matter what I think any longer?' he asked. 'Anyway, we'll probably never get another chance.'

He was right in this at least, though that may have been her doing rather than his. She was shrewd enough to see that the man was so hurt in his pride that he would almost have welcomed pressure from her to break altogether with his past. But she saw too that it was the responsible man in him, not the rebel, who had revolted against things as he found them and now when at last he was free and could have the sort of wife and home he longed for, it was only the responsible man that remained. She had some notion of the tragedy it represented for him, but she knew as well that it would be a much worse tragedy if now he were to try and live out his life with a personality that was no longer his own.

The Face of Evil

"The Face of Evil" begins deceptively as light-hearted nostalgia told by a typical O'Connor boy—pious, diligent, and naïve. It soon grows darker as the narrator's confidence in himself crumbles. Written in 1953, the story springs from an incident in O'Connor's childhood but is characteristically transformed: "I heard that a young fellow I knew—a wild, handsome boy whose father beat him savagely—had run away from home and was being searched for by the police. The story was told in whispers. He would be picked up and sent to a reformatory. That evening I found him myself, lurking in an alleyway, his long face dirty with tears, and tried to make him come home with me. He wouldn't, and I could not leave him there like that, lonely and lost and crying. I made it clear that I would stay with him, and at last he agreed to return home if I went with him and pleaded for him. When I knocked at the door he stood against the wall, his hands in his pockets and his head bent. His elder sister opened the door, and I made my little speech, and she promised to see that he wasn't punished. Then I went home in a glow of self-righteousness, feeling that I had saved him from the fate I had always dreaded myself. I felt sure he would be grateful, and that from this out we would be good friends, but it didn't happen like that at all. When we met again he would not look at me; instead, he turned away with a sneer, and I knew his father had beaten him again, and that it was all my fault. As a protector of the weak, I was never worth a damn" (An Only Child, 128).

I could never understand all the old talk about how hard it is to be a saint. I was a saint for quite a bit of my life and I never saw anything hard in it. And when I stopped being a saint, it wasn't because the life was too hard.

157

I fancy it is the sissies who make it seem like that. We had quite a few of them in school, fellows whose mothers intended them to be saints, and who hadn't the nerve to be anything else. I never enjoyed the society of chaps who wouldn't commit sin for the same reason that they wouldn't dirty their new suits. That was never what sanctity meant to me, and I doubt if it is what it means to other saints. The companions I liked were the tough gang down the road, and I enjoyed going down of an evening and talking with them under the gaslamp about football matches and school, even if they did sometimes say things I wouldn't say myself. I was never one for criticising; I had enough to do criticising myself, and I knew they were decent chaps and didn't really mean much harm by the things they said about girls.

No, for me the main attraction of being a saint was the way it always gave you something to do. You could never say you felt time hanging on your hands. It was like having a room of your own to keep tidy; you'd scour it, and put everything neatly back in its place, and within an hour or two it was beginning to look as untidy as ever. It was a full-time job that began when you woke and stopped only when you fell asleep.

I would wake in the morning, for instance, and think how nice it was to lie in bed, and congratulate myself on not having to get up for another half-hour. That was enough. Instantly a sort of alarm clock would go off in my mind; the mere thought that I could enjoy half an hour's comfort would make me aware of an alternative, and I'd begin an argument with myself. I had a voice in me that was almost the voice of a stranger, the way it nagged and jeered. Sometimes I could almost visualise it, and then it took on the appearance of a fat and sneering teacher I had some years before at school—a man I really hated. I hated that voice. It always began in the same way, smooth and calm and dangerous. I could see the teacher rubbing his fat hands and smirking.

'Don't get alarmed, boy. You're in no hurry. You have another half-hour.'

'I know well I have another half-hour,' I would reply, trying to keep my temper. 'What harm am I doing? I'm only imagining I'm down in a submarine. Is there anything wrong in that?

'Oho, not the least in the world. I'd say there's been a heavy frost. Just the sort of morning when there's ice in the bucket.'

'And what has that to do with it?'

'Nothing, I tell you. Of course, for people like you it's easy enough in the summer months, but the least touch of frost in the air soon makes you feel different. I wouldn't worry trying to keep it up. You haven't the stuff for this sort of life at all.'

And gradually my own voice grew weaker as that of my tormentor grew stronger, till all at once I would strip the clothes from off myself and lie in my night-shirt, shivering and muttering, 'So I haven't the stuff in me, haven't I?' Then I would go downstairs before my parents were awake, strip and wash in the bucket, ice or no ice, and when Mother came down she would cry in alarm, 'Child of Grace, what has you up at this hour? Sure, 'tis only half past seven.' She almost took it as a reproach to herself, poor woman, and I couldn't tell her the reason, and even if I could have done so, I wouldn't. How could you say to anybody 'I want to be a saint'?

Then I went to Mass and enjoyed again the mystery of the streets and lanes in the early morning; the frost which made your feet clatter off the walls at either side of you like falling masonry, and the different look that everything wore, as though, like yourself, it was all cold and scrubbed and new. In the winter the lights would still be burning red in the little cottages, and in summer they were ablaze with sunshine so that their interiors were dimmed to shadows. Then there were the different people, all of whom recognised one another, like Mrs. MacEntee, who used to be a stewardess on the boats, and Macken, the tall postman, people who seemed ordinary enough when you met them during the day, but carried something of their mystery with them at Mass, as though they, too, were re-born.

I can't pretend I was ever very good at school, but even there it was a help. I might not be clever, but I had always a secret reserve of strength to call on in the fact that I had what I wanted, and that beside it I wanted nothing. People frequently gave me things, like fountain pens or pencil-sharpeners, and I would suddenly find myself becoming attached to them and immediately know I must give them away, and then feel the richer for it. Even without throwing my weight around I could help and protect kids younger than myself, and yet not become involved in their quarrels. Not to become involved, to remain detached—that was the great thing; to care for things and for people, yet not to care for them so much that your happiness became dependent on them.

It was like no other hobby, because you never really got the better of yourself, and all at once you would suddenly find yourself reverting to childish attitudes; flaring up in a wax with some fellow, or sulking when Mother asked you to go for a message, and then it all came back; the nagging of the infernal alarm clock which grew louder with every moment until it incarnated as a smooth, fat, jeering face.

'Now, that's the first time you've behaved sensibly for months, boy. That was the right way to behave to your mother.'

'Well, it *was* the right way. Why can't she let me alone, once in a while? I only want to read. I suppose I'm entitled to a bit of peace some time?'

'Ah, of course you are, my dear fellow. Isn't that what I'm saying? Go on with your book! Imagine you're a cowboy, riding to the rescue of a beautiful girl in a cabin in the woods, and let that silly woman go for the messages herself. She probably hasn't long to live anyway, and when she dies you'll be able to do all the weeping you like.'

And suddenly tears of exasperation would come to my eyes and I'd heave the story-book to the other side of the room and shout back at the voice that gave me no rest, 'Cripes, I might as well be dead and buried. I have no blooming life.' After that I would apologise to Mother (who, poor woman, was more embarrassed than anything else and assured me that it was all her fault), go on the message, and write another tick in my notebook against the heading of 'Bad Temper' so as to be able to confess it to Father O'Regan when I went to Confession on Saturday. Not that he was ever severe with me, no matter what I did; he thought I was the last word in holiness, and was always asking me to pray for some special intention of his own. And though I was depressed, I never lost interest, for no matter what I did I could scarcely ever reduce the total of times I had to tick off that item in my notebook.

Oh, I don't pretend it was any joke, but it did give you the feeling that your life had some meaning; that inside you, you had a real source of strength; that there was nothing you could not do without, and yet remain sweet, self-sufficient, and content. Sometimes too, there was the feeling of something more than mere content, as though your body were transparent, like a window, and light shone through it as well as on it, onto the road, the houses, and the playing children, as though it were you who was shining on them, and tears of happiness would come into my eyes, and I would hurl myself among the playing children just to forget it.

But, as I say, I had no inclination to mix with other kids who might be saints as well. The fellow who really fascinated me was a policeman's son named Dalton, who was easily the most vicious kid in the locality. The Daltons lived on the terrace above ours. Mrs. Dalton was dead; there was a younger brother called Stevie, who was next door to an imbecile, and there was something about that kid's cheerful grin that was even more frightening than the malice on Charlie's broad face. Their father was a tall, melancholy man, with a big black moustache, and the nearest thing imaginable to one of the Keystone cops. Everyone was sorry for his loss in his wife, but you knew that if it hadn't been that it would have been something else—maybe the fact that he hadn't lost her. Charlie was only an additional grief. He was always getting into trouble, stealing and running away from home; and only his father's being a policeman prevented his being sent to an industrial school. One of my most vivid recollections is that of Charlie's education. I'd hear a shriek, and there would be Mr. Dalton, dragging Charlie along the pavement to school, and whenever the names his son called him grew a little more obscene than usual, pausing to give Charlie a good going-over with the belt which he carried loose in his hand. It is an exceptional father who can do this without getting some pleasure out of it, but Mr. Dalton looked as though even that were an additional burden. Charlie's screams could always fetch me out.

'What is it?' Mother would cry after me.

'Ah, nothing. Only Charlie Dalton again.'

'Come in! Come in!'

'I won't be seen.'

'Come in, I say. 'Tis never right.'

And even when Charlie uttered the most atrocious indecencies, she only joined her hands as if in prayer and muttered, 'The poor child! The poor unfortunate child!' I never could understand the way she felt about Charlie. He wouldn't have been Charlie if it hadn't been for the leatherings and the threats of the industrial school.

Looking back on it, the funniest thing is that I seemed to be the only fellow on the road he didn't hate. The rest were all terrified of him, and some of the kids would go a mile to avoid him. He was completely unclassed: being a policeman's son, he should have been way up the social scale, but he hated the respectable kids worse than the others. When we stood under the gaslamp at night and saw him coming up the road, everybody fell silent. He looked suspiciously at the group, ready to spring at anyone's throat if he saw the shadow of offence; ready even when there wasn't a shadow. He fought like an animal, by instinct, without judgement, and without ever reckoning the odds, and he was terribly strong. He wasn't clever; several of the older chaps could beat him to a frazzle when it was merely a question of boxing or wrestling, but it never was that with Dalton. He was out for blood and usually got it. Yet he was never that way with me. We weren't friends. All that ever happened when we passed one another was that I smiled at him and got a cold, cagey nod in return. Sometimes we stopped and exchanged a few words, but it was an ordeal because we never had anything to say to one another.

It was like the signalling of ships, or more accurately, the courtesies of great powers. I tried, like Mother, to be sorry for him in having no proper home, and getting all those leatherings, but the feeling which came uppermost in me was never pity but respect: respect for a fellow who had done all the things I would never do: stolen money, stolen bicycles, run away from home, slept with tramps and criminals in barns and doss-houses, and ridden without a ticket on trains and on buses. It filled my imagination. I have a vivid recollection of one summer morning when I was going up the hill to Mass. Just as I reached the top and saw the low, sandstone church perched high up ahead of me, he poked his bare head round the corner of a lane to see who was coming. It startled me. He was standing with his back to the gable of a house; his face was dirty and strained; it was broad and lined, and the eyes were very small, furtive and flickering, and sometimes a sort of spasm would come over them and they flickered madly for half a minute on end.

'Hullo, Charlie,' I said. 'Where were you?'

'Out,' he replied shortly.

'All night?' I asked in astonishment.

'Yeh,' he replied with a nod.

'What are you doing now?'

He gave a short, bitter laugh.

'Waiting till my old bastard of a father goes out to work and I can go home.'

His eyes flickered again, and selfconsciously he drew his hand across them as though pretending they were tired.

'I'll be late for Mass,' I said uneasily. 'So long.'

'So long.'

That was all, but all the time at Mass, among the flowers and the candles, watching the beautiful, sad old face of Mrs. MacEntee and the plump, smooth, handsome face of Macken, the postman, I was haunted by the image of that other face, wild and furtive and dirty, peering round a corner like an animal looking from its burrow. When I came out, the morning was brilliant over the valley below me; the air was punctuated with bugle calls from the cliff where the barrack stood, and Charlie Dalton was gone. No, it wasn't pity I felt for him. It wasn't even respect. It was almost like envy.

Then, one Saturday evening, an incident occurred which changed my attitude to him; indeed, changed my attitude to myself, though it wasn't until long after that I realised it. I was on my way to Confession, preparatory to Communion next morning. I always went to Confession at the parish church in town where Father O'Regan was. As I passed the tramway terminus at the Cross, I saw Charlie sitting on the low wall above the Protestant church, furtively smoking the butt-end of a cigarette which somebody had dropped getting on the tram. Another tram arrived as I reached the Cross, and a number of people alighted and went off in different directions. I crossed the road to Charlie and he gave me his most distant nod.

'Hullo.'

'Hullo, Cha. Waiting for somebody?'

'No. Where are you off to?'

'Confession.'

'Huh.' He inhaled the cigarette butt deeply and then tossed it over his shoulder into the sunken road beneath without looking where it alighted. 'You go a lot.'

'Every week,' I said modestly.

'Jesus!' he said with a short laugh. 'I wasn't there for twelve months.'

I shrugged my shoulders. As I say, I never went in much for criticising others, and, anyway, Charlie wouldn't have been Charlie if he had gone to Confession every week.

'Why do you go so often?' he asked challengingly.

'Oh, I don't know,' I said doubtfully. 'I suppose it keeps you out of harm's way.'

'But you don't do any harm,' he growled, just as though he were defending me against someone who had been attacking me.

'Ah, we all do harm.'

'But, Jesus Christ, you don't do anything,' he said almost angrily, and his eyes flickered again in that curious nervous spasm, and almost as if they put him into a rage, he drove his knuckles into them.

'We all do things,' I said. 'Different things.'

'Well, what do you do?'

'I lose my temper a lot,' I admitted.

'Jesus!' he said again and rolled his eyes.

'It's a sin just the same,' I said obstinately.

'A sin? Losing your temper? Jesus, I want to kill people. I want to kill my bloody old father, for one. I will too, one of those days. Take a knife to him.'

'I know, I know,' I said, at a loss to explain what I meant. 'But that's just the same thing as me.'

I wished to God I could talk better. It wasn't any missionary zeal. I was excited because for the first time I knew that Charlie felt about me exactly as I felt about him, with a sort of envy, and I wanted to explain to him that he didn't have to envy me, and that he could be as much a saint as I was just as I could be as much a sinner as he was. I wanted to explain that it wasn't a matter of tuppence ha'penny worth of sanctity as opposed to tuppence worth that made the difference, that it wasn't what you did, but what you lost by doing it, that mattered. The whole Cross had become a place of mystery; the grey light, drained of warmth; the trees hanging over the old crumbling walls, the tram, shaking like a boat when someone mounted it. It was the way I sometimes felt afterwards with a girl, as though everything about you melted and fused and became one with a central mystery.

'But when what you do isn't any harm?' he repeated angrily, with that flickering of the eyes I had almost come to dread.

'Look, Cha,' I said, 'you can't say a thing isn't any harm. Everything is harm. It might be losing my temper with me and murder with you, like you say, but it would only come to the same thing. If I show you something, will you promise not to tell?'

'Why would I tell?'

'But promise.'

'Oh, all right.'

Then I took out my little notebook and showed it to him. It was extraordinary, and I knew it was extraordinary. I found myself, sitting on that wall, showing a notebook I wouldn't have shown to anyone else in the world to Charlie Dalton, a fellow any kid on the road would go a long way to avoid, and yet I had the feeling that he would understand it as no one else would do. My whole life was there, under different headings—Disobedience, Bad Temper, Bad Thoughts, Selfishness, and Laziness—and he looked through it quietly, studying the ticks I had placed against each count.

'You see,' I said, 'you talk about your father, but look at all the things I do against my mother. I know she's a good mother, but if she's sick or if she can't walk fast when I'm in town with her, I get mad just as you do. It doesn't matter what sort of mother or father you have. It's what you do to yourself when you do things like that.'

'What do you do to yourself?' he asked quietly.

'It's hard to explain. It's only a sort of peace you have inside yourself. And you can't be just good, no matter how hard you try. You can only do your best, and if you do your best you feel peaceful inside. It's like when I miss Mass of a morning. Things mightn't be any harder on me that day than any other day, but I'm not as well able to stand up to them. It makes things a bit different for the rest of the day. You don't mind it so much if you get a hammering. You know there's something else in the world besides the hammering.'

I knew it was a feeble description of what morning Mass really meant to me, the feeling of strangeness which lasted throughout the whole day, and reduced reality to its real proportions, but it was the best I could do. I hated leaving him.

'I'll be late for Confession,' I said regretfully, getting off the wall.

'I'll go down a bit of the way with you,' he said, giving a last glance at my notebook and handing it back to me. I knew he was being tempted to come to Confession along with me, but my pleasure had nothing to do with that. As I say, I never had any missionary zeal. It was the pleasure of understanding rather than that of conversion.

He came down the steps to the church with me and we went in together.

'I'll wait here for you,' he whispered, and sat in one of the back pews.

It was dark there; there were just a couple of small, unshaded lights in the aisles above the confessionals. There was a crowd of old women outside Father O'Regan's box, so I knew I had a long time to wait. Old women never got done with their confessions. For the first time I felt it long, but when my turn came it was all over in a couple of minutes: the usual 'Bless you, my child. Say a prayer for me, won't you?' When I came out, I saw Charlie Dalton sitting among the old women outside the confessional, waiting to go in. I felt very happy about it in a quiet way, and when I said my penance I said a special prayer for him.

It struck me that he was a long time inside, and I began to grow worried. Then he came out, and I saw by his face that it was no good. It was the expression of someone who is saying to himself with a sort of evil triumph, 'There, I told you what it was like.'

'It's all right,' he whispered, giving his belt a hitch. 'You go home.'

'I'll wait for you,' I said.

'I'll be a good while.'

I knew then Father O'Regan had given him a heavy penance, and my heart sank.

'It doesn't matter,' I said. 'I'll wait.'

And it was only long afterwards that it occurred to me that I might have taken one of the major decisions of my life without being aware of it. I sat at the back of the church in the dusk and waited for him. He was kneeling up in front, before the altar, and I knew it was no good. At first I was too stunned to feel. All I knew was that my happiness had all gone. I admired Father O'Regan; I knew that Charlie must have done things that I couldn't even imagine—terrible things—but the resentment grew in me. What right had Father O'Regan or anyone to treat him like that? Because he was down, people couldn't help wanting to crush him further. For the first time in my life I knew real temptation. I wanted to go with Charlie and share his fate. For the first time I realised that the life before me would have complexities of emotion which I couldn't even imagine.

The following week he ran away from home again, took a bicycle, broke into a shop to steal cigarettes, and, after being arrested seventy-five miles from Cork in a little village on the coast, was sent to an industrial school.

Lonely Rock

"Lonely Rock" (1946) depicts an unusual household—a man, his wife, his lover, and his mother, all devoted to him, much to his discomfort— and it focuses on the emotions that the characters, their allegiances shifting, evoke. It is autobiographical, comic, mournful, even puzzled. Mrs. Courtenay, Jack's mother, who claims our ultimate sympathies, is an affectionate version of O'Connor's beloved mother, and the narrator, Phil, does not spare Jack (a version of the role O'Connor took in real life) critical assessment. Like "The Holy Door," this story focuses on "adult" problems, the nuances of loyalty, jealousy, affection, leaving the physical details of love to others.

In England during the war I had a great friend called Jack Courtenay who was assistant manager in one of the local factories. His job was sufficiently important to secure his exemption from military service. His family was originally from Cork, but he had come to work in England when he was about eighteen and married an English girl called Sylvia, a school-teacher. Sylvia was tall, thin, fair, and vivacious, and they got on very well together. They had two small boys, of seven and nine. Jack was big-built, handsome, and solemn-looking, with a gravity which in public enabled him to escape from the usual English suspicion of Irish temperament and in private to get away with a schoolboy mania for practical joking. I have known him invite someone he liked to his office to discuss an entirely imaginary report from the police, accusing the unfortunate man of bigamy and deserting a large family. He could carry on a joke like that for a long time without a shadow of a smile, and end up by promising his victim to try and persuade the police that it was all a case of mistaken identity.

167

He was an athlete, with an athlete's good nature when he was well and an athlete's hysteria when he wasn't. A toothache or a cold in the head could drive him stark, staring mad. Then he retired to bed (except when he could create more inconvenience by not doing so) and conducted guerrilla warfare against the whole household, particularly the children, who were diverting the attention which should have come to himself. His face, normally expressionless, could convey indescribable agonies on such occasions, and even I felt that Sylvia went too far with her air of indifference and boredom. "Do stop that shouting!" or "Why don't you see the dentist?" were remarks that caused me almost as much pain as they caused her husband.

Fortunately, his ailments were neither serious nor protracted, and Sylvia didn't seem to mind so much about his other weakness, which was girls. He had a really good eye for a girl and a corresponding vanity about the ravages he could create in them, so he was forever involved with some absolutely stunning blonde. At Christmas I was either dispatching or receiving presents that Sylvia wasn't supposed to know about. These flirtations (they were nothing more serious) never went too far. The man was a born philanderer. Because I was fresh from Ireland and disliked his schoolboy jokes, he regarded me as a puritan and gave me friendly lectures with a view to broadening my mind and helping me to enjoy life. Sylvia's mind he had apparently broadened already.

"Did you know that Jack's got a new girl, Phil?" she asked, while he beamed proudly on both of us. "Such a relief after the last! Didn't he show you the last one's photo? Oh, my dear, the commonest-looking piece."

"Now, now, who's jealous?" Jack would say severely, wagging his finger at her.

"Really, Jack," she would reply with bland insolence, "I'd have to have a very poor opinion of myself to be jealous of that. Didn't you say she was something in Woolworth's?"

To complete the picture of an entirely emancipated household, I was supposed to be in love with her and to indulge in all sorts of escapades behind his back. We did our best to keep up the game, but I am afraid she found me rather heavy going.

There was a third adult in the house; this was Jack's mother, whom Sylvia, with characteristic generosity, had invited to live with them. At the same time I don't think she had had any idea what she was letting herself in for. It was rather like inviting a phase of history. Mrs. Courtenay was a big, bossy, cheerful woman and an excellent housekeeper, so Jack and Sylvia had at least the advantage of being able to get away together whenever they liked. The children were fond of her and she spoiled them, but at the same time her heart was not in them. They had grown up outside her scope and atmosphere. Her heart was all the time in the little house in Douglas Street in Cork, with the long garden and the apple trees, the old cronies who dropped in for a cup of tea and a game of cards, and the convent where she went to Mass and to visit the lifelong friend whom Sylvia persisted in calling Sister Mary Misery. Sister Mary Misery was always in some trouble and always inviting the prayers of her friends. Mrs. Courtenay's nostalgia was almost entirely analogical, and the precise degree of pleasure she received from anything was conditioned by its resemblance to something or somebody in Cork. Her field of analogy was exceedingly wide, as when she admired a photograph of St. Paul's because it reminded her of the Dominican Church in Cork.

Jack stood in great awe of his mother, and this was something Sylvia found it difficult to understand. He did not, for instance, like drinking spirits before her, and if he had to entertain while she was there, he drank sherry. When at ten o'clock sharp the old woman rose and said: "Wisha, do you know, I think I'll go to my old doss; good night to ye," he relaxed and started on the whisky.

There was hardly a day, wet or fine, well or ill, but Mrs. Courtenay was up for morning Mass. This was practically her whole social existence, as her only company, apart from me, was Father Whelan, the parish priest; a nice, simple poor man, but from Waterford—"not at all the same thing," as Sylvia observed. For a Waterford man he did his best. He lent her the papers from home; sometimes newspapers, but mostly religious papers: "simple papers for simple people," he explained to Sylvia, just to show that he wasn't taken in.

But if he implied that Mrs. Courtenay was simple, he was wrong.

"Wisha, hasn't Father Tom a beautiful face, Phil?" she would exclaim with childish pleasure as she held out the photograph of some mountainous sky-pilot. "You'd never again want to hear another Passion sermon after Father Tom. Poor Father Whelan does his best, but of course he hasn't the intellect."

"How could he?" Sylvia would say gravely. "We must remember he's from Waterford."

Mrs. Courtenay never knew when Sylvia was pulling her leg.

"Why then, indeed, Sylvia," she said, giving a reproving look over her spectacles, "some very nice people came from Waterford."

Though Mrs. Courtenay couldn't discuss it with Sylvia, who might have thought her prejudiced, she let me know how shocked she was by the character of the English, who seemed from the age of fifteen on to do nothing but fall in and out of love. Mrs. Courtenay had heard of love; she was still very much in love with her own husband, who had been dead for years, but this was a serious matter and had nothing whatever in common with those addle-pated affairs you read of in the newspapers. Fortunately, she never knew the worst, owing to her lack of familiarity with the details. Once an old schoolmistress friend of Sylvia's with a son the one age with Jack tried to start a little chat with her about the dangers young men had to endure, but broke down under the concentrated fire of Mrs. Courtenay's innocence.

"Willie's going to London worries me a lot," she said darkly.

"Why, then, indeed, ma'am, I wouldn't blame you," said Mrs. Courtenay. "The one time I was there, the traffic nearly took the sight out of my eyes."

"And it's not the traffic only, is it, Mrs. Courtenay?" asked the schoolmistress, a bit taken aback. "I mean, we send them out into the world healthy, and we want them to come back to us healthy."

"Ah, indeed," said Mrs. Courtenay triumphantly, "wasn't it only the other day I was saying the same thing to you, Sylvia? Whatever he gets to eat in London, Jack's digestion is never the same."

Not to wrong her, I must admit that she wasn't entirely ignorant of the subject, for she mentioned it herself to me (very confidentially while Sylvia was out of the room) in connection with a really nice sodality man from the Watercourse Road who got it through leaning against the side of a ship.

Sylvia simply did not know what to make of her mother-in-law's ingenuousness, which occasionally bordered on imbecility, but she was a sufficiently good housekeeper herself to realize that the old woman had plenty of intelligence, and she respected the will-power that kept her going, cheerful and uncomplaining, through the trials of loneliness and old age.

"We're very busy these days," she would sigh after Mrs. Courtenay had gone to bed, and she was enjoying what her husband called "the first pussful." "We're doing another novena for Sister Mary Misery's sciatica. The last one misfired, but we'll wear Him down yet! Really, she talks as if God were a Corkman!"

"Well," said Jack, "some very nice people came from Cork."

"But it's fantastic, Jack! It's simply fantastic!" Sylvia cried, slamming her palm on the arm-rest of her chair. "She's upstairs now, talking to God as she talked to us. She feels she will wear Him down, exactly as she says."

"She probably will," said I.

"I shouldn't be in the least surprised," Sylvia added viciously. "She's worn me down."

·   ·   ·

Naturally, Jack and Sylvia both told me of the absolutely stunning brunette he had met in Manchester, driving a Ministry car. Then, for some reason, the flow of confidences dried up. I guessed that something had gone wrong with the romance, but knew better than to ask questions. I knew that Jack would tell me in his own good time. He did too, one grey winter evening when we had walked for miles up the hills and taken refuge from the wind in a little bar-parlour where a big fire was roaring. When he brought in the pints, he told me in a slightly superior way with a smile that didn't seem quite genuine that he was having trouble about Margaret.

"Serious?" I asked.

"Well, she's had a baby," he said with a shrug.

He expected me to be shocked, and I was, but not for his reasons. It was clear that he was badly shaken, did not know how his philandering could have gone so far or had such consequences, and was blaming the drink or something equally irrelevant.

"That's rotten luck," I said.

"That's the worst of it," he said. "It's not luck."

"Oh!" I said. I was beginning to realize vaguely the mess in which he had landed himself. "You mean she———?"

"Yes," he cut in. "She wanted it. Now she wants to keep it, and her family won't let her, so she's left home."

"Oh," I said again. "That is rotten."

"It's not very pleasant," he said, unconsciously trying to reassert himself in his old part as a man of the world by lowering the key of the conversation.

"Does Sylvia know?"

"Good Lord, no," he exclaimed with a frown, and this time it was he who was shocked. "There's no point in upsetting her."

"She'll be a damn sight more upset if she hears of it from someone else," I said.

"Yes," he replied after a moment. "I see your point."

I don't know whether he did or not. He had the sort of sensitiveness which leads men into the most preposterous situations in the desire not to give pain to people they love. It never minimizes the pain in the long run, of course, or so it seemed to me. I had no experience of that sort of situation and was all for giving the pain at once and getting it over. I should even have been prepared to break the news to Sylvia myself, just to be sure she had someone substantial to bawl on. Nowadays I wouldn't rush into it so eagerly.

Instead, Sylvia talked to me about it, in her official tone. It was a couple of months later. She had managed to get rid of her mother-in-law for half an hour, and we were drinking cocktails.

"Did you know Jack's got himself into a scrape with the brunette, Phil?" she said lightly, crossing her legs and smoothing her skirt. "Has he told you?"

I could have shaken her. There was no need to do the stiff upper lip on me, and at any rate I couldn't reply to it. I like a bit more intimacy myself.

"He has," I said uncomfortably. "How are things going?"

"Baby's ill, and she's had to chuck her job. Jack is really quite worried."

"I don't wonder," I said. "What's he going to do?"

"What can he do?" she exclaimed with a shrug and a mow. "He should look after the girl. I've told him I'll divorce him."

I hardly knew what to say to this. Sweet reasonableness may be all very well, but usually it bears no relation to the human facts.

"Is that what you want to do?"

"Well, my feelings don't count for much in this."

"That's scarcely how Jack looks at it," I said.

"So he says," she muttered with a shrug.

"Oh, don't be silly, Sylvia!" I said.

She looked at me for a moment as though she might throw something at me, and I almost wished she would.

"Oh, well," she said at last, "if that's how he feels he should bring her here. You can't even imagine what girls in her position have to go through. It'll simply drive her to suicide, and then he will have something to worry about. I do wish you'd speak to him, Phil."

"What's his objection?"

"Mother doesn't know we drink," she said maliciously. "Anyhow, as if it would ever cross her mind that he was responsible! She probably thinks it's something you catch from leaning against a tree."

"I'll talk to him," I said. I had a feeling that between them they would be bound to make a mess of it.

"Tell him Granny need never know," she said. "He doesn't even have to pretend he knows the girl. She can be a friend of mine. And at a time like this, who's going to inquire about her husband? We can kill him off in the most horrible manner. She just loves tragedies."

This was more difficult than it sounded. Jack didn't want to talk at all, and when he talked he was in a bad humour. I had had to take him out to the local pub, and we talked in low voices between the family parties and the dart-players. Jack's masculine complacency revolted as much at taking advice from me as at taking help from Sylvia. He listened in a peculiar way he had, frowning with one side of his face, as if with half his mind he was considering your motion while with the other he ruled it out of order.

"I'm afraid it's impossible," he said stiffly.

"Well, what are you going to do?"

"Sylvia said she'd divorce me," he replied in a sulky voice that showed it would be a long time before he forgave Sylvia for her high-minded offer.

"Is that what you want?"

"But, my dear fellow, it's not a matter of what I want," he said scoffingly.

"You mean you won't accept Sylvia's kindness, is that it?"

"I won't go on my knees to anybody, for anything."

"Do you want her to go on her knees to you?"

"Oh," he replied ungraciously, "if that's how she feels————"

"You wouldn't like me to get a note from her?" I asked. (I knew it was mean, but I couldn't resist it.)

.   .   .

That was how Margaret came to be invited to the Courtenays'. I promised to look in, the evening she came. It was wet, and the narrow sloping High Street with its rattling inn-signs looked the last word in misery. As I turned up the avenue to the Courtenays', the wind was rising. In the distance it had blown a great gap through the cloud, and the brilliant sky had every tint of metal from blue steel at the top to bronze below. Mrs. Courtenay opened the door to me.

"They're not back from the station yet," she said cheerfully. "Would you have a cup of tea?"

"No," I said. "All I want is to get warm."

"I suppose they'll be having it when they come in," she said. "The train must be late."

Just then the taxi drove up, and Sylvia came in with Margaret, a short, slight girl with a rather long, fine-featured face; the sort of face that seems to have been slightly shrunken to give its features a certain precision and delicacy. Jack came in, carrying the baby's basket, and set it on a chair in the hall. His mother went straight to it, as though she could see nothing else.

"Isn't he lovely, God bless him?" she said, showing her gums while her whole face lit up.

"I'd better get him settled down," Margaret said nervously with a quick, bright smile.

"Yes," Sylvia said. "Margaret and I will take him up. Will you pour her a drink first, Jack?"

"Certainly," said Jack, beginning to beam. "Nothing I like so much. Whisky, Mrs. Harding?"

"Oh, whisky—Mr. Courtenay," she replied with her sudden, brilliant laugh.

"Won't you call me Jack?" he asked with a mock-languishing air. I think he was almost enjoying the mystification, which had something in common with his own practical jokes.

While the girls went upstairs with the baby, Mrs. Courtenay sat before the fire, her hands joined in her lap. Her eyes had a faraway look.

"God help us!" she sighed. "Isn't she young to be a widow?"

At ten Mrs. Courtenay drew the shawl about her shoulders, said as usual "I'll go to my old doss," and went upstairs. Some time later we were interrupted by a sickly little whine. Margaret jumped up with an apologetic smile.

"That's Teddy," she said. "I shan't be a minute."

"I shouldn't trouble, dear," Sylvia said in her bland, insolent way, and we heard a door open softly. "I rather thought Granny would come to the rescue," she explained.

"He'll be afraid of a stranger," Margaret said tensely, and we all listened again. We heard the old woman's voice, soft and almost continuous, and the crying ceased abruptly. Apparently Teddy didn't consider Mrs. Courtenay a stranger. I noticed as if for the first time the billows of wind break over the house.

Next morning, when Teddy had been settled in the garden in his pram, Mrs. Courtenay said: "I think I'll take him for a little walk. They get very tired of the one place." She apparently knew things about babies that weren't in any textbook, and uttered them in a tone of quiet authority which made textbooks an impertinence. She didn't appear again until lunch-time, having taken him to the park—"they're very fond of trees." His father's death in an air-crash in the Middle East had proved a safe introduction to the other women, and Mrs. Courtenay, who usually complained of the stand-offishness of the English, returned in high good humour, full of gossip—the untold numbers blinded, drowned, and burned to death, and the wrecked lives of young women who became too intimate with foreigners. The Poles, in particular, were a great disappointment to her—such a grand Catholic nation, but so unreliable.

That evening, when we heard the shriek from the bedroom, there was no question about who was to deal with it. "Don't upset yourselves," Mrs. Courtenay said modestly, pulled the shawl firmly about her, and went upstairs. Margaret, a very modern young woman, had Teddy's day worked out to a time-table, stipulating when he should be fed, lifted, and loved, but it had taken that baby no time to discover that Mrs. Courtenay read nothing but holy books and believed that babies should be fed, lifted, and loved when it suited themselves. Margaret frowned and shook herself in her frock.

"I'm sure it's bad for him, Sylvia," she said.

"Oh, dreadful," Sylvia sighed with her heartless air as she threw one long leg over the arm of the chair. "But Granny is thriving on it. Haven't you noticed?"

A curious situation was developing in the house, which I watched with fascination. Sylvia, who had very little use for sentiment, was quite attracted by Margaret. "She really is charming, Phil," she told me in her bland way. "Really, Jack has remarkably good taste." Margaret, a much more dependent type, after hesitating for a week, developed quite a crush on Sylvia. It was Jack who was odd man out. Their friendship was a puzzle to him, and what they said and thought about him when they were together was more than he could imagine, but judging by the frown that frequently drew down one side of his face, he felt it couldn't be very nice.

Sylvia was older, shrewder, more practical, and Margaret's guileless-ness took her breath away. Margaret's experience of love had been very limited; she had fluttered round with some highly inappropriate charac-ters, and from them drew vast generalizations, mostly derogatory, which included all races and men. Jack had been the first real man in her life, and she had grabbed at the chance of having his child. Now she envis-aged nothing but a future dedicated to the memory of a couple of week-ends with him and to the upbringing of his child. Sylvia in her cool way tried to make her see things more realistically.

"Really, Phil," she told me, "she is the sweetest girl, but, oh, dear, she's such an impossible romantic. What she really needs is a husband to knock some of the romance out of her."

I had a shrewd idea that she regarded me as a likely candidate for the honours of knocking the romance out of Margaret, but I felt the situation was already complicated enough. At the same time, it struck me as ironic that the world should be full of men who would be glad of a decent wife, while a girl like Margaret, whom any man could be proud of, made a fool of herself over a married man.

·   ·   ·

One Saturday afternoon, I went up early, just after lunch, for my walk with Jack. He wasn't ready, so I sat in the front room with Sylvia, Margaret, and Mrs. Courtenay. I had the impression that there were feelings, at least on the old lady's part, and I was right. It had taken Teddy a week to discover that she had a bedroom of her own, and when he did, he took full advantage of it. She had now become his devoted slave, and when we met, I had to be careful that she didn't suspect me of treating him with insufficient respect. Two old women on the road had made a mortal enemy of her because of that. And it wasn't only strang-ers. Margaret too came in for criticism.

The criticism this afternoon had been provoked first by Margaret's inhuman refusal to feed him half an hour before his feeding time, and secondly by the pointed way the two younger women went on with their talk instead of joining her in keeping him company. In Margaret this was only assumed. She was inclined to resent the total occupation of her baby by Mrs. Courtenay, but this was qualified by Teddy's antics and quite suddenly she would smile and then a quick frown would follow the smile. Sylvia was quite genuinely uninterested. She had the capacity for surrounding herself in her own good manners.

The old woman could, of course, have monopolized me, but it gave her more satisfaction to throw me to the girls and make their monstrous inhumanity obvious even to themselves.

"Wisha, go on, Phil," she said with her sweet, distraught smile. "You'll want to be talking. He'll be getting his dinner soon anyway. The poor child is famished."

Most of this went over my head, and I joined the girls gladly enough, while Mrs. Courtenay, playing quietly with Teddy, suffered in silence. Just then the door opened quietly behind her and Jack came in. She started and looked up.

"Ah, here's Daddy now!" she said triumphantly. "Daddy will play with us."

"Daddy will do nothing of the sort," retorted Jack with remarkable presence of mind. "Daddy wants somebody to play with him. Ready, Phil?"

But even this didn't relax the tension in the room. Margaret looked dumbfounded. She looked at Jack and grinned; then frowned and looked at me. Sylvia raised her shoulders. Meanwhile her mother-in-law, apparently quite unaware of the effect she had created, was making Teddy sit up and show off his tricks. Sylvia followed us to the door.

"Does she suspect anything?" she asked anxiously with one hand on the jamb.

"Oh, not at all," Jack said with a shocked expression that almost caused one side of his face to fold up. "That's only her way of speaking."

"Hm," grunted Sylvia. "Curious way of speaking."

"Not really, Sylvia," I said. "If she suspected anything, that's the last thing in the world she'd have said."

"Like leaning against a ship?" Sylvia said. "I dare say you're right."

But she wasn't sure. Jack walked down the avenue without speaking, and I knew he was shaken too.

"Awkward situation," he said between his teeth.

Since Margaret's arrival he had become what for him was almost forthcoming. It was mainly the need for someone to confide in. He couldn't any longer confide in Margaret or Sylvia because of their friendship.

"I don't think it meant what Sylvia imagined," I said as we set off briskly up the hill. We both liked the hilly country behind the town, the strong thrust of the landscape that made walking like a bird's flight on a stormy day.

"I dare say not, but still, it's awkward—two women in a house!"

"I suppose so."

"You know what I mean?"

I thought I did, and I liked his delicacy. Being a chap who never cared to hurt people's feelings, he probably left both girls very much alone. Having had so much to do with them both, and being the sort who is accustomed to having a lot to do with women, he probably found this a strain. They must have found it so likewise, because their behaviour had grown decidedly obstreperous. One evening I had watched them, with their arms about one another's waists, guying him, and realized that behind it there was an element of hysteria. The situation was becoming impossible.

We had come out on the common, with the little red houses to one side, and the uplands sweeping away from them.

"Last night Sylvia woke me when the alert went, to keep Margaret company," he went on in a tone in which pain, bewilderment, and amusement were about equally blended. It was as though he were fastidiously holding up something small, frail, and not quite clean for your inspection. "She said she'd go if I didn't. I'd have preferred her to go, but then she got quite cross. She said: 'Margaret won't like it, and you've shown her little enough consideration since she came.' "

"Rather tactless of Sylvia," I said.

"I know," he added with a bewildered air. "And it's so unlike her. She said I didn't understand women."

"And did you go?"

"I had to."

I could fill in the gaps in his narrative and appreciate his embarrassment. Obviously, before he went to Margaret's room, he had to go to his mother's to explain Sylvia's anxiety for her old school friend, and

having done everything a man could do to spare the feelings of three
women, had probably returned to bed with the feeling that they were all
laughing at him. And though he told it lightly, I had the feeling that it
was loneliness which made him tell it at all, and that he would never
again be quite comfortable with either Sylvia or Margaret. "Now your
days of philandering are over," was running through my head. I wasn't
sure that he would be quite such a pleasant friend.

Margaret remained for some months until the baby was quite well
and she had both got a job and found a home where Teddy would be
looked after. She was full of gaiety and courage, but I had the feeling
that her way was not an easy one either. Even without the aid of a
husband, the romance had been knocked out of her. It was marked by
the transference of her allegiance from Jack to Sylvia. And Sylvia was
lonesome too. She kept pressing me to come to the house when Jack was
away. She corresponded with Margaret and went to stay with her when
she was in town. They were linked by something which excluded Jack.
To each of them her moment of sacrifice had come, and each had risen
to it, but nobody can live on that plane forever, and now there stretched
before them the commonplace of life with no prospect that ever again
would it call on them in the same way. Never again would Sylvia and
Jack be able to joke about his philandering, and the house seemed the
gloomier for it, as though it had lost a safety valve.

Mrs. Courtenay too was lonely after Teddy, though with her usual
stoicism she made light of it. "Wisha, you get very used to them, Phil,"
she said to me as she pulled her shawl about her. Now she felt that she
had no proper introduction when she went to the park, was jealous of
the mothers and grandmothers who met there, and decided that the
English were as queer and stand-offish as she had always supposed them
to be. For weeks she slept badly and talked with resignation of "being in
the way" and "going to her long home." She never asked about Teddy,
always about his mother, and when Margaret, who seemed suddenly to
have got over her dislike of the old woman, sent her a photo of the child,
she put it away in a drawer and did not refer to it again.

One evening, while Sylvia was in the kitchen, she startled me by a
sudden question.

"You never hear about Mrs. Harding?" she asked.

"I believe she's all right," I said. "Sylvia could tell you. She hears from
her regularly."

"They don't tell me," she said resignedly, folding her arms and looking broodingly into the fire—it was one of her fictions that no one ever
told her anything. "Wisha, Phil," she added with a smile, "you don't
think she noticed me calling Jack his daddy?"

She turned a searching look on me. It was one of those occasions
when whatever you say is bound to be wrong.

"Who's that, Mrs. Courtenay?"

"Sylvia. She didn't notice?"

"I wouldn't say so. Why?"

"It worries me," she replied, looking into the fire again. "It could
make mischief."

"I doubt it," I said. "I don't think Sylvia noticed anything."

"I hope not. I made a novena that she wouldn't. She's a nice, simple
poor girl."

"She's one in a thousand," I said.

"Why then, indeed, Phil, there aren't many like her," she agreed
humbly. "I could have bitten my tongue out when I said it. But, of
course, I knew from the first minute I saw him in the hall. Didn't you?"

"Know what?" I stammered, wondering if I looked as red as I felt.

"That Jack was his daddy," she said in a low voice. "Sure you must."

"Oh, yes," I said. "He mentioned it."

"He didn't say anything to me," she said, but without reproach. You
could see she knew that Jack would have good reason for not telling her.
"I suppose he thought I'd tell Sylvia, but of course I wouldn't dream of
making mischief. And the two of them such great friends too—wisha,
isn't life queer, Phil?"

In the kitchen Sylvia suddenly began to sing "Lili Marlene." It was
then the real poignancy of the situation struck me. I had seen it only as
the tragedy of Jack and Sylvia and Margaret, but what was their loneliness to that of the old woman, to whom tragedy presented itself as in a
foreign tongue? Now I realized why she did not care to look at the
photograph of Margaret's son.

"It might be God's will her poor husband was killed," Mrs. Courtenay said. "God help us, I can never get the poor boy out of my head. I
pray for him night and morning. 'Twould be such a shock to him if he
ever found out. And the baby so lovely and all—oh, the dead image of
Jack at his age!"

Sylvia accompanied me to the door as usual. Now when we kissed good-night it wasn't such an act on her part; not because she cared any more for me but because she was already seeking for support in the world outside. The bubble in which she lived was broken. I was tempted to tell her about her mother-in-law, but something held me back. Women like their own mystifications, which give them a feeling of power; they dislike other people's, which they always describe as slyness. Besides, it would have seemed like a betrayal. I had shifted my allegiance.

A Minority

This 1957 story suggests that O'Connor had greater political sensitivity than he was ever credited with, yet its emotional center is still the impulses that make humans act in ways they cannot explain to themselves. It also echoes the narrator's relation to Charlie Dalton in "The Face of Evil," where, although that story is apparently about Dalton, it is more about the narrator's contact with an atypical individual, who forces him to revelations about the world and himself.

Denis Halligan noticed Willy Stein for the first time one Sunday when the other fellows were at Mass. As Denis was a Protestant, he didn't go to Mass. Instead, he sat on the steps outside the chapel with Willy. Willy was a thin, seedy little chap with long, wild hair. It was an autumn morning; there was mist on the trees, and you could scarcely see the great ring of mountains that cut them off there in the middle of Ireland, miles from anywhere.

'Why did they send you here if you're a Proddy?' asked Willy.

'I don't know,' said Denis, who felt his background was so queer that he didn't want to explain it to anybody. 'I suppose because it was cheap.'

'Is your old fellow a Catholic?' asked Willy.

'No,' replied Denis. 'Is yours?'

'No,' Willy said contemptuously. 'He was a Proddy. My old one was a Proddy, too.'

'Where do they live?' asked Denis.

'They're dead,' Willy said, making the motion of spitting. 'The bloody Germans killed them.'

'Oh, cripes!' Denis said regretfully. Denis had a great admiration for everything German, particularly tank generals, and when he grew up he wanted to be a tank general himself, but it seemed a pity that they had

182

to kill Willy's father and mother. Bad as it was to have your parents separated, as his own were, it was worse having them dead. 'Was it a bomb?' he asked.

'No,' Willy replied without undue emotion. 'They were killed in a camp. They sent me over to the Cumminses in Dublin or I'd have been killed, too. The Cumminses are Catholics. That's why I was sent here.'

'Do you like it here?' asked Denis.

'I do not,' Willy said scornfully in his slummy Dublin accent, and then took out a slingshot and fitted a stone in it. 'I'd sooner Vienna. Vienna was gas. When I grow up I'm going to get out of this blooming place.'

'But what will you do?'

'Aw, go to sea, or something. I don't care.'

Denis was interested in Willy. Apart from the fact that they were the only Proddies in the school, Willy struck him as being really tough, and Denis admired toughness. He was always trying to be tough himself, but there was a soft streak in him that kept breaking out. It was breaking out now, and he knew it. Though he saw that Willy didn't give a rap about his parents, Denis couldn't help being sorry for him, alone in the middle of Ireland with his father and mother dead half a world away. He said as much to his friend Nigel Healy, from Cork, that afternoon, but Nigel only gave a superior sniff.

'But that fellow is mad,' he said, in his reasonable way.

'How is he mad?' asked Denis.

'He's not even left go home on holidays,' explained Nigel. 'He has to stay here all during the summer. Those people were nice to him, and what does he do? Breaks every window in the place. They had the police to the house twice. He's mad on slingshots.'

'He had one this morning,' said Denis.

'Last time he was caught with one he got flogged,' said Nigel. 'You see, the fellow has no sense. I even saw him putting sugar on his meat.'

'But why did he do that?' asked Denis.

'Said he liked it,' replied Nigel with a smile and a shrug. 'He's bound to get expelled one of these days. You'd want to mind yourself with him.'

But for some reason that only made Denis more interested in Willy Stein, and he looked forward to meeting him again by himself the following Sunday. He was curious to know why the Germans would want to kill Stein's father and mother. That seemed to him a funny thing to do—unless, of course, they were spies for the English.

Again they sat on the steps, but this morning the sun was warm and bright, and the mountains all round them were a brilliant blue. If Stein's parents were really spies, the idea of it did not seem to have occurred to him. According to him, his father had been a lawyer and his mother something on a newspaper, and he didn't seem to remember much about them except that they were both 'gas'. Everything with Stein was 'gas'. His mother was gentle and timid, and let him have everything he wanted, so she was 'great gas'. His father was sure she was ruining him, and was always on to him to study and be better than other kids, and when his father got like that he used to weep and shout and wave his hands, but that was only now and then. He was gas, too, though not, Denis gathered, great gas. Willy suddenly waved his hands and shouted something in a foreign language.

'What's that?' asked Denis with the deepest admiration.

'German,' Stein replied, in his graceless way.

'What does it mean?' asked Denis.

'I dunno,' Stein said lightly.

Denis was disappointed. For a fellow like himself, who was interested in tanks, a spatter of German might one day be useful. He had the impression that Stein was only letting on to remember parents he had lost before he was really old enough to remember them.

Their talk was interrupted by Father Houlihan, a tall, morose-looking priest. He had a bad belly and a worse temper, but Denis knew Father Houlihan liked him, and he admired Father Houlihan. He was violent, but he wasn't a stinker.

'Hah!' he said, in his mocking way. 'And what do you two cock sparrows think you're doing out here?'

'We're excused, Father,' Denis said brightly, leaping to his feet.

'No one is excused anything in this place till I excuse him,' snarled Father Houlihan cheerfully, 'and I don't excuse much. Run into Mass now, ye pair of heathens!'

'But we're Protestants, Father!' Stein cried, and Denis was half afraid of seeing the red flush on Father Houlihan's forehead that showed he was out for blood.

'Aha, what fine Protestants we have in ye!' he snorted good-humouredly. 'I suppose you have a Protestant slingshot in your pocket at this very minute, you scoundrel, you!'

'I have not!' Stein shouted. 'You know Murphy took it off me.'

'Mr. Murphy to you, Willy Stein,' said the priest, pinching his ear playfully and pushing him towards the chapel. 'And next time I catch you with a slingshot I'll give you a Catholic cane on your fat Protestant backside.'

The two boys went into chapel and sat together on a bench at the back. Willy was muttering indignantly to himself, but he waited until everyone was kneeling with bowed head. Then, to Denis's horror, he took out a slingshot and a bit of paper, which he chewed up into a wet ball. There was nothing hasty or spontaneous about this. Stein went about it with a concentration that was almost pious. As the bell rang for the Consecration, there was a *ping,* and a seminarist kneeling at the side of the chapel put his hand to his ear and looked angrily round. But by this time Stein had thrown himself on his knees, and his eyes were shut in a look of rapt devotion. It gave Denis quite a turn. Even if he wasn't a Catholic, he had been brought up to respect every form of religion.

The business of going to Mass and feeling out of it made Denis Halligan completely fed up with being a Proddy. He had never liked it anyway, even at home, as a kid. He was gregarious, and a born gang leader, a promoter of organisation, and it cut him to the heart to feel that at any moment he might be deserted by his gang because, through no fault of his own, he was not a Catholic and might accidentally say or do the wrong thing. He even resented the quiet persuasion that the school authorities exercised on him. A senior called Hanley, whom Nigel described sarcastically as 'Halligan's angel', was attached to Denis—not to proselytise, but to give him an intelligent understanding of the religious life of the group. Hanley had previously been attached to Stein, but that had proved hopeless, because Stein seemed to take Hanley's company as a guarantee of immunity from punishment, so he merely involved Hanley in every form of forbidden activity, from smoking to stealing. One day when Stein stole a gold tie-pin from a master's room, Hanley had to report him. On Hanley's account, he was not flogged, but told to put the tie-pin back in the place from which he had taken it. Stein did so, and seized the opportunity to pinch five shillings instead, and this theft was discovered only when someone saw Stein fast asleep in bed with his mouth open and the two half-crowns in his jaw. As Hanley, a sweet and saintly boy, said to Denis, it wasn't Stein's fault. He was just unbalanced.

In any other circumstances Denis would have enjoyed Hanley's attention, but it made him mad to be singled out like this and looked after like some kid who couldn't undo his own buttons.

'Listen, Hanley,' he said angrily one day when he and Nigel were discussing football and Hanley had slipped a little homily into the conversation. 'It's no good preaching at me. It's not my fault that I'm a Proddy.'

'Well, you don't have to be a Proddy if you don't want to be,' Hanley said with a smile. 'Do you?'

'How can I help it?' asked Denis.

'Well, who'd stop you?'

'My mother would, for one.'

'Did you try?'

'What do you mean, Hanley?'

'I mean, why don't you ask her?' Hanley went on, in the same bland way. 'I wouldn't be too sure she wants you to be a Proddy.'

'How could I ask her?'

'You could write. Or phone,' Hanley added hastily, seeing the look on Denis's face at the notion of writing an extra letter. 'Father Houlihan would let you use the telephone, if you asked him. Or I'll ask him, if you like.'

'Do if you want to,' said Denis. 'I don't care.'

He didn't really believe his mother would agree to something he wanted, just like that, but he had no objection to a free telephone call that would enable him to hear her voice again. To his astonishment, she made no difficulty about it.

'Why, of course, darling,' she said sweetly. 'If that's how you feel and Father Houlihan has no objection, I don't mind. You know I only want you to be happy at school.'

It was a colossal relief. Overnight, his whole position in the school changed. He had ceased to be an outsider. He was one of the gang. He might even be Chief Gang Leader in the course of time. He was a warm-hearted boy, and he had the feeling that by a simple gesture he had conferred an immense benefit on everybody. The only person who didn't seem too enthusiastic was Father Houlihan, but then he was not much of an enthusiast anyway. 'My bold young convert,' he said, pulling Denis's ear, 'I suppose any day now you'll start paying attention to your lessons.'

Yet the moment he had made his decision, he began to feel guilty about young Stein. As has been said, he was not only gregarious—but he was also a born gang leader, and had the feeling that someone might think he had deserted an ally to secure his own advantage. He was suddenly filled with a wild desire to convert Willy as well, so that the pair of them could be received as a group. He saw it as even more of a duty of Willy's than of his own. Willy had been saved from his parents' fate by a good kind Catholic family, and it was the least they could expect that Willy should show his gratitude to them, to the school, and to Ireland.

But Willy seemed to have a deplorable head for theology. All the time they talked Denis had the impression that Willy was only planning some fresh mischief.

'Ah, come on, Willy,' he said authoritatively, 'you don't want to be a blooming old Proddy.'

'I don't want to be a Cat either,' said Willy with a shrug.

'Don't you want to be like the other fellows in the school?'

'Why don't they want to be like me?' asked Stein.

'Because there's only two of us, and there's hundreds of them. And they're right.'

'And if there were hundreds of us and two of them, we'd be right, I suppose?' Stein said with a sneer. 'You want to be like the rest of them. All right, be like the rest of them, but let me alone.'

'I'm only speaking for your own good,' Denis said, getting mad. What really made him mad was the feeling that somehow Stein wasn't speaking to him at all; that inside, he was as lonely and lost as Denis would have been in similar circumstances, and he wouldn't admit to it, wouldn't break down as Denis would have done. What he really wanted to do was to give Stein a sock in the gob, but he knew that even this was no good. Stein was always being beaten, and he always yelled bloody murder, and next day he came back and did the same thing again. Everyone was thinking exclusively of Stein's good, and it always ended up by their beating him, and it never did him any good at all.

Denis confided his difficulties to Hanley, who was also full of concern for Stein's good, but Hanley only smiled sadly and shook his head.

'I know more about that than you do, Denis,' he said, in his fatherly way. 'I'll tell you if you promise not to repeat it to a living soul.'

'What is it?' asked Denis eagerly.

'Promise! Mind, this is serious!'

'Oh, I promise.'

'The fact is that Stein isn't a Proddy at all,' Hanley said sadly.

'But what is he?'

'Stein is a Jew,' Hanley said in a low voice. 'That's why his father and mother were killed. Nobody knows that, though.'

'But does Stein know he's a Jew?' Denis asked excitedly.

'No. And mind, we're not supposed to know it, either. Nobody knows it, except the priests and ourselves.'

'But why doesn't somebody tell him?'

'Because if they did, he might blab about it—you know, he's not very smart—and then all the fellows would be jeering at him. Remember, Denis, if you ever mentioned it, Father Houlihan would skin you alive. He says Stein is after suffering enough. He's sorry for Stein. Mind, I'm only warning you.'

'But won't it be awful for him when he finds out?'

'When he's older and has a job, he won't mind it so much,' said Hanley.

But Denis wasn't sure. Somehow, he had an idea that Stein wanted to stay a Proddy simply because that was what his father and mother had been and it was now the only link he had with them, and if someone would just tell him, he wouldn't care so much and would probably become a Catholic, like Denis. Afterwards, when he did find out that everything he had done was mistaken, it might be too late. And this—and the fact that Father Houlihan whom Denis admired, was also sorry for Willy Stein—increased his feeling of guilt, and he almost wished he hadn't been in such a hurry himself about being converted. Denis wasn't a bright student, but he was a born officer and he would never have deserted his men.

The excitement of his own reception into the Church almost banished the thought of Stein from his mind. On the Sunday he was received he was allowed to sleep late, and Murphy, the seminarist, even brought him comics to read in bed. This was real style! Then he dressed in his best suit and went down to meet his mother, who arrived, with his sister, Martha, in a hired car. For once, Martha was deferential. She was impressed, and the sight of the chapel impressed her even more. In front of the High Altar there was an isolated prie-dieu for Denis himself, and behind him a special pew was reserved for her and his mother.

Denis knew afterwards that he hadn't made a single false move. Only once was his exaltation disturbed, and that was when he heard the *ping* of a slingshot and realised that Stein, sitting by himself in the back row, was whiling away the time by getting into fresh mischief. The rage rose up in Denis, in spite of all his holy thoughts, and for a moment he resolved that when it was all over he would find Willy Stein and beat him to a jelly.

Instead, when it was over he suddenly felt weary. Martha had ceased to be impressed by him. Now she was just a sister a bare year younger who was mad with him for having stolen the attention of everybody. She knew only too well what a figure she would have cut as a convert, and was crazy with jealousy.

'I won't stand it,' she said. 'I'm going to be a Catholic, too.'

'Well, who's stopping you?' Denis asked.

'Nobody's going to stop me,' said Martha. 'Just because Daddy is fond of you doesn't mean that I can't be a Catholic.'

'What has Daddy to do with it?' asked Denis with a feeling of alarm.

'Because now that you're a Catholic, the courts wouldn't let him have you,' Martha said excitedly. 'Because Daddy is an atheist, or something, and he wanted to get hold of you. He tried to get you away from Mummy. I don't care about Daddy. I'm going to be converted, too.'

'Go on!' growled Denis, feeling sadly how his mood of exaltation was fading. 'You're only an old copycat.'

'I am not a copycat, Denis Halligan,' she said bitterly. 'It's only that you always sucked up to Daddy and I didn't, and he doesn't care about me. I don't care about him, either, so there!'

Denis felt a sudden pang of terror at her words. In a dim sort of way he realised that what he had done might have consequences he had never contemplated. He had no wish to live with his father, but his father came to the school to see him sometimes, and he had always had the feeling that if he ever got fed up with living at home with his mother and Martha, his father would always have him. Nobody had told him that by becoming a Catholic he had made it impossible for his father to have him. He glanced round and saw Stein, thin and pale and furtive, slouching away from the chapel with his hand in his pocket clutching his slingshot. He gave Denis a grin in which there was no malice, but Denis scowled and looked away.

'Who's that?' asked Martha inquisitively.

'Oh, him!' Denis said contemptuously. 'That's only a dirty Jew-boy.'

Yet even as he spoke the words he knew they were false. What he really felt towards Willy Stein was an aching envy. Nobody had told him that by changing his faith he might be unfaithful to his father, but nobody had told Stein, either, and, alone and despairing, he still clung to a faith that was not his own for the sake of a father and mother he had already almost forgotten, who had been murdered half a world away and whom he would never see again. For a single moment Denis saw the dirty little delinquent whom everyone pitied and despised transfigured by a glory that he himself would never know.

The Man of the World

O'Connor loved to transform the facts of a heard anecdote, the charac-
ters, personalities, and situation, remolding them into forms that would
stimulate creation; thus, the little boy in this 1956 story (Larry Delaney
of Cork) was, in real life, Harriet Sheehy's cousin's wife ("Listening to
Frank O'Connor," 151).

As much of his fiction focuses on "what the neighbors think," this
story contains a reversal of expectations when the anticipated forbidden
spectacle turns out surprisingly. It is private and intimate, but familiar
and pious rather than erotic, making the voyeur feel ashamed, not gra-
tified. The story also confounds the expectations of readers, page-turning
voyeurs: what salacious delights do we expect Jimmy Leary to share
with us? Do we share the narrator's surprise, disappointment, guilt? As
O'Connor said in his Paris Review *interview, "Dragging the reader in,*
making the reader a part of the story—the reader is a part of the story.
You're saying all the time, 'This story is about you—de te fabula' "
(Cowley, Writers at Work, *181). As Larry Delaney relives the incident*
"forty years later," we might consider how subtly O'Connor, like
Jimmy, has invited us to join him, peering at the new couple in their
bedroom, and then made us reexamine our own eagerness to do so.

When I was a kid there were no such things as holidays for me and my
likes, and I have no feeling of grievance about it because, in the way of
kids, I simply invented them, which was much more satisfactory. One
year, my summer holiday was a couple of nights I spent at the house of
a friend called Jimmy Leary, who lived at the other side of the road from
us. His parents sometimes went away for a couple of days to visit a sick
relative in Bantry, and he was given permission to have a friend in to

keep him company. I took my holiday with the greatest seriousness, insisted on the loan of Father's old travelling bag and dragged it myself down our lane past the neighbours standing at their doors.

"Are you off somewhere, Larry?" asked one.

"Yes, Mrs. Rooney," I said with great pride. "Off for my holidays to the Learys'."

"Wisha, aren't you very lucky?" she said with amusement.

"Lucky" seemed an absurd description of my good fortune. The Learys' house was a big one with a high flight of steps up to the front door, which was always kept shut.

They had a piano in the front room, a pair of binoculars on a table near the window, and a toilet on the stairs that seemed to me to be the last word in elegance and immodesty. We brought the binoculars up to the bedroom with us. From the window you could see the whole road up and down, from the quarry at its foot with the tiny houses perched on top of it to the open fields at the other end, where the last gas lamp rose against the sky. Each morning I was up with the first light, leaning out the window in my nightshirt and watching through the glasses all the mysterious figures you never saw from our lane: policemen, railway-men, and farmers on their way to market.

I admired Jimmy almost as much as I admired his house, and for much the same reasons. He was a year older than I, was well-mannered and well-dressed, and would not associate with most of the kids on the road at all. He had a way when any of them joined us of resting against a wall with his hands in his trousers pockets and listening to them with a sort of well-bred smile, a knowing smile, that seemed to me the height of elegance. And it was not that he was a softy, because he was an excellent boxer and wrestler and could easily have held his own with them any time, but he did not wish to. He was superior to them. He was —there is only one word that still describes it for me—sophisticated.

I attributed his sophistication to the piano, the binoculars, and the indoor john, and felt that if only I had the same advantages I could have been sophisticated, too. I knew I wasn't, because I was always being deceived by the world of appearances. I would take a sudden violent liking to some boy, and when I went to his house my admiration would spread to his parents and sisters, and I would think how wonderful it must be to have such a home; but when I told Jimmy he would smile in that knowing way of his and say quietly: "I believe they had the bailiffs in a few weeks ago," and, even though I didn't know what bailiffs were, bang would go the whole world of appearances, and I would realize that once again I had been deceived.

It was the same with fellows and girls. Seeing some bigger chap we knew walking out with a girl for the first time, Jimmy would say casually: "He'd better mind himself: that one is dynamite." And, even though I knew as little of girls who were dynamite as I did of bailiffs, his tone would be sufficient to indicate that I had been taken in by sweet voices, broad-brimmed hats, gaslight and evening smells from gardens.

Forty years later I can still measure the extent of my obsession, for, though my own handwriting is almost illegible, I sometimes find myself scribbling idly on a pad in a small, stiff, perfectly legible hand that I recognize with amusement as a reasonably good forgery of Jimmy's. My admiration still lies there somewhere, a fossil in my memory, but Jimmy's knowing smile is something I have never managed to acquire.

And it all goes back to my curiosity about fellows and girls. As I say, I only imagined things about them, but Jimmy knew. I was excluded from knowledge by the world of appearances that blinded and deafened me with emotion. The least thing could excite or depress me: the trees in the morning when I went to early Mass, the stained-glass windows in the church, the blue hilly streets at evening with the green flare of the gas lamps, the smells of cooking and perfume—even the smell of a cigarette packet that I had picked up from the gutter and crushed to my nose— all kept me at this side of the world of appearances, while Jimmy, by right of birth or breeding, was always at the other. I wanted him to tell me what it was like, but he didn't seem to be able.

Then one evening he was listening to me talk while he leant against the pillar of his gate, his pale neat hair framing his pale, good-humoured face. My excitability seemed to rouse in him a mixture of amusement and pity.

"Why don't you come over some night the family is away and I'll show you a few things?" he asked lightly.

"What'll you show me, Jimmy?" I asked eagerly.

"Noticed the new couple that's come to live next door?" he asked with a nod in the direction of the house above his own.

"No," I admitted in disappointment. It wasn't only that I never knew anything but I never noticed anything either. And when he described the new family that was lodging there, I realized with chagrin that I didn't even know Mrs. MacCarthy, who owned the house.

"Oh, they're just a newly married couple," he said. "They don't know that they can be seen from our house."

"But how, Jimmy?"

"Don't look up now," he said with a dreamy smile while his eyes strayed over my shoulder in the direction of the lane. "Wait till you're going away. Their end wall is only a couple of feet from ours. You can see right into the bedroom from our attic."

"And what do they do, Jimmy?"

"Oh," he said with a pleasant laugh, "everything. You really should come."

"You bet I'll come," I said, trying to sound tougher than I felt. It wasn't that I saw anything wrong in it. It was rather that, for all my desire to become like Jimmy, I was afraid of what it might do to me.

But it wasn't enough for me to get behind the world of appearances. I had to study the appearances themselves, and for three evenings I stood under the gas lamp at the foot of our lane, across the road from the MacCarthys', till I had identified the new lodgers. The husband was the first I spotted, because he came from his work at a regular hour. He was tall, with stiff jet-black hair and a big black guardsman's moustache that somehow failed to conceal the youthfulness and ingenuousness of his face, which was long and lean. Usually, he came accompanied by an older man, and stood chatting for a few minutes outside his door—a black-coated, bowler-hatted figure who made large, sweeping gestures with his evening paper and sometimes doubled up in an explosion of loud laughter.

On the third evening I saw his wife—for she had obviously been waiting for him, looking from behind the parlour curtains, and when she saw him she scurried down the steps to join in the conversation. She had thrown an old jacket about her shoulders and stood there, her arms folded as though to protect herself further from the cold wind that blew down the hill from the open country, while her husband rested one hand fondly on her shoulder.

For the first time, I began to feel qualms about what I proposed to do. It was one thing to do it to people you didn't know or care about, but, for me, even to recognize people was to adopt an emotional attitude towards them, and my attitude to this pair was already one of approval.

They looked like people who might approve of me, too. That night I remained awake, thinking out the terms of an anonymous letter that would put them on their guard, till I had worked myself up into a fever of eloquence and indignation.

But I knew only too well that they would recognize the villain of the letter and that the villain would recognize me, so I did not write it. Instead, I gave way to fits of anger and moodiness against my parents. Yet even these were unreal, because on Saturday night when Mother made a parcel of my nightshirt—I had now become sufficiently self-conscious not to take a bag—I nearly broke down. There was something about my own house that night that upset me all over again. Father, with his cap over his eyes, was sitting under the wall-lamp, reading the paper, and Mother, a shawl about her shoulders, was crouched over the fire from her little wickerwork chair, listening; and I realized that they, too, were part of the world of appearances I was planning to destroy, and as I said good-night I almost felt that I was saying good-bye to them as well.

But once inside Jimmy's house I did not care so much. It always had that effect on me, of blowing me up to twice the size, as though I were expanding to greet the piano, the binoculars, and the indoor toilet. I tried to pick out a tune on the piano with one hand, and Jimmy, having listened with amusement for some time, sat down and played it himself as I felt it should be played, and this, too, seemed to be part of his superiority.

"I suppose we'd better put in an appearance of going to bed," he said disdainfully. "Someone across the road might notice and tell. *They're* in town, so I don't suppose they'll be back till late."

We had a glass of milk in the kitchen, went upstairs, undressed, and lay down, though we put our overcoats beside the bed. Jimmy had a packet of sweets but insisted on keeping them till later. "We may need these before we're done," he said with his knowing smile, and again I admired his orderliness and restraint. We talked in bed for a quarter of an hour; then put out the light, got up again, donned our overcoats and socks, and tiptoed upstairs to the attic. Jimmy led the way with an electric torch. He was a fellow who thought of everything. The attic had been arranged for our vigil. Two trunks had been drawn up to the little window to act as seats, and there were even cushions on them. Looking out, you could at first see nothing but an expanse of blank wall topped with chimney stacks, but gradually you could make out the outline of a single window, eight or ten feet below. Jimmy sat beside me and opened his packet of sweets, which he laid between us.

"Of course, we could have stayed in bed till we heard them come in," he whispered. "Usually you can hear them at the front door, but they might have come in quietly or we might have fallen asleep. It's always best to make sure."

"But why don't they draw the blind?" I asked as my heart began to beat uncomfortably.

"Because there isn't a blind," he said with a quiet chuckle. "Old Mrs. MacCarthy never had one, and she's not going to put one in for lodgers who may be gone tomorrow. People like that never rest till they get a house of their own."

I envied him his nonchalance as he sat back with his legs crossed, sucking a sweet just as though he were waiting in the cinema for the show to begin. I was scared by the darkness and the mystery, and by the sounds that came to us from the road with such extraordinary clarity. Besides, of course, it wasn't my house and I didn't feel at home there. At any moment I expected the front door to open and his parents to come in and catch us.

We must have been waiting for half an hour before we heard voices in the roadway, the sound of a key in the latch and, then, of a door opening and closing softly. Jimmy reached out and touched my arm lightly. "This is probably our pair," he whispered. "We better not speak any more in case they might hear us." I nodded, wishing I had never come. At that moment a faint light became visible in the great expanse of black wall, a faint, yellow starlight that was just sufficient to silhouette the window frame beneath us. Suddenly the whole room lit up. The man I had seen in the street stood by the doorway, his hand still on the switch. I could see it all plainly now, an ordinary small, suburban bedroom with flowery wallpaper, a coloured picture of the Sacred Heart over the double bed with the big brass knobs, a wardrobe, and a dressing-table.

The man stood there till the woman came in, removing her hat in a single wide gesture and tossing it from her into a corner of the room. He still stood by the door, taking off his tie. Then he struggled with his collar, his head raised and his face set in an agonized expression. His wife kicked off her shoes, sat on a chair by the bed, and began to take off her stockings. All the time she seemed to be talking because her head was raised, looking at him, though you couldn't hear a word she said. I glanced at Jimmy. The light from the window below softly illumined his face as he sucked with tranquil enjoyment.

The woman rose as her husband sat on the bed with his back to us and began to take off his shoes and socks in the same slow, agonized way. At one point he held up his left foot and looked at it with what might have been concern. His wife looked at it, too, for a moment and then swung half-way round as she unbuttoned her skirt. She undressed in swift, jerky movements, twisting and turning and apparently talking all the time. At one moment she looked into the mirror on the dressing-table and touched her cheek lightly. She crouched as she took off her slip, and then pulled her nightdress over her head and finished her undressing beneath it. As she removed her underclothes she seemed to throw them anywhere at all, and I had a strong impression that there was something haphazard and disorderly about her. Her husband was different. Everything he removed seemed to be removed in order and then put carefully where he could find it most readily in the morning. I watched him take out his watch, look at it carefully, wind it, and then hang it neatly over the bed.

Then, to my surprise, she knelt by the bed, facing towards the window, glanced up at the picture of the Sacred Heart, made a large hasty Sign of the Cross, and, covering her face with her hands, buried her head in the bedclothes. I looked at Jimmy in dismay, but he did not seem to be embarrassed by the sight. The husband, his folded trousers in his hand, moved about the room slowly and carefully, as though he did not wish to disturb his wife's devotions, and when he pulled on the trousers of his pyjamas he turned away. After that he put on his pyjama jacket, buttoned it carefully, and knelt beside her. He, too, glanced respectfully at the picture and crossed himself slowly and reverently, but he did not bury his face and head as she had done. He knelt upright with nothing of the abandonment suggested by her pose, and with an expression that combined reverence and self-respect. It was the expression of an employee who, while admitting that he might have a few little weaknesses like the rest of the staff, prided himself on having deserved well of the management. Women, his slightly complacent air seemed to indicate, had to adopt these emotional attitudes, but he spoke to God as one man to another. He finished his prayers before his wife; again he crossed himself slowly, rose, and climbed into bed, glancing again at his watch as he did so.

Several minutes passed before she put her hands out before her on the bed, blessed herself in her wide, sweeping way, and rose. She crossed the room in a swift movement that almost escaped me, and next moment the light went out—it was as if the window through which we had watched the scene had disappeared with it by magic, till nothing was left but a blank black wall mounting to the chimney pots.

Jimmy rose slowly and pointed the way out to me with his flashlight. When we got downstairs we put on the bedroom light, and I saw on his face the virtuous and sophisticated air of a collector who has shown you all his treasures in the best possible light. Faced with that look, I could not bring myself to mention the woman at prayer, though I felt her image would be impressed on my memory till the day I died. I could not have explained to him how at that moment everything had changed for me, how, beyond us watching the young married couple from ambush, I had felt someone else watching us, so that at once we ceased to be the observers and became the observed. And the observed in such a humiliating position that nothing I could imagine our victims doing would have been so degrading.

I wanted to pray myself but found I couldn't. Instead, I lay in bed in the darkness, covering my eyes with my hand, and I think that even then I knew that I should never be sophisticated like Jimmy, never be able to put on a knowing smile, because always behind the world of appearances I would see only eternity watching.

"Sometimes, of course, it's better than that," Jimmy's drowsy voice said from the darkness. "You shouldn't judge it by tonight."

The Genius

Like "Old Fellows" and "The Face of Evil" this is intensely autobiographical although "Larry Delaney" was a persona through which O'Connor could relive his own perceptions and reconsider them at arm's length. What transcends unembellished memory is the intensity of Larry's passions—made more painful by his inability to master his feelings by shaping them in language or acting on them. "The Genius" is more than the comedy of a proud, precocious little boy who knows less than he thinks. It is a tragicomedy enacted by schoolchildren, and we presume wrongly if we think Larry's emotions less powerful than an adult's.

Some kids are sissies by nature but I was a sissy by conviction. Mother had told me about geniuses; I wanted to be one, and I could see for myself that fighting, as well as being sinful, was dangerous. The kids round the Barrack where I lived were always fighting. Mother said they were savages, that I needed proper friends, and that once I was old enough to go to school I would meet them.

My way, when someone wanted to fight and I could not get away, was to climb on the nearest wall and argue like hell in a shrill voice about Our Blessed Lord and good manners. This was a way of attracting attention, and it usually worked because the enemy, having stared incredulously at me for several minutes, wondering if he would have time to hammer my head on the pavement before someone came out to him, yelled something like "blooming sissy" and went away in disgust. I didn't like being called a sissy but I preferred it to fighting. I felt very like one of those poor mongrels who slunk through our neighbourhood and took to their heels when anyone came near them, and I always tried to make friends with them.

I toyed with games, and enjoyed kicking a ball gently before me along the pavement till I discovered that any boy who joined me grew violent and started to shoulder me out of the way. I preferred little girls because they didn't fight so much, but otherwise I found them insipid and lacking in any solid basis of information. The only women I cared for were grown-ups, and my most intimate friend was an old washerwoman called Miss Cooney who had been in the lunatic asylum and was very religious. It was she who had told me all about dogs. She would run a mile after anyone she saw hurting an animal and even went to the police about them, but the police knew she was mad and paid no attention.

She was a sad-looking woman with grey hair, high cheekbones, and toothless gums. While she ironed, I would sit for hours in the steaming, damp kitchen, turning over the pages of her religious books. She was fond of me, too, and told me she was sure I would be a priest. I agreed that I might be a Bishop, but she didn't seem to think so highly of Bishops. I told her there were so many other things I might be that I couldn't make up my mind but she only smiled at this. Miss Cooney thought there was only one thing a genius could be and that was a priest.

On the whole, I thought an explorer was what I would be. Our house was in a square between two roads, one terraced above the other, and I could leave home, follow the upper road for a mile past the Barrack, turn left on any of the intervening roads and lanes, and return almost without leaving the pavement. It was astonishing what valuable information you could pick up on a trip like that. When I came home I wrote down my adventures in a book called *The Voyages of Johnson Martin*, with Many Maps and Illustrations, Irishtown University Press, 3s.6d. nett. I was also compiling *The Irishtown Song Book for Use in Schools and Institutions*, by Johnson Martin, which had the words and music of my favourite songs. I could not read music yet but I copied it from anything that came handy, preferring staff to solfa because it looked better on the page. But I still wasn't sure what I would be. All I knew was that I intended to be famous and have a statue put up to me near that of Father Matthew in Patrick Street. Father Matthew was called the Apostle of Temperance, but I didn't think much of temperance. So far our town hadn't a proper genius and I intended to supply the deficiency.

But my work continued to bring home to me the great gaps in my knowledge. Mother understood my difficulty and worried herself endlessly finding answers to my questions, but neither she nor Miss Cooney had a great store of the sort of information I needed, and Father was more a hindrance than a help. He was talkative enough about subjects that interested himself but they did not greatly interest me. "Ballybeg," he would say brightly. "Market Town. Population 648. Nearest station, Rathkeale." He was also forthcoming enough about other things, but later Mother would take me aside and explain that he was only joking again. This made me mad because I never knew when he was joking and when he wasn't.

I can see now, of course, that he didn't really like me. It was not the poor man's fault. He had never expected to be the father of a genius and it filled him with forebodings. He looked round him at all his contemporaries who had normal, bloodthirsty, illiterate children, and shuddered at the thought that I would never be good for anything but being a genius. To give him his due, it wasn't himself he worried about, but there had never been anything like it in the family before and he dreaded the shame of it. He would come in from the front door with his cap over his eyes and his hands in his trousers pockets and stare moodily at me while I sat at the kitchen table, surrounded by papers, producing fresh maps and illustrations for my book of voyages or copying the music of "The Minstrel Boy."

"Why can't you go out and play with the Horgans?" he would ask wheedlingly, trying to make it sound attractive.

"I don't like the Horgans, Daddy," I would reply politely.

"But what's wrong with them?" he would ask testily. "They're fine, manly young fellows."

"They're always fighting, Daddy."

"And what harm is fighting? Can't you fight them back?"

"I don't like fighting, Daddy, thank you," I would say, still with perfect politeness.

"The dear knows, the child is right," Mother would say, coming to my defence. "I don't know what sort those children are."

"Ah, you have him as bad as yourself," Father would snort and stalk to the front door again, to scald his heart with thoughts of the nice natural son he might have had if only he hadn't married the wrong woman. Granny had always said Mother was the wrong woman for him and now she was being proved right.

She was being proved so right that the poor man couldn't keep his eyes off me, waiting for the insanity to break out. One of the things he didn't like was my Opera House. The Opera House was a cardboard box I had mounted on two chairs in the dark hallway. It had a proscenium cut in it, and I had painted some backdrops of mountain and sea with wings that represented trees and rocks. The characters were pictures cut out, mounted and coloured and moved on bits of stick. It was lit with candles for which I had made coloured screens, greased so that they were transparent, and I made up operas from story-books and bits of songs. I was singing a passionate duet for two of the characters while twiddling the screens to produce the effect of moonlight when one of the screens caught fire and everything went up in a mass of flames. I screamed and Father came to stamp out the blaze, and he cursed me till even Mother lost her temper with him and told him he was worse than six children, after which he wouldn't speak to her for a week.

Another time I was so impressed with a lame teacher I knew that I decided to have a lame leg myself, and there was hell in the home for days because Mother had no difficulty at all in seeing that my foot was already out of shape while Father only looked at it and sniffed contemptuously. I was furious with him, and Mother decided he wasn't much better than a monster. They quarrelled for days over that until it became quite an embarrassment to me because, though I was bored stiff with limping, I felt I should be letting her down by getting better. When I went down the Square, lurching from side to side, Father stood at the gate, looking after me with a malicious knowing smile, and when I had discarded my limp, the way he mocked Mother was positively disgusting.

.   .   .

As I say, they squabbled endlessly about what I should be told. Father was for telling me nothing.

"But, Mick," Mother would say earnestly, "the child must learn."

"He'll learn soon enough when he goes to school," he snarled. "Why do you be always at him, putting ideas into his head? Isn't he bad enough? I'd sooner the boy would grow up a bit natural."

But either Mother didn't like children to be natural or she thought I was natural enough as I was. Women, of course, don't object to geniuses half as much as men do. I suppose they find them a relief.

Now, one of the things I wanted badly to know was where babies came from but this was something that no one seemed to be able to explain to me. When I asked Mother she got upset and talked about birds and flowers, and I decided that if she had ever known she must have forgotten it and was ashamed to say so. Miss Cooney when I asked her only smiled wistfully and said: "You'll know all about it soon enough, child."

"But, Miss Cooney," I said with great dignity, "I have to know now. It's for my work, you see."

"Keep your innocence while you can, child," she said in the same tone. "Soon enough the world will rob you of it, and once 'tis gone 'tis gone forever."

But whatever the world wanted to rob me of, it was welcome to it from my point of view, if only I could get a few facts to work on. I appealed to Father and he told me that babies were dropped out of aeroplanes and if you caught one you could keep it. "By para- chute?" I asked, but he only looked pained and said: "Oh, no, you don't want to begin by spoiling them." Afterwards, Mother took me aside again and explained that he was only joking. I went quite dotty with rage and told her that one of these days he would go too far with his jokes.

All the same, it was a great worry to Mother. It wasn't every mother who had a genius for a son, and she dreaded that she might be wronging me. She suggested timidly to Father that he should tell me something about it, and he danced with rage. I heard them because I was supposed to be playing with the Opera House upstairs at the time. He said she was going out of her mind, and that she was driving me out of my mind as well. She was very upset because she had considerable respect for his judgement.

At the same time when it was a matter of duty she could be very, very obstinate. It was a heavy responsibility, and she disliked it intensely—a deeply pious woman who never mentioned the subject at all to anybody if she could avoid it—but it had to be done. She took an awful long time over it—it was a summer day, and we were sitting on the bank of a stream in the Glen—but at last I managed to detach the fact that mum- mies had an engine in their tummies and daddies had a starting handle that made it work, and once it started it went on until it made a baby. That certainly explained an awful lot I had not understood up to this— for instance, why fathers were necessary and why Mother had buffers on her chest while Father had none. It made her almost as interesting as a locomotive, and for days I went round deploring my own rotten luck that I wasn't a girl and couldn't have an engine and buffers instead of a measly old starting handle like Father.

Soon afterwards I went to school and disliked it intensely. I was too small to be moved up to the big boys, and the other "infants" were still at the stage of spelling "cat" and "dog." I tried to tell the old teacher about my work, but she only smiled and said: "Hush, Larry!" I hated being told to hush. Father was always saying it to me.

One day I was standing at the playground gate, feeling very lonely and dissatisfied, when a tall girl from the Senior Girls' School spoke to me. She had a plump, dark face and black pigtails.

"What's your name, little boy?" she asked.

I told her.

"Is this your first time at school?" she asked.

"Yes."

"And do you like it?"

"No, I hate it," I replied gravely. "The children can't spell and the old woman talks too much."

Then I talked myself, for a change, and she listened attentively while I told her about myself, my voyages, my books, and the time of the trains from all the city stations. As she seemed so interested I told her I would meet her after school and tell her some more.

I was as good as my word. When I had eaten my lunch, instead of going on further voyages I went back to the Girls' School and waited for her to come out. She seemed as pleased to see me because she took my hand and brought me home with her. She lived up Gardiner's Hill, a steep, demure suburban road with trees that overhung the walls at either side. She lived in a small house on top of the hill and was one of a family of three girls. Her little brother, John Joe, had been killed the previous year by a car. "Look at what I brought home with me!" she said when we went into the kitchen, and her mother, a tall, thin woman, made a great fuss of me and wanted me to have my dinner with Una. That was the girl's name. I didn't take anything but while she ate I sat by the range and told her mother about myself. She seemed to like it as much as Una, and when dinner was over Una took me out in the fields behind the house for a walk.

When I went home at teatime, Mother was delighted.

"Ah," she said, "I knew you wouldn't be long making nice friends at school. It's about time for you, the dear knows."

I felt much the same about it, and every fine day at three I waited for Una outside the school. When it rained and Mother would not let me out I was miserable.

One day while I was waiting for her there were two senior girls outside the gate.

"Your girl isn't out yet, Larry," said one with a giggle. "And do you mean to tell me Larry has a girl?" the other asked with a shocked air.

"Oh, yes," said the first. "Una Dwyer is Larry's girl. He goes with Una, don't you, Larry?"

I replied politely that I did, but in fact I was seriously alarmed. I had not realized that Una would be considered my girl. It had never happened to me before, and I had not understood that my waiting for her would be regarded in such a grave light. Now, I think the girls were probably right anyhow, for that is always the way it has been with me. A woman has only to shut up and let me talk long enough for me to fall head and ears in love with her. But then I did not recognize the symptoms. All I knew was that going with somebody meant you intended to marry them. I had always planned on marrying Mother; now it seemed as if I was expected to marry someone else, and I wasn't sure if I should like it or if, like football, it would prove to be one of those games that two people could not play without pushing.

A couple of weeks later I went to a party at Una's house. By this time it was almost as much mine as theirs. All the girls liked me and Mrs. Dwyer talked to me by the hour. I saw nothing unusual about this except a proper appreciation of geniuses. Una had warned me that I should be expected to sing, so I was ready for the occasion. I sang the Gregorian *Credo,* and some of the little girls laughed but Mrs. Dwyer only looked at me fondly.

"I suppose you'll be a priest when you grow up, Larry?" she asked.

"No, Mrs. Dwyer," I replied firmly. "As a matter of fact, I intend to be a composer. Priests can't marry, you see, and I want to get married."

That seemed to surprise her quite a bit. I was quite prepared to continue discussing my plans for the future, but all the children talked together. I was used to planning discussions so that they went on for a long time, but I found that whenever I began one in the Dwyers', it was immediately interrupted so that I found it hard to concentrate. Besides, all the children shouted, and Mrs. Dwyer, for all her gentleness, shouted with them and at them. At first, I was somewhat alarmed, but I soon saw that they meant no particular harm, and when the party ended I was jumping up and down on the sofa, shrieking louder than anyone, while Una, in hysterics of giggling, encouraged me. She seemed to think I was the funniest thing ever.

It was a moonlit November night, and lights were burning in the little cottages along the road when Una brought me home. On the road outside she stopped uncertainly and said: "This is where little John Joe was killed."

There was nothing remarkable about the spot, and I saw no chance of acquiring any useful information.

"Was it a Ford or a Morris?" I asked, more out of politeness than anything else.

"I don't know," she replied with smouldering anger. "It was Donegans' old car. They can never look where they're going, the old shows!"

"Our Lord probably wanted him," I said perfunctorily.

"I dare say He did," Una replied, though she showed no particular conviction. "That old fool Donegan—I could kill him whenever I think of it."

"You should get your mother to make you another," I suggested helpfully.

"Make me a what?" Una exclaimed in consternation.

"Make you another brother," I repeated earnestly. "It's quite easy, really. She has an engine in her tummy, and all your daddy has to do is to start it with his starting handle."

"Cripes!" Una said and clapped her hand over her mouth in an explosion of giggles. "Imagine me telling her that!"

"But it's true, Una," I said obstinately. "It only takes nine months. She could make you another little brother by next summer."

"Oh, Jay!" exclaimed Una in another fit of giggles. "Who told you all that?"

"Mummy did. Didn't your mother tell you?"

"Oh, she says you buy them from Nurse Daly," said Una and began to giggle again.

"I wouldn't really believe that," I said with as much dignity as I could muster.

But the truth was I felt I had made a fool of myself again. I realized now that I had never been convinced by Mother's explanation. It was too simple. If there was anything that woman could get wrong she did so without fail. And it upset me, because for the first time I found myself wanting to make a really good impression. The Dwyers had managed to convince me that, whatever else I wanted to be, I did not want to be a priest. I didn't even want to be an explorer, a career which would take me away for long periods from my wife and family. I was prepared to be a composer and nothing but a composer.

That night in bed I sounded Mother on the subject of marriage. I tried to be tactful because it had always been agreed between us that I should marry her and I did not wish her to see that my feelings had changed.

"Mummy," I asked, "if a gentleman asks a lady to marry him, what does he say?"

"Oh," she replied shortly, "some of them say a lot. They say more than they mean."

She was so irritable that I guessed she had divined my secret and I felt really sorry for her.

"If a gentleman said 'Excuse me, will you marry me?' would that be all right?" I persisted.

"Ah, well, he'd have to tell her first that he was fond of her," said Mother, who, no matter what she felt, could never bring herself to deceive me on any major issue.

But about the other matter I saw that it was hopeless to ask her any more. For days I made the most pertinacious inquiries at school and received some startling information. One boy had actually come floating down on a snowflake, wearing a bright blue dress, but, to his chagrin and mine, the dress had been given away to a poor child in the North Main Street. I grieved long and deeply over this wanton destruction of evidence. The balance of opinion favoured Mrs. Dwyer's solution, but of the theory of engines and starting handles no one in the school had ever heard. That theory might have been all right when Mother was a girl but it was now definitely out of fashion.

And because of it I had been exposed to ridicule before the family whose good opinion I valued most! It was hard enough to keep up my dignity with a girl who was doing algebra while I hadn't got beyond long division without falling into childish errors that made her laugh. That is another thing I still cannot stand, being made fun of by women. Once they begin they never stop. Once when we were going up Gardiner's Hill together after school she stopped to look at a baby in a pram. The baby grinned at her and she gave him her finger to suck. He waved his fists and sucked like mad and she went off into giggles again.

"I suppose that was another engine?" she said.

Four times at least she mentioned my silliness, twice in front of other girls, and each time, though I pretended to ignore it, I was pierced to the heart. It made me determined not to be exposed again. Once Mother asked Una and her younger sister, Joan, to tea and all the time I was in an agony of self-consciousness, dreading what she would say next. I felt that a woman who had said such things about babies was capable of anything. Then the talk turned on the death of little John Joe, and it all flowed back into my mind on a wave of mortification. I made two efforts to change the conversation, but Mother returned to it. She was full of pity for the Dwyers, full of sympathy for the little boy, and had almost reduced herself to tears. Finally, I got up and ordered Una and Joan to play with me. Then Mother got angry.

"For goodness' sake, Larry, let the children finish their tea!" she snapped.

"It's all right, Mrs. Delaney," Una said good-naturedly. "I'll go with him."

"Nonsense, Una!" Mother said sharply. "Finish your tea and go on with what you were saying. It's a wonder to me your poor mother didn't go out of her mind. How can they let people like that drive cars?"

At this I set up a loud wail. At any moment now, I felt, she was going to get on to babies and advise Una about what her mother ought to do.

"Will you behave yourself, Larry!" Mother said in a quivering voice. "Or what's come over you in the past few weeks? You used to have such nice manners, and now look at you! A little corner boy! I'm ashamed of you!"

How could she know what had come over me? How could she realize that I was imagining the family circle in the Dwyers' house and Una, between fits of laughter, describing my old-fashioned mother who still talked about babies coming out of people's stomachs? It must have been real love, for I have never known true love in which I wasn't ashamed of Mother.

And she knew it and was hurt. I still enjoyed going home with Una in the afternoons and, while she ate her dinner, I sat at the piano and pretended to play my own compositions, but whenever she called at our house for me I grabbed her by the hand and tried to drag her away so that she and Mother shouldn't start talking.

"Ah, I'm disgusted with you," Mother said one day. "One would think you were ashamed of me in front of that little girl. I'll engage she doesn't treat her mother like that."

Then one day I was waiting for Una at the school gate as usual. Another boy was waiting there as well—one of the seniors. When he heard the screams of the school breaking up he strolled away and stationed himself at the foot of the hill by the crossroads. Then Una herself came rushing out in her wide-brimmed felt hat, swinging her satchel, and approached me with a conspiratorial air.

"Oh, Larry, guess what's happened!" she whispered. "I can't bring you home with me today. I'll come down and see you during the week, though. Will that do?"

"Yes, thank you," I said in a dead cold voice. Even at the most tragic moment of my life I could be nothing but polite. I watched her scamper down the hill to where the big boy was waiting. He looked over his shoulder with a grin, and then the two of them went off together.

Instead of following them, I went back up the hill alone and stood leaning over the quarry wall, looking at the roadway and the valley of the city beneath me. I knew this was the end. I was too young to marry Una. I didn't know where babies came from and I didn't understand algebra. The fellow she had gone home with probably knew everything about both. I was full of gloom and revengeful thoughts. I, who had considered it sinful and dangerous to fight, was now regretting that I hadn't gone after him to batter his teeth in and jump on his face. It wouldn't even have mattered to me that I was too young and weak and that he would have done all the battering. I saw that love was a game that two people couldn't play at without pushing, just like football.

I went home and without saying a word took out the work I had been neglecting so long. That, too, seemed to have lost its appeal. Moodily, I ruled five lines and began to trace the difficult sign of the treble clef.

"Didn't you see Una, Larry?" Mother asked in surprise, looking up from her sewing.

"No, mummy," I said, too full for speech.

"Wisha, 'twasn't a falling-out ye had?" she asked in dismay, coming towards me. I put my head on my hands and sobbed. "Wisha, never mind, childeen!" she murmured, running her hand through my hair. "She was a bit old for you. You reminded her of her little brother that was killed, of course—that was why. You'll soon make new friends, take my word for it."

But I did not believe her. That evening there was no comfort for me. My great work meant nothing to me and I knew it was all I would ever have. For all the difference it made, I might as well become a priest. I felt it was a poor, sad, lonesome thing being nothing but a genius.

Music When Soft Voices Die

Echoing "What's Wrong with The Country," "Music When Soft Voices Die" appears to lack plot, but the plot's bony structure lies beneath the surface of the conversations, teacups, entrances and exits—the conflict between the passionate individual (as in "The Holy Door") and the respectability demanded by the community. O'Connor, writing of "The Ugly Duckling," could say that it "isn't even supposed to be a story but a piece of pure lyricism in which the characters are regarded merely as voices in a bit of instrumental music. It's one of the odd things I do for my own satisfaction, without expecting anybody in the world to like it except myself" (Michael/Frank, 146), yet the voices in this story are the drama, and they can only hint at what is unsaid and may be unsayable, even among friends. Why, one might ask, has Nora been crying? Note, as well, the richness of the narrator's double perspective: both the young man, oblivious to the significance of what he overhears, and the mature man, who remembers and understands all too well but who chooses to leave the interpretations to us.

During the lunch hour the male clerks usually went out, leaving myself and the three girls behind. While they ate their sandwiches and drank their tea, they chattered away, thirteen to the dozen. Half their conversation I didn't understand at all, and the other half bored me to tears. I usually drifted into the hallway with a Western. As a boy, I acted out whatever I was reading—taking steady aim, drawing rein, spurring to the rescue, and clutching at my shoulder where an Indian arrow had lodged—and the girls interrupted me with their comments.

They were nice girls, though. Joan, who was nineteen, was my favourite. She was masterful and warmhearted; she would take my part

211

when I got in trouble, and whenever she saw me with the sign of tears, she would put her arm round me and say, 'Look, Larry—*you* tell Mr. Scally if he says *another* word to you, I'll tear his *eyes* out.' She talked like that, all in italics. I liked Nora, too, but not so much. Sometimes she was very sweet and sometimes she didn't see you, and you never knew which it would be. Marie I didn't really like at all in those days. She was the prettiest of the three—thin, tall, and nunlike, with a queer stiff way of holding herself and an ironic intonation in her beautiful voice. Marie usually just didn't see you. I thought she was an old snob.

The three girls had fellows, and I knew these, too, mostly from seeing them hang about the office in the evening. Joan was going with a long-haired medical student called Mick Shea, with no hat and no religion, and she was always making novenas for his conversion. Nora went with a dressy fellow in Montenotte, the classy quarter of Cork, but she had a sort of underground understanding with a good-looking postman called Paddy Lacy, who used to stop me in the street and give me gallant messages for her. She never walked out with him that I knew of, but he was certain she loved him, and it shocked me that a superior fellow like a postman would not have more sense. Marie was going strong with a chap called Jim Holbrook, a rather snobbish intellectual type, who lived up my way.

Thirty years has turned the girls and myself into old friends. Only Nora is still at the office. Joan owns a private hotel, and Marie is the harassed mother of two wild children. She is still beautiful, sedate, and caustic. Not one word of their conversation ever seemed to register in my memory, which was full of valuable information about American states and Indian nations, wigwams, colts, derringers, and coyotes; yet now that I cannot remember anything of what I read, it seems to me that I can hear the girls as though they were in the same room with me, like the voices of Shelley's poem, trembling on the edge of pure music.

'Do you know, I have a *great* admiration for that girl?' Joan begins in her eager italics.

'Go on!' Nora says lightly. 'What did she do?'

'I admire her pluck, Nora,' Joan says, emphasising three syllables out of seven. 'When I *think* what she went through!'

'Ah, for God's sake, what did she go through?' Nora asks sceptically.

'That's all you know, Nora,' Joan says in a bloodcurdling voice. 'You never had an illegitimate kid to support, and Susie had.'

'Good job, too,' Nora says. 'I can't support myself.'

'What did you say she had, Joan?' Marie asks incredulously.

'A kid.'

'Well!' Marie exclaims, looking brightly from one to the other. 'The friends some people have!'

'Oh, it's true, Marie.'

'That's what makes it so peculiar, Joan,' Marie says with a shrug.

'What did she do with it?' Nora asks inquisitively.

'I suppose I really shouldn't say it, Nora, but of course it's really no secret. With the way the police watch girls like that, everything leaks out eventually. She had to farm him out in Rochestown. He must be about twelve now.'

'And does he know who his mother is?' asks Nora.

'Not at all, girl,' says Joan. 'How could she tell him? I suppose she's never even seen him. Gosh, I'm sorry for that girl!'

'I'd be sorrier for the kid,' Nora says.

'Oh, I know, Nora, I know,' Joan says earnestly. 'But what could the poor girl do? I mean, what would *we* do if we were in her place?'

And now that the voices grow clearer in my mind, I realise that Joan is the leader of the trio. It is she who sets the tempo, and it is her violin that holds it all together. Marie, with her deep beautiful voice, is the viola; Nora, for all that her voice sounds thin and squeaky, is the cello.

'Honestly, Joan, the things you say!' Marie cries, but without indignation. Marie sometimes behaves as though Joan is not really right in the head, and manages to suggest that she herself alone, with her nunlike air and caustic tongue, represents normality.

But Joan, who believes that Marie cultivates a blind spot for anything it doesn't suit her to see, only smiles knowingly. 'Well, we're all human, girl,' she says.

'Ah, nonsense, Joan!' says Marie. 'There must be something wrong with a girl like that.'

'There's something wrong with every girl or else she'd be a man,' says Nora.

'Ah, with the best will in the world, girl, I couldn't imagine myself going on like that,' says Marie. 'I suppose I mustn't be human,' she adds with a shrug, meaning that if this is what it's like to be human, so much the worse for humanity. 'Of course,' she ends, to show she has feelings, like anyone else, 'we all like a bit of sport, but that's different.'

'Oh, but it's not different, Marie,' Joan says warmly, and again the fiddle proclaims the theme. 'That's where you make your big mistake. What you call "a bit of sport" is only a matter of degree. God knows, I'm not what you'd call a public menace, but if I didn't watch my step, I could very easily see it happening to me.'

'So could I,' Nora says, and then begins to blush. 'And I don't know what I'd do about it, either.'

'Well, what could you do?' asks Marie. 'Assuming that such a thing could happen, which is assuming quite a lot.'

'I suppose I'd have to go to England and have it there,' says Nora gloomily.

'England?' says Marie.

'That would be all right if you knew someone in England, Nora,' says Joan. 'I mean, someone you could rely on.'

' "All right"?' echoes Marie. 'I should think starting life again in a foreign country with a baby, like that, would hardly be described as "all right." Or maybe I'm lacking in initiative?'

'Well, it would either be that or make him marry you,' says Nora.

'I was wondering when you'd think of marriage,' says Marie.

'That mightn't be as easy as it sounds, either, Marie,' says Joan. 'I think Nora means the fellow wouldn't want to marry you.'

'Yes, and I think it's rotten!' says Nora. 'A fellow pretending to a girl that she's the only thing in the world he cares for, till she makes a fool of herself for him, and then he cuts his hook.'

'Well,' Joan says practically, 'I suppose we're all the same when we get what we want.'

'If that's all a man wants, couldn't somebody give it to him on a spoon?' says Nora.

'I'd simply say in a case like that that the man began to see what sort the girl was,' Marie says, having completely misunderstood Nora's remark.

'And what sort would you say *he* was?' Nora asks.

'Ah, well,' Marie replies comfortably, 'that's different, Nora. Considering the sort of sheltered lives women lead, it's up to them to set a standard. You can't expect the same sort of thing from men. Of course, I think he should be made to marry her.'

'But who'd make him, Marie?' asks Joan.

'Well, I suppose his family would, if it was for nothing but to avoid a scandal.'

'Ask any mother in Cork would she sooner a scandal or a daughter-in-law,' Nora says cynically.

'Then of course the priest would have to make him,' says Marie, still unperturbed.

'That's what I find so hard to imagine, though,' Joan says, and then her tone changes, and she becomes brilliant and mocking. 'I mean, it's all very well talking about it like this in the peace and quiet of the office, but imagine if I had to go up tonight after dark to the presbytery and talk to old Canon Cremin about it. "Excuse me, Canon, but I've been keeping company with a boy called Mick Shea, and it just so happens that he made a bit too free with me, and I was wondering would you ever mind running down and telling him to marry me." Cripes, if I was the Canon, I'd take my stick to a one like that!'

'Lovely marriage 'twould be anyway,' says Nora.

'Exactly, Nora,' Joan says, in her dramatic way, laying her hand on Nora's arm. 'That's just what I mean. How on earth could you spend the rest of your life with a man after having to do that to get him to marry you?'

'How he could spend the rest of his life with me is what I'd be worrying about,' says Nora. 'After all, I'd be the one that was to blame.'

'Never mind about him at all, now, girl,' Joan says with a jolly laugh. 'It's my own troubles that I'm thinking about. Honestly, do you know, I don't think I could face it!'

'I'm full sure I couldn't,' says Nora, lighting a cigarette.

'But what else could you do?' Marie asks. She obviously thinks they are two very peculiar girls, and no wonder. They were peculiar, like all delightful girls.

'Do you know, Marie,' says Joan, 'I think I'd sooner marry the first poor devil that came the way.'

'Aren't you lucky, being able to pick them up like that?' Marie asks dryly.

'Ah, well, Marie,' says Joan, 'a girl would be in a bad way entirely if there wasn't one man that would take her on.'

'Like Paddy Lacy,' says Nora, with a giggle. 'He stopped me on the road the other day while he was delivering the letters, and I declare to God I didn't know which way to look.'

'I see,' says Marie. 'So that's why you keep Paddy Lacy on. I was wondering about that.'

'You needn't,' Nora says with sudden temper. 'I'm pretty sure Paddy Lacy would be just as tough as the rest of them if I went along and told him a thing like that.'

'But why would you have to tell him, Nora?' Joan asks anxiously. 'Wouldn't you let him find out for himself?'

'And a nice situation I'd be in when he did!'

'Oh, I wouldn't be too sure,' Joan says with another laugh. 'Before a man made up his mind about a thing like that, I'd like him to have a chance of seeing the full beauty of my character. Like the boatman in Glengarriff, I'm at my best on a long stretch.'

'I think I'd as soon live with a man I forced to marry me as one I tricked into marrying me,' Nora says. 'And I'd sooner do either than what your pal did—farm out a child. I don't think I'd ever have a day's luck after.'

'Now, you're misjudging the girl there, Nora,' Joan says earnestly. 'You are, really! It's not the same thing when you never have the chance of getting attached to a child. And when there isn't a blessed thing you can do about it, I don't honestly believe that there's any moral responsibility.'

'Responsibility?' Nora says, getting up. 'Who's talking about responsibility? I'd live in dread of my own shadow for the rest of my days. I wouldn't be able to see a barefooted kid in the street without getting sick. Every knock that came to the door, I'd be in dread to open it. Every body that was picked out of the river, I'd feel it was my kid, and I was the one to blame. For God's sake, don't talk to me!'

'There's another cup of tea left, Nora,' Joan says, a little too brightly. 'Would you like it?'

'In a minute, Joan,' says Nora, and goes out to the Ladies'. When she returns a few minutes later, she looks as though she had been crying. To me it is a great mystery, because no one speaks crossly to her. I assume that, like myself, she has a father who drinks.

'Cripes, I'm sorry for poor May Jenkins,' Joan begins on another day, after Nora has poured out the tea. That is her time for a new theme, when there is no serious danger of interruption.

'Who's *she* when she's at home?' Nora asks lightly.

'May Jenkins? You'd hardly know her, Nora. She's from the South Side.'

'And what ails her now didn't ail her before?' asks Nora, who is full of local quips and phrases.

'Oh, the usual thing,' says Joan with a shrug. 'Phil Macken, her husband, is knocking round with the Archer girl, on the Wellington Road —the Yellow Peril.'

'Really, Joan,' Marie says, 'I don't know where you come across all those extraordinary people.'

'I don't see what's so extraordinary about that at all,' Nora says. 'People are always doing it.'

'And people are always getting terrible diseases, only we don't go out of our way to inquire,' says Marie primly. 'Really, there must be something wrong with a woman like that.'

'Like May, Marie?' Joan asks in mock surprise.

'No, like that other creature—whatever you said her name was.'

'Oh, I wouldn't say that at all, Marie,' says Joan. 'Some very respectable people live on the Wellington Road. And a lot of men find her attractive.'

'Then there must be something wrong with the men.'

'Or the wife, why don't you say?' cries Nora.

'Or the wife,' Marie agrees, with perfect placidity. 'She should be able to mind her own husband.'

'She'd want roller skates,' says Joan, and again I hear the high note of the violin, driving the trio onward. 'No, Marie, girl,' she says, resting her chin on her hands, 'you have to face the facts. A lot of women do get unattractive after marriage. Of course, I'm not blaming them. We'd be the same ourselves, with kids to mind and jobs to do. They can't waste time dancing and dolling themselves up like Maeve Archer, and if they did, their houses would soon show it. You see, it's something we all have to be prepared for.'

'If I felt that way, Joan, I'd go into a convent,' Marie says severely.

'But after all, Marie,' says Joan, 'what could you do? Suppose you were married to Jim and a thing like that happened?'

'What could I do?' Marie echoes, smiling at the thought of anything of the sort happening with Jim. 'Well, I suppose I could walk out of the house.'

'Ah, come now, Marie,' Joan says. 'It's not as easy as all that. Where would you walk to, in the first place?'

'What's wrong with going home?'

'With a houseful of kids?' says Joan. 'Of course, I know your father is very fond of you and all the rest of it, but all the same, we have to be reasonable.'

'I could go somewhere else,' says Marie. 'After all, Jim would have to support me—and the kids, as you say.'

'Of course he would. That's if you didn't mind spending the rest of your days as a grass widow. You know, Marie, I saw one or two women who did that, and it didn't look too promising to me. No, in the way of husbands and fathers and so on, I don't think you can beat men. A dog won't do.'

'But do you mean you'd let him go on seeing a filthy creature like that?' asks Marie. 'Really, Joan, I don't think you can be serious.'

'Oh, I never said that,' Joan says hastily. 'I'm sure I'd make it pretty uncomfortable for him.'

'Which mightn't be such a bad way of making the other woman more attractive,' Nora says dryly.

'Oh, we all know what Nora would do,' Joan retorts with affectionate mockery. 'She'd sit down and have a good cry. Wouldn't you, love?'

'I might,' Nora replies doubtfully. 'I'd sooner that than calling in the neighbours.'

'Oh, I admit you'd have to keep your dignity, Nora,' Marie says, being particularly susceptible to any appeal to her ladyhood. 'But surely someone would have to interfere.'

'I saw too much interference, Marie,' Nora says grimly. 'It's mad enough thinking you can spend your whole life with a man and still be in love with him, but 'tis dotty entirely if you imagine you can do it with half Cork acting as referee.'

'All the same, Nora,' Joan says, in her practical way, 'before I saw a woman like that making off with a husband of mine, I'd get a fistful of her hair, and I wouldn't mind who knew it, either. I'd read and spell her, I give you my word.'

'I certainly wouldn't degrade myself by quarrelling with a creature like that,' says Marie.

'I wouldn't have the nerve,' says Nora, lighting a cigarette. 'Look, it's all very well to talk about it like that, but suppose it was the other way around? Suppose you were making a fool of yourself over another man, and your husband disgraced you all over Cork by fighting him?'

'Really, Nora,' says Marie, with her Mona Lisa smile, 'you have a remarkably vivid imagination.'

'Oh, I don't know that that's all imagination, either, Marie,' says Joan, who enjoys nothing better than imagining things. 'That could happen, too, mind you!'

'But that would make you no better than the woman you're just talking about,' says Marie.

'Who said we were any better?' asks Nora. 'I might be worse, for all anyone knows.'

'But do you know, Nora,' Joan says, 'I'm not at all sure but I'd like Mick to do it.'

'To shame you all over Cork?' Nora asks.

'Oh, no. Just to stand up for his rights. Nobody wants a doormat.'

'Give me doormats every time,' says Nora, with a sinister pull at her cigarette.

'But, Nora,' Marie asks in horror, 'you don't mean you'd just sit at home and do nothing?'

'I don't know, girl. What could you do?'

'And wait till he changed his mind and came back to you?'

'Maybe,' says Nora, with a shrug. 'I mightn't be there when he got back. I might have a fellow, too.'

'Really,' Marie says, scratching her long neck. 'I'm beginning to see a number of uses for this Paddy Lacy of yours.'

'That's where women have the worst of it,' Joan says quickly, to head off a reply from Nora about Paddy Lacy. 'It's not as easy for a married woman with a couple of kids to find someone to go off with. It's too chancy giving children a stepfather, no matter how fond you might be of him. No, what I can't imagine,' she adds earnestly, 'is what you'd do when he did change his mind. I often wonder could you ever behave in the same way to him.'

'Of course not, Joan,' Marie says. 'Naturally, if there were children, I could understand remaining in the same house with him, just for their sake, but living with him as husband and wife is a thing I could never imagine doing.'

'Ah, now, Marie, you're a girl of great character,' Joan says. 'But that sounds to me too much like giving up sweets in a sweetshop. Of course, I know people do it when they get tired of one another, but it never seems natural to me. I wouldn't do it just for fun,' she adds gravely. 'I'd want to be pretty sure that he was still fond of me.'

'I'm afraid I wouldn't have much faith in the affections of a man like that,' Marie says.

'What about you, Nora?' Joan asks.

'Me?' Nora says, blushing. 'Oh, I suppose 'twould depend.'

'You mean, depend on how he behaved to you?'

'Yes,' Nora replies with a frightened air. 'And how he behaved to the other one.'

'Well, really, Nora, this is going beyond the beyonds!' Marie exclaims, putting down her cup with a ladylike air of finality. 'Are we supposed to take *her* feelings into consideration as well?'

'I suppose she might have feelings, too?' Nora replies gloomily.

'I know what Nora would do!' Joan says triumphantly, bringing her hand down flat on the table. 'I know it just as if I was there. She'd tell her husband to go to blazes, and skelp off to the other woman's house to console her.'

'By the way she's talking, it sounds as if she'd leave her husband and live with the other one,' Marie says.

'I might even do that,' says Nora, moving towards the door.

'Ah, go on, girl!' Joan says boisterously. 'Don't you know we're only making fun of you? I know what's going to happen to you,' she adds comfortingly. 'You'll marry a fine steady slob of a man that'll stick his two heels on the mantelpiece and never look at the side of the road another woman is walking at. Look, there's a cup of tea in the pot still!'

'I don't want it, Joanie, thanks,' says Nora, and goes off to the Ladies'.

Marie gives a shrug. 'For an intelligent girl, Nora does talk the most extraordinary nonsense,' she says with finality.

'Oh, I wouldn't be too sure it was nonsense, Marie,' Joan says, in her loyal way. 'I think Nora might surprise us all.'

But Nora, worse luck, has never had the opportunity of surprising anyone; nor has Joan—two fine women who have never met with men astute enough to grab them. As for Marie, she rules her husband gently but firmly, like a Reverend Mother dealing with a rather dull under-gardener. Of the three, she is now the one I am most intimate with. Sometimes I even think that if I were to forget myself and make advances to her, instead of slapping my face indignantly she would only laugh and say, 'Ah, Larry, will you have a bit of sense?'—which from Marie would be almost like a declaration of love. And I think the reason is that like me, she hears those voices 'vibrate in the memory' and wonders over them.

'Ah, Larry,' she says, grabbing me eagerly by the hands, 'do you remember all the old nonsense we used to talk in the office, and Joan saying what she'd do with an illegitimate baby, and me saying what I'd do if Jim went off with another woman? And look at us now—three old women!'

No doubt she realises that she can afford to say things like that to me, for while the music of those voices lingers in my mind she and they will never be old.

The Party

*Although not O'Connor's last story, this is an appropriate ending, fo-
cusing on a character who must distance himself from his comfortable
life to see it and his role in it. Many O'Connor stories deal with the
isolated population, the lonely outsider; "The Party" makes the meta-
phorical tangible, if only for a few hours: from across the street, in the
watchman's box, Mr. Hardy bitterly observes the party at his own house.*

*That in itself might seem slender inspiration, but much of the reader's
pleasure is in observing Johnny, Tim Coakley, and Mrs. Coakley, the
watchman, postman, and his wife, cheerfully confident amateur psychol-
ogists, offer solutions to this emotional mystery whose answer may be
beyond them, although their instincts are occasionally right.*

Old Johnny, one of the Gas Company's watchmen, was a man with a
real appreciation of his job. Most of the time, of course, it was a cold,
comfortless job, with no one to talk to, and he envied his younger friend
Tim Coakley, the postman. Postmen had a cushy time of it—always
watched and waited for, bringing good news or bad news, often called
in to advise, and (according to Tim, at least) occasionally called in for
more intimate purposes. Tim, of course, was an excitable man, and he
could be imagining a lot of that, though Johnny gave him the benefit of
the doubt. At the same time, queer things happened to Johnny now and
again that were stranger than anything Tim could tell. As it seemed to
Johnny, people got it worse at night; the wild ones grew wilder, the
gloomy ones gloomier. Whatever it was in them that had light in it
burned more clearly, the way the stars and moon did when the sun went
down. It was the darkness that did it. Johnny would be sitting in his hut
for hours in the daylight and no one even gave him a second glance, but

222

once darkness fell, people would cross the street to look at his brazier, and even stop to speak to him.

One night, for instance, in the week before Christmas, he was watching in a big Dublin square, with a railed-off park in the middle of it and doctors' and lawyers' houses on all the streets about it. That suited Johnny fine, particularly at that time of year, when there was lots of visiting and entertaining. He liked to be at the centre of things, and he always appreciated the touch of elegance: the stone steps leading up to the tall door, with the figures entering and leaving looking small in the lighted doorway, and the slight voices echoing on the great brick sounding board of the square.

One house in particular attracted him. It was all lit up as if for a party, and the curtains were pulled back to reveal the tall, handsome rooms with decorated plaster ceilings. A boy with a basket came and rang, and a young man in evening dress leaned out of the window and told the boy to leave the stuff in the basement. As he did so, a girl came and rested her hand on his shoulder, and she was in evening dress too. Johnny liked that. He liked people with a bit of style. If he had had the good fortune to grow up in a house like that, he would have done the right thing too. And even though he hadn't, it pleased him to watch the show. Johnny, who came of a generation before trade unions, knew that in many ways it is pleasanter to observe than to participate. He only hoped there would be singing; he was very partial to a bit of music.

But this night a thing happened the like of which had never happened to Johnny before. The door of the house opened and closed, and a man in a big cloth coat like fur came across the road to him. When he came closer, Johnny saw that he was a tall, thin man with greying hair and a pale discontented face.

'Like to go home to bed for a couple of hours?' the man asked in a low voice.

'What's that?' said Johnny, in astonishment.

'I'll stay here and mind your box.'

'Oh, you would, would you?' Johnny said, under the impression that the man must have drink taken.

'I'm not joking,' said the man shortly.

The grin faded on Johnny's face, and he hoped God would direct him to say the right thing. This could be dangerous. It suggested only one thing—a check-up—though in this season of good will you'd think people would be a bit more charitable, even if a man had slipped away for a few minutes for a drink. But that was the way of bosses everywhere. Even Christmas wasn't sacred to them. Johnny put on an appearance of great sternness. 'Oho,' he said. 'I can't afford to do things like that. There's valuable property here belonging to the Gas Company. I could lose my job over a thing like that.'

'You won't lose your job,' the man said. 'I won't leave here till you come back. If there's any trouble about it, I'll get you another job. I suppose it's money you want.'

'I never asked you for anything,' Johnny replied indignantly. 'And I can't go home at this hour, with no bus to bring me back.'

'I suppose there's other places you can go,' the man replied. 'There's a quid, and I won't expect you till two.'

The sight of the money changed Johnny's view of the matter. If a rich man wanted to amuse himself doing Johnny's job for a while—a little weakness of rich men that Johnny had heard of in other connections—and was willing to pay for it, that was all right. Rich men had to have their little jokes. Or of course, it could be a bet.

'Oh, well,' he said, rising and giving himself a shake, 'so long as there's no harm in it!' He hadn't seen the man go into the house where they were having the party, so he must live there. 'I suppose it's a joke?' he added, looking at the man out of the corner of his eye.

'It's no joke to me,' the man said gloomily.

'Oh, I wasn't being inquisitive, of course,' Johnny said hastily. 'But I see there was to be a party in the house. I thought it might be something to do with that.'

'There's your quid,' said the man. 'You needn't be back till three unless you want to. I won't get much sleep anyway.'

Johnny thanked him profusely and left in high good humour. He foresaw that the man would probably be of great use to him some time. A man who could offer to get you a job just like that was not to be slighted. And besides he had an idea of how he was going to spend the next hour or so, at least, and a very pleasant way it was. He took a bus to Ringstead to the house of Tim Coakley, the postman. Tim, though a good deal younger, was very friendly with him, and he was an expansive man who loved any excuse for a party.

As Johnny expected, Tim, already on his way to bed, welcomed him with his two arms out and a great shout of laughter. He was bald and fat, with a high-pitched voice. Johnny showed Tim and his wife the money, and announced that he was treating them to a dozen of stout. Like the decent man he was, Tim didn't want to take the money for the stout from Johnny, but Johnny insisted. 'Wait till I tell you, man!' he said triumphantly. 'The like of it never happened before in the whole history of the Gas Company.'

As Johnny told the story, it took close on half an hour, though this included Mrs. Coakley's departure and return with the dozen of stout. And then the real pleasure began, because the three of them had to discuss what it all meant. Why was the gentleman in the big coat sitting in the cold of the square looking at the lights and listening to the noise of the party in his own home? It was a real joy to Johnny to hear his friend analyse it, for Tim had a powerful intellect, full of novel ideas, and in no time what had begun as a curious incident in a watchman's life was beginning to expand into a romance, a newspaper case. Tim at once ruled out the idea of a joke. What would be the point in a joke like that? A bet was the more likely possibility. It could be that the man had bet someone he could take the watchman's place for the best part of the night without being detected, but in Tim's view there was one fatal flaw in this explanation. Why would the man wear a coat as conspicuous as the one that Johnny had described? There would be big money on a wager like that, and the man would be bound to try and disguise himself better. No, there must be another explanation, and as Tim drank more stout, his imagination played over the theme with greater audacity and logic, till Johnny himself began to feel uncomfortable. He began to perceive that it might be a more serious matter than he had thought.

'We've agreed that it isn't a joke,' said Tim, holding up one finger. 'We've agreed that it isn't a bet,' he added, holding up another finger. 'There is only one explanation that covers the whole facts,' he said, holding up his open hand. 'The man is watching the house.'

'Watching his own house?' Johnny asked incredulously.

'Exactly. Why else would he pay you good money to sit in your box? A man like that, that could go to his club and be drinking champagne and playing cards all night in the best of company? Isn't it plain that he's doing it only to have cover?'

'So 'twould seem,' said Johnny meekly, like any interlocutor of Socrates.

'Now, the next question is: Who is he watching?' said Tim.

'Just so,' said Johnny with a mystified air.

'So we ask ourselves: Who would a man like that be watching?' Tim went on triumphantly.

'Burglars,' said Mrs. Coakley.

'Burglars?' her husband asked with quiet scorn. 'I suppose they'd walk in the front door?'

'He might be watching the cars, though,' Johnny said. 'There's a lot of them young hooligans around, breaking into cars. I seen them.'

'Ah, Johnny, will you have sense?' Tim asked wearily. 'Look, if that was all the man wanted, couldn't he give you a couple of bob to keep an eye on the cars? For the matter of that, couldn't he have a couple of plainclothesmen round the square? Not at all, man! He's watching some-body, and what I say is, the one he's watching is his own wife.'

'His wife?' Johnny exclaimed, aghast. 'What would he want to watch his wife for?'

'Because he thinks someone is going to that house tonight that should not be there. Someone that wouldn't come at all unless he knew the husband was out. So what does the husband do? He pretends to go out, but instead of that he hides in a watchman's box across the road and waits for him. What other explanation is there?'

'Now, couldn't it be someone after his daughter?' said Johnny.

'What daughter?' Tim asked, hurt at Johnny's lack of logic. 'What would a well-to-do man like that do if his daughter was going with a fellow he considered unsuitable? First, he would give the daughter a clock in the jaw, and then he would say to the maid or butler or whoever he have, "If a Mr. Murphy comes to this house again looking for Miss Alice, kindly tell him she is not at home." That's all he'd do, and that would be the end of your man. No, Johnny, the one he's watching is the wife, and I can only hope it won't get you into any trouble.'

'You don't think I should tell the bobbies about it?' Johnny asked in alarm.

'What *could* you tell the bobbies, though?' Tim asked. 'That there was a man in your box that paid you a quid to let him use it? What proof have you that a crime is going to be committed? None! And this is only suspicion. There's nothing you can do now, only let things take their course till two o'clock, and then I'll go round with you and see what really happened.'

'But what could happen?' Johnny asked irritably.

'He sounds to me like a desperate man,' Tim said gravely.

'Oh, desperate entirely,' agreed his wife, who was swallowing it all like a box of creams.

'You don't mean you think he might do him in?' asked Johnny.

'Him, or the wife, Johnny,' said Tim. 'Or both. Of course, it's nothing to do with you what he does,' he added comfortingly. 'Whatever it is, you had neither hand, act, nor part in it. It is only the annoyance of seeing your name in the papers.'

'A man should never take advice from anybody,' Johnny commented bitterly, opening another bottle of stout. Johnny was not a drinking man, but he was worried. He valued his own blameless character, and he knew there were people bad enough to pretend he ought not to have left his post for a couple of hours, even at Christmastime, when everybody was visiting friends. He was not a scholar like Tim, and nobody had warned him of the desperate steps that rich men took when their wives acted flighty.

'Come on,' Tim said, putting on his coat. 'I'm coming with you.'

'Now, I don't want your name dragged into this,' Johnny protested. 'You have a family to think of, too.'

'I'm coming with you, Johnny,' Tim said in a deep voice, laying his hand on Johnny's arm. 'We're old friends, and friends stick together. Besides, as a postman, I'm more accustomed to this sort of thing than you are. You're a simple man. You might say the wrong thing. Leave it to me to answer the questions.'

Johnny was grateful and said so. He was a simple man, as Tim said, and, walking back through the sleeping town, expecting to see police cordons and dead bodies all over the place, he was relieved to have a level-headed fellow like Tim along with him. As they approached the square and their steps perceptibly slowed, Tim suggested in a low voice that Johnny should stand at the corner of the square while he himself scouted round to see if everything was all right. Johnny agreed, and stopped at the corner. Everything seemed quiet enough. There were only two cars outside the house. There were lights still burning in it, but though the windows were open, as though to clear the air, there was no sound from within. His brazier still burned bright and even in the darkness under the trees of the park. Johnny wished he had never left it.

He saw Tim cross to the other side of the road and go slowly by the brazier. Then Tim stopped and said something, but Johnny could not catch the words. After a few moments, Tim went on, turned the corner, and came back round the square. It took him close on ten minutes, and when he reached Johnny it was clear that something was wrong.

'What is it?' Johnny asked in agony.

'Nothing, Johnny,' Tim said sadly. 'But do you know who the man is?'

'Sure I told you I never saw him before,' said Johnny.

'I know him,' said Tim. 'That's Hardy that owns the big stores in George's Street. It's his house. The man must be worth hundreds of thousands.'

'But what about his wife, man?' asked Johnny.

'Ah, his wife died ten years ago. He's a most respectable man. I don't know what he's doing here, but it's nothing for you to fret about. I'm glad for everyone's sake. Good night, Johnny.'

'Good night, Tim, and thanks, thanks!' cried Johnny, his heart already lighter.

The Gas Company's property and his reputation were both secure. The strange man had not killed his wife or his wife's admirer, because the poor soul, having been dead for ten years, couldn't have an admirer for her husband or anyone else to kill. And now he could sit in peace by his brazier and watch the dawn come up over the decent city of Dublin. The relief was so sharp that he felt himself superior to Tim. It was all very well for postmen to talk about the interesting life they led, but they hadn't the same experiences as watchmen. Watchmen might seem simple to postmen, but they had a wisdom of their own, a wisdom that came of the silence and darkness when a man is left alone with his thoughts, like a sailor aboard ship. Thinking of the poor man sitting like that in the cold under the stars watching a party at his own house, Johnny wondered that he could ever have paid attention to Tim. He approached his brazier smiling.

'Everything nice and quiet for you?' he asked.

'Except for some gasbag that stopped for a chat five minutes ago,' the other replied with rancour. Johnny felt rather pleased to hear Tim described as a gasbag.

'I know the very man you mean,' he said with a nod. 'He's a nice poor fellow but he talks too much. Party all over?'

'Except for one couple,' the other man said, rising from his box. 'It's no use waiting for them. They'll probably be at it till morning.'

'I dare say,' said Johnny. 'Why wouldn't you go in and have a chat with them yourself? You could do with a drink by this time, I suppose.'

'A lot they care whether I could or not,' the man said bitterly. 'All that would happen is that they'd say "Delighted to see you, Mr. Hardy" and then wait for me to go to bed.'

'Ah, now, I wouldn't say that,' said Johnny.

'I'm not asking whether you'd say it or not,' said the other savagely. 'I know it. Here I am, that paid for the party, sitting out here all night, getting my death of cold, and did my daughter or my son as much as come to the door to look for me? Did they even notice I wasn't there?'

'Oh, no, no,' Johnny said politely, talking to him as if he were a ten-year-old in a tantrum—which, in a sense, Johnny felt he was. The man might have hundreds of thousands, as Tim said, but there was no difference in the world between him and a little boy sitting out in the back on a frosty night, deliberately trying to give himself pneumonia because his younger brother had got a penny and he hadn't. It was no use being hard on a man like that. 'Children are very selfish, of course, but what you must remember is that fathers are selfish, too.'

'Selfish?' the other exclaimed angrily. 'Do you know what those two cost me between private schools and colleges? Do you know what that one party tonight cost me? As much as you'd earn in a year!'

'Oh, I know, I know!' said Johnny, holding his hands up in distress. 'I used to feel the same myself, after the wife died. I'd look at the son putting grease on his hair in front of the mirror, and I'd say to myself, "That's my grease and that's my mirror, and he's going out to amuse himself with some little piece from the lanes, not caring whether I'm alive or dead!" And daughters are worse. You'd expect more from a daughter somehow.'

'You'd expect what you wouldn't get,' the other said gloomily. 'There's that girl inside that I gave everything to, and she'd think more of some spotty college boy that never earned a pound in his life. And if I open my mouth, my children look at me as if they didn't know was I a fool or a lunatic.'

'They think you're old-fashioned, of course,' said Johnny. 'I know. But all the same you're not being fair to them. Children can be fond enough of you, only you'd never see it till you didn't care whether they were or not. That was the mistake I made. If I might have got an old woman for myself after the Missis died, I'd have enjoyed myself more and seen it sooner. That's what you should do. You're a well-to-do man. You could knock down a very good time for yourself. Get some lively little piece to spend your money on who'll make a fuss over you, and then you won't begrudge it to them so much.'

'Yes,' said the other, 'to have more of them wishing I was dead so that they could get at the rest of it.'

He strode across the street without even a good night, and Johnny saw the flood of light on the high steps and heard the dull thud of the big door behind him.

Sitting by his brazier, waiting for the dawn over the city square, Johnny felt very fortunate, wise, and good. If ever the man listened to what he had said, he might be very good to Johnny: he might get him a proper job as an indoor watchman; he might even give him a little pension to show his appreciation. If only he took the advice—and it might sink in after a time—it would be worth every penny of it to him. Anyway, if only the job continued for another couple of days, the man would be bound to give him a Christmas box. Five bob. Ten bob. Even a quid. It would be nothing to a man like that.

Though a realist by conviction, Johnny, too, had his dreams.

Poetry—Translations

I Am Stretched on Your Grave

O'Connor's translation of this anonymous eighteenth-century Irish poem exemplifies the vivid freshness of his work. Fidelity to the original and preserving its emotional complexity were both essential. In "Adventures in Translation," he stated that "the problem for the translator is, how to give the reader the feeling that he 'was there' " (159). Translating earlier Irish literature had its own moral imperative for him, as David Greene saw: "Some people learn for their own private satisfaction, others for the pleasure of displaying their erudition; to Frank O'Connor such attitudes were incomprehensible. He had learned the older language so that he could tell the Irish people about it; after reading a poem that had especially moved him he would look up and say: 'Isn't it grand? Think how the kids down the country would love that!' (Michael/Frank, 139).

I am stretched on your grave
   And would lie there forever;
If your hands were in mine
   I'd be sure we'd not sever.
My apple tree, my brightness,
   'Tis time we were together
For I smell of the earth
   And am stained by the weather.

When my family thinks
   That I'm safe in my bed
From night until morning
   I am stretched at your head,

Calling out to the air
With tears hot and wild
My grief for the girl
That I loved as a child.

Do you remember
The night we were lost
In the shade of the blackthorn
And the chill of the frost?
Thanks be to Jesus
We did what was right,
And your maidenhead still
Is your pillar of light.

The priests and the friars
Approach me in dread
Because I still love you
My love and you dead,
And would still be your shelter
From rain and from storm,
And with you in the cold grave
I cannot sleep warm.

Kilcash

Introducing this eighteenth-century poem, O'Connor noted that "In the English clearances after 1691 the woodlands were the first things to be destroyed because they sheltered the now landless men of Sarsfield's armies," thus this lament, whose mood Daniel Binchy characterized as "bewildered despair" (Michael/Frank, 20). "Kilcash" is also closely connected to Yeats; "it was the home of one branch of the Butler family," although Yeats may not have known it. O'Connor noted that "it was one of his favorite poems, and there was a good deal of his work in it" (Kings 98, 100). The symbiosis between Yeats and O'Connor on translations such as this was remarkable: " . . . wild horses could not have kept Yeats from helping with them, and sometimes, having supplied some felicitous line of his own, he promptly stole it back for one of his original poems. Hence the 'influence' of these poems on Yeats's later poems. . . . Yeats's suggestions [in "Kilcash"] . . . seem to me not only to have enriched the poem, but also to have made it closer in feeling to the original" (Kings, v).

W̲hat shall we do for timber?
   The last of the woods is down.
Kilcash and the house of its glory
   And the bell of the house are gone,
The spot where that lady waited
   Who shamed all women for grace
When earls came sailing to greet her
   And Mass was said in the place.

My grief and my affliction
   Your gates are taken away,
Your avenue needs attention,
   Goats in the garden stray.
The courtyard's filled with water
   And the great earls where are they?
The earls, the lady, the people
   Beaten into the clay.

No sound of duck or geese there,
   Hawk's cry or eagle's call,
No humming of the bees there
   That brought honey and wax for all,
Nor even the song of the birds there
   When the sun goes down in the west,
No cuckoo on top of the boughs there,
   Singing the world to rest.

There's mist there tumbling from branches,
   Unstirred by night and by day,
And darkness falling from heaven,
   For our fortune has ebbed away,
There's no holly nor hazel nor ash there,
   The pasture's rock and stone,
The crown of the forest has withered,
   And the last of its game is gone.

I beseech of Mary and Jesus
   That the great come home again
With long dances danced in the garden,
   Fiddle music and mirth among men,
That Kilcash the home of our fathers
   Be lifted on high again,
And from that to the deluge of waters
   In bounty and peace remain.

The Lament for Art O'Leary

"Arthur or Art O'Leary, a colonel in the Austrian army, outlawed and killed in Carriganimma, County Cork in 1773 for refusing to sell his famous mare to a Protestant named Morris for £5.0.0 (Catholics were not permitted by law to possess a horse of greater value than this), is buried in the ruined abbey of Kilcrea under an epitaph probably composed by his wife, the author of this lament, and aunt of Daniel O'Connell.

> *Lo Arthur Leary, generous, handsome, brave,*
> *Slain in his bloom lies in this humble grave.*

She is said to have followed up his murderers as she threatened and to have had the soldiers who shot him transported. Morris himself is supposed to have been shot in Cork by O'Leary's brother. The curious intervention of O'Leary's sister in the lament strongly suggests that she had originally composed a lament for her brother in which Eileen O'Connell was taunted, and that the widow seized on this as a theme and developed it into the fine poem we know. There is a defensive note about even the opening lines.

The members of her family—the O'Connells of Derrynane—whom she mentions are her father, Donal, her brother Connell, who was drowned in 1765, and her sister Abby, married to another Austrian officer named O'Sullivan. Abby is the girl who is supposed to have been the companion of Maria Theresa. Her twin sister, Maire, also named, was married to a man named Baldwin in Macroom, who appears to have surrendered the mare to Morris in order to avoid legal complications. The markethouse of the first verse is in Macroom, and the Mill of the penultimate verse is Millstreet, County Cork" (Kings, 109).

237

[See "Ireland," the last essay in this collection, for another discussion of the poem O'Connor called "the history of every great Irish family, and not mere history . . . but burned into the racial memory of the people."]

My love and my delight,
The day I saw you first
Beside the markethouse
I had eyes for nothing else
And love for none but you.

I left my father's house
And ran away with you,
And that was no bad choice;
You gave me everything.
There were parlours whitened for me
Bedrooms painted for me,
Ovens reddened for me,
Loaves baked for me,
Joints spitted for me,
Beds made for me
To take my ease on flock
Until the milking time
And later if I pleased.

My mind remembers
That bright spring day,
How your hat with its band
Of gold became you,
Your silver-hilted sword,
Your manly right hand,
Your horse on her mettle
And foes around you
Cowed by your air;
For when you rode by
On your white-nosed mare
The English lowered their head before you

Not out of love for you
But hate and fear,
For, sweetheart of my soul,
The English killed you.

My love and my calf
Of the race of the Earls of Antrim
And the Barrys of Eemokilly,
How well a sword became you,
A hat with a band,
A slender foreign shoe
And a suit of yarn
Woven over the water!

My love and my darling
When I go home
The little lad, Conor,
And Fiach the baby
Will surely ask me
Where I left their father,
I'll say with anguish
'Twas in Kilnamartyr;
They will call the father
Who will never answer.

My love and my mate
That I never thought dead
Till your horse came to me
With bridle trailing,
All blood from forehead
To polished saddle
Where you should be,
Either sitting or standing;
I gave one leap to the threshold,
A second to the gate,
A third upon its back.
I clapped my hands,
And off at a gallop;

I never lingered
Till I found you lying
By a little furze-bush
Without pope or bishop
Or priest or cleric
One prayer to whisper
But an old, old woman,
And her cloak about you,
And your blood in torrents—
Art O'Leary—
I did not wipe it off, I drank it from my palms.

My love and my delight
Stand up now beside me,
And let me lead you home
Until I make a feast,
And I will roast the meat
And send for company
And call the harpers in,
And I shall make your bed
Of soft and snowy sheets
And blankets dark and rough
To warm the beloved limbs
An autumn blast has chilled.

(His sister speaks.)

My little love, my calf,
This is the image
That last night brought me
In Cork all lonely
On my bed sleeping,
That the white courtyard
And the tall mansion
That we two played in
As children had fallen,
Ballingeary withered
And your hounds were silent,

Your birds were songless
While people found you
On the open mountain
Without priest or cleric
But an old, old woman
And her coat about you
When the earth caught you—
Art O'Leary—
And your life-blood stiffened
The white shirt on you.

My love and treasure,
Where is the woman
From Cork of the white sails
To the bridge of Tomey
With her dowry gathered
And cows at pasture
Would sleep alone
The night they waked you?

(His wife replies.)

My darling, do not believe
One word she is saying,
It is a falsehood
That I slept while others
Sat up to wake you—
'Twas no sleep that took me
But the children crying;
They would not rest
Without me beside them.

O people, do not believe
Any lying story!
There is no woman in Ireland
Who had slept beside him
And borne him three children
But would cry out

After Art O'Leary
Who lies dead before me
Since yesterday morning.

Grief on you, Morris!
Heart's blood and bowels' blood!
May your eyes go blind
And your knees be broken!
You killed my darling
And no man in Ireland
Will fire the shot at you.

Destruction pursue you,
Morris the traitor
Who brought death to my husband!
Father of three children—
Two on the hearth
And one in the womb
That I shall not bring forth.

It is my sorrow
That I was not by
When they fired the shots
To catch them in my dress
Or in my heart, who cares?
If you but reached the hills
Rider of the ready hands.

My love and my fortune
'Tis an evil portion
To lay for a giant—
A shroud and a coffin—
For a big-hearted hero
Who fished in the hill-streams
And drank in bright halls
With white-breasted women.

My comfort and my friend,
Master of the bright sword,
'Tis time you left your sleep;
Yonder hangs your whip,
Your horse is at the door,
Follow the lane to the east
Where every bush will bend
And every stream dry up,
And man and woman bow
If things have manners yet
That have them not I fear.

My love and my sweetness,
'Tis not the death of my people,
Donal Mor O'Connell,
Connell who died by drowning,
Or the girl of six and twenty
Who went across the water
To be a queen's companion—
'Tis not all these I speak of
And call in accents broken
But noble Art O'Leary,
Art of hair so golden,
Art of wit and courage,
Art the brown mare's master,
Swept last night to nothing
Here in Carriganimma—
Perish it, name and people!

My love and my treasure,
Though I bring with me
No throng of mourners,
'Tis no shame for me,
For my kinsmen are wrapped in
A sleep beyond waking,
In narrow coffins
Walled up in stone.

Though but for the smallpox,
And the black death,
And the spotted fever,
That host of riders
With bridles shaking
Would wake the echoes,
Coming to your waking,
Art of the white breast.

Could my calls but wake my kindred
In Derrynane beyond the mountains,
Or Capling of the yellow apples,
Many a proud and stately rider,
Many a girl with spotless kerchief,
Would be here before tomorrow,
Shedding tears about your body,
Art O'Leary, once so merry.

My love and my secret,
Your corn is stacked,
Your cows are milking;
On me is the grief
There's no cure for in Munster.
Till Art O'Leary rise
This grief will never yield
That's bruising all my heart
Yet shut up fast in it,
As 'twere in a locked trunk
With the key gone astray,
And rust grown on the wards.

My love and my calf,
Noble Art O'Leary,
Son of Conor, son of Cady,
Son of Lewis O'Leary,
West of the Valley
And east of Greenane
Where berries grow thickly

And nuts crowd on branches
And apples in heaps fall
In their own season;
What wonder to any
If Iveleary lighted
And Ballingeary
And Gougane of the saints
For the smooth-palmed rider,
The unwearying huntsman
That I would see spurring
From Grenagh without halting
When quick hounds had faltered?
My rider of the bright eyes,
What happened you yesterday?
I thought you in my heart,
When I bought you your fine clothes,
A man the world could not slay.

'Tis known to Jesus Christ
Nor cap upon my head,
Nor shift upon my back
Nor shoe upon my foot,
Nor gear in all my house,
Nor bridle for the mare
But I will spend at law;
And I'll go oversea
To plead before the King,
And if the King be deaf
I'll settle things alone
With the black-blooded rogue
That killed my man on me.

Rider of the white palms,
Go in to Baldwin,
And face the schemer,
The bandy-legged monster—
God rot him and his children!
(Wishing no harm to Maire,

Yet of no love for her,
But that my mother's body
Was a bed to her for three seasons
And to me beside her.)

Take my heart's love,
Dark women of the Mill,
For the sharp rhymes ye shed
On the rider of the brown mare.

But cease your weeping now,
Women of the soft, wet eyes
Till Art O'Leary drink
Ere he go to the dark school—
Not to learn music or song
But to prop the earth and the stone.

The Midnight Court

"The Midnight Court" was doubly important to O'Connor: for Bryan Merryman's slashing wit, and for the official attack on O'Connor's translation—banning it as "indecent or obscene" yet permitting the original to be published without restriction. Brendan Kennelly, poet and scholar, calls O'Connor's translation "vibrant with a kind of visionary bawdiness and uproarious spiritual gusto, perfectly capturing the curious mixture of verbal license and emotional inhibition, of audacity and frustration, that Merryman discovered in eighteenth-century Gaelic Ireland. O'Connor's uncanny insight into the poetry of that time and that society enabled him to bring a remote eighteenth-century poet right into the heart of our times, portraying both the frustration and the ebullience with a vitality of language that Merryman himself would have loved" (Michael/Frank, 103). O'Connor loved the poem for its raucous spirit, its blunt eloquence, yet equally for its theme—Irish loneliness (marriage providing no immunity) as a truth more durable than any illusion of love —which resonated in his own fiction.

O'Connor's comments on the poet and poem are valuable: "Merryman . . . had ideas about what was wrong with Irish poetry and Irish life, and even if one does not share them, one should admire the fierce intellectual energy with which they are expressed. The translation of his long poem is doubly banned in Ireland, and I believe the best authorities hold that it is almost entirely my own work, the one compliment Ireland ever has paid me. Had Merryman been able to write in English—an English with the magnificence of his Irish—his work would probably have been more famous than that of Burns, for I think he was a greater master of language." (Kings, xii–xiii).

I liked to walk in the river meadows
In the thick of the dew and the morning shadows,
At the edge of the woods in a deep defile
At peace with myself in the first sunshine.
When I looked at Lough Graney my heart grew bright,
Ploughed lands and green in the morning light,
Mountains in rows with crimson borders
Peering above their neighbours' shoulders.
The heart that never had known relief
In a lonesome old man distraught with grief,
Without money or home or friends or ease,
Would quicken to glimpse beyond the trees
The ducks sail by on a mistless bay
And a swan before them lead the way;
A speckled trout that in their track
Splashed in the air with arching back;
The grey of the lake and the waves around
That foamed at its edge with a hollow sound.
Birds in the trees sang merry and loud;
A fawn flashed out of the shadowy wood;
The horns rang out with the huntsman's cry
And the belling of hounds while the fox slipped by.

Yesterday morning the sky was clear,
The sun fell hot on river and mere,
Its horses fresh and with gamesome eye
Harnessed again to assail the sky;
The leaves were thick upon every bough
And ferns and grass were thick below,
Sheltering bowers of herbs and flowers
That would comfort a man in his dreariest hours.
Longing for sleep bore down my head,
And in the grass I scooped a bed
With a hollow behind to house my back,
A prop for my head and my limbs stretched slack.
What more could one ask? I covered my face
To avert the flies as I dozed a space,

But my mind in dreams was filled with grief
And I tossed and groaned as I sought relief.

I had only begun when I felt a shock,
And all the landscape seemed to rock;
A north wind made my senses tingle
And thunder crackled along the shingle.
As I looked up—as I thought, awake—
I seemed to see at the edge of the lake
As ugly a brute as man could see
In the shape of woman approaching me;
For, if I calculated right,
She must have been twenty feet in height,
With yards and yards of hairy cloak
Trailing behind her in the muck.
There never was seen such a freak of nature;
Without a single presentable feature;
Her grinning jaws with the fangs stuck out
Would be cause sufficient to start a rout,
And in a hand like a weaver's beam
She raised a staff that it might be seen
She was coming on a legal errand,
For nailed to the staff was a bailiff's warrant.

She cried in a voice with a brassy ring:
"Get up out of that, you lazy thing!
That a man like you could think 'tis fitting
To lie in a ditch while the court is sitting!
A decenter court than e'er you knew,
And far too good for the likes of you.
Justice and Mercy hand in hand
Sit in the courts of Fairyland.
Let Ireland think when her trouble's ended
Of those by whom she was befriended.
In Moy Graney palace twelve days and nights
They've sat discussing your wrongs and rights.
All mourned that follow in his train,
Like the king himself, that in his reign

Such unimaginable disaster
Should follow your people, man and master.
Old stock uprooted on every hand
Without claim to rent or law or land;
Nothing to see in a land defiled
Where the flowers were plucked but the weeds and wild;
The best of your breed in foreign places,
And upstart rogues with impudent faces,
Planning with all their guile and spleen
To pick the bones of the Irish clean.
But worst of all those bad reports
Was that truth was darkened in their courts,
And nothing to back a poor man's case
But whispers, intrigue and the lust for place;
The lawyer's craft and the rich man's might,
Cozening, favour, greed and spite;
Maddened with jobs and bribes and malice,
Anarchy loose on cot and palace.

" 'Twas all discussed, and along with the rest
There were women in scores who came to attest—
A plea that concerns yourself as well—
That the youth of the country's gone to hell,
And men's increase is a sort of crime,
Which only happened within our time;
Nothing but weeds for want of tillage
Since famine and war assailed the village,
And a flighty king and emigration—
And what have you done to restore the nation?
Shame on you without chick nor child
With women in thousands running wild!
The blossoming tree and the young green shoot,
The strap that would sleep with any old root,
The little white saint at the altar rail,
And the proud, cold girl like a ship in sail—
What matter to you if their beauty founder,
If belly and breast will never be rounder,
If, ready and glad to be mother and wife,
They drop unplucked from the boughs of life?

"And having considered all reports,
They agreed that in place of the English courts,
They should select a judge by lot
Who'd hold enquiry on the spot.
Then Eevul, Queen of the Grey Rock,
Who rules all Munster herd and flock,
Arose, and offered to do her share
By putting an end to injustice there.
She took an oath to the council then
To judge the women and the men,
Stand by the poor though all ignore them
And humble the pride of the rich before them;
Make might without right conceal its face
And use her might to give right its place.
Her favour money will not buy,
No lawyer will pull the truth awry,
The smoothest perjurer will not dare
To make a show of falsehood there.
The court is sitting today in Feakle,
So off with you now as quick as you're able!
Come on, I say, and give no back chat,
Or I'll take my stick and knock you flat."
With the crook of her staff she hooked my cape,
And we went at a speed to make Christians gape
Away through the glens in one wild rush
Till we stood in Moinmoy by the ruined church.

Then I saw with an awesome feeling
A building aglow from floor to ceiling,
Lighted within by guttering torches
Among massive walls and echoing arches.
The Queen of the Fairies sat alone
At the end of the hall on a gilded throne,
While keeping back the thronged beholders
Was a great array of guns and soldiers.
I stared at it all, the lighted hall,
Crammed with faces from wall to wall,
And a young woman with downcast eye,
Attractive, good-looking and shy,

With long and sweeping golden locks
Who was standing alone in the witness box.
The cut of her spoke of some disgrace;
I saw misfortune in her face;
Her tearful eyes were red and hot,
And her passions bubbled as in a pot;
But whatever on earth it was provoked her
She was silent, all but the sobs that choked her.
You could see from the way the speaking failed her
She'd sooner death than the thing that ailed her,
But, unable to express her meaning,
She wrung her hands and pursued her grieving
While all we could do was stand and gaze
Till sobs gave place to a broken phrase,
And bit by bit she mastered her sorrows,
And dried her eyes, and spoke as follows—

"Yourself is the woman we're glad to see,
Eevul, Queen of Carriglee,
Our moon at night, our morning light,
Our comfort in the teeth of spite;
Mistress of the host of delight,
Munster and Ireland stand in your sight.
My chief complaint and principal grief,
The thing that gives me no relief,
Sweeps me from harbour in my mind
And blows me like smoke on every wind
Is all the girls whose charms miscarry
Throughout the land and who'll never marry;
Bitter old maids without house or home,
Put on one side through no fault of their own.
I know myself from the things I've seen
Enough and to spare of the sort I mean,
And to give an example, here am I
While the tide is flowing, left high and dry.
Wouldn't you think I must be a fright,
To be shelved before I get started right;
Heartsick, bitter, dour and wan,

Unable to sleep for the want of a man?
But how can I lie in a lukewarm bed
With all the thoughts that come into my head?
Indeed, 'tis time that somebody stated
The way that the women are situated,
For if men go on their path to destruction
There will nothing be left to us but abduction.
Their appetite wakes with age and blindness
When you'd let them cover you only from kindness,
And offer it up for the wrongs you'd done
In hopes of reward in the life to come:
And if one of them weds in the heat of youth
When the first down is on his mouth
It isn't some woman of his own sort,
Well-shaped, well-mannered or well-taught;
Some mettlesome girl who studied behavior,
To sit and stand and amuse a neighbour,
But some pious old prude or dour defamer
Who sweated the couple of pounds that shame her.
There you have it! It has me melted,
And makes me feel that the world's demented:
A county's choice for brains and muscle,
Fond of a lark and not scared of a tussle,
Decent and merry and sober and steady,
Good-looking, gamesome, rakish and ready;
A boy in the blush of his youthful vigour
With a gracious flush and a passable figure
Finds a fortune the best attraction
And sires himself off on some bitter extraction;
Some fretful old maid with her heels in the dung,
Pious airs and venomous tongue,
Vicious and envious, nagging and whining,
Snoozing and snivelling, plotting, contriving—
Hell to her soul, an unmannerly sow
With a pair of bow legs and hair like tow
Went off this morning to the altar
And here am I still without hope of the halter!
Couldn't some man love me as well?

Amn't I plump and sound as a bell?
Lips for kissing and teeth for smiling,
Blossomy skin and forehead shining?
My eyes are blue and my hair is thick
And coils in streams about my neck—
A man who's looking for a wife,
Here's a face that will keep for life!
Hand and arm and neck and breast,
Each is better than the rest.
Look at that waist! My legs are long,
Limber as willows and light and strong.
There's bottom and belly that claim attention,
And the best concealed that I needn't mention.
I'm the sort a natural man desires,
Not a freak or a death-on-wires,
A sloven that comes to life in flashes,
A creature of moods with her heels in the ashes,
Or a sluggard stewing in her own grease,
But a good-looking girl that's bound to please.
If I was as slow as some I know
To stand up for my rights and my dress a show,
Some brainless, illbred, country mope
You could understand if I lost hope;
But ask the first you meet by chance:
Hurling match or race or dance,
Pattern or party, market or fair,
Whatever it was, was I not there?
And didn't I make a good impression
Turning up in the height of fashion?
My hair was washed and combed and powdered,
My coif like snow and stiffly laundered;
I'd a little white hood with ribbons and ruff
On a spotted dress of the finest stuff,
And facings to show off the line
Of a cardinal cloak the colour of wine;
A cambric apron filled with showers
Of fruit and birds and trees and flowers;
Neatly-fitting, expensive shoes

With the highest of heels pegged up with screws;
Silken gloves, and myself in spangles
Of brooches, buckles, rings and bangles.
And you mustn't imagine I was shy,
The sort that slinks with a downcast eye,
Solitary, lonesome, cold and wild,
Like a mountainy girl or an only child.
I tossed my cap at the crowds of the races
And kept my head in the toughest places.
Am I not always on the watch
At bonfire, dance or hurling match,
Or outside the chapel after Mass
To coax a smile from fellows that pass?
But I'm wasting my time on a wildgoose-chase,
And my spirit's broken—and that's my case!
After all my shaping, sulks and passions
All my aping of styles and fashions,
All the times that my cards were spread
And my hands were read and my cup was read;
Every old rhyme, pishrogue and rune,
Crescent, full moon and harvest moon,
Whit and All Souls and the First of May,
I've nothing to show for all they say.
Every night when I went to bed
I'd a stocking of apples beneath my head;
I fasted three canonical hours
To try and come round the heavenly powers;
I washed my shift where the stream was deep
To hear a lover's voice in sleep;
Often I swept the woodstack bare,
Burned bits of my frock, my nails, my hair,
Up the chimney stuck the flail,
Slept with a spade without avail;
Hid my wool in the lime-kiln late
And my distaff behind the churchyard gate;
I had flax on the road to halt coach or carriage
And haycocks stuffed with heads of cabbage,
And night and day on the proper occasions

Invoked Old Nick and all his legions;
But 'twas all no good and I'm broken-hearted
For here I'm back at the place I started;
And this is the cause of all my tears
I am fast in the rope of the rushing years,
With age and need in lessening span,
And death beyond, and no hopes of a man.
But whatever misfortunes God may send
May He spare me at least that lonesome end,
Nor leave me at last to cross alone
Without chick nor child when my looks are gone
As an old maid counting the things I lack
Scowling thresholds that warn me back!
God, by the lightning and the thunder,
The thought of it makes me ripe for murder!
Every idiot in the country
With a man of her own has the right to insult me.
Sal' has a slob with a well-stocked farm,
And Molly goes round on a husband's arm,
There's Min and Margery leaping with glee
And never done with their jokes at me.
And the bounce of Sue! and Kitty and Anne
Have children in droves and a proper man,
And all with their kind can mix and mingle
While I go savage and sour and single.

"Now I know in my heart that I've been too quiet
With a remedy there though I scorned to try it
In the matter of draughts and poisonous weeds
And medicine men and darksome deeds
That I know would fetch me a sweetheart plighted
Who'd love me, whether or not invited.
Oh, I see 'tis the thing that most prevails
And I'll give it a trial if all fruit fails—
A powerful aid to the making of splices
Is powdered herbs on apples in slices.
A girl I know had the neighbours yapping
When she caught the best match in the county napping,

And 'twas she that told me under a vow
That from Shrove to All Souls—and she's married now—
She was eating hay like a horse by the pail
With bog-roots burned and stuped in ale—
I've waited too long and was too resigned,
And nothing you say can change my mind;
I'll give you a chance to help me first
And I'm off after that to do my worst."

2

Then up there jumps from a neighbouring chair
A little old man with a spiteful air,
Staggering legs and panting breath,
And a look in his eye like poison and death;
And this apparition stumps up the hall
And says to the girl in the hearing of all:
"Damnation take you, you bastard's bitch,
Got by a tinkerman under a ditch!
No wonder the seasons are all upsot,
Nor every beating Ireland got;
Decline in decency and manners,
And the cows gone dry and the price of bonhams!
Mavrone! what more can we expect
With Doll and Moll and the way they're decked?
You slut of ill-fame, allow your betters
To tell the court how you learned your letters!
Your seed and breed for all your brag
Were tramps to a man with rag and bag;
I knew your da and what passed for his wife,
And he shouldered his traps to the end of his life,
An aimless lout without friend or neighbour,
Knowledge or niceness, wit or favour:
The breeches he wore were riddled with holes
And his boots without a tack of the soles.
Believe me, friends, if you sold at a fair,
Himself and his wife, his kids and gear,
When the costs were met, by the Holy Martyr,

You'd still go short for a glass of porter.
But the devil's child has the devil's cheek—
You that never owned cow nor sheep,
With buckles and brogues and rings to order—
You that were reared in the reek of solder!
However the rest of the world is gypped
I knew you when you went half-stripped;
And I'd venture a guess that in what you lack
A shift would still astonish your back;
And, shy as you seem, an inquisitive gent
Might study the same with your full consent.
Bosom and back are tightly laced,
Or is it the stays that gives you the waist?
Oh, all can see the way you shine,
But your looks are no concern of mine.
Now tell us the truth and don't be shy
How long are you eating your dinner dry?
A meal of spuds without butter or milk,
And dirt in layers beneath the silk.
Bragging and gab are yours by right,
But I know too where you sleep at night,
And blanket or quilt you never saw
But a strip of old mat and a bundle of straw,
In a hovel of mud without a seat,
And slime that settles about your feet,
A carpet of weeds from door to wall
And hens inscribing their tracks on all;
The rafters in with a broken back
And brown rain lashing through every crack
'Twas there you learned to look so nice,—
But now may we ask how you came by the price?
We all admired the way you spoke,
But whisper, treasure, who paid for the cloak?
A sparrow with you would die of hunger—
How did you come by all the grandeur,
All the tassels and all the lace—
Would you have us believe they were got in grace?
The frock made a hole in somebody's pocket,

And it wasn't you that paid for the jacket;
But assuming that and the rest no news,
How the hell did you come by the shoes?

"Your worship, 'tis women's sinful pride
And that alone has the world destroyed.
Every young man that's ripe for marriage
Is hooked like this by some tricky baggage,
And no one is secure, for a friend of my own,
As nice a boy as ever I've known
That lives from me only a perch or two—
God help him!—married misfortune too.
It breaks my heart when she passes by
With her saucy looks and head held high,
Cows to pasture and fields of wheat,
And money to spare—and all deceit!
Well-fitted to rear a tinker's clan,
She waggles her hips at every man,
With her brazen face and bullock's hide,
And such airs and graces, and mad with pride.
And—that God may judge me!—only I hate
A scandalous tongue, I could relate
Things of that woman's previous state
As one with whom every man could mate
In any convenient field or gate
As the chance might come to him early or late!
But now, of course, we must all forget
Her galloping days and the pace she set;
The race she ran in Ibrackane,
In Manishmore and Teermaclane,
With young and old of the meanest rabble
Of Ennis, Clareabbey and Quin astraddle!
Toughs from Tradree out on a fling,
And Cratlee cutthroats sure to swing;
But still I'd say 'twas the neighbours' spite,
And the girl did nothing but what was right,
But the devil take her and all she showed!
I found her myself on the public road,

On the naked earth with a bare backside
And a Garus turf-cutter astride!
Is it any wonder my heart is failing,
That I feel that the end of the world is nearing,
When, ploughed and sown to all men's knowledge,
She can manage the child to arrive with marriage,
And even then, put to the pinch,
Begrudges Charity an inch;
For, counting from the final prayer
With the candles quenched and the altar bare
To the day when her offspring takes the air
Is a full nine months with a week to spare?

"But you see the troubles a man takes on!
From the minute he marries his peace is gone;
Forever in fear of a neighbour's sneer—
And my own experience cost me dear.
I lived alone as happy as Larry
Till I took it into my head to marry,
Tilling my fields with an easy mind,
Going wherever I felt inclined,
Welcomed by all as a man of price,
Always ready with good advice.
The neighbours listened—they couldn't refuse
For I'd money and stock to uphold my views—
Everything came at my beck and call
Till a woman appeared and destroyed it all:
A beautiful girl with ripening bosom,
Cheeks as bright as apple-blossom,
Hair that glimmered and foamed in the wind,
And a face that blazed with the light behind;
A tinkling laugh and a modest carriage
And a twinkling eye that was ripe for marriage.
I goggled and gaped like one born mindless
Till I took her face for a form of kindness,
Though that wasn't quite what the Lord intended
For He marked me down like a man offended
For a vengeance that wouldn't be easy mended
With my folly exposed and my comfort ended.

"Not to detain you here all day
I married the girl without more delay,
And took my share in the fun that followed.
There was plenty for all and nothing borrowed.
Be fair to me now! There was no one slighted;
The beggarmen took the road delighted;
The clerk and mummers were elated;
The priest went home with his pocket weighted.
The lamps were lit, the guests arrived;
The supper was ready, the drink was plied;
The fiddles were flayed, and, the night advancing,
The neighbours joined in the sport and dancing.

"A pity to God I didn't smother
When first I took the milk from my mother,
Or any day I ever broke bread
Before I brought that woman to bed!
For though everyone talked of her carouses
As a scratching post of the publichouses
That as sure as ever the glasses would jingle
Flattened herself to married and single,
Admitting no modesty to mention,
I never believed but 'twas all invention.
They added, in view of the life she led,
I might take to the roads and beg my bread,
But I took it for talk and hardly minded—
Sure, a man like me could never be blinded!—
And I smiled and nodded and off I tripped
Till my wedding night when I saw her stripped,
And knew too late that this was no libel
Spread in the pub by some jealous rival—
By God, 'twas a fact, and well-supported:
I was a father before I started!

"So there I was in the cold daylight,
A family man after one short night!
The women around me, scolding, preaching,
The wife in bed and the baby screeching.
I stirred the milk as the kettle boiled

Making a bottle to give the child;
All the old hags at the hob were cooing
As if they believed it was all my doing—
Flattery worse than ever you heard:
'Glory and praise to our blessed Lord,
Though he came in a hurry, the poor little creature,
He's the spit of his da in every feature.
Sal, will you look at the cut of that lip!
There's fingers for you! Feel his grip!
Would you measure the legs and the rolls of fat!
Was there ever a seven month child like that?'
And they traced away with great preciseness
My matchless face in the baby's likeness;
The same snub nose and frolicsome air,
And the way I laugh and the way I stare;
And they swore that never from head to toe
Was a child that resembled his father so.
But they wouldn't let me go near the wonder—
'Sure, a draught would blow the poor child asunder!'
All of them out to blind me further—
'The least little breath would be noonday murder!'
Malice and lies! So I took the floor,
Mad with rage and I cursed and swore,
And bade them all to leave my sight.
They shrank away with faces white,
And moaned as they handed me the baby:
'Don't crush him now! Can't you handle him easy?
The least thing hurts them. Treat him kindly!
Some fall she got brought it on untimely.
Don't lift his head but leave him lying!
Poor innocent scrap, and to think he's dying!
If he lives at all till the end of day
Till the priest can come 'tis the most we'll pray!'

"I off with the rags and set him free,
And studied him well as he lay on my knee.
That too, by God, was nothing but lies
For he staggered myself with his kicks and cries.

A pair of shoulders like my own,
Legs like sausages, hair fullgrown;
His ears stuck out and his nails were long,
His hands and wrists and elbows strong;
His eyes were bright, his nostrils wide,
And the knee-caps showing beneath his hide—
A champion, begod, a powerful whelp,
As healthy and hearty as myself!

"Young woman, I've made my case entire.
Justice is all that I require.
Once consider the terrible life
We lead from the minute we take a wife,
And you'll find and see that marriage must stop
And the men unmarried must be let off.
And, child of grace, don't think of the race;
Plenty will follow to take our place;
There are ways and means to make lovers agree
Without making a show of men like me.
There's no excuse for all the exploiters;
Cornerboys, clerks and priests and pipers—
Idle fellows that leave you broke
With the jars of malt and the beer they soak,
When the Mother of God herself could breed
Without asking the views of clerk or creed.
Healthy and happy, wholesome and sound,
The come-by-twilight sort abound;
No one assumes but their lungs are ample,
And their hearts as sound as the best example.
When did Nature display unkindness
To the bastard child in disease or blindness?
Are they not handsomer, better-bred
Than many that come of a lawful bed?

"I needn't go far to look for proof
For I've one of the sort beneath my roof—
Let him come here for all to view!
Look at him now! You see 'tis true.

Agreed, we don't know his father's name,
But his mother admires him just the same,
And if in all things else he shines
Who cares for his baptismal lines?
He isn't a dwarf or an old man's error,
A paralytic or walking terror,
He isn't a hunchback or a cripple
But a lightsome, laughing gay young divil.
'Tis easy to see he's no flash in the pan;
No sleepy, good-natured, respectable man,
Without sinew or bone or belly or bust,
Or venom or vice or love or lust,
Buckled and braced in every limb
Spouted the seed that flowered in him:
For back and leg and chest and height
Prove him to all in the teeth of spite
A child begotten in fear and wonder
In the blood's millrace and the body's thunder.

"Down with marriage! It's out of date;
It exhausts the stock and cripples the state.
The priest has failed with whip and blinker
Now give a chance to Tom the Tinker,
And mix and mash in Nature's can
The tinker and the gentleman!
Let lovers in every lane extended
Struggle and strain as God intended
And locked in frenzy bring to birth
The morning glory of the earth;
The starry litter, girl and boy
Who'll see the world once more with joy.
Clouds will break and skies will brighten,
Mountains bloom and spirits lighten,
And men and women praise your might,
You who restore the old delight."

3

The girl had listened without dissembling,
Then up she started, hot and trembling,
And answered him with eyes alight
And a voice that shook with squalls of spite:
"By the Crown of the Rock, I thought in time
Of your age and folly and known decline,
And the manners I owe to people and place
Or I'd dye my nails in your ugly face;
Scatter your guts and tan your hide
And ferry your soul to the other side.
I'd honour you much if I gave the lie
To an impudent speech that needs no reply;
'Tis enough if I tell the sort of life
You led your unfortunate, decent wife.

"This girl was poor, she hadn't a home,
Or a single thing she could call her own,
Drifting about in the saddest of lives,
Doing odd jobs for other men's wives,
As if for drudgery created,
Begging a crust from women she hated.
He pretended her troubles were over;
Married to him she'd live in clover;
The cows she milked would be her own,
The feather bed and the decent home,
The stack of turf, the lamp to light,
The good earth wall of a winter's night,
Flax and wool to weave and wind,
The womanly things for which she pined.
Even his friends could not have said
That his looks were such that she lost her head.
How else would he come by such a wife
But that ease was the alms she asked of life?
What possible use could she have at night
For dourness, dropsy, bother and blight,
A basket of bones with thighs of lead,

Knees absconded from the dead,
Fire-speckled shanks and temples whitening,
Looking like one that was struck by lightning?
Is there living a girl who could grow fat
Tied to a travelling corpse like that
Who twice a year wouldn't find a wish
To see what was she, flesh or fish
But draggd the clothes about his head
Like a wintry wind to a woman in bed?

"Now was it too much to expect as right
A little attention once a night?
From all I know she was never accounted
A woman too modest to be mounted.
Gentle, good-humoured and Godfearing
Why should we think she'd deny her rearing?
Whatever the lengths his fancy ran
She wouldn't take fright from a mettlesome man,
And would sooner a boy would be aged a score
Than himself on the job for a week or more;
And an allnight dance or Mass at morning,
Fiddle or flute or choir or organ,
She'd sooner the tune that boy would play
As midnight struck or at break of day.
Damn it, you know we're all the same,
A woman nine months in terror and pain,
The minute that Death has lost the game—
Good morrow my love, and she's off again!
And how could one who longed to please
Feel with a fellow who'd sooner freeze
Than warm himself in a natural way
From All Souls Night to St. Brigid's day?
You'd all agree 'twas a terrible fate—
Sixty winters on his pate,
A starved old gelding, blind and lamed
And a twenty year old with her parts untamed.
It wasn't her fault if things went wrong,
She closed her eyes and held her tongue;

She was no ignorant girl from school
To whine for her mother and play the fool
But a competent bedmate smooth and warm
Who cushioned him like a sheaf of corn.
Line by line she bade him linger
With gummy lips and groping finger,
Gripping his thighs in a wild embrace
Rubbing her brush from knee to waist
Stripping him bare to the cold night air,
Everything done with love and care.
But she'd nothing to show for all her labour;
There wasn't a jump in the old deceiver,
And all I could say would give no notion
Of that poor distracted girl's emotion,
Her knees cocked up and the bedposts shaking,
Chattering teeth and sinews aching,
While she sobbed and tossed through a joyless night
And gave it up with the morning light.

"I think you'll agree from the little I've said
A man like this must be off his head
To live like a monk to the end of his life
Muddle his marriage and blame his wife.
The talk about women comes well from him,
Without hope in body or help in limb;
If the creature that found him such a sell
Has a lover today she deserves him well:
A benefit Nature never denies
To anything born that swims or flies;
Tell me of one that ever went empty
And died of want in the midst of plenty.
In all the wonders west and east
Where will you hear of a breed of beast
That will turn away from fern and hay
To feed on briars and roots and clay?
You silly old fool, you can't reply
And give us at least one reason why
If your supper is there when you come back late

You've such talk of someone that used the plate.
Will it lessen your store, will you sigh for more
If twenty millions cleaned it before?
You must think that women are all like you
To believe they'll go dry for a man or two;
You might as well drink the ocean up
Or empty the Shannon with a cup.
Ah, you must see that you're half insane;
Try cold compresses, avoid all strain,
And stop complaining about the neighbours,
If every one of them owed her favours,
Men by the hundred beneath her shawl
Would take nothing from you in the heel of all.

"If your jealousy even was based on fact
In some hardy young whelp that could keep her packed;
Covetous, quarrelsome, keen on scoring,
Or some hairy old villain hardened with whoring;
A vigorous pusher, a rank outsider,
A jockey of note or a gentleman rider—
But a man disposed in the wrong direction
With a poor mouth shown on a sham erection!

"But oye, my heart will grow grey hairs
Brooding forever on idle cares,
Has the Catholic Church a glimmer of sense
That the priests won't come to the girls' defense?
Is it any wonder the way I moan,
Out of my mind for a man of my own
While there's men around can afford one well
But shun a girl as they shun Hell.
The full of a fair of primest beef,
Warranted to afford relief;
Cherry-red cheeks and bull-like voices
And bellies dripping with fat in slices;
Backs erect and huge hind-quarters,
Hot-blooded men, the best of partners,
Freshness and charm, youth and good looks
And nothing to ease their mind but books!

The best-fed men that travel the country,
With beef and mutton, game and poultry,
Whiskey and wine forever in stock,
Sides of bacon and beds of flock.
Mostly they're hardy under the hood,
And we know like ourselves they're flesh and blood.
I wouldn't ask much of the old campaigners,
Good-for-nothings and born complainers
But petticoat-tossers aloof and idle
And fillies gone wild for bit and bridle!

"Of course I admit that some, more sprightly,
Would like to repent, and I'd treat them lightly.
A pardon and a job for life
To every priest that takes a wife!
For many a good man's chance miscarries
If you scuttle the ship for the crooks it carries;
And though some as we know were always savage,
Gnashing their teeth at the thought of marriage,
And, modest beyond the needs of merit,
Invoked hell-fire on girls of spirit,
Yet some who took to their pastoral labours
Made very good priests and the best of neighbours.
Many a girl filled byre and stall
And furnished her house through a clerical call.
Everyone's heard some priest extolled
For the lonesome women that he consoled;
People I've known throughout the county
Have nothing but praise for the curate's bounty,
Or uphold the canon to lasting fame
For the children he reared in another man's name;
But I hate to think of their lonely lives,
The passions they waste on middle-aged wives
While the girls they'd choose if the choice was theirs
Go by the wall and comb grey hairs.

"I leave it to you, O Nut of Knowledge,
The girls at home and the boys in college,
You cannot persuade me it's a crime

If they make love while they still have time,
But you who for learning have no rival,
Tell us the teachings of the Bible;
Where are we taught to pervert our senses
And make our natural needs offences?
To fly from lust as in Saint Paul
Doesn't mean flight from life and all,
But to leave home and friends behind
And stick to one who pleased one's mind.
But I'm at it again! I'll keep my place;
It isn't for me to judge the case,
When you, a spirit born and queen
Remember the texts and what they mean,
With apt quotations well-supplied
From the prophets who took the woman's side,
And the words of Christ that were never belied
Who chose for His Mother an earthly bride.

"But oye, what use are pishrogue and spell
To one like myself in the fires of Hell?
What chance can there be for girls like me
With husbands for only one in three?
When there's famine abroad the need advises
To look after yourself as chance arises,
And since crops are thin and weeds are plenty,
And the young without heart and Ireland empty,
And to fill it again is a hopeless job,
Get me some old fellow to sit by the hob;
Tie him down there as best you can—
And leave it to me to make him a man."

4

The day crept in and the lights grew pale,
The girl sat down as she ended her tale;
The princess rose with face aglow
And her voice when she spoke was grave and slow.
"Oyez!" said the clerk to quell the riot,

And wielded his mace till all were quiet,
Then from her lips as we sat hushed
Speech like a rainbow glory gushed.
"My child," she said, "I will not deny
That you've reason enough to scold and cry,
And, as a woman, I can't but grieve
To see girls like you, and Moll and Maeve,
With your dues diminished and favours gone,
And none to enjoy a likely man
But misers sucking a lonely bone
Or hairy old harpies living alone.
I do enact according then
That all the present unmarried men
Shall be arrested by the guard,
Detained inside the chapel yard
And stripped and tied beside the gate
Until you decide upon their fate.
Those that you find whom the years have thwarted
With masculine parts that were never exerted
To the palpable loss of some woman's employment,
The thrill of the milk and their own enjoyment;
Who, having the chance of wife and home
Went wild and took to the hills to roam,
Are only a burden on the earth
So give it to them for all you're worth.
Roast or pickle them, some reflection
Will frame a suitable correction,
But this you can choose at your own tribunal,
And whatever you do will have my approval.
Fully grown men too old to function
As I say you can punish without compunction;
Nothing you do can have consequences
For middle-aged men with failing senses,
And, whatever is lost or whatever survives,
We need never suppose will affect their wives—
Young men, of course, are another affair;
They still are of use, so strike with care!

"There are poor men working in rain and sleet,
Out of their minds with the troubles they meet,
But, men in name and in deed according,
They quarry their women at night and morning—
A fine traditional consolation!—
And these I would keep in circulation.
In the matter of priests a change is due,
And I think I may say it's coming, too.
Any day now it may be revealed
That the cardinals have it signed and sealed,
And we'll hear no more of the ban on marriage
Before the priests go entirely savage.
Then the cry of the blood in the body's fire
You can quicken or quell to your heart's desire,
But anyone else of woman born,
Flay him alive if he won't reform!
Abolish wherever my judgment reaches
The nancy boy and the flapper in breeches,
And when their rule is utterly ended
We can see the world that the Lord intended.

"The rest of the work must only wait.
I'm due elsewhere and already late;
I've business afoot that I must attend
Though you and I are far from the end,
For I'll sit next month and God help the men
If they haven't improved their ways by then!
But mostly those who sin from pride
With women whose names they do not hide,
Who keep their tally of ruined lives
In whispers, nudges, winks and gibes.
Was ever vanity more misplaced
Than in married women and girls disgraced?
It isn't desire that gives the thrust,
The smoking blood and the ache of lust,
Weakness of love and the body's blindness
But to punish the fools who show them kindness.
Thousands are born without a name

That braggarts may boast of their mothers' shame—
Men lost to Nature through conceit,
And their manhood killed by their own deceit,
For 'tis sure that however their wives may weep
It's never because they go short of sleep."

I'd listened to every word she uttered,
And then as she stopped my midriff fluttered;
I was took with a sort of sudden reeling
Till my feet seemed resting on the ceiling;
People and place went round and round,
And her words came back as a blur of sound.
Then the bailiff strode along the aisle
And reached for me with an ugly smile;
She nipped my ear as if in sport
And dragged me up before the court.
Then the girl who'd complained of how she was slighted,
Spotted my face and sprang up, excited.
"Is it you?" says she. "Of all the old crocks!
I'm waiting for years to comb your locks.
You had your chance and you missed your shot,
And devil's cure to you now you're caught!
Will anyone here speak in your favour
Or even think you worth the labour?
What little affair would you care to mention
Or what girl did you honour with your attention?
We'll all agree that the man's no beauty,
But, damn it, he's clearly fit for duty.
I know, he's ill-made and ugly as hell,
But he'd match some poor misfortunate well.
I'd sooner him pale and not quite so fat,
But the hump's no harm; I'd make nothing of that
For it isn't a thing you'd notice much
Or one that goes with the puritan touch.
You'll find bandy legs on men of vigour
And arms like pegs on a frolicsome figure.
Of course there must be some shameful reason
That kept him single out of season.

He's welcome at the country houses,
And at the villagers' carouses,
Called in wherever the fun is going,
And fiddles being tuned and whiskey flowing—
I'll never believe there's truth in a name:
A wonder the Merrymans stand the shame!
The doggedest devil that tramps the hill
With grey in his hair and a virgin still!
Leave me alone to settle the savage!
You can spare your breath to cool your porridge!
The truth of it's plain upon your forehead;
You're thirty at least and still unmarried!
Listen to me, O Fount of Luck,
This fellow's the worst that ever I struck.
All the spite I have locked inside
Won't let me at peace till I've tanned his hide.
Can't ye all help me? Catch him! Mind him!
Winnie, girl, run and get ropes to bind him!
Where are you, Annie, or are you blind?
Sally, tie up his hands behind!
Molly and Maeve, you fools what ails you?
Isn't it soon the courage fails you?
Hand me the rope till I give him a crack;
I'll earth it up in the small of his back.
That, young man, is the place to hurt you;
I'll teach you to respect your virtue!
Steady now, till we give him a sample!
Women alive, he's a grand example!
Set to it now and we'll nourish him well!
One good clout and ye'll hear him yell!
Tan him the more the more he'll yell
Till we teach his friends good manners as well.
And as this is the law to restore the nation
We'll write the date as a great occasion—
'The First of January, Seventeen Eighty——' "

And while I stood there, stripped and crazy,
Knowing that nothing could save my skin,

She opened her book, immersed her pen,
And wrote it down with careful art,
As the girls all sighed for the fun to start.
And then I shivered and gave a shake,
Opened my eyes, and was wide awake.

Self-portraits

Only Child

This October 11, 1950, broadcast can only hint at the magic of O'Connor's memoirs. It is characteristically serious and witty, revealing much about himself and what his experience suggests of ours. Readers heartened by his insight and openness will find the first volume of his autobiography, An Only Child, *unforgettable in itself, and it provides another perspective on his fiction, because similarities between O'Connor as a child and "Larry Delaney" and other precocious boys of his stories are not accidental. The new teacher mentioned here is Daniel Corkery (1878–1964), O'Connor's early mentor, a poet, novelist, short story writer, and literary critic* (The Threshold of Quiet, The Hidden Ireland)*.*

I believe statistics have proved that genius occurs most frequently in younger sons of large families. That may be, but I'm sure the *conviction* of genius occurs mainly among only children. They have no brothers and sisters to shake it. In fact, so rooted is their conviction that it rarely occurs to them that they are geniuses at all. They merely know, as geniuses do, that they are unique and irreplaceable, and take up the occupation for want of anything better to do.

That's one of the troubles of being an only child; it's not pleasant, particularly on wet days. We lived near the barrack in Cork, next door to my grandmother who washed for the officers. She was an old country-woman who never wore boots indoors and lived mainly on potatoes and porter. Socially she was a sore trial to me. My father, who had been a soldier, was worse, because he diverted so much of my mother's attention. I was the victim of what Freud calls an Oedipus complex—a shocking misnomer because Oedipus must have been the only only child who never suffered from that complaint. There is no evidence whatever that Oedipus wanted to kill his father and marry his mother. I did. I shouldn't have much minded getting rid of my grandmother at the same time.

I can't remember a time when as an escape from these domestic trials I hadn't books, paints and a private theatre. The theatre was usually a bootbox with a proscenium arch cut in one end, and my company of actors were cut from illustrations in books, mounted on pasteboard and stuck in sticks. Apart from the Passion Play at Oberammergau I had no playbooks, and my plays tended to be of the composite type with Prince Charlie and Buffalo Bill as contemporaries. In those days I devoted less attention than I should now on dramatic construction or even acting; my main interests were in decor and lighting. Like many entrepreneurs my real difficulty was to find plays worthy of my art. Coloured paper well greased made wonderful filters. Never again have I seen in any theatre moonlit woodlands with solitary cottage windows aglow that equalled mine. I particularly liked producing grand opera because it gave scope to my skill as a singer as well. The experiments led to trouble in the home; the greased paper blazed and my theatres went up with the regularity of mediaeval towns, but with mediaeval pertinacity I went on.

Books were a trial too. With my pocket money I could buy only a 'Gem' or at most a 'Gem' and a 'Scout,' and even eked out by judicious swapping these were not enough. The Carnegie Library was right at the other side of the town, on the quay beyond the second branch of the river, and I tramped there almost every second day. In the reading room you could get the 'Boy's Own Paper,' a most superior magazine with illustrations in half tone—as an artist myself, I had a poor opinion of line drawings. It was in the days before open access, and unless you could nab a good book on the counter, just as it was brought back, you had to choose from the catalogue. Library catalogues—I've *never* made them myself—are an invention of the devil. A title that suggested Rockies or Himalayas proved to be a pious tract, and back I tramped over the two bridges in the dusk with death in my heart. I couldn't change it until next day at the earliest, and for some reason I was afraid of changing a book the day after for fear one of the assistants would think I wasn't able to read and cancel my ticket. I don't know if there was any basis for this fear other than the fact that I was kept rigorously law-abiding by endlessly trying and sentencing myself for imaginary crimes. I don't think I ever pinched an illustration from a library book, though I was often sorely tempted for the sake of the theatre. Usually, I confined myself to tracing.

You see, if only children escape one sort of crisis by retreating into fantasy, it's only to find another one waiting them inside. For instance, I was convinced that the authors of the books I read were all realists like myself. Their characters protected the weak, endured endless suffering rather than betray a companion, and always told the truth. Could the authors do less? Could their books contain falsehoods? As the fellows in the school where I went told lies, beat up smaller boys and put the blame on someone else, they were obviously no class. Once, a teacher gave the leather to a chap I'd been fighting with and told him to slap me. Would Tom Merry stand for punishment from a bounder? Would even a bounder take the leather to Tom Merry? I made it plain that I'd die rather than be licked in that ignoble manner, and of course, I only got licked worse and was regarded as a fool for my pains. That was what always happened when I stood on principle.

The second crisis was more serious. These were the good old days of the Liberal Alliance, and the atmosphere we grew up in might have been that of any small Scotch town of the time. But when I was eight or nine a new teacher came. He took down the grimy educational prints from the schoolroom wall and hung up two watercolours of his own. As a bit of an artist myself, I felt I was going to like him. He stopped us singing 'When through life unblest we rove' and made us sing instead 'Breathes there a man with soul so dead,' a change I disliked, because I loved sentimental songs, the dolefuller the better. Then one day he kept us in after school, wrote something on the blackboard in an unfamiliar script, and gave us our first lesson in an unfamiliar language. I noticed that he refrained from translating the words on the blackboard, so being a studious sort of chap I went afterwards and asked him what they meant. After a moment's hesitation he said 'Waken your courage, Ireland.' I thought this most peculiar. I thought it more peculiar still when I went home and discovered that the strange language was spoken by my grandmother, the washer-woman. In fact, what was taught in secrecy, almost, after school hours, was Gaelic, 'Breathes there a man with soul so dead' was a disguised appeal to our patriotic sentiments (very disguised so far as I was concerned), and the words which the teacher hadn't translated were probably an exhortation to himself. That was my introduction to the Irish Renaissance, so called.

Still, I was glad I hadn't murdered my grandmother, because she now enabled me to take the head of the class. The new teacher gave me books. He hadn't it seemed heard of E. S. Ellis or Gunby Hadath, but he gave me books about Irish heroes like Cu Chulainn and Finn McCool. I saw that Cu Chulainn and I had a great deal in common. At the age of six he set out from home to the royal palace with a dart, a hurley stick and a ball. He threw the dart, pucked the ball, tossed the stick after them and caught all three before they reached the ground. I practised that single simple trick endlessly but never succeeded in catching even the dart. Naturally, it never struck me that any more than Frank Richards or Gunby Hadath, wasn't the author telling the truth. I put it down to a general decline in vigour and felt I had to do something about it.

Then came the 1914 war, and my father and uncle were back in the army, and I followed our army on a map. I was at a new school with a lot of Belgian refugees. I forgot Cu Chulainn, I forgot my Gaelic; all my time was taken up learning Flemish from the Belgian lads. And after that came the Easter Rebellion, and Cu Chulainn and Gaelic came back, and I didn't even understand how I could have been so heartless as to desert them. At the same time I saw in a shop window a book with my old teacher's name on it. It cost a shilling—a small fortune!—but I was in a fever until I got it. It turned out to be a book of short stories, not, of course up to the standard of E. S. Ellis or Gunby Hadath—in fact, most of them I couldn't make head or tail of—but a trifle of incomprehension has never worried me when I felt really enthusiastic. That book sunk me. Between Tom Merry, Cu Chulainn, the theatre and short stories, the course of my life had already been mapped out, and never since have I been for long out of hot water.

That's the major drawback of being an only child. 'Just when we're safest' as Browning says, but it isn't a 'sunset touch or a chorus ending from Euripides,' it's Tom Merry, Buffalo Bill, Bonnie Prince Charlie or Cu Chulainn, and all at once you begin to behave in a way that drives the children of large families wild. Their invisible playmates, their extemporised playthings, if they ever had any, have long been banished by the mockery of brothers and sisters. They assume you are behaving like that to please some audience other than themselves—a galling thought. They assume that you're not doing it for nothing—'three thousand a year or more' is the last figure I heard quoted for myself,—and they hate it. They make it hot for you. Ah, yes, the way of the only child is hard, especially in Ireland. Ireland is *full* of large families.

The Writer and the Welfare State

THE WELFARE STATE AND I

This September 1960 talk, given in Copenhagen, seems to return to the territory of "Only Child," but its darker tone and purpose are quickly evident. Here O'Connor moves from a somber depiction of the misery, poverty, and repression of his childhood environment to incisive political observations. His references to Eisenhower and Russia are no longer current, but his concerns are still relevant.

When I was asked to speak at this Conference I sat down and with great labour wrote a paper which I hoped might interest my audience. I tried to explain what I thought was the true purpose of the Welfare State. I analysed its relation to the Industrial Revolution and tried to give an answer to the gigantic problem that is now facing Russia and is threatening to isolate her from her ally, China—the problem of whether in fact you can create the potentiality of wealth without distributing it. In fact, I tried to do what every writer today must be attempting to do —to define what is wrong with our world. And then I realised that this was not the way I thought at all. I am a writer and I can think only in experiences. Yeats was correct. "We have no gift to set a statesman right." We have, of course, but only when we are not trying to exercise it. Finally, I tore up what I had written and sat down to write something quite different, something about myself.

.   .   .

In the autobiography which is being published next Spring I have recounted the facts of my life up to the age of twenty. I grew up in Cork, a small city, in Ireland, a small country—a Catholic country too I must

283

add for that has a lot to do with the story. My mother was an orphan. Her father died when she was about four, and my grandmother and her four children were thrown out on the roadside before their little cabin because they could not pay the rent. My mother, my aunt and my uncle were put into orphanages; the youngest child, a baby of a few months old, was taken in by neighbours and disappeared—disappeared forever as far as her brother and sisters were concerned. Under the strain my grandmother went mad, and after her release from the lunatic Asylum, went to the workhouse to die. My aunt died soon after in the orphanage, and my mother was sent out as an unpaid maid to various lodging houses where she was half starved, overworked, and in one house at least, treated with great cruelty. When she was about thirty-five she married my father, a labouring man who indulged in long, wild bouts of drinking. I was their only child. Those were the very early days of Irish trade nationalism, and I remember the statement by the head of the Dublin Employers that any man should be able to bring up a family on twelve shillings a week. I don't suppose my father earned much more than that, and my mother had to work as a charwoman to eke out his wages. For part of the time, when my father was drinking, we had no other means, and I lived largely on the scraps she was permitted to take from houses where she worked. She was never strong; she suffered all her life from migraines and chronic appendicitis, but she could not afford to be seriously ill. If she became seriously ill, I starved; that was all there was to it. There was a rudimentary health service. When she was ill I had to go to a Poor Law Guardian—a member of the local welfare service—who was also the undertaker—and he gave me a red ticket which entitled us to a visit from the doctor and to free medicine. The medicine I suspect was of a very simple kind for we knew it only in three forms—the pink bottle, the yellow bottle and the black bottle. If she had ever become really ill she would have had to go to the workhouse hospital, the hospital attached to the paupers' home, where my grandmother had died, and poor people dreaded this terrible place, which was like something out of Dickens. There was, of course, no provision whatever for dental service. If one got a toothache, one pulled out the tooth oneself. Only once was my mother able to afford to send me to a dentist, and then it had to be an extraction without anaesthetic, which would have cost her too much. Only the wealthy could have their teeth filled. As a result we all lost our teeth early, and a number of the people among whom I grew up were never able to afford dentures and ate with their gums, dipping every morsel of bread into the tea.

.   .   .

My mother was a woman of quite unusual character and refinement, and she did not wish me to stay in the gutter to which life had condemned her, but it wasn't easy to get out of. The state, which had provided for our health had provided, in much the same way for our education. I attended the state school where the children, particularly the poorer ones, were savagely beaten and flogged, and I didn't learn anything there. For a while I attended the Christian Brothers school where the children were beaten almost as much, and I didn't learn anything there either. The monks decided that I was too stupid to take the ordinary state examinations, and put me into what was called the Trades School, though they didn't teach me any trade. I don't think I was an abnormally slow or stupid child, and I desperately wanted to learn. For a few months I had as teacher a poet and novelist called Daniel Corkery, and I must have been a fairly apt pupil because at the end of the term he gave me a special prize, the only prize I ever won. He taught me my first words of Irish, and when I went home and repeated this it turned out that my grandmother's language was Irish. My grandmother was illiterate but she knew thousands of lines of poetry by heart, and when she was dying she consoled herself by reciting poetry. I remember the beginning of one of the poems which had been written by a neighbour of hers, a woman whose son had joined the English Army. The poor woman considered this a great disgrace and called in the neighbours exactly as though he were dead, and then recited the elegy she had composed for him. It is interesting to hear poetry discussed as though it were a great mystery. I have known scores of the old people who would be astonished to hear that the emotions had any language other than poetry.

.   .   .

When I was about twelve or thirteen I realised that I was never going to learn anything, so I left school to look for work as a messenger boy. Meanwhile, I tried to educate myself as best I could. My education was mostly conducted through the public library, an institution that strikes me now as probably having been as valuable as the state school. There was a card catalogue and what was called an Indicator; a big glass case with thousands of little numbers shown on it in red or blue. If the number of your book was in blue it was available, and then you wrote out a slip and got it. After that, you couldn't change it until the following day. If you were clever at judging the quality of books by their titles you might get something you could read; if you guessed wrong, as I so often did, you tramped home, realising that you had had a four mile walk for nothing.

.   .   .

All the light I had on education was from the stories of an Irish priest called Canon Sheehan, and from these I gathered that German was the great language of culture and Goethe the most cultured person, so I set out to learn German and read all Goethe through in English in the hope of becoming cultured too. The trouble with German, and with other languages I felt I should know, was that I did not understand the simplest grammatical term. I was close on twenty and in an internment camp for political prisoners when one day, glancing through a German grammar, I suddenly realised exactly what the dative and accusative cases meant. It was a great day in my life because for the first time I felt I had an objective basis for something that previously had been little better than day-dreaming. When I came out of prison I became a librarian, which was at that particular moment the one job I could get without paper qualifications. Things have improved enormously since then, and now I doubt if you could get a position as librarian without a degree and a library diploma, certifying that you are qualified to prevent anybody's making practical use of your library. When I had a children's library of my own I tried to make it as different as possible from the sort of library I had known. We had gramophone concerts, talks on pictures, on folk-lore and history; we had competitions in poetry and painting, and the police had to control the mobs of children who wanted to join in. The thing was a success, so the authorities decided to apply it generally. Its management was handed over to a language organisation, and each week a paid lecturer was sent out from a central post to talk to the children in a language they didn't know—Irish. I have never forgotten one evening when the children laughed without stopping for minutes until the lecturer sat down in confusion. They knew as I did that he hadn't come to talk to them. They had ceased to be children and become an institution. That evening taught me one thing; that welfare schemes are all very well, but they are only as good as the people who operate them.

. . .

It certainly doesn't mean they are misconceived. I am recounting these particulars of my own life not because I think them significant but because they are facts, and theories interest me only in so far as they apply to facts. You can look at these facts in various ways. You may say as Mr. Eisenhower seemed to be saying recently in his criticism of the Welfare State in Scandinavia that I am a shining example of private enterprise, and far superior to my English son who has grown up in a real Welfare State, has had free medical and dental treatment and learned Greek—a subject I have never succeeded in mastering, much as I wished to. For him, if I understand Mr. Eisenhower correctly, there is nothing in store but a career of idleness and drunkenness, terminated by suicide. Mr. Eisenhower I suspect is exaggerating. If extreme poverty is so very beneficial in producing talent, energy and enterprise why on earth are its benefits reserved for the very poor? Why are they not taken advantage of by those who seem best fitted to appreciate them? Why are the children of well-to-do parents never deliberately sent to bad schools where skilled hands can flog and frustrate them every time they show a tendency to scholarship or culture? Why, when their teeth decay are they sent to expensive dentists instead of being told to pull out the teeth themselves in order to improve their character? The whole discussion of the Welfare State seems to me unreal. To any sane person who has the responsibility of bringing up children, elementary nourishment, care and instruction are merely the tools of the good life, not, as Mr. Eisenhower and the Soviet technician whose "What now?" has been quoted to us, assume, an end in themselves. As for that nameless Soviet technician, I suspect that his attitude is already out of date in his own country, or if it isn't that the Soviet technician, whenever the subject is discussed, would now prefer to remain nameless. Certainly the problem of what Russia will do with the accumulated technical resources of forty-four years is not going to be decided in his happy-go-lucky manner. Chekhov put it all in a sentence when he defined the only reality of progress, "When I was a child they used to beat me; when I grew up they stopped beating me. *That* is progress."

. . .

That doesn't mean that things have not changed since I was a boy, nor does it mean that I don't think that in some ways they have changed for the worse. Let me resume my modest autobiography. I grew up a socialist and a rationalist, and, like a lot of young intellectuals of my day, a great admirer of France and things French. We lived for eleven and a half months of the year in some outpost of Europe for the sake of a fortnight in Paris or in one of the French provinces, and brought back with us some French books, a Picasso print and a few packets of French cigarettes to exist on until the next holiday came round. Those who could do it created little Latin Quarters of their own in places like Chelsea in London and Greenwich Village in New York where they could live cheaply, live freely and discuss the things that mattered most to them with kindred spirits. When Chelsea became too expensive they moved to little hamlets in the districts round London where you could get a cottage for fifteen or twenty pounds a year. Last year I lectured on this at a big American university and asked one simple question—What do the young intellectuals think of now as their spiritual homeland? The result was fascinating. The older members of the audience remembered quite clearly the period of which I was speaking, but nobody, old or young, seemed to visualise any place that represented a utopia for intellectuals. Even in France itself it seems to me, the idea of the artists' colony is disappearing. Young people are more and more imitating things American. America doesn't have the same quality as France, but it is much, much bigger. And within that change it seems to me that there has been another change, particularly since the sputniks and luniks. Russia is even bigger than America, even if the quality of life there is far inferior, and I swear I believe that at the back of the intellectuals' minds is the notion that China is really the coming country.

.   .   .

This is part of the change that came with the last European war and the emergence of America and Russia as super-states. That emergence was itself so obvious that it now seems extraordinary that we didn't all anticipate it. It was implicit in the Industrial Revolution, for at that point as we have since learned, life ceased to be a matter of the most skillful exploitation of resources and became one of the extent of these resources, a matter of scale versus quality. We can now truthfully say that never since the days of the mastodons has size mattered so much in the world as it does today. Never has quality seemed to matter so little. The individual sees himself as almost powerless between great organisations of one sort or another. To influence anything at all it would appear that one must be a member of such an organisation, and yet in becoming a member one loses the personal freedom which is the most valuable thing we possess as human beings. Denmark has not escaped that curse. In Copenhagen I met a very intelligent hotel worker who spoke English and German excellently. He regarded Danish as a blight—'a language that's spoken by only five million people is no use.' It never occurred to him that because it was a language spoken by five million *civilised* people he was a better linguist than I should ever be. And I have been told of an important resolution which should have been submitted to the United Nations. It wasn't submitted because the United Nations would pay no attention to the opinion of a mere five million people. Of course fifty million savages could command attention.

.   .   .

In politics the educated man feels himself as powerless before the mastodon states as a writer feels before the mastodon mediums of communication—the film, radio, television. They are too big, too unwieldy, they involve the expenditure of too much money to be trusted in the hands of idealists and artists. As a theatre manager I know that Shakespeare's "Henry V" as he produced it didn't cost much—a hundred pounds or so invested by a half dozen actors like himself. Laurence Olivier's "Henry V" cost a million, but it was not what Shakespeare wrote, for it had also to be seen by millions, and with all that good capital involved the producers could not take the risk of offending a few cranks in some backward town. And so the play had to be doctored like an old tom cat to prevent its disturbing an old maid's dreams by its animal passion.

.   .   .

As for television, there is probably no form of entertainment in the world today baser than American television, and every serious American critic has said as much without being able to change it in the least degree for the better. Even in England where cultural and educational organisations have so much more say than they have in America, television is still subject to the grading system by which nameless people are telephoned and asked what they are looking at and how they like it. Nobody asks them what their qualifications are to give an opinion, and merely by inviting it one undermines the natural process by which they would eventually come to accept the opinion of their superiors on matters outside their experience and knowledge. That has always been a weakness of democracy in politics. In morals and taste it is not a weakness; it is a disaster. Because the alternative is tyranny one is compelled to assume the existence of innate good sense in any group of people; one cannot assume the existence of innate knowledge or taste, and to assume its existence is to destroy the whole validity of one's assumption of good sense.

.   .   .

What can the artists and intellectuals do? Nothing that I can see except to reassert authority in their own spheres. Authority is not merely, as we now tend to think, the biggest population with the biggest nuclear bomb; it is fundamentally the individual and, in his communal character, the civilisation of the small unit. At the time the United Nations was established, I was accused of cynicism because I attacked it. I felt that three or four small countries like the Scandinavian countries, with no territorial ambitions, should establish a real world government, no matter how small or weak it might be, or how often it was beaten up by bigger powers. I knew that a world state, flying a world flag, would act as a centre for all the unfocussed idealism of the world. Though I still have regrets for that experiment that was never tried, I suspect now that I was probably wrong. It would merely have added another mastodon to the group of mastodons. You cannot fight quantity with quantity; you can only lose whatever quality you possess.

.   .   .

I am beginning to think that the laws of biology are operating once more, almost unknown to us, and that the super-states have almost reached the end of their development. I don't know how that end will come, whether it will be by conflict between themselves or by their own sheer unwieldiness and over-specialisation, but I feel sure that the future of life on this earth will be with a much smaller, less specialised, more adaptable unit, above all with a unit that concerns itself with quality rather than quantity. That change will involve a restoration of authority in the spheres to which authority belongs. Above all it will involve the restoration of the concept of God—the "God theory," as Sir Julian

Huxley calls it. It isn't of course a theory, and has never been a theory except in the minds of the most simple-minded worshippers and scientists. It is a concept, the concept of completeness, of the absolute opposed to the relative, of a dark sun towards which all life turns. "On earth the broken arcs, in Heaven the perfect round."

A Boy in Prison

*Written in the summer of 1934, this is one of O'Connor's darkest rec-
ollections—of his year's imprisonment in an internment camp during the
Troubles—perhaps too close to the 1923 experience for its bitterness
and pain to be transformed. For another version of that time, twenty-
five years later, see* An Only Child, *242–274.*

A friend had promised to send me Heine's poems. To my disappointment he failed to get them and sent instead a school edition of *Hermann
und Dorotea.* Those fine spring days, while the others were exercising, I
lay on the floor of my cell and read and re-read it; two lines of it are still
in my head, because in the days that followed I tried to take them as a
precept.

> *Menschen lernten wir kennen, und Nationen, so lasst uns Unser eigenes
> Herz kennend uns dessen erfreun.*

The cell, condemned as inadequate for one, contained four; three slept
on the floor and one across the radiator. My cell-mates were, Cronin, an
ex-soldier and a very good-tempered fellow; Johnson, a big man with a
laughing rogue's face, and a country boy whose name I have forgotten,
dark, square-headed, handsome, silent and stupid. By day Cronin made
rings out of shilling pieces and in the evenings he amused himself with
me, singing.

On my first night in the prison I was wakened by the officer of the
guard flashing his torch in my face. Somewhere down the passage I heard
him, his voice echoing, say that there had been a raid and that one of
our men had been captured—with a revolver. That meant death, and for

a long time I remained awake thinking of death and what it meant, and of the man who would die so soon. I saw him as an embodiment of us all, young, poor, bewildered, struggling against we knew not what; his mother perhaps making a miserable living as a laundress in some slum. Then I thought of her; imagined her sitting by the fire at that moment, now screaming and struggling, now hushed and quiet, while the neighbours tried to comfort and reassure her. I imagined how she would go to the priest and beg him to intercede for her son, and how at last, wearied by her appeals, he would promise (perhaps with no intention of keeping his promise); then she, in the style of poor people like ourselves, would write to her boy to tell him that Father McCarthy or Father Maguire would speak for him, that the Blessed Virgin would intercede for him and the Sacred Heart watch over him. I imagined her going to early Mass, stumbling down the lane with the plaid shawl drawn tight about her face: kneeling far back in the darkness under the oblong gallery, her eyes fixed upon the suffering Christ and his weeping mother in their gaudy grandeur of crimson and blue. And she would pray half-aloud in a tortured whisper until to her tear-dimmed eyes the actor's face of Christ would seem to break into a pitying smile and she would be comforted . . . and at the same moment a green-clad officer with a pale dissolute face would put his revolver to the head of the bleeding figure writhing beside the prison wall . . . And that was life.

Early that morning I was wakened by Johnson, whose harsh and sneering voice was curiously subdued. He led me across the grey cylindrical building balconied and echoing, its tall barred windows aglow and framed in the half light of sloping stone. We went down another corridor which was quite dark. In one of the cells the morning light, cast upwards on to the arched and whitewashed ceiling and down again on the wall, picked out an officer, standing there, silent and very sinister in his grey-green uniform. Just as we entered what seemed a bundle of rags rose heavily from the tall square of darkness under the high window. There was a low growl from two or three men standing in the shadows. It took me some time to distinguish anything; then I noticed that the face of the man who had risen was swollen and black with beating.

'Ready?' asked the officer in an expressionless voice.

'Is this how you treat your prisoners?' snarled Johnson, clenching his fists.

'He should have thought of that when he was pouring petrol on the children last night.'

It was a lie, and we knew it, and we knew too what folly it was to speak. I held out my hand first, and the boy who was to die took it. To this day I remember the touch of his hand, and how it was swollen like his face and there seemed to be no bones in it. In silence we leaned over the balcony and through the suicide net watched him stumble down the clanking winding stair after the officer, past the heap of refuse stinking beside the high, barred gate, and disappear for ever from our sight through the little door that led to the world and eternity.

That night when I hung up my coat it was thick with vermin.

Sometimes—not often, for those periods of comparative silence were too precious—I took exercise with the others. It was very crowded outside; we had scarcely room to move in the yard, and the concrete circle round which convicts had walked served Ned and his gang for their rounders. What I did come to see was the nun. Behind the prison was a penitentiary for fallen women, and beside it the convent where the nuns who administered it lived; and every day when we were at exercise a nun sat beside an open window and waved to us. One only, never more; I felt the other nuns disapproved of us, and how much more of her! And in the solitary figure of that nun who had not yet detached herself from the world of passions that we represented, there was for me something terribly lonely and heartbroken, and for years the thought of her made me lonely too until at last I put her into a story called Nightpiece with Figures. But a number of the men preferred the back of the prison which was overlooked by the penitents' garden, and when the women were walking there in their wide French caps of starched linen, half a dozen faces would be pressed between the bars and whistles and cat-calls would ring out until the soldiers below raised their rifles. At a meeting of the prisoners a small, dark, talkative man made a very bitter speech against this indecency, and I suddenly started awake, for the man who was speaking might have been the original Baburin of Turgenev's greatest story. At the other end of the scale from these fanatical Baburins was my favourite, Ned, a ragged, toothless, underfed-looking man with blue eyes and a cropped skull, who invented a hundred follies to keep the men gay and remained himself, or so I think, a lonely, melancholy figure, a Pantaloon with a tragic heart. I should have loved to know more about him but he never responded to my overtures. I met him only once after, that was during an election and he looked more ragged and underfed than ever, and I felt that through his unswerving loyalty there was breaking a terrible disillusionment. Later I heard he tried to drown himself.

Cronin and I continued our singing. One night Matt Lenihan joined us. Matt was a gay lad with a melancholy voice. The three of us gave some offence by not joining in the Rosary. When Matt realized that we had missed it he was very depressed. He returned to his own cell groaning. We went to bed. Lights were quenched. The whole great prison sank into a sort of repose, broken by distant sniping. Then I heard stockinged feet come up the passage. It was Lenihan.

'O'Connor, kneel up and say the Rosary.'

'What's wrong with you, you mad bastard?' asked Cronin.

'I can't sleep. Honest to God, I can't. Listen, there were red and blue devils and every sort of thing tearing round the cell. We'll be damned if we don't say the Rosary. Do you hear me, O'Connor?'

Cronin struck a match. He was laughing and it was clear that he thought it a new and amusing prank. Lenihan was laughing too but there was a wild gleam in his eyes.

'Cronin, kneel up! Kneel up, O'Connor!'

'Go away to bloody hell from this!' shouted Johnson angrily.

'I won't go away until they say the Rosary. I won't stir a bloody foot until they say the Rosary. Lord God, is it destroyed you want me to be?'

He was dragging frenziedly at the pair of us, laughing all the while. At last he got us to our knees but he had scarcely got past 'In the name of the Father' when Cronin began to giggle. I giggled too. The country boy began to shake with half-suppressed laughter; next to join in was Johnson whose bad temper gave way before the spectacle of myself and Cronin on our knees and Lenihan giving out the Rosary. At last Lenihan himself joined in.

'Ah, Christ,' he protested, shaking helplessly with laughter and glauming wildly at myself and Cronin in the darkness, 'don't, don't, ah don't, leave ye! We'll all be damned I tell ye. Ye bastards, will ye stop laughing? Ah, say the prayer, can't ye? Say the bloody prayer. Cronin, kneel up or so help me God I'll choke the life out of you.'

There was renewed scuffling and shouting and somebody began to knock on the cell wall. Stupid with mirth, Cronin was dragged once more to his knees; I slid back on to the mattress. Once more in tones that he tried to make deadly solemn Lenihan gave out 'In the name of the Father.' Then we all exploded in concert. Pausing for an instant I heard it about me, and thought I had never before heard such strange laughter. There was shouting all along the passage. 'What's up?' 'What's wrong with them?' 'Shut up, blast ye!' and so on.

'Oh, God,' groaned Lenihan. 'I'm destroyed. O'Connor, O'Connor, kneel up! Maybe you'll die to-night. Maybe they'll shoot you to-morrow morning. Kneel up! Oh, God, we'll have the sentries atop of us!'

A boot clattered in the corridor. Lenihan rose and fumbled his way out of the cell, groaning. I heard him replying to questions at every cell door, shouting, his melancholy voice broken by wild bursts of hysterical laughter.

'The Rosary. They kept me from saying the Rosary and now I won't sleep a wink. Oh, God, what'll I do?'

.   .   .

In the early morning we were lined up, some hundreds of us, in the grey yard before the governor's house. From that we were taken in lorries through the barely-wakened city. After an hour in the train we were marched through another town to the terminus behind a blown-up viaduct. It was April, and even that few minutes under the sun and so close to the green fields was unforgettable.

In the train again we were served with tinned fish. I ate none of it, for which afterwards I was thankful as it created a thirst there was no way of appeasing. Midnight came and we were still imprisoned in the train. Finally we reached a wayside station. It was flat country, not a hill anywhere. In the distance a searchlight moved up and down the sky and over the quiet fields, picking out whitewashed cottages and trees and flattening them against the night with sharp edges like pieces of theatre scenery, garish in their greens and whites. We moved towards it and it went with us, half-human in its mechanical precision. I was fascinated, watching it reveal the faces of my companions as they staggered on under their burdens, and the monstrous shadows, spreading and contracting, that drifted like smoke over the cardboard trees and hedges. It became almost a new sensation with hunger and thirst and weariness, and like a hallucination it made a fantasy of these; bursting upon us like a March wind, rising, falling, blooming upon the dark sky like a flower until its beams were blunted upon the shaggy side of some low cloud. Gradually we began to perceive what it was leading us to. Changing like the shapes of a kaleidoscope under that restless eye, there emerged a block of low irregular buildings. These too became part of the fantasy; now it was a long cement hall, its broken window-panes seeming like holes burned in canvas; now a group of small brown wooden huts, every board in them sharp as in an old woodcut, their canvas roofs shining like slates; now great red-brick buildings that looked like what they were, aerodromes. The image never remained still. The only fixtures in this fantastic world were the barbed-wire entanglements and the main gate which were lit with great arc lamps and the little wooden hut outside which we halted and in which we must be received. We stood there for hours; it was bitterly cold. It was early morning when I was admitted. I was marched to the quartermaster's hut and served out with a spring bed, a mattress and blankets. I lifted them and collapsed. Some of the prisoners carried my bedding while two tall military policemen helped me to my hut and saw me into bed.

When I opened my eyes next morning I saw a long, many-windowed building, divided, at about the height of a man, into two aisles, in each of which were two rows of beds, iron and trestle. Everyone round me was asleep, rolled up in brown prison blankets like my own, and the place suggested a Franciscan dormitory. Through the clerestory windows over my head I saw blue clouds. I was only a few yards from the door and through it and the side-door of the concrete porch outside it that someone had left unlatched I caught my first view of the compound. And there, beyond the sunken wire, glowed the fields!

It is the same picture I always see whenever I hear the Good Friday music from Parsifal; Parsifal's *Wie duenkt mich doch die Aue heut' so schoen* alone expresses the astonishment and delight of that waking. Everything was bright; there was a high wind blowing and it brought the breath of the fields about me; the prison and its horrors were far away.

. . .

The interior life of a place or a human being is so indescribable that I wonder we ever attempt it. Eleven years later I revisited this internment camp, now deserted, only to find I had lost my bearings in it. Then the framework of a gate started the engine of memory and I shot off. Suddenly the friend who was with me caught me by the arm and asked, 'What's wrong with you? Why did you do that?' It was some time before I realized what I had done that astonished him: I had made a sharp turn in one open place, had picked my way along a path once fenced with barbed wire, though now the path was obliterated and the barbed wire gone. That is what I mean by an interior life.

In the camp I soon lost touch with my old companions and made friends among the new. After prison with its rowdy and indiscriminate contacts this was a place of privacy and culture. There were a thousand internees but one came to know very few; in a town twice its size everyone would have known everyone else, but left to themselves men are unsociable and incurious. For the first few months it was easy to maintain the illusion that one was in a town; there were classes, lectures, plays, concerts, debates, books; the great dining hall in the North Camp had been rigged up as theatre and church with a stage at one end and an altar at the other.

In the mornings I was often first to wake, had a shower bath and a stroll and put in an hour's work at my books before old Dan came through the huts blowing reveille. Soon after that came first count. Military policemen stationed themselves outside while we stood at the foot of our beds and listened to the whistles coming nearer. Then one blew at our door, the hutleader called us to attention and one of the camp command with a Free State officer stamped through the files, tapping each man as they passed. Sometimes counting and recounting went on for an hour till we were sick of it. Next came Mass. It was a crippled service because we were all under ban, and only one man who served Mass communicated. When Mass was over the whistle went for breakfast, and after breakfast there were fatigues for those whose turn it was. I as a teacher was exempt from fatigues, and when I hadn't a class put in my morning at work. Except in the summer work was not easy, because in our great barrack of a hut there was a continuous hum of talk and tapping of improvised hammers, and men were all the time going and coming and stopping to ask questions or start aimless conversations. After dinner if it were fine there was a procession to the playing-field, a wide field overlooking the sea from which you could watch the trains puffing north and south. Then tea and finally that evening warmth of relaxation and debate of men who all their lives have been used to work, before the whistle sounded for second count and we rushed to the cookhouse for hot water for our tea or cocoa. When the light had gone out for the last time the hutleader gave out the rosary and then there was silence. It was a monastic existence, devoid of responsibility and care, and at first, particularly while fighting still went on outside and there was still chance of an honourable peace, I was happy enough.

My best friend was a country lad from the coast of Clare. I had been in camp only a day or two when he spoke to me and told me that he remembered poems I had contributed to a children's paper at the age of twelve or thirteen. He was a heavy youth with a more than labouring awkwardness; he can have been no more than nineteen, but his body was hunched and twisted like an old man's; he always shambled with eyes on the ground, a lock of jet-black hair hanging over one eye, his thick black brows knitted. His massive features that would have been the joy of a sculptor's heart had a sort of shimmering delicacy that suggested an intense interior conflict; he had a slight stammer that exaggerated the slowness of his speech, and when he spoke earnestly there appeared on each temple a faint pallor that somehow caught the light and made him seem transfigured. His smile, sometimes candid and wistful, sometimes brilliant and passionate, suggested lightning over a moor.

Neither of us had yet framed any criticism of our companions, but it was not long before we discovered that we differed from them in a certain robustness of outlook which we had in common. We both loved life. I first began to appreciate the distinction when I noticed in the autograph books that were always circulating in the camp the number of quotations from Shelley, a poet I disliked. But it was not only Shelley, it was Shelley's period and type and all it stood for, Mazzini and Terence McSwiney and Pearse and a gospel of liberty and self-sacrifice and heroworship which in Ireland has degenerated into a sickly idealism that covers every reality with a sort of syrup of legend. Against these abstractions that reduce life to a tedious morality O'Neill opposed his knowledge of simple people and I the philosophy I had been acquiring from Goethe. To McSwiney's dictum that victory comes not to those who inflict most but to those who endure most I retorted in Goethe's phrase that a man must be either a hammer or an anvil.

. . .

One began by feeling this idealism as a harmony: one ended by doubting the existence of a treble. When the whistle blew for count it was nominally for our own and not the enemy officer that we paraded and stood to attention. Later on that struck me as a rather silly evasion. And there was the astonishing tale of John Mahoney (let us call him that) which, in the beginning, seemed no more than the very funny incident it was.

John frequently disagreed with his hutleader. The hutleader said John was insubordinate, John retorted that the hutleader was favouring the other men at his expense. What the right and wrong of it were I don't profess to remember. At any rate, by way of protest John refused to do his fatigues.

So one day two policemen, that is to say two prisoners wearing armlets, brought John before the command court which consisted of several prisoners like himself, and the command court sentenced him to extra fatigues by way of punishment. These also he refused to perform and in a day or two he was up before the court once more. One would imagine that sensible men faced with the simple fact that John and his hutleader could not agree would simply send one or the other to a different hut. But no! Discipline must be preserved. So John was sent to prison.

Now 'the prison' was a tiny hut isolated on a knoll at the eastern end of the camp. That day the rumour spread and the compound was in an uproar. O'Neill and I rejoiced. It gave us the same feeling of moral relief we had experienced when we had found in some autograph book, cheek by jowl with a quotation from Shelley, those lines about the kiss 'that broke the mainspring of her heart and left her mouth wide open.'

But John, the doubly-imprisoned, was far from being beaten. He did something that staggered us all. He declared a hunger-strike. Not against the Free State, mark you, not against imprisonment in the camp, but against the Irish Republic and imprisonment in the isolation. And how was one to disentangle two causes from one creature? How could the Free State, with such a trifling complaint against so good a man, stand aside and allow him to be done to death by the wicked Republic, which at any rate it did not recognize? And how could John, who had seen his country's liberties pocketed by the Free State (which he did not recognize) and been its prisoner for a year, how could he accept the protection of a usurping authority against the legitimate Republic? John's challenge was double-edge, infuriating logic.

How exactly it ended for him I forget, but his hash was settled at a mass meeting of the prisoners where the sacred principle of majority rule was proclaimed by the camp intelligentsia. Since we were ourselves a minority at war with the state I thought this illogical, but I must confess that I made very little effort to follow the speeches; my sympathies were too wholeheartedly with the outcast.

I became friendly with a big-boned, wild-faced man with a shaven skeleton head and a bare hairy chest. I called him the Prophet because he talked politics in a deep, thrilling rumble-bumble of a voice that tickled the drums of your ears. Both studious, we were condemned to exist apart in the large huts that were becoming increasingly difficult to work in. Besides, the fighting was over, releases took place every day, and an appalling restlessness had begun to invade the camp. One day we discovered that a group of men were being ejected from their room for insubordination. It was a charming room, warm and quiet and large enough for three: in an evil hour we applied for it.

I have called my friend the Prophet, but we were both prophets—and martyrs. For no sooner had we applied than we realized that we had committed in Irish eyes the unforgivable sin, and we were too proud to withdraw. If we hadn't applied no one else would have done so; the men would have been formally ejected, the room would have been vacant for a day or two, and then one evening they would have reappeared and taken up their old quarters without question. No discipline, no law can withstand that anarchic Irish personal factor that eats up principles as an old goat eats up a fence. You think you can build up a personal life, can sit at home and mind your garden? Just try. Sooner or later that old goat, for all the long stick that knocks so forbiddingly between his horns, will come through your fences and trample your flower beds and munch your fairest posies.

But we hadn't realized it. And solitary and dignified we carried our mattresses and beds and books into the new hut under a fire of taunts and threats from the ejected and their friends. There was vague talk of reprisals, beatings and police protection that pleased the camp for a fortnight.

And for a while my friend and I were very happy. We foregathered with our new hutmates at night over the stove, sang songs, swapped stories, debated. But disagreements arose between myself and the prophet, and oftener and oftener I heard the prophetic note in his voice, and less and less the lilting scatter-brained one that had enchanted me. Boom-boom-boom it went all day and the triangle between his brows became more marked, and I began to realize, dimly and helplessly, that my charming comrade looked on me as a devil incarnate. Why was that? I asked myself.

One day I arrived to find the prophet had posted over his bed a very romantic poem, full of fine sentiments about liberty and martyrdom and recreants and what not else. It was not as bad a poem as I thought then, seeing in it nothing but a sermon directed against myself. That evening I wrote over my own bed in small but firm letters:

Neither in death nor life has the just man anything to fear.

And that evening the prophet's brow was like a thunderstorm. When he spoke to me his voice was choked with passion. Nor, though I felt a distinctly just man, did I feel I had nothing to fear. Next day there was another poem over the prophet's bed, and the same evening I wrote over my own:

Grey, my dear friend, is all your theory,
And green the golden tree of life.

After that we had a terrible row nor did we speak to one another again until the tragi-comedy ended, a few days later.

.   .   .

A young fellow from the south received a wire to say his mother was dying and begging him to come home. One could secure parole only by signing a declaration of allegiance (a savage condition, having regard to opinion within the camp which was dead against signing). It was a pity, I said, that God hadn't made mothers with the durability of principles. The mother, being of softer material, died, and the lad began to mope. Worse news came; his brothers and sisters had been left homeless, but this was kept from him. One evening he overheard a conversation about it and threw himself on the wires under the rifles of the sentries. When they brought him back to his room he said 'They wouldn't even shoot me!'

One morning the doctor ordered me to hospital. On the same day the great hunger strike was announced. It was decided, very cleverly, to put the issue, for and against, to the men at county meetings: this meant that the few like myself who opposed it were practically unheard. So close on a thousand men solemnly pledged themselves to abstain from food until they either died or were released. That evening I went into hospital.

On the same evening while I lay in my bed, rejoicing again in the feeling of clean linen and the myriad virtues of pillows, a military police-man brought in a tall lad with a vacant face who had to be undressed and put to bed. Then the policeman sat down by the bed and lit his pipe. It was the man whose mother had died; I had fresh reason to admire the durability of principles.

I did not sleep that night. A sigh, a stir of clothes and the tall lad slipped quietly out of bed and padded across the floor to the window beside me. He stood on the windowsill, gripping the bars with his hands, his face crushed between them. God only knows what he saw. Once I dozed and woke to find him standing there, fixed by the searchlight, crucified against the bars, his grey shirt reaching half-way down his thighs. Another sigh and he padded back to bed again.

A few days later I left the hospital to be with O'Neill and the other objectors. It was a bitter, black day, the compound, almost deserted, was a sea of mud. I entered one hut to see a friend. The men were lying every way; some in bed, some dressed but unshaven; they did not look at me. Partitions and doors and lavatory seats, everything wooden had been torn away to make fires, round which groups of them sat gloomily, watching the pot of salt water that simmered there; the only sustenance they allowed themselves. But what struck me most forcibly was the silence: all that busy hammering and shouting was gone. As I left the hut I was followed by a general hiss—objectors were not popular.

Then it began to break: first in ones and twos, and then in small groups. These men's rations had to be claimed; that took a full day, so we objectors divided our food amongst them. The first-comers were treated with derision and contempt by the cookhouse staff, and it amused me to observe how with numbers they attained dignity: soon it was they who were bullying the cookhouse. The day after my return a big group of my county men broke, and the command hut which obviously rated my influence higher than I did ordered me to occupy a deserted hut and to enter no other.

But the agitator who was speaking now was one much more eloquent than I, and him they could not lock up. In the next few days the break became an avalanche. Then came surrender. The soldiers brought buckets of soup to the wires and men tore themselves to dip their mugs in it. Bleeding, famished, ill, half-crazy, and yet happy seeing relief come, they snapped and fought like mad dogs while the soldiers sweated under the steaming buckets, the sentries lowered their rifles and the officers stood about smiling. O'Neill's face was very pale, and he spoke almost in a whisper. We both knew that what we were watching was the end of a period; the end, in our day at least, of something noble, priceless and irreplaceable. Afterwards there was another mass meeting. The command thanked and complimented the men; it was a splendid moral victory: the men cheered like mad, but all the same the camp remained what it was then, a grave, and a ruined grave at that. The national impossibilism had produced its deadly aftermath, apathy: it was not the weariness of a healthy man, it was the deadly thing with which we had been familiar in our childhood and with which unless a miracle happens we must die—the moral stagnation of a people who at every turn reject life.

. . .

It was a November day, bright and cold. I was sitting in O'Neill's room when a man burst in and called 'O'Connor, you're wanted. There's an officer looking for you.' I did not stir. It was a favourite and cruel joke. 'You're wanted, I tell you,' he continued. 'You're wanted,' said O'Neill with a wistful smile. And even then I only half-believed it. O'Neill and I went to my hut. The officer we were told had been and gone. I sat down, trembling, overcome by a sudden feeling of despair. And then a green-clad figure appeared in the doorway; it reminded me of another such I had seen in a dark cell in a city prison, but that had been a call to death, this was a call to life. 'Is O'Connor back yet?' asked the voice. 'Yes,' I answered weakly, 'Here I am.'

Meet Frank O'Connor

*Both interviews, "Meet Frank O'Connor" (*The Bell, *1951) and "Talk With the Author" (*Newsweek, *1961), fall short of an imagined ideal. Often the questions seem designed only to goad him into being quotably controversial. Larry Morrow's 1951 impressionistic word-portrait, admiring and sly, succeeds more although its background—O'Connor, prosecuted as immoral and thwarted by provincialism—accounts for much of its sharpness. William Flynn's queries, although limited, stimulate some memorable responses. The interviews may also have been shaped by what Harriet Sheehy described (in a 1990 interview of her own) as O'Connor's shyness, which revealed itself paradoxically: "When we went to a party, Michael would be the one who would say, 'Oh, Auden? He never wrote a word that anybody ever wanted to read!' or some really wild statement like that, so people thought he was arrogant and that he didn't have any patience about anything. He'd come home from a party like that and say, 'Oh, God, I made a fool out of myself. I talked too much. I blathered such rubbish,' and that was partly because he was shy."*

Still, we must be glad that these interviews exist, for—aside from the Paris Review *interview and one given in 1963 to Michael Longley, then a Trinity College undergraduate—we have few glimpses of O'Connor in these circumstances. [Jimmy Montgomery, referred to at the end of "Meet Frank O'Connor," was the Dublin film censor, "one of the greatest of the Dublin wits, and, though I had no great liking for wit and detested the Dublin brand, I was very attached to Montgomery" (*My Father's Son, *136).]*

306 / Frank O'Connor

A label-minded American might pin-point Frank O'Connor as, variously, The Voice, the Profile, or The Pain. For O'Connor is all these things, besides (need one say?) much more. Personally (one fancies) he'd prefer to be known as The Pain—in almost anyone's neck—a position which, despite serious opposition from many quarters, he has succeeded in holding for twenty years, since, in fact, his first book of short stories, *Guests of the Nation*.

Only a major prophet—and O'Connor, poet, playwright, novelist, short-story-writer, topographer, critic, and student of Architecture, has somehow never gone in professionally for Prophecy—could have achieved such reeking unpopularity in his own country. Few Irish writers have managed to maintain at sullen heat, and for so long, such personal antipathies against themselves: fewer still extracted such sweet-savoured bemusement from doing so. How else account for the fact that while England and America are doors open for his 'exile', O'Connor chooses to remain not merely in Ireland—how pleasant to 'retire' to one's native County Cork!—but in suburban Dublin, unclubable, almost unpubable, aloof with the aloofness of a yogi, with an almost physical horror of droppers-in or (if they exist) would-be disciples? It is almost as if, after *Finnegans Wake*, Joyce had returned to Dublin, set up in Ballsbridge and refused the house even to the Chevalier McGreevy.

All of which, oddly, is not to suggest that O'Connor is anything other than what you'd expect from his best stories—a writer so passionately interested in the common life around him that in *Who's Who* he admits as his sole recreation: 'Cycling.' Could anything, these days, symbolise Democracy more vividly than the bicycle-clipped trouser, the flattened back-tyre? For only the wealthy-eccentric and the utterly dispossessed can nowadays afford to walk.

Even in the dehydrated prose of *Who's Who* O'Connor (now forty-eight) manages to strike the defiant note—one auralises it as being somewhat in the key of F sharp major. Nimbly side-tracking his Dublin (and other) detractors, he inscribes his occupation in plain pitch-pine: 'Writer and journalist', as if it were no more than 'painter and glazier'; and then follows it with: 'by profession librarian.' Reference to his by no means negligible part in the Civil War he modestly suppresses, but rolls out as reason for resigning from the Board of the Abbey Theatre in 1939: 'protest against attitude of fellow-directors on censorship and other issues affecting the theatre'. And, again, what could be more deliberately down-written than: 'Educ., Christian Brothers, Cork'? Or is that being merely Old School Tie in reverse? With O'Connor one never knows. He is at once, and so often the *garçon* gagging the *gorsoon*. And *vice versa*. To hear him appraise a Gothic arch or a tale of Turgenev's with what sounds like 'Verray, verray lahvly!' for instance, is often (to the uninitiated) to confuse the trilling, almost aspirated West Cork 'R' with the throat-clearings of the *haut-monde* Parisien—the sound which has made many a foreigner to Macroom imagine himself in Montmartre.

In Horse Show week, when Dublin takes on the air of an Edwardian exhibition at Earl's Court, Frank O'Connor might pass for almost any distinguished non-Western visitor—with the egregious exception of the Agha Khan. How he achieves this may be an optical illusion, but there it is. Maybe it's the clothes-the bawneen jacket and tussore trousers, the suggestion of sandal-shod feet. There is a whiff of black coffee and Burmese cheroots about him, something of the hieratic, dynastic, figure on an Egyptian fresco, as if he were always, only, to be seen, like all the best-period Egyptians, in profile. Even the crumpled fisherman's hat (minus dry-flies) somehow adds to the orientation. Hatless (as in the Dog Days), his head, flung back, fiercely-proud, flashes a startling suggestion of the Yeats of thirty years ago—the silvered Arab steed freed from its snaffle, sniffing the air, the lips peeled, domino-teeth in grin-grimace. And in the darkness under the ostrich-egg brows chestnut eyes glow, burn, brazier-bright.

And The Voice? If it was once said of a famous soprano that her top notes were so high that there was snow on them half the year round it can be more truthfully said of O'Connor that his voice is so low that barnacles cling to it *all* the year round and that deep-sea divers in conversation with him have put aside their plummets and organ-tuners boomingly despaired of their diapasons. It is, in some senses, the voices of Plançon, Chaliapin and Kipnis put end to end. One feels that with him *Boris* is really not quite good enough.

O'Connor has a plethora of passions. They range (as stated) from cycling to the drinking of libations of tea, the like of which even that thirty-two cup man, Doctor Johnson, would hem at. Indeed if you would bait O'Connor, tea is your man. And so, setting about trapping him, you'd best lay your snares in Bewley's or Robert's. Which—guess which you like—is where we found him, nose-flickering, ready for the job of questioning, being questioned, rather. After a brisk 'Good morning' we settled uncomfortably to the job, beginning with the old dodge of: Why and how the pseudonym of 'Frank O'Connor' when your intimates know you by your real name of Michael O'Donovan? The victim inspected his deep cup before answering—to make sure that it was of the brew he prefers: upon which a mouse can be trotted.

My mother was an O'Connor—no O'Connors that anybody would know—and my Communion name is Francis Xavier, not Assisi, hence the violent streak in my nature. As a Carnegie librarian I was forced to adopt a pen-name, so what better than 'Frank O'Connor'?

Irish fiction to-day? Escapist? Not reflecting the life of our times? Why has there never been one really great Irish novel? Unlike the British, aren't Irish novelists living in and writing about a romantic past that may indeed never have existed?

When I was taking up literature as a career I told Osborn Bergin and he asked 'What are you going to write?' I said 'Novels.' Bergin shook his head. 'There isn't a novel in this country.' 'Short stories, so,' I said. 'You might get some short stories out of it,' said Bergin.

As O'Connor has told us elsewhere, his parents were poor and he was an only child, which meant that from the beginning he was thrown very much upon himself. He is by no means immodest when probed about his precocity.

'I was born reading,' he drawls, puffing long and confidentially at his cigarette. 'I don't know when I started to write, but I published—privately—a collected edition of my works at the age of twelve.' The large eyes roll and pop. The thickly-sculptured lips purse. Only the closest of scrutinies reveals the twinkle in the eyes, the faintest of faint flickers of the lips. O'Connor is enjoying the leg-pull, the irony, rather, as much as his listener. He goes on:

At that time I wasn't quite sure whether I wanted to be a writer, a painter or a musician, but soon after I decided on the writing because the raw materials cost less. If I'd had the money for a piano nobody would have been able to ban me now.

Recollecting *Who's Who* again, one fiddles a little with a question about the Abbey. How did he find himself there, for instance? The eyes again have it. This time the lip curls perceptibly.

I got connected with the theatre because Yeats was in a hole for someone to go on his Board and I'm a man of weak and amiable character. The experience left me considerably stronger, but much less amiable.

And so one plunges. 'Would you regard yourself as the *Homme Terrible* of present-day Irish letters?' A firm-clenched hand all but strikes the table, arrests itself in mid-air.

I'm not 'terrible.' It's the Society that's 'terrible.' In a country like this, 'Pious without Enthusiasm,' like the epitaph I once came on in an English churchyard, without any standards of any sort—moral or intellectual—any normal human being appears 'terrible.'

Fearing a little for the eavesdropper—those who hear no good of themselves, not even in Bewley's—one skirts off Morals and the like into the maybe less skiddy terrain of Politics, to ask whether a great novel might not, conceivably, spring from, say, Partition or the squabblings of our politicians both in and out of the Dáil? To which a mountainous shrugging of the shoulders and in the ensuing silence:

'There aren't any Irish politics left. The last Irish politician, Mr. de Valera, began his career in Boland's Bakery and ended it in———' At which moment, luckily, the waitress at a nearby table tripped and crashed her tray of crockery. Where Mr. de Valera is presumed to have ended his career I didn't quite catch. Or did I?

O'Connor's deep diapason rises and falls, mighty Wurlitzer. There is no improvisation, no impromptu stuff here. Remove the snaffle and his talk assumes the intricate pattern of a Bach three-part invention. He is one of the few living Irishmen whose conversation is capable of being parsed: one of the very few who, in their talk, employ not only the full stop and common comma, but the colon and semi-colon. And only one who had once contemplated becoming a musician could so delicately employ italics. These, properly, he reserves for his 'Sayings of the Week' moments, when suddenly out of the boom into the blue he floats, filigreed in italics, some such *obiter dictum* as: 'A great novel doesn't exist in a writer; it exists in a Society. To produce a novel you need a Society with an aristocracy—of intellect or birth.'

Which for virtually a tea-totaller—and at eleven o'clock on a wet Monday morning—is about as good a scrap of table-talk as one is likely to find. Even in Dublin where so much of it has (shades of Joyce and Jimmy Montgomery!) become under-the-table talk.

Talk with the Author

O'Connor lives near the Stanford campus in Palo Alto with his wife and their two-year-old daughter Harriet. Tall and urbane, with unruly white hair, pink cheeks, and a finely trimmed mustache, he talks with casual force and only a hint of brogue. His creative writing course, he recently told *Newsweek*'s William Flynn, will occupy him fully until June. "When one teaches," O'Connor said, "the writer loses the competitive spirit that is necessary to write. You forget your own work when you teach writing. You become too wrapped up in the writing of your students. Therefore, you can't teach and write at the same time."

O'Connor found the situation rather questionable. "I don't think it is good for the writer to teach," he continued. "The good writer is a bad teacher. If he is a good writer he doesn't give a damn about the success of other writers. So he is not a good teacher. If he is a good teacher, cares about the other writers, he can't write himself. I become so enthusiastic about the writers in the class that I don't think of my own work."

Americans: He was less impressed by the state of American writing in general. "You have loads of talent in this country," he said. "But the tragedy of the American writer is multiple talents. The best American writer I know is not only a writer but he is an economist, a boxer, an artist.* And there is the great enthusiasm of America. That may inspire the use of the multiple talents. The United States is exciting."

O'Connor made his objections to that fact perfectly clear: "The real writer has to be ruthless. He has to be able to say to other people: 'I don't have to read your manuscript or revise it.' The writer has to have a good streak of solid selfishness to get his own work done. He should

---

* Richard Thomas Gill, assistant professor of economics at Harvard, who has published short stories in *The New Yorker*.

throw his wife out and make his children go out and work to support themselves at a really early age so he will be able to concentrate on his own writing. If his best friend drops in when he is writing, he should say: 'Get the hell out.' Real dear friends won't mind."

On the subject of TV and the movies as contributors to literature, O'Connor was pointed. Stressing that both mediums in their present form depend on "organization and money," he went on: "Literature has got to be done on a small budget. But the small budget is not involved in pictures or television. The result is that both completely kill creative imagination. Even in England, television has vulgarized literature. Pay-TV won't make any difference. The result will be that the salesman will be out telling people what they like and the people eventually will believe it. That is what the motion pictures have done." O'Connor freely admitted that he would welcome a fat Hollywood check for the screen rights to "An Only Child," and he had his comments to make on that: "Money does not corrupt the individual. It corrupts any organization. I would be enchanted to sell to Hollywood. I would take the money but I don't think the picture would be a work of art."

Writing a Story—One Man's Way

This June 1959 BBC broadcast has O'Connor happily explicating his creative process—his devotion to the four-line theme, the "treatment," obsessive revision—and illustrating it with his own work ("First Confession," "Michael's Wife") and that of students enrolled in his writing classes. (O'Connor's students remembered him as an enthralling teacher, and this talk shows why.) Valuable also are his comments on the short story's form and the work of some of its masters developed more fully in The Lonely Voice *(an entertaining book, even when the reader is positive that O'Connor's eloquent assertions can be disproved!)*

Once when I was lecturing in America and, as usual, could not think of a title for my lecture, someone advertised it as 'One Man's Way,' and that seemed to me such a good title that I wanted to use it again. Because short-story writing is my job, and, as all of us who write stories will know, there is only one way to do a job and that is the way you do it yourself.

I am dealing here with one man's way of writing a story, and the thing this man likes best in the story is the story itself. A story begins when someone grabs you by the lapel and says: 'The most extraordinary thing happened to me yesterday.' I don't like the sort of story that begins with someone saying: 'I don't know if it's a matter of any interest to you but I'd like to describe my emotions while observing sunset last evening.' I am not saying the second man may not have important things to say, things far more important than those the first has to say, but that particular tone gives me the shivers. I like the feeling that the story-teller has something to communicate, and if he doesn't communicate it he'll bust.

The story can be anything from the latest shaggy dog story to an incident so complex that for the rest of your life you will be wondering what the meaning of it was. Let me tell you a story that has made me wonder. Once when my father and I were staying in a little seaside place in County Cork we got into conversation with a farmer whose son had emigrated to America. There he had married a North of Ireland girl, and soon after she fell very ill and was advised to go home and recuperate. Before she went to her own family she spent six weeks with her husband's family in County Cork, and they all fell in love with her. It was only when she had left that they discovered from friends in America that their son had been dead before she left America at all.

'Now, why would she do a thing like that to us?' the old farmer asked, and for years I asked myself the same question.

Sometimes a story leaves you with a question. Sometimes it answers a question that has been in your mind. I had always felt ashamed of the horrible, snobbish attitude I had adopted to my own father and mother when I was growing up—an attitude for which there was no justification. Then a couple of years ago my wife and I were out walking in the little American city where we lived and we came on my son standing at a street corner with a girl—his first girl. I was wearing an Aran Island beret which I found very comfortable in the American winters. Instantly his face grew black and her face lit up, and it was as plain as though the pair of them had said it that he was mortified by the spectacle of his degraded old father who knew no better than to wear a knitted cap in the street, and she was thrilled at the thought of a father who did not dress like every other American father.

At that moment I understood my own horrible snobbery, and realized that falling in love always means being a bit ashamed of one's own parents and a bit enthusiastic about others'. At the age of seventeen we all have ambitions to be adopted.

But before I wrote that story, or would allow any student of mine to write it, I had to see exactly what it looked like. I find it easier to see it if it is written in four lines. Four is only an ideal, of course; I don't really quarrel with five, and sometimes a difficult subject may require six. But four is the best length; four is a seed: anything more is a cutting from somebody else's garden.

I mean the sort of subject that begins like this: 'Mary Martin, unmarried, aged twenty-two, is a school-teacher in Belfast. She is the daughter of respectable parents; her father being employed in the shipyards and her mother a dressmaker.' Instantly I feel tied hand and foot, by school-teaching, Belfast, ship-building and dressmaking, and have the impression that I am never going to see the subject through all the trimmings. That is why I want to see it cut to four lines, even if this involves using algebraic symbols. In that way the story I told you about the old farmer in County Cork would read something like this: 'X marries Y abroad. After Y's death, X returns home to Y's parents, but does not tell them Y is dead.'

That method looks crude, but from my point of view it has its advantages. It enables me to forget all about County Cork and farming, and the North of Ireland and the United States, even to forget the sex of the people concerned, so that I can imagine what the consequences would be if X were a man instead of a woman. It gives me freedom—freedom to try out the story in terms of any place or group of people who happen to interest me at the moment, and who may, perhaps, illustrate the subject better than those to whom it originally related.

Obviously, there are limitations to this. You could not write a story like my little 'First Confession' about a Protestant family. But I always feel that there is something wrong with the poetic quality of any short story that adheres too closely to one place or nationality or religion or profession. One of the stories of mine that I like best was told to me originally about a well-known English actor and a London girl, but I did not know anything about English actors and very little about London girls, so I set the story in Dublin, and just because I was able to do that without seriously affecting the subject, I felt it was a better story as I told it.

This necessity for freedom seems to me to hold for every aspect of storytelling. Take clergymen, for instance. When I write about clergymen I try not to think of clergymen; the same with lawyers and the same with policemen. A man's profession should be demonstrated by the circumstances of the story, and the writer's business is to get past the given circumstances, and find in the clergyman, the lawyer, or the policeman whatever it is that makes him a recognizable, individual human being and not a mere professional figure—whatever makes the clergyman have, maybe, a passion for amateur theatricals, the lawyer for roses, and makes the policeman sing in the parish choir on Sunday. That is what gives a story by Chekhov what I call 'interior perspective,' so that instead of a flat surface of narrative, you get a texture like life itself, something you can walk in and out of, and move about in, and catch people in from odd angles.

Before I start the serious business of writing a story I like to sketch it out in a rough sort of way. I like to block in the general outlines and see how many sections it falls into, which scenes are necessary and which are not, and which characters it lights up most strongly. At this stage it is comparatively easy to change scenes about in order to change the lighting so as to make it fall where you want it. At a later stage it requires considerably more fortitude. Of course, a close examination of the four lines of subject should give a fair idea of what this treatment should be like, but it is surprising how often it does not.

Here, for example, are two themes handled by students of mine. One described how, when he was a schoolboy, his mother took him out of school one day and brought him to a suburban railway station where she pointed out to him a good-looking girl. 'Follow her wherever she goes,' said his mother. The girl got on a train, and the boy got into the same compartment. A few stops up the line she got out and he followed her off the train and down a ramp leading from an upstairs platform to the street. Below him in the street he suddenly saw his father's car and realized what his mother had made him do.

The other story was told by a student from New York. It was about the only son of a Jewish widow who kept a mean little shop in a New York slum. For close to a year the boy had been robbing the till of quarters and fifty-cent pieces to keep himself in movies and cokes. One day he came home from school to find that his mother had been coshed and the till robbed by a Jewish thug. Instantly the boy wanted to call the police and report the thief, whom his mother had recognized, but his mother said in horror: 'Isn't it bad enough for poor Mrs. Solomons to have a son like that without my handing him over to the police?' A little while later the boy noticed that he had stopped stealing.

Both of these were excellent themes, the second a beautiful one, but for the life of me I couldn't have said without working them out in class whether they should be told in the first person or the third. That is one of the hardest choices a young writer has to make. By using the first person you can get effects of depth and feeling that are impossible by any other method. You can see it for yourself in the first subject: 'I saw my father's car standing below in the street' has many times the emotional effect of 'Peter saw his father's car standing below in the street';

in the second 'I stole money from my mother' is stronger than 'Isaac stole money from his mother.'

In fact, in the second subject it seems to me so strong that I should find it hard to treat the story in any other way. If you think of it in the third person there is little to choose between the boy and Solomons, and all you can do is mark the analogy as Joyce does in 'Counterparts.' But the fact is that the boy who is really acted on in the story clearly sees the distinction; it is only gradually and almost unconsciously that he becomes aware of the analogy.

But the first subject is a much more difficult problem. You can get the same effect only by almost obliterating the whole relationship of the parents, and ignoring whatever diabolical fury there was in the mother that made her involve her innocent son in such a sordid episode. Can you afford to ignore that? Can you ignore the possibility that the father was really a decent man who was driven into devious courses by his wife's hysterical character?

This is the reason why in class I insist on this blocking out of the story, which I call a treatment. The students all hate it. They always want to begin right away with 'It was a spring evening, and under ice-cold skies the crowds were hurrying homeward along Third Avenue where the neon signs on the bars were beginning to be reflected in the exhausted eyes of office workers.' This is the sort of thing that makes me tear my hair out, because I know it is ten to one that that story should not begin on Third Avenue at all, and that whatever I may say later about the necessity for putting it in the first or third person, somehow or other the student is going to work that story back to Third Avenue on a spring evening when the neon lights were beginning to be reflected in the exhausted eyes, etc.

Now that you know something about my shocking character, you probably have already perceived the difficulty the student has put me in. He has already surrendered his liberty for the sake of a pretty paragraph, and young writers love pretty paragraphs, so it is going to take something like a major operation to cut that pretty paragraph out and let him begin to think again about his subject. The time for fine writing comes when everything else is correct, when you know how the story should be told and whom the characters are that you want to tell it about; and the light falls not on the eyes of office workers but where you as a story-teller want it to fall—dead on the crisis, the moment after which everything changes; the moment in the first subject when the boy realizes what his mother had made him do to his father, and that in the second when the old Jewish lady says the words that will in time reveal to her son that he too is a thief.

Those of you who know something about my work will realize that even then, when you have taken every precaution against wasting your time, when everything is organized, and, according to the rules, there is nothing left for you but produce a perfect story, you often produce nothing of the kind. My own evidence for that comes from a story I once wrote called 'First Confession.' It is a story about a little boy who goes to confession for the first time and confesses that he had planned to kill his grandmother. I wrote the story twenty-five years ago, and it was published and I was paid for it. I should have been happy, but I was not. No sooner did I begin to re-read the story than I knew I had missed the point. It was too spread out in time.

Many years later a selection of my stories was being published, and I re-wrote the story, concentrating it into an hour. This again was published, and became so popular that I made more money out of it than I'd ever made out of a story before. You'd think that at least would have satisfied me. It didn't.

Years later, I took that story and re-wrote it in the first person because I realized it was one of those stories where it was more important to say 'I planned to kill my grandmother' than to say 'Jackie planned to kill his grandmother.' And since then, you will be glad to know, whenever I wake up at four in the morning and think of my sins, I do not any longer think of the crime I committed against Jackie in describing his first confession. The story is as finished as it is ever going to be, and, to end on a note of confidence, I would wish you to believe that if you work hard at a story over a period of twenty-five or thirty years, there is a reasonable chance that at last you will get it right.

Why Don't You Write About America?

Written in 1961 but published posthumously, this essay moves far from its title to self-portrait, discussions of character, literary technique, Ireland and America. Note particularly O'Connor's remarks on the individual's revolt against family and community; they are the basis of many notable stories of young men and women.

Ever since I came to this country I have been haunted by that question, "Why don't you write about America?" It has always made me feel awkward, like a failure to repay hospitality, or worse a deliberate flouting of it. It was as though I didn't think America worth writing about, when indeed it was modesty more than anything else. It is a peculiarity of Americans that they welcome people's writing of them. An Irishman shudders every time Honor Tracy writes a book about Ireland. "What does that one know about it?" they ask passionately, till one has to remind oneself that knowledge is not what makes a book. Affection too has its share, and even, while we are speaking of Miss Tracy, good, old-fashioned spitefulness. I too have said that I didn't know enough about America, but the answer satisfied nobody. Lots of American writers know less. Look at the sorts of novels they write!

Then there is the defense of language. I have an exceedingly weak visual imagination, and have the greatest difficulty in keeping my characters within a consistent scenic background. The houses are always turning from two storeys to three, and laneways suddenly appear where no laneways were. But I have a very strong auditory imagination, and when I have to read a student's story to a class my casual recollection of how Americans speak—stage Yankee mixed up with Virginia—fills even myself with gloom. But that, of course, is likewise not conclusive. Synge,

318

Yeats, and Lady Gregory were all great writers, but they could not record the everyday speech of Ireland.

There is also the matter of manners and customs. It was my small boy, then aged 14, who after a month of America put his finger on one of the major differences. "When you get in a fight in Ireland some man separates you," he said. "When you do it in England, someone separates you, makes you shake hands, and gives you sixpence, but when you do it in America people cross to the other side of the street."

But now, after five years of experience, I know that the best defense is attack. "Why do you want me to write about America?" stops the questioner dead. Because usually his reason for wanting me to do it resembles mine in not wishing to do it; to neither of us is the subject of literature merely a country, merely a different set of facts, words, and manners. Usually, the questioner's experience has been like my own, and like that of the Joyce of *A Portrait of the Artist as a Young Man;* it is that of an exceptional people, and consists of two ordeals, ordeal by family and ordeal by community. In fact, we first come to identify the community merely as a pleasant relief from the family. The community consists largely of a number of delightful people with delightful families. We, the exceptional ones, are unique in having such a terrible family. It drinks, it quarrels in public, it has the wrong views, and it wears awful clothes. It says things like "I suppose you think you're clever?" or "Why do you waste your time with that silly book?" or "Why do you go round with that dreadful boy? I suppose he can't afford to get his hair cut?" Rapidly we are driven to the conclusion that we are orphans or illegitimates or both, which gives us superior airs that involve us in further trouble. One parent is mainly responsible for our orphaned or illegitimate state. In Europe it is frequently the mother. In Ireland, England, and America it seems to be always the father. (Look at the horrible indictment of the American father in Arthur Miller's *All My Sons.*)

So we make our escape to the community, and discover too late that it is out of the frying pan into the fire. We buy a framed print of the Picasso "White Lady" and hang it in our room as a symbol of our uniqueness and detachment from the sordid life about us. Miss Mary McCarthy has recently been making fun of the White Lady, though I can't see why she should be so superior about it. My own choice was a Degas, but I am writing this in a room with the White Lady over the fireplace. Now she is part of the high road, but at one time she was a very narrow, dark laneway indeed, and something of the magic lingers. I cannot patronize my own youth, and must be content with memories of the French coffee, and French cigarettes and wine, the wide-brimmed black hat (made in Birmingham) and the flowing bow tie, the folk songs and night-long arguments about free love, and the refusal to attend church. And then there was the little local dramatic society, and one's efforts to make it perform Ibsen or Chekhov instead of the latest West End or Broadway farce. And always the natural differences became more acute, the more criticism one incurred.

In the main, the revolt (against the family and the community) was innocent and funny, but it had a tragic side that Sherwood Anderson revealed in *Winesburg, Ohio*. Anderson's descriptions are more convincing than Joyce's, because Anderson knew it was not only the artist who suffered from the pettiness of the community, but the exceptional person generally, and he knew that sometimes the White Lady looked down on suicide and madness.

So the exceptional person retreats, if he can, to Metropolis. Metropolis is wherever he is most free to be himself, but to Joyce and the generation that succeeded him, it was the Latin Quarter of Paris. The Latin Quarter was a direct result of the industrial revolution, but it was in the last half of the century that it became world famous. George Moore lived there; Synge, too, went there and met Joyce and Yeats. You needed little money; like Synge you "walked to spare your sack of coals," and a little cold and hunger was a small price to pay for the freedom to wear a big black hat, to let your hair grow, not to go to church, and (if you were that way inclined) to practice as well as discuss free love. Success might come in time; you would have a butler and a fashionable wife, but your thoughts would go back to some Paris attic and the good company you had enjoyed there.

That dream of an artist's homeland—one of the most moving of 19th-century fantasies—penetrated to England and America and produced Chelsea and Greenwich Village, it was the first time that artists and writers detached themselves from the world, and there was something in it that resembled the great monastic dream of the 10th century. Willa Cather movingly describes the artists' colonies in *Youth and the Bright Medusa*. More than any of the other writers, Willa Cather had a sense of dedication to the community; again and again in those stories she returns to her American country folk with their courage and generosity.

Because of course sooner or later the revolt against family and community breaks down. If it isn't the butler, it's the bank manager. We find that our parents are not the ogres they seemed to be; usually, indeed, they turn out to be wise and kindly folk, far superior to their neighbors. In our youth we make them into symbols of the conflict in ourselves between reason and judgment, and this is the guise in which they return to us in dreams. Arthur Miller's *Death of a Salesman* inters the American father with full military honors.

And what has happened to the artists' colonies? I doubt if today there is any real Latin Quarter or Chelsea or Greenwich Village. They existed on into the 20s, though even then most of the real writers lived in little villages in Buckinghamshire or Connecticut in 17th-or 18th-century cottages with original oak beams and no plumbing, or in caravans or barges on the river. If the literature of the colony was largely town literature, this was rural literature, its most characteristic voice A. E. Coppard, its most powerful Robert Frost.

But today commuters have caught up with the colonies, and the original oak beams decorate the weekend cottage of a film director. When I talk to young people of talent they seem to have no particular desire to go anywhere, except to some capital to earn a living. America alone still has a refuge for its talented young people in the universities where they can live cheaply, dress informally, and discuss the universe late into the night. Europe has no such refuges.

But in talking to myself about the question I began with, I find I have answered it, for the loyalties of the exceptional person are not so much to any country, but to the place or places where he endured the two ordeals and to whatever ideal homeland gave them birth.

Essays and Portraits

W. B. Yeats

In the last decade of Yeats's life, O'Connor worked closely with him in a variety of situations. He may have known Yeats better than anyone else and observed him—in the Abbey Theatre and at home—with great affection and to great effect. His devotion to Yeats did not prevent them from arguing, and some of his best portraits of Yeats humanize the man while celebrating the poet, the Irish genius, even the man of action. A passage from My Father's Son *shows this well: "I knew the apparent childish selfishness of Yeats, because once when I was seeing him home, he went to his club, and told me that George was ill with some infectious disease and that he couldn't go home. I, thinking of George by herself in the house, said 'Oh, that's awful!' and Yeats replied mournfully, 'Yes. You see, I can't even get at my books.' But I also saw the other side. . . . when we went in a taxi to some Board meeting, I paid the taxi driver and Yeats grabbed the money frantically from his hand and created a scene while he tried to find money of his own—always a difficult task for him as he never could make out where his pockets were. I said, 'Oh, stop it, W. B.,' and he turned on me. 'You don't understand, O'Connor,' he gasped. 'I wouldn't mind, but my wife would never forgive me.' Maybe only a story-teller can understand this, but I knew that a man who worried about what he was going to tell his wife about who paid the taxi fare was a man in love, whatever anybody else might think" (217–18). We are fortunate indeed that O'Connor saw, understood, and recorded such moments. This essay, published in 1948 and discovered recently by Ruth Sherry, is a fine example of O'Connor on Yeats, assessing the achievement and evoking the singular individual.*

The return of Yeats's remains to Ireland is an occasion for celebration. If they had come home nine years ago, we should probably have been thinking of our loss rather than of his achievement. To-day we can think of his return only as the completion of a work long-planned, the crowning of a life which was like a great work of art, nobly conceived, nobly executed, and now brought to a triumphant conclusion.

For it was part of the work of art as he saw it that he who took his inspiration from the landscape and people of Sligo should return to them in the end.

> Under bare Ben Bulben's head
> In Drumcliffe churchyard Yeats is laid . . .
> On limestone quarried near the spot
> By his commands these words are cut:
>   Cast a cold eye
>   On life, on death.
>   Horseman, pass by!

For the life of me I do not know what he meant by that epitaph, because of all the men I have met there never was one who threw a warmer eye on both life and death. On the evening when I heard of his death I said to my wife: "Eternity never had a new arrival who expected it more confidently."

It used to be said of the Celts that they believed in the next world so passionately that you could borrow money from them and arrange to pay it back there. I have known a couple of old Irish-speaking country-women who had that belief. Yeats had it. I sometimes wondered what on earth he could make of Hamlet's lines about "the fear of something after death."

He had the same noble attitude to life. For me he will always be the poet of friendship. How often, when I have arranged some little party which went wrong I have found myself quoting:—

> Always we'd have the new friend meet the old,
> And we are hurt if either friend seem cold.

Or when a friend has disappointed me:—

> But thoughts rise up unbid
> On generous things that he did,
> And I grow half-contented to be blind.

Once when he told me of a thing like that about somebody we both admired he suddenly caught himself up and pointed a warning finger at me. "But that was So-and-So, the intriguer," he said, "not So-and-So, your friend and mine!" That was the sort of sudden burst of generosity, like sunlight through a cloud, which sometimes made my heart jump when I was with him.

"John Quinn," Yeats's father reported, "says you are the straightest and most generous Irishman he ever met. He says you are always generous." I think anyone who knew him would agree. He was generous with money, but that is not rare in Ireland; he was equally generous with his opinions; that *is* rare.

Like the old Greeks, I have always believed that a great man must also be a good man. I never had any doubts of Yeats's goodness, but in a leader such as he was it matters less what his virtues are than that they should make a good roaring blaze. And Yeats was a leader as well as an artist.

I think he must be unique in this: I can't think of anyone else who combined the executive artist and the leader as he did, and it was one of the most Irish things about him.

It was not enough for him to win fame for himself; he had to win it for his country as well. As well as being a sensitive poet he was also an I. R. B. man, and what he or his friends did had somehow or other to be made to serve Ireland. Like Swift, whom he resembled, like Parnell whom he greatly resembled and admired, he realised that the damage done to our social institutions through the centuries left him with no alternative but to be himself whatever he wanted Ireland to be. He traced all our evils to the fact that our leadership became infected by the ruin of our institutions like some blitzed town by the bodies buried in its ruins.

He would never allow you to criticize Mr. de Valera's statement that when he wanted to know what Ireland thought he looked into his own heart. "Where else *could* the man look?" Yeats would growl.

It was a dangerous creed, and might easily have led him into the arrogance and inhumanity his father feared for him. He was saved by his own splendid balance. He had all the virtues which I call middle-class (he would have hated me for using the word, but the day will come when it will be fashionable again). He was sober, industrious; a man accustomed to the exercise of responsibility and scrupulous in every detail of it.

He was a solid man; the artist's fancy and flightiness never went very deep, and wherever you dug you struck rock.

He made his ideal Ireland out of folklore and the great sagas of the eighth and ninth centuries before the Danish invasions had destroyed a growing culture. He knew them mostly through inferior translations, but he knew them in the same way as his ancestors knew their Bible. He frequently surprised me by quoting some Gaelic story or poem which I either didn't know or knew superficially.

In later years he got a lot from Swift and Berkeley, but he never lost his veneration for the sagas, and even on his death-bed continued to dramatise his own life in terms of Cú Chulainn's. Cú Chulainn was always the man he tried to be, and the ideal he set for himself is that which Cú Roi Mac Daire crowns in Cú Chulainn:—

And I choose the laughing lip,
That shall not turn from laughing, whatever rise or fall,
The heart that grows no bitterer although betrayed by all,
The hand that loves to scatter, the life like a gambler's throw,
And these things I make prosper.

To the preservation of this integrity of his, this image of the ideal Irishman and the ideal Ireland, he devoted all his craft and pertinacity. You could go to Yeats and confess all the crimes in the calendar. But go to him, even in the noblest cause, as the representative of the Society for the Preservation of This or the Suppression of That, and all you were likely to get was a rocket. As an individual, even though you were in the wrong, you enriched his experience; as the mouthpiece of a group you attacked his integrity. When the Cosgrave Government established the Military Tribunal I tried to get him to join in a protest and got a typical Yeats reply—a rocket with a bouquet attached: "I have been reading your translations with admiration."

I knew what the "admiration" meant! "Why doesn't that fellow get on with his proper job instead of interfering in politics?"

But by preserving his integrity he created real liberty for us and those who come after us.

He broke forever in Ireland the tyranny of public opinion and ended the cruel dichotomy which said to the young writer: "You must be a good Irishman or a good writer; you cannot be both."

By audacity, pertinacity and craft, Yeats succeeded in being both.

Whether it was Cú Roi Mac Daire or some higher power, his ideals certainly prospered. As we see under Parnell the emergence of a formidable political intelligence, so with Yeats, who took over where Parnell left off, we see the emergence of a literary genius which placed Ireland intellectually where Parnell had placed it politically. You cannot say Parnell created Dillon, O'Brien, Sexton or Healy; all you can say is that there was no such constellation of talent before him.

Yeats did not create Synge, Augusta Gregory, Robinson, O'Casey or the rest, but he did give them the blaze of light by which they worked, and he was so much the leader that he threw overboard all concern for his own fame, and served theirs, even when, as with Synge and O'Casey, it became temporarily greater than his own.

The leader is a man so great that he doesn't have to be jealous.

Yeats was probably the most fortunate of all great poets; fortunate in his father, in his friends, in his marriage, and in his children.

Beginning as playwright in a small hall, he lived to see his theatre recognised as the National Theatre of Ireland (I wish it would learn to live up to that name).

Beginning as a revolutionary conspirator in a country enslaved, he lived to become a member of its Parliament, and now after his death will be brought home by the Irish Navy, received by the Irish Army.

That much he might perhaps in some fanciful moment have anticipated, but even he couldn't have guessed that the ship which brought him back would be called after Macha, the Celtic divinity who presided over Emain Macha, Cú Chulainn's capital, or that the Minister of State who would receive back his body from the French Government would be the son of the woman he had loved in his youth and who had inspired some of his loveliest poetry.

You can call that a coincidence if you like; I prefer to think of it as a "tilly," to use a good old Irish word; a last rose tossed from eternity to crown the completed work of art in time.

All the Olympians

O'Connor's literary criticism benefits from his energetic willingness to diverge from accepted critical wisdom and, as well, from his immersion in the works and their world. Who else, writing of the relationships between Yeats, Lady Gregory, and John Synge, had the advantage of being a director of the Abbey Theater in the 1930s, meeting Lady Gregory, knowing Yeats well, and working on productions of Synge's plays?

Nobody will ever understand much about modern Irish literature who does not grasp the fact that one cannot really deal with any of its three great writers in isolation. Synge and Lady Gregory are as much part of Yeats' life-work as are his plays, and until his death he proudly linked their names with his own. They are converts, not imitators, and what they share with him is a religion as much as an aesthetic. The death of Synge came very close to being the end of the others as writers: Yeats' work between 1909 and his marriage is the least important part of his work, and all Lady Gregory's best work was written during Synge's lifetime. In many ways she was temperamentally closer to him than she was to Yeats, and in a peculiar way he seems to have acted as a challenge to her.

It is because the relationship of the three was a conversion rather than a conspiracy that it does not really affect the originality of Synge and Lady Gregory. That it was a true conversion we can see if we consider what they were like about the year 1895. Lady Gregory was a London literary hostess who seemed to model herself on Queen Victoria. In 1886 the English poet Scawen Blunt wrote of her:

> It is curious that she, who could see so clearly in Egypt when it was a case between the Circassian pashas and the Arab fellahin, should be blind now

330

that the case is between English landlords and Irish tenants in Galway. But property blinds all eyes, and it is easier for a camel to pass through the eye of a needle, than for an Irish landlord to enter the kingdom of Home Rule. She comes of a family, too, who are 'bitter Protestants', and has surrounded herself with people of her class from Ireland, so that there is no longer room for me in her house (*Land War in Ireland,* 146).

Synge was a shy and sickly young man who was quietly starving in a Paris attic, producing badly written little articles which editors fought shy of. A couple of years later the London hostess was hard at work learning Irish, writing down folk-stories in the cottages of the poor peasants she had cut Blunt for trying to assist, and indeed was being restrained only by Yeats himself from turning Catholic as well. Synge, dressed in homespuns, was living a comfortless life on a barren island on the edge of Europe. The conversion was complete, but within, both remained very much what they had always been.

Not that I find Synge very easy to understand either before or after conversion. Yeats' autobiography, Lady Gregory's journals, George Moore's gossip, Professor D. H. Greene's *Life,* Dr. Henn's criticism all leave him completely opaque to me. The only passage I can think of that suggests a real man is in Miss Walker's reminiscences.

At the first opportunity, he would lever his huge frame out of a chair and come up on the stage, a half-rolled cigarette in each hand. Then he would look enquiringly round and thrust the little paper cylinders forward towards whoever was going to smoke them. In later years he became the terror of fire-conscious Abbey stage managers. He used to sit timidly in the wings during plays, rolling cigarettes and handing them to the players as they made their exits (MacShiubhlaigh and Kenny, *The Splendid Years,* 1955).

At least the shy man in that little sketch is alive, even if one cannot exactly see him as author of *The Playboy of the Western World.*

So one must fall back on the work, and even here I find myself mystified. In every writer there are certain key words that give you some clue to what he is about. Words like 'friend' and 'friendship' are valuable when one is reading Yeats, but in Synge all I can find are words that suggest carrion.

> Yet these are rotten—I ask their pardon—
> And we've the sun on rock and garden;
> These are rotten, so you're the Queen
> Of all are living, or have been.

If this is how he usually addressed girls it is hardly surprising that he had to spend so much time rolling cigarettes. When he escaped for a while from this carrion view of life it was into a sort of Wordsworthian pantheism. Clearly he was deeply influenced by Wordsworth, and Wordsworth need hardly have been ashamed of signing some of his poems.

> Still south I went and west and south again,
> Through Wicklow from the morning till the night,
> And far from cities, and the sites of men,
> Lived with the sunshine, and the moon's delight.
>
> I knew the stars, the flowers, and the birds,
> The grey and wintry sides of many glens,
> And did but half remember human words,
> In converse with the mountains, moors, and fens.

How Yeats managed to persuade him at all is a mystery. Yeats had not a glimmer of carrion consciousness. I get the feeling that he carefully avoided the whole subject as being exaggerated, dull, and totally irrelevant. Where he may have managed to communicate with Synge is through Wordsworthianism. Not that Yeats had much time for Wordsworth—'the only great poet who was cut down and used for timber'—but when he preached about the Aran Islands, the necessity for writing about peasants and for adopting peasant speech, a student of Wordsworth could easily have caught what seemed to be echoes of the English poet.

> Low and rustic life was generally chosen because in that situation the essential passions of the heart find a better soil in which they can attain their maturity, are less under restraint, and speak a plainer and more emphatic language; because in that situation our elementary feelings exist in a state of greater simplicity and consequently may be more accurately contemplated and more forcibly communicated; because the manners of

rural life germinate from those elementary feelings; and from the necessary character of rural occupations are more easily comprehended and are more durable; and lastly, because in that situation the passions of men are incorporated with the beautiful and permanent forms of nature. The language, too, of these men is adopted (purified indeed from what appear to be its real defects from all lasting and rational causes of dislike or disgust) because such men hourly communicate with the best objects from which the best part of language is originally derived; and because from their rank in society and the sameness and narrow circle of their intercourse, being less under the action of social vanity they convey their feelings and notions in simple and unelaborated expressions (Wordsworth, Preface to *Lyrical Ballads*).

It seems to me possible that when we read Synge's prefaces, which so often seem to echo Yeats, we may find that they are really—saving the syntax—echoing Wordsworth.

The material of Synge's plays is slight, and, for the most part, according to Yeats' formula. What is extraordinary is the impact the plays themselves made by comparison with Yeats' and Lady Gregory's. *In the Shadow of the Glen,* for instance, is a folk-story about a flighty wife whose husband pretends to be dead so as to expose her. At the end of the play she goes off with a tramp who, as so often in these plays, represents the Wordsworthian compromise. It is a harmless little play that barely holds interest on the stage, but Arthur Griffith screamed his head off about it as about everything else Synge wrote. 'His play is not a work of genius, Irish or otherwise. It is a foul echo from degenerate Greece.'

It is hard to understand the ferocity of the Catholic reaction to Synge, so much fiercer than the reaction to Joyce. Though it is doubtful if Yeats himself understood it, instinct seems to have warned him that his theories stood or fell by Synge's work.

It must have been instinct too that warned Arthur Griffith what to attack. Essentially Synge seems to have been, as everyone describes him, gentle, and I should say with little self-confidence. He was willing to write folk plays, mystery plays, or mythological plays to order, though they always turned out to be much the same play. Yeats describes him somewhere as the most 'unpolitical' man who ever lived, but he was 'anti-political' rather than 'unpolitical.'

Once some group of patriotic people persuaded him to write a really patriotic play about the heroes of 1798 and the wickedness of the English soldiery. In his obliging way Synge came back with a most extraordinary scenario. The characters were two girls, one Protestant, the other Catholic, who in fear of being raped took shelter in a mountain cave. During the play they discuss the cruel and immoral behaviour of both sides, the Catholic girl defending the rebels and the Protestant the military, till they begin to pull one another's hair out. Finally they separate, the Catholic declaring that she would prefer to be raped by an Englishman than listen to further heresy; and the Protestant that she would prefer to be raped by a rebel than listen to Catholic lies.

Much chance there was that a man like that would write a play to reunite everybody!

In the Shadow of the Glen fails because the story on which it is based is farcical, while the play itself is serious. *Riders to the Sea* succeeds brilliantly because, though it is a Yeatsian miracle, one can watch it without even being aware that a miracle is involved. We can perceive its originality best if we study Lawrence's imitation of it in 'Odour of Chrysanthemums.' A fisherman's death, a miner's death represent the whole of life concentrated in a limited society. Both are anti-political, and in neither is there any reference to the price of fish or coal, or any demand for safety regulations. In these two worlds there is no safety except a clean burial. 'What more can we want than that? No man at all can be living for ever, and we must be satisfied.'

The Tinker's Wedding fails as a play because it has no Synge in it; *The Well of the Saints* because it has too much. The truth is that neither Yeats himself nor any of his followers ever really mastered the problems of extended form, and once they went beyond the one-act play they made the most extraordinary mistakes—I have already pointed out Synge's mistake in the first act of the *Playboy*. (Moore noticed this weakness in Lady Gregory's plays. See *Hail and Farewell!* iii. *Vale*, chap. viii.) In a one-act play dealing with a miracle, it is the miracle which automatically establishes itself as the crisis, the point towards which a playwright must build and then work away from; but in *The Well of the Saints* there are two miracles, neither of which is the real crisis.

The Playboy of the Western World is Synge's masterpiece because it contains more of the real Synge than anything else he wrote, and naturally, it created a greater storm. Synge himself is the shy and sickly young man who scandalizes the world by a crime he has not committed at all, but he remains a hero even when he is shown up, because he has at last learned to live with his image of himself. Unfortunately he discovered what life was like only as death caught up with him. When the *Playboy* appeared he was world-famous and dying.

His greatest achievement as a writer was his elaboration of a style. It was he who really came to grips with the problems posed by Hyde in *Beside the Fire*—the problems of adapting folk speech to literary ends. Yet Synge's own ear for folk speech cannot have been very good. Though he describes himself recording the conversation in the kitchen below his bedroom in Wicklow he never seems to have studied Hyde's introduction to *Beside the Fire,* where he points out the most obvious fact about English spoken in Ireland: the absence of the pluperfect. In Modern Irish, unlike Old Irish, there are no perfect tenses, so they rarely occur in spoken English. We do not normally say 'He had been there an hour' or 'I shall have discussed it with him.' If we need to supply the missing tense we use the adverb 'after' with the verbal noun: 'He was after being there an hour' or 'I'll be after discussing it with him.'

Synge could never get this quite straight. He dropped the relative pronoun, as in the lines I quoted earlier, 'Of all are living or have been,' a construction that in my experience does not occur at all, and rounded it off with a past perfect; and twice at the climax of *Riders to the Sea* he uses improbable tenses: 'It isn't that I haven't prayed for you, Bartley, to the Almighty God. It isn't that I haven't said prayers in the dark night till you wouldn't know what I'd be saying.' Even in the very opening scene he gives us the English use of 'shall' in 'Shall I open it now?'

What he did succeed in was giving Anglo-Irish speech a strong cadence structure. The dialogue in Lady Gregory's *Spreading the News* is enchanting, but it is prose, and in the passionate moments of real drama there is no reserve of language upon which to draw. Lady Gregory herself must have been keenly aware of what he had achieved because in a play that she obviously intended as a rival to *Riders to the Sea, The Gaol Gate,* she used an irregular ballad metre, which she then concealed by writing it as prose; but this is a clumsy device because if the actor becomes aware of the metre he can scarcely avoid falling into sing-song, while if he is not, he is just as liable to break up the cadences as though they were nothing but prose. Hyde had given Irish prose writers a medium by which they could keep their distance from English writers; Synge went one better and invented a medium which enabled them to keep the whole modern prose theatre at a distance.

Nobody that I know of has analysed this cadence structure. One obvious cadence fades out on an unimportant word like 'only' or 'surely.' Another of the same sort ends on a temporal clause, which in modern English would be placed at the beginning of the phrase, and this is emphasized by the modern Irish use of the conjunction 'and' as an adverb. Thus, where an English speaker would be inclined to say, 'When I was coming home it was dark,' we tend to say, 'It was dark and I coming home,' and Synge tends to use it for its slightly melancholy colour.

> MAURYA: Isn't it a hard and cruel man won't hear a word from an old woman, and she holding him from the sea?
> CATHLEEN: It's the life of a young man to be going on the sea, and who would listen to an old woman with one thing and she saying it over?

A notable cadence seems to end on a single accented long vowel, often a monosyllable which is preceded by another long and a short—cretics alternating with choriambs is perhaps how it might be described. Synge makes very effective use of it in the great love scene in the *Playboy*—'in the heat of noon,' 'when our banns is called,' 'in four months or five,' and 'in his golden chair.'

If Synge remains a mysterious figure, there is nothing whatever mysterious about Lady Gregory. If there is one word that sums her up it is complacency—Victorian complacency at that. To please Yeats she rewrote the early sagas and romances that had been edited by famous scholars in English, French and German, but when she came to a line such as 'Will we ask her to sleep with you?' in 'The Voyage of Mael Dúin', Lady Gregory, remembering what the Dear Queen would have felt, turned it into 'Will we ask her would she maybe be your wife?'

Yet I think the critic in the *Times Literary Supplement* who not so long ago told us that there would be no Lady Gregory revival was probably wrong. If ever we get a national theatre again I should expect more revivals of *Spreading the News*, *The Rising of the Moon*, *The Travelling Man*, and *The Gaol Gate* than of *Riders to the Sea* or *On Baile's Strand*. We have to learn to appreciate the work of Yeats and Synge, and in doing so lose something of its original freshness, but anyone can appreciate a Lady Gregory play just as anyone can enjoy watching a children's game. Under the Victorian complacency is the Victorian innocence, and this is a quality that does not easily date.

I do not mean that she is unsophisticated. If Yeats had his Corneille for master and Synge his Racine, she has her Molière, and anyone who knows Molière will notice his little tricks in her comedies; as for instance the slow passages of elaborate exposition that suddenly give place to the slapstick stichomythia.

> MR. QUIRKE: The man that preserved me!
> HYACINTH: That preserved you?
> MR. QUIRKE: That kept me from ruin!
> HYACINTH: From ruin?
> MR. QUIRKE: That saved me from disgrace!
> HYACINTH: *(To Mrs. Delane.)* What is he saying at all?
> MR. QUIRKE: From the Inspector!
> HYACINTH: What is he talking about?

But in spite of the Victorian complacency she had a genuine tragic sense. Naturally it was a very limited one. She had a tendency to repeat a phrase of Yeats': 'Tragedy must be a joy to the man that dies.' Even as stated it is a very doubtful critical principle, because we do not go to the theatre to see Oedipus enjoy himself, but as she applied it it was even more restricting because it tended to turn into 'Tragedy must be a *pleasure* to the man who dies,' which is a very Victorian notion indeed and somewhat reminiscent of the Father of All putting his creatures across his knee and saying, 'This hurts me more than it hurts you.'

But within that Victorian framework she achieves remarkable results, as she does for instance in *The Gaol Gate*. When the play opens we see two poor countrywomen, mother and daughter-in-law, at the gate of Galway Gaol, waiting for the release of a young man who is supposed to have betrayed his comrades in some agrarian outrage. Instead, when the gaol gate opens, they are informed that his comrades have been released and that he has been hanged; and as they walk back through the streets of the town the old mother bursts into a great song of praise. Lady Gregory had been studying *Riders to the Sea* and old Maurya's great tragic tirade at the curtain, and to make certain of a poetic effect has deliberately chosen to write in a loose and ungainly metre. But even more striking is the contrast between the two climaxes, Synge's haunted by the imminence of death, Lady Gregory's by the triumph of life.

MARY CAHEL: *(Holding out her hands.)* Are there any people in the streets
at all till I call on them to come hither? Did they ever hear in Galway
such a thing to be done, a man to die for his neighbour?

Tell it out in the streets for the people to hear, Denis Cahel from Slieve
Echtge is dead. It was Denis Cahel from Daire-caol that died in the
place of his neighbour! . . .

Gather up, Mary Cushin, the clothes for your child; they'll be wanted by
this one and that one. The boys crossing the sea in the springtime will
be craving a thread for a memory. . . .

The child he left in the house that is shook, it is great will be his boast of
his father! All Ireland will have a welcome before him, and all the
people in Boston.

I to stoop on a stick through half a hundred years, I will never be tired
with praising! Come hither, Mary Cushin, till we'll shout it through
the roads, Denis Cahel died for his neighbour!

Apart from the fact that this is as great as anything in classical tragedy, it is also one of the most astonishing things in the Irish Literary
Revival, for it is the work of a Protestant landowner, whose own son
would die as an officer in the British Air Force and who had broken off
an old friendship with Scawen Blunt because he himself had occupied a
cell in Galway Gaol with the Denis Cahels of his day. It makes everything
else written in Ireland in our time seem like the work of a foreigner.

There is an even more haunting tragic climax in *Dervorgilla* of the
following year, 1908. Dervorgilla keeps on attracting romantic writers
since Thomas Moore called her 'falsest of women,' and in *The Dreaming
of the Bones* even Yeats denies her forgiveness for her imaginary crime.
According to the chestnut, which is served up even in the most recent
histories and guide-books she was the wife of O'Rourke of Breany and
eloped with MacMurrough of Leinster, thus precipitating the Norman
invasion. The writers have most peculiar notions of Irish dynastic marriages: Dervorgilla was a woman famous for her piety whose 'marriages'
to two unmitigated ruffians like O'Rourke and MacMurrough she had
nothing whatever to say to.

But what we are dealing with in Lady Gregory's play is the legend of
the unfaithful woman who sacrificed Ireland to her passions, and we see
her in retirement and repentance at Mellifont Abbey, acting Lady Boun-
tiful to the young people of the countryside till her identity comes to
light. Her last great speech is as noble as anything in Irish literature; in

a sense we may, I think, read it as Lady Gregory's own apology for her withdrawal from Kiltartan Cross.

> DERVORGILLA: Since you were born and before you were born I have been here, kneeling and praying, kneeling and praying, fasting and asking forgiveness of God. I think my father God has forgiven me. They tell me my mother the Church has forgiven me. That old man had forgiven me, and he had suffered by the Gall. The old—the old—that old woman, even in her grief, she called out no word against me. You are young. You will surely forgive me, for you are young. *(They are all silent. Then Owen comes over and lays down his cup at her feet, then turns and walks slowly away.)* It is not your hand that has done this, but the righteous hand of God that has moved your hand. *(Other lads lay down their gifts.)* I take this shame for the shame in the west I put on O'Rourke of Breffny and the death I brought upon him by the hand of the Gall. *(The youngest boy, who has hesitated, comes and lays down his hurl and silver ball, and goes away, his head drooping.)* I take this reproach for the reproach in the east I brought upon Diarmuid, King of Leinster, trusting upon him wars and attacks and battles, till for his defence and to defend Leinster he called in the strangers that have devoured Ireland. *(The young men have gone. Mamie comes as if to lay down her gift, but draws back. Dervorgilla turns to her.)* Do not be afraid to give back my gifts, do not separate yourself from your companions for my sake. For there is little of my life but is spent, and there has come upon me this day all the pain of the world and its anguish, seeing and knowing that a deed once done has no undoing, and the lasting trouble my unfaithfulness has brought upon you and your children for ever. *(Mamie lays down her necklace and goes away sadly.)* There is kindness in your unkindness, not leaving me to go and face Michael and the scales of judgement wrapped in comfortable words, and the praises of the poor, and the lulling of psalms, but from the swift, unflinching, terrible judgement of the young.

I have quoted that great speech, partly that you may understand why the first play I insisted on reviving when I became a director of the Abbey Theatre was *Dervorgilla,* partly to pass on the terrible lesson I learned from it. The play was produced by a young English producer I admired, and the part of Dervorgilla acted by an exceptionally intelligent young actress, and I did not attend the theatre until the dress rehearsal. I listened in bewilderment and horror, and it was only in the last few minutes that I could bring myself to moan, 'For God's sake, stop that infernal snivelling!' It was that evening that I asked Yeats if it was ever permissible for an actor to weep at the curtain of a play and he wrote his answer into 'Lapis Lazuli.'

But my mistake, of course, went deeper than production or acting. It was that in post–Civil War Ireland I expected the atmosphere of that whole dazzling decade; a decade in which Kuno Meyer could casually edit 'King and Hermit' and 'Liadan and Cuirithir' and George Moore in the same year produce the Irish version of *The Untilled Field;* when people acted superbly who had never acted before and in a single year one might have joined in the *Playboy* riots and seen *The Rising of the Moon* and *Dervorgilla* itself, while English and American critics wondered what would happen next.

Only a literary historian will ever be able to capture again anything of that magic—'All the Olympians, a thing never known again.'

Introduction to *A Portrait of the Artist as a Young Man*

Well before Joyce was accepted into the undergraduate curriculum, O'Connor had studied him thoroughly, his admiration tempered with reservations (and vice versa). In April 1930, he praised Joyce's "third period," approving of Work in Progress; *in a July 1937 broadcast, he linked Joyce with Lawrence as "our two greatest; and they seemed to me to have failed" (Cohn and Peterson, 220). His 1943 "post-mortem" in* The Bell *was even more frankly ambivalent: "I think I almost said 'Thank God' when Joyce died. . . . I can think of no other writer, unless perhaps Rousseau, who wielded such an influence; who was so much the pool of Narcissus to his generation, as Cyril Connolly put it" (363). This 1964 preface is better-mannered, but no less complex. Most fascinating is the mingling of perspectives—O'Connor as the young reader of* Portrait, *the young writer on a pilgrimage to Joyce in Paris, seeing Cork and cork, and as a mature artist of sixty.*

A Portrait of the Artist as a Young Man should be compulsory reading for every young man and woman. I doubt if I was 17 when I read it first, in a copy removed from the Students' Library at University College, Cork, because of its indecency. Though I had had a more sheltered childhood than most boys, I wasn't in the least shocked or disturbed by it. I felt too strongly that Joyce had understood as no one else seemed to do the problems of the serious adolescent growing up in squalid circumstances. Young people are like that. What they get out of a book is more often what they need for their own adjustment to life than what the author intends. What I got out of Dostoevsky at the same time was not the sadism—I never noticed it—but a realization that the lies I told

341

almost automatically were more comic than serious, and this gradually made me stop telling lies at all.

After this, Joyce was the Irish writer who influenced me most. I came on *Ulysses* also in an erratic way and was moved and excited by everything in it that dealt with Stephen Dedalus, not so much by the chapters that dealt with Bloom. From what I knew of Russian fiction I got the impression that Bloom was a flat figure. I still find him rather flat. When "Work in Progress"—later titled *Finnegans Wake*—began to appear in print, I learned parts of it by heart and wrote in praise of it in *The Irish Statesman,* though the editor, George Russell, tried in private to restrain my enthusiasm. "You shouldn't say Joyce is a genius, you know," he said reprovingly. "An enormous talent, of course; a colossal talent, but not a genius. Now, James Stephens is a genius." In those days I looked down on Stephens and repeated Russell's verdict with derision; which shows not only that you can't put an old head on young shoulders but that you shouldn't try.

I even made a youthful pilgrimage to see Joyce and liked him a lot, though I was disturbed by the remark he made when I was leaving. The story of the cork frame has been argued and argued by Joyceans since Desmond MacCarthy first printed it, and the reader must argue it for himself. I had admired an old print of the city of Cork in a peculiar frame and, touching the frame, asked "What's that?" "Cork," said Joyce. "I know that," I said, "but what's the frame?" "Cork," replied Joyce. "I had great difficulty in getting a French frame maker to make it."

The main significance of that silly little anecdote relates to myself, for after that I began to see cork frames all over Joyce's work, and they always gave me the same slight shock I got when he said "cork" for the second time. *Finnegans Wake* was the first book of his I lost interest in, because, though I knew it much better than those who criticized it, I always had a lingering doubt whether what I was defending was really supreme artistry or plain associative mania. Later, I stopped rereading great chunks of *Ulysses* which had always bored me—the parodies, the chapter of errors, the scientific catechism—till I was left with only 25 per cent of the book and had to admit that Joyce not only had no sense of organic design but—what was much worse—no vision of human life that had developed beyond the age of 21.

On the other hand, I began to see that he was the greatest master of rhetoric who had ever lived. By rhetoric I mean the technique of literary composition, the relationship of the written word to the object. This, I think, is the aspect of *A Portrait of the Artist* that should appeal most to middle-aged people. His brother, Stanislaus, was shocked when Joyce told him that he was interested in nothing but style, because Stanislaus was a moralist, and his principal interest was in the material and the viewpoint. But Joyce was telling the literal truth; by that time he had ceased to care for anything but the art of writing.

It had not always been so, and this was the tragedy of the relationship between those two brilliant brothers, as it so often is between two strong characters who grow up side by side, mutually dependent. There had been another James Joyce, much closer to Stanislaus, and whom only Stanislaus remembered—poor, angry and idealistic—and to him the material had mattered intensely. One can find this earlier Joyce in *Stephen Hero*, a fragment of the rejected early draft of *A Portrait of the Artist*. Before its publication, I had been hearing of it for years from acquaintances. One of them had told me it was written in the manner of Meredith, and, indeed, it contains a number of awkward ironic references to the hero, like "this fantastic idealist" and "this heaven-ascending essayist," which recall Meredith at his archest. But it is not the style of *Stephen Hero* that matters, for it has none; it is the rage, the anguish, the pity, the awkwardness in it. I remember thinking when I read it first, "This is the worst book ever written, but after it I shall never be able to read *A Portrait of the Artist* again."

This, of course, was an exaggerated reaction; in fact, I find it hard to reread *Stephen Hero*, while I can always read *A Portrait of the Artist* again, though never in the same way. Less and less do I hear the echoes of my own tormented youth in Cork, and more and more do I find myself admiring the devices of the great master of rhetoric. This is not so much a description of a tormented childhood and youth as a reconstitution of it in another form that excites all the detective instinct in me. I do not know what the total pattern is, but I recognize sections of a total pattern here and there as, when I am out archeologizing, I can identify portions of some great building from humps and hollows in the ground. First, there is the over-all rhetorical pattern by which the book is divided into three sections—lyric, epic and dramatic. While the character of Stephen is still fluid, his experiences are expressed in lyric form, each ending in a cry; when he finally takes shape as an individual, he speaks in his own particular voice, through his diary.

Under that is the basic psychological development that accompanies and sustains the artistic one, and this has to be understood in terms of Aristotle's *De Anima*. It is not for nothing that young Stephen Dedalus notices the two faucets in the men's room in the Wicklow Hotel which are hot and cold, or the school badges which are red and white—hot and cold—or the illness which makes him sweat and shiver; for these are the extremes between which the individual lives who is neither hot nor cold. "The mean," says Aristotle, "is capable of judgment, for it becomes in reference to each of the extremes another extreme. And as that which is to perceive white or black must not itself be actually white or black, but both of these potentially . . . so also in the case of touch, it must not be either hot or cold in itself." So, too, when Dante says, "A priest would not be a priest if he did not tell his flock what is right and what is wrong," and Stephen thinks, "It was wrong; it was unfair and cruel," we are present at the birth of a mind which alone decides what is right and wrong and differentiates us from the world of sensation. Aristotle adds: "Neither is thought, in which right and wrong are determined —*i.e.* right in the sense of practical judgment, scientific knowledge and true opinion, and wrong in the sense of the opposite of these—thought in this signification is not identical with sensation."

I have no illusion that I have said the last word on the matter, nor do I think that Joyce stuck to Aristotle any more closely than he stuck to Homer or Vico—in fact, I should be very much surprised if he had. I should suggest that the reader might follow a pattern leading from "heart" through "mind," "soul," "spirit" and "imagination" to "freedom," and see how it works out for him. One of the best student papers I ever read in America was by a young poet who analyzed the book in terms of the rubrics.

"Analyzed"—the very word is like a knell. Why should a work of art have to be subjected to analysis? And where is the Joyce whom Stanislaus knew and who cared deeply about the things Stanislaus and myself and so many others have cared about and who never grew up? My friend V. S. Pritchett has called Joyce "a mad grammarian," and I have said myself that his work is "a rhetorician's dream," saying little more than Joyce himself said to his brother when he told him he was interested only in style. Joyce believed, as Yeats did not, that "words alone are certain good" and that all that happens to human beings can be expressed fully in language. This, as we say in Ireland, is where the ferryboat left him, because it can't. Experience, as older people know, is always drifting into a world where language cannot follow, where, as Turgenev says, "perhaps only music can follow." Robert Browning wrote:

> A fancy from a flower-bell, someone's death,
> A chorus-ending from Euripides,—
> And that's enough for fifty hopes and fears
> As old and new at once as nature's self,
> To rap and knock and enter in our soul,
> Take hands and dance there, a fantastic thing,
> Round the ancient idol, on his base again,—
> The grand Perhaps!

Younger readers will read, careless of Aristotle and Thomas Aquinas, the pattern of human life and how rhetoric may follow it, and not notice how every word has been brooded upon until nothing can be neglected; and older readers will read, pursuing every hint, in the hope that they may understand their children's revolt. But this great book is one about which they can both hope to be right, because, as an elderly man, I can still think back on the boy who read it first in a provincial town 40-odd years ago and was comforted by it, and almost wish I were 16 again.

For a Two-Hundredth Birthday

Although this essay shows O'Connor was as perceptive about music as literature, it is, unfortunately, his only published work on the subject. His celebration of Mozart is illuminated by his feeling for the "Mozartean" temperament that colored his own writing and perspectives. It also shows O'Connor's assurance, as he moves from anecdote to biography, from literary references to discerning musical commentary.

A short time ago I was dining with some friends when a discussion arose about Dylan Thomas. Thomas had been a friend of our hosts, and they continued to regret the sheer waste of his early death. An Indian woman writer opposed this view in what I can think of only as an Eastern way. Who after all were we to judge what was waste? "All things fall and are built again." Soon the party broke into two camps: the Indian lady and two Americans in one; host, hostess and myself, Jewish and Irish, in the other. The Americans, like the Indian lady, scoffed at our passion for history, for exemplary individuals, for monuments, and the importance that we attached to these things in our own lives. Later, one of the Americans developed a conscience. "Of course," she said, "if anyone had asked what a world without Mozart would be like, I shouldn't have known what to say."

There was good reason why she should understand the argument in terms of Mozart rather than of Socrates or Shakespeare who had come up only to be dismissed; why he alone should have defined our hosts' idea of the unique, irreplaceable individual. Mozart's name naturally and easily forms an adjective that describes a whole aspect of human existence that cannot be better delineated. When we say "Wagnerian" we mean something very limited, and usually something not in the least like Wagner; but when we say "Mozartean" we call up a vision of

346

something spring-like, graceful, evanescent, of girls in flower, of young soldiers, or of certain passages in literature like Millamant's surrender in *The Way of the World* or the flower scene in *The Winter's Tale*.

It is a way of seeing things which revokes the tragic attitude without turning into comedy, which says, not "Life is beautiful but so sad" but "Life is sad but so beautiful" and this way of seeing things, half way between tragedy and comedy, represents a human norm. When I wondered where last I had used the adjective, I remembered that it was to describe a letter of the Irish rebel, Lord Edward Fitzgerald, to his mother. "I long for a little walk with you," runs one passage, "leaning on me, or to have a long talk with you, sitting out in some pretty spot, of a fine day, with your long cane in your hand, working at some little weed at your feet, and looking down, talking all the time." Reading it again to see what I meant, I feel that the emotion, for all its sincerity, has turned under one's eyes to grace and charm.

This exemplary quality has nothing in particular to do with Mozart's place as a musician, though I think it does mean that his reputation can never be the sport of fashion, like Bach's or Wagner's. He will always keep the place he has held since his death, not perhaps as the greatest (if superlatives have any meaning in such a discussion) but certainly among the greatest since he represents a human norm by which the greatest must be judged. Just as there are certain people born with perfect pitch, so there are people like Mozart born with a tuning fork in their fingers, whose business it is to render the middle C of human life.

Mozart's own life was anything but Mozartean. When he was dying he thought of it himself as having begun "under such favourable auspices"; and indeed, he might seem the most fortunate of geniuses, educated and protected by the best of fathers, led about Europe from court to court like an infant prodigy, pitting his skill against the great men of his time. Actually, through no fault of his father's, it was a deplorable upbringing, which left him ill-equipped for the rough and tumble of a creative artist's life, imprudent, arrogant and extravagant. What was worse, it left him, in his teens, with an absolute knowledge of music that put him outside the ranks of ordinary musicians and was even an obstacle to his development as a composer.

Again, I can describe this only in literary terms. His plight might be compared with that of certain writers who are "naturals"; who develop rapidly and certainly, and whose first books are as excellent as their last. Maturity comes to them too soon, and they are incapable of the astonishing developments of a Shakespeare or a Yeats who change as their lives change. Mozart did not succumb to this danger but neither did he entirely escape it. There are certain early works of his like the slow movement of the A Major Violin Concerto, written before he was twenty, which leave one wondering where he could go from there. And there is a great mass of his work which shows that frequently he did not know himself. He can be empty more than any other great musician. It is a skill too big, too overworked, for the inspiration; and the inspiration when it comes is inventive rather than constructive. Inspiration comes to Beethoven in fragmentary form, no more than a phrase capable of development; but it comes to Mozart in the form of a perfect, finished melody.

It was in opera that he found himself, for opera, more than any other musical form, depends on invention. The composer must go not where the music takes him but where the action takes him. His own criticism of *The Abduction from the Seraglio* is the epitaph of most other operas—"At that time I was never tired of hearing myself." Above all, it meant he could go where the characters took him, and it is in his ability to do this that he leaves every other composer behind. There are better symphonies than his, better chamber music, perhaps; but there are no operas to compare with *The Marriage of Figaro, Don Giovanni* or even *Cosi fan tutte* for not only does the music interpret the action, but it actually sets itself up as an alternative to the words in the interpretation of character. Each of the enchanting tunes exists in its own right, but, at the same time, it also belongs to the character who sings it, in the situation in which he finds himself. *Voi che sapete* is Cherubino's tune, and could not be Figaro's; Figaro's *Non andrai* is his own, not only because of the words but because Mozart deliberately composed the tune as a novelist composes a speech, delimiting it to the frame of the character. Like a novelist's dialogue, it diminishes the character, but at the same time gives it the consistency of people we have known in everyday life. Let me admit that the cascade of sensuous melody in Susanna's *Deh vieni* always gives me a slight shock. I had not thought nice girls behaved like that; it is as though Elizabeth Bennet were to say to Mr. Darcy, "We have the house to ourselves."

The Magic Flute is a thing apart among the operas, and I am not sure that even yet I fully understand it. In a literary man's way I explain it to myself as Mozart's last struggle with his own premature development. Traditional Catholicism was no longer enough for him. No doubt he loved it as he loved the forms of absolute music and his father's wise and gentle nagging, but he was searching for something different. Like Pierre Bezukhov in *War and Peace* he found it in Freemasonry, though what Freemasonry meant to him, or indeed to Pierre, it would take a greater than Tolstoy to tell us.

All we can see is that it involved an intense simplification of religious patterns; a reduction of them to something as uncomplicated as a schoolboy's code of honor. Schikaneder was another Mason, and his illiterate libretto inspired Mozart as much as Da Ponte's charming librettos had done, though in an entirely different way. Almost every scene reveals a new Mozart, and a puzzling one. Critics ask if it is possible that Mozart, the greatest of musical dramatists, meant *"Bei Maennern welche Liebe fuehlen"* to sound as exalted as the music suggests, though one of the characters is Papageno, the clown. The answer would seem to be that here music transcends characterization. It is hard to say, for the new Mozart was a man who knew that he was dying, and believed that he was dying before having reached the fruition of his talent.

Yet this does not explain the opera as a whole. The human misery of the dying man is expressed rather in the unfinished *Requiem Mass* than in *The Magic Flute*. The abiding impression of the opera is one of joy. We can feel it in Sarastro's two great arias, the first of which Bernard Shaw described as "the only music which might be put into the mouth of God without blasphemy." They are religious music but not in the way of Mozart's church music, not even in the way of the B Minor Mass. They are simple, almost without decoration; their themes are human love and human brotherhood. *O Isis und Osiris* probably owes its extraordinary exaltation to the fact that it deals with love as the key to the ordeal, and for Mozart, at the time he wrote it, the ordeal meant only one thing. For me, the greatest moment in Mozart's music is when the lovers pass through the ordeal of fire and water, accompanied only by the mysterious sound of the flute and the distant rumbling of the drums. Even Schikaneder's doggerel seems for the time being to catch the glory of the music,

> And so we pass through Music's might
> Safe through the horror of Death's night.

It is as though before he himself passed through its horror, the man whose mind was a tuning fork had set himself to sound the middle C of faith.

A Walk in New York

These last four essays could be called "travel writing," but that name would limit them, for O'Connor's writing about places and the lives of their inhabitants—Cork, Brooklyn, or Irish and English pubs—goes beyond our expectations of travel prose. Three of these essays (except "The Conversion") were originally published in Holiday, *whose audience may have been startled by what O'Connor offered.*

He lived intermittently in Brooklyn Heights from 1954 to 1961, and this 1958 essay begins with observations and reminiscences of bridges, vistas, and skyscrapers—a European viewing America so that Americans may newly see it. His thoughts take surprising turns as he describes American loneliness and piety, eccentricity, and acquisition ("the Gimmies"). It is not the expected polemic against "ugly Americans"; it is fascinated and rueful, perhaps still more valid than not.

The Battery is one of the most inspiring places in New York, particularly for a European. It is always full of watery life; the handsome red ferryboats running to Staten Island, the improbable ferryboats to Governors Island which look as though they had strayed out of the pages of Mark Twain; the brilliant, fussy tugboats pulling whole trains of wagons or great barges full of coal and contemptuously butting them through any obstacle that presents itself. There are so many things here on the European scale—the charming buildings on Governors Island, for instance, and the Battery itself, built at the beginning of the 19th Century, and capable of being vaulted today by any well-trained commando unit. It is an earlier America, an America that had not yet begun to dwell on grandiose conceptions like the Statue of Liberty, who stands out there in the harbor with her lamp, like a referee with his pistol, giving the starting signal for the liners in their race across the Atlantic.

These, too, are a breath of home. They come along at intervals in their black-and-cream uniforms and the crimson shakos of their funnels; sticking out their great chests, the drum majors of the Hudson, and one's heart rises to them not only because they remind one of home but because they are living symbols of democracy. Not democracy as our unfortunate politicians try to define it, but the true democracy defined by Thucydides, the democracy of trade. That wise Greek, writing twenty-four centuries ago, knew that people who lacked access to the great ocean route must necessarily be governed autocratically, while those with the sea in their blood must venture abroad, must trade, must welcome other venturers, must create a citizenship not of race or class but of initiative and wealth, and must try to govern themselves, however imperfectly, by their own methods of give and take. Not Liberty, handsome and moving though she is, but the water about her decides what this people is and how it is to live.

For freedom's real throne is on the sea, and that is half the pleasure of sleeping in this island city, lulled to rest by the yapping of the never-silent steamers and tugs.

And then I look over my shoulder and see another inspiring sight, the towers of Lower Manhattan. At first they are a real shock because I have become accustomed to the human levels of the buildings on Governors Island. Looking in this direction, I am anywhere, in a commercial community under a democratic government—in England, Ireland, Holland, Denmark, Sweden. But when I turn my head I can be nowhere but in America.

I know it did not begin this way. I shall retrace my steps along Broadway and linger around St. Paul's, which is one of the most beautiful churches to be found anywhere, in Europe or America, and watch the effect of that enchanting red-brown spire against the great pasty cliffs of masonry that threaten to crush it, and feel myself at home. For it is not only a perfect building of a century which thought in terms of human scales, but it is the church of the exiled Irish of the period, and its churchyard, like Trinity's, is full of soil that belongs to Ireland. There, to remind me, is the monument to Emmett and the other to McNevin, and in the porch the tomb and monument of Richard Montgomery, the rebel general.

And at once I am cycling outside of Drogheda, on the east coast of Ireland, and see a beautiful Late Renaissance mansion off the road and prowl about it till a woman asks me in, and there, over the mantelpiece is a fine portrait of a dashing young officer. "Good Lord!" I say incredulously. "Wolfe Tone!" And she retorts rather tartly: "No, not Wolfe Tone. Richard Montgomery. This was his home." And because of him and the others, this particular church feels like a bit of home to me, but what would he and they say of the fairytale nonsense that now looks down on their resting place?

I know all the physical reasons for the extraordinary development of New York, but they do not satisfy me. Anyone can see them for himself who stands for half an hour on one of the bridges over the East River. I have spent a lot of my time on them. When first I came to live in New York I was tormented by the handsome bridge which apparently rose at the end of my street. But when I inquired about it, I found that though there was general agreement that it was the Brooklyn Bridge, nobody seemed to know how a pedestrian could get on to it, or indeed, if a pedestrian could get on to it at all. I wandered about it for two days until I met an intelligent policeman who could tell me that pedestrians had not been permitted for about a year, though the bridge might now be open to them, and could give me directions as to how I could get on it. I followed the directions carefully and found myself on the Manhattan Bridge.

Now, this is not so dumb as it sounds. One day after I had got to know my way, I was crossing the Brooklyn Bridge when I saw two pretty girls hanging over the fence between the boardwalk and the driveway.

"Say, how do we get on to that?" asked one.

"How the hell did you get on to the other?" I asked in astonishment.

"Well, we hired a taxi and told the driver we wanted to walk on Brooklyn Bridge. How do you get on to it?"

"That," I said, "is a secret. The Public Works people and myself are keeping it under our hats. But I *could* lift you over."

So you see it is not so easy as it looks. I searched the exits for days before discovering where the Brooklyn entrance was. It was winter, and for weeks I had the bridge almost to myself. I was in such a state of delirium that I took rolls of photographs, and only realized later that the bridge was plastered with notices saying that I mustn't. I am a law-abiding man, and being a European, I cannot see anybody breaking the law without at once wanting to go up and point out the notices to him, (which would be almost bound to get me into trouble) except that I cannot feel that in this case the law is reasonable. It is like putting up similar notices on the Grand Canal at Venice. In fact, it is not too much to say that anyone who doesn't want to take photographs from Brooklyn Bridge must have tendencies that are un-American and may well prove to be an enemy spy.

The view from the bridge is beautiful in any light, and in some lights it is incredible. This is largely because of the raised boardwalk which lifts you above the roar of the traffic with nothing between you and Lower Manhattan but the delicate patterns of cables from the great lancets of the superstructure. It is a peculiarly exalted feeling. On the Manhattan Bridge on the other hand you are on a level with the subway cars. At the same time each of the bridges has its own poetry. The Manhattan looks down into streets over which I can linger for hours and under its girders lives a whole colony of cats which is fed by old women from the Bowery. The Williamsburg, which takes off from the Jewish quarter, actually has a toilet with a sign in Hebrew—which revealed to me that in certain circumstances Hebrew can be as much a vernacular to me as Irish. Apart from that, it is a most frightening bridge.

One winter evening I was crossing it when I saw a man come toward me, behaving in a most suspicious manner. He ran a little and then stopped. Then he retreated to the side farthest from me and slunk along, pulling down his hat. He made another, farther run. By this time I had ceased to admire that wonderful view from the elbow of the East River and was walking close to the side, studying the suspicious character. My American wife lives in dread of my Irish temper. She knows that I have no great concern about being robbed because, as I never know how much money I have, this will make little difference to my temper. What does worry her is that the gunman may fail to be polite, in which case I shall be almost bound to push his face in. I wished this fellow, if he was a gunman, would stop slinking and scurrying because it was beginning to make me nervous, and when I am nervous I am easily moved to anger. As well as I could in the dusk, I fixed him with my eye. This, which was intended to reassure him, only made him scuttle and crouch in a way that positively caused me to jump. Then as we passed each other he took to his heels and fled like the wind. He was merely scared of me.

.　　.　　.

But all these bridges, even the Brooklyn, which is the classic of great bridges, have a scary, non-human feeling which attracts to them the poor devils who are tired of the simple things of life. I feel it most on the

Queensboro Bridge where the footpath is out over the river and every car that passes makes you rock gently. You leave the familiar street and mount, and as you mount you see the roofs of the old brownstone houses with their extraordinary collections of chimney pots fall below you until you are ten stories up, and when you look at the sky line of Manhattan and tell yourself that the bridge is here only to relieve the pressure that forever bubbles and blasts within the skyscrapers, you realize that this is only partly true, and that neither the skyscrapers nor the bridges are really necessary. They are both a reckless act of defiance of those limits within which humanity for thousands of years has contracted itself; like the Gothic cathedrals, they express an inner compulsion far more than they express the solution of an engineering problem. They are not there because they are physically necessary but because they are psychologically necessary, and that, ultimately, is what makes them beautiful even when, as in the skyscrapers of Lower Manhattan, they ignore the laws of beauty.

Personally, though my historian friends shake their heads over me, I date it all from Whitman, who gave the whole population a sort of elephantiasis of the imagination. Whoever conceived of the idea of the Statue of Liberty out there in the river, raising her torch to the poor and outcast, had it bad. So had the builders of the Lincoln Memorial in Washington. These things may be inferior art, but they certainly overawe the imagination. They are not all of America, for the classical, anthropocentric American attitude runs clear from the earliest days through Emily Dickinson to Robert Frost and E. B. White, but it has an awful, late Romantic antithesis to counter. It has not really countered it yet, and every American has somewhere or other in him an obstreperous bit of Whitman and a detached bit of Robert Frost, and one of these days the two will fight it out and there will be one unholy bang.

.   .   .

One winter day I was walking in New York when another pedestrian, a stranger, came up to me and addressed me without ceremony. "This damn city!" he said angrily, with a wave of his hand generally at all of Manhattan. "The people in it have forgotten how to walk."

It probably had not occurred to him that walking in the European sense of the word is possible only in a city with public conveniences. Americans, for some reason, ignore the necessity for them. But it isn't only that. Let me explain. I came to America for the first time with one suit. Of that trip I possess a great number of photographs of myself; looking at the tower of the R.C.A. Building with an approving air, watching the skaters in Rockefeller Plaza with a knowing smile; standing among the spring flowers as if they were all my own work. There are many, many poses, but only one suit. I had no interest in clothes. The only lust I had ever really known was the literary man's lust for writing materials. I cannot see a notebook without seeing at once the short story that would suit it best, or a fountain pen without feeling that a certain dramatic incident which is somewhere in the back of my head could never be rendered in all its delicacy except with that particular pen. I cadge pencils in every office I enter—I once cadged two dozen—and when that doesn't work I steal them. But clothes are always safe with me.

Anyhow, coming back to the matter of walking, I remember going to see a great collection of American art. (I had better explain that I like very few American pictures after the great period of Sloan and Bellows.) I looked at the art, grew pale, and said, "I'm going out." Which I did because I was afraid I was going to be sick; and once outside, I was too upset to do anything but walk.

Then I noticed myself behaving in a peculiar way, a peculiar way for me, that is, and I had to stop in the middle of the sidewalk and ask myself what I was doing that I did not normally do. Then I realized that I was sauntering slowly past an array of shop windows devoted to spring clothes for young ladies, and stopping at each window to look. I also realized why I was doing it, because the art that had been absent from the art collections was here in the shop windows, in the design of a window, the play of a light, the cut of a skirt. I also understood why, in reading American magazines, I tended to linger over the advertisements rather than over the short stories of Mr.———. But the name does not matter.

This was a revelation to me, but like most revelations it had small effect on my character. Two years later I came back with one suit—the same suit. At this point I began to covet a leather coat. I wasn't really alarmed at this because I had coveted things before but it had never led to any rash behavior. I even went into a store and tried on a leather coat but left it because it was too dear. Forty dollars! I had never spent as much on anything except a typewriter. That settled it, or so I thought. But I still found myself stopping in front of shop windows that displayed leather jackets. Finally my wife reported that she had found the perfect leather jacket for me. I went with her, loathed the leather jacket at sight, and then bought myself another which was only a shade less offensive. I no longer wanted a leather jacket. All I wanted was to rid myself of this gnawing craving inside me. Now I have three suits and a raincoat of the most superior kind that does at least half a dozen things other than keep out the rain—the only claim made for the cheaper types.

In other words, I have now got the great American disease—the Gimmies. The principal symptom of the Gimmies is, of course, window shopping, and you can't walk and window-shop. Walking, to the New Yorker—and alas to me nowadays—is only a still imperfect method of getting from one shop window to the next. In a perfect America the shopper will sit still, and the vast buildings, running on rubber-tired wheels and driven by silent motors, will circulate perpetually about him. But to me the Gimmies are a quite pleasant disease. They rarely flare up into the violent neurosis I experienced about the leather coat. They merely keep me permanently slowed down. I drift from shop window to shop window, and have learned the art of enjoying things that I shall never own, of appreciating other people's necessities. I shall never, I hope, need the services of the shopkeeper in Chinatown who advertises BLACK EYES MADE TO LOOK NATURAL, but I am glad for the sake of certain of my friends who regularly deserve black eyes even if they do not acquire them. All my youthful socialism is dying away in my admiration for Mr. Rockefeller who, after Napoleon, has given me the greatest amount of free pleasure. I sit in his gardens and smell his hyacinths; I look approvingly up at his tower in which his architects have solved the problem of the relations between eye and severity that were left unsolved in the skyscrapers of Lower Manhattan; I study the outstretched leg of the good-looking girl on his ice, and take a small tour of Switzerland, France and Great Britain in the windows of his travel agencies, and go home feeling sated, "as if on honeydew I fed and drank the milk of Paradise."

·   ·   ·

New York is a city of the most extraordinary extremes. Has no one noticed that it is the most pious of all great cities? One night, or rather one morning about one o'clock, I picked up a taxi and the driver said with resignation, "You caught me by accident. I was just coming out of Mass." "Mass at this hour?" I said. "Yes," he said, "I can catch it almost any hour of day or night," and then and there, he took me on a regular timetable of all the New York churches. And that, let me tell you, is something that would not happen to you in London or Paris.

Is it because the human thing is very lonely and frightened in the middle of this vast inhuman compulsion, and clings to the images that are related to man's inescapable condition? Or is it that a man's religion is associated with his homeland? Even in colonial days there must have been a terrible feeling of homesickness about New York, and that, too, represents a real conflict in the American character; the pride in one's own achievement battling with the conception of some Great Good Place where everything was better. It is part of the incredible charm of this city that within a few streets one can pass from Canton to Milan, from Milan to Warsaw, from Warsaw to New Orleans. My first impression of Switzerland was that Europe should be handed over to it as a going concern. One of my strongest impressions of New York is that the whole world has been handed over to it as a going concern, and that it goes remarkably well. If I had to show a European what it is I think America has really achieved, I should take him for a nice long stroll through the Negro quarter and let him see the happy faces of the men cleaning their cars—cars that he and his like can barely dream of—and if that did not give him a new outlook on international politics nothing would.

Yet it seems only to palliate the underlying nostalgia and loneliness. Where on earth do all the homesick songs come from if not from New York? And not only the Old Kentucky Homes and the Little Gray Homes in the West, but those eternal Mammas of the singers in pubs—Mother Machree and My Yiddish Mamma. Does any crooner ever sing about Father Machree? The dominance of Mamma in American life is much better explained in terms of the dream image it really represents; the dream of the motherland and the womb. Newcomers like myself don't have it, and tend to be cynical about it. The only Irish bar on Third Avenue that I frequent is run by another Irishman who was born and brought up in Ireland and who turns a cold eye on anyone who even mentions the Old Sod.

The nostalgia is inevitable, for New York is undoubtedly the loneliest city in the world, and in the subways and streets and in the drugstores you can study every known form of nervous obsession. One night, for instance, I was passing by the Plaza Hotel when a woman in an old-fashioned hat and dress came by. I had gone a few yards when I heard someone speaking French in a shrill voice, and when I looked round, there was the same woman in the old-fashioned attire, standing at the corner of the hotel, speaking into a telephone. She was in a state of acute excitement, and was apparently quarreling with some man about his neglect of her, and it struck me as surprising that she should do it there at the street corner with people passing by. Then I got a slight feeling of the willies because I realized that there was no telephone and no man, either, and that something about that particular corner had started off the gramophone record of a scene that had been played out many years before, when the clothes she wore were still fashionable, perhaps in another country, and which must now forever repeat itself behind the eyes of a somnambulist. Nobody but myself stopped to stare at her. The people went by, their eyes straight ahead, for New Yorkers know how to avoid the difficult and unpleasant. When I asked my small boy what he noticed most about the city he replied that, if he and another boy fought in the streets, no one interfered. In Ireland or in England, the passers-by would have separated them at once. In England they would have been compelled to shake hands and even—as he wistfully implied —given sixpence apiece to atone for injured pride. But here they could fight forever without disturbing anyone.

For the passers-by, too, are lonely. "Sex, sex, sex!" a lone woman cries as she stalks by me, glancing into a bookshop window. "I'd sex the whole damn lot of them to Hell if I'd my way." A man comes toward me, shrinking timidly against the wall of a broad sidewalk and grinning ingratiatingly as he says, "Plenty of room! Plenty of room!" One evening I even saw a whole subway car of people with tics. There was a man reading a life of Gandhi in a way that showed he wasn't reading, but watching himself being watched reading. There was a tall woman with red-rimmed eyes who must once have been beautiful, who occasionally dipped into her handbag and took out a letter, shrugging her shoulders and smiling with mock indifference. Whatever her private drama was she seemed to be saying: "Well, really, dear, if this is how you feel about me, then perhaps the best thing is that we should separate." The door opened and two men got in. One, dressed in blue, was normal-looking, but the other, a tall handsome Negro, kept his hand stiffly in his right-hand pocket as though he were carrying a knife. He had an attaché case and took out some papers which he began to study carefully, forgetting that he was wearing dark glasses. Then he filled his pipe without looking at it, holding it and the pouch stiff by his side while he read. It was only when he had filled his pipe that he realized he was supposed to be reading and that he was in a badly lit subway with dark glasses on, and with a great flourish he whipped out a pair of reading glasses. I felt as if I had walked in on a futurist film. I looked at the man who had come in with him, the man in blue. Nice, nice, normal man, I thought, please forgive me if I rest my eyes on you, because otherwise I shall be doing something peculiar myself. I know I shall. I feel it coming on. Suddenly the man in blue rapped out a message in Morse on his heel. Then he looked at me defiantly and removed his hand from his leg. But it was only for a moment, for as I looked sadly away, trying to see nothing, I saw the telltale hand steal out again to the heel, the fingers sketching a stealthy rat-tat-tat.

. . .

But the real loneliness of New York comes out at night. I had seen it but failed to read the signs correctly one morning when a party of commuters was entering the subway. One man came along with a Gladstone bag. He was followed by a dog. Just before he reached the ticket office he opened the bag and laid it on the ground. The dog, without waiting for a word or a glance, popped in and lay down; the man nonchalantly closed the bag and went to the ticket office for his token.

So, just when the daily roar of the traffic begins to die down, and the lowing of ships and tugs becomes more perceptible, there is another noise —of dogs scenting perambulating cats and struggling furiously with their leashes. Down every street they come, sniffing, staring up at their owners, driving indignantly or affectionately at other dogs. In the shadows, quiet, specialized friendships are struck up between dog lovers who meet night after night like policemen on their beats, and gradually the city is pervaded by a peculiar, pungent, doggy smell.

It is a strange, nostalgic hour for the European in New York. Outside the doors of apartment buildings superintendents and their assistants deposit the most amazing collection of furniture: sofas, armchairs, radio sets, which indicate that the owners are suffering from the Gimmies and are replacing things which in Europe would become heirlooms. And the poor European, measuring the big old-fashioned armchair and wondering if he could stagger home with it without mishap, and marveling at the wealth of this fabulous city which can throw such treasures out with the rubbish, hears the padding of delicate paws behind him; and realizes that behind all the wealth and luxury there is the ache of loneliness that nothing can satisfy but these useless, helpless, foolish, affectionate creatures.

In Quest of Beer

This 1957 essay is again typical O'Connor; in its first page, a reader meets dream-interpretation, the connections between modern pubs and medieval alehouses, O'Connor's alcoholic father, the stories "Old Fellows" and "The Drunkard." He also offers gleeful insights on the "schizoid" Irish attitude toward drink and its English counterpart, and the establishments that result.

It was a great relief to me when I took up the study of dreams to find that when I dreamed of an inn or a pub I was dreaming about a wife. I don't suppose the temperance societies go in much for dream language, but they would be well advised to remember that pubs and beer are as deeply rooted in a man's world as marriage itself. This goes back to the days when forests covered the earth, the roads were only tracks and the lighted alehouse was the very image of Life itself. All the great abbeys were inns as well, and if ever you find yourself on the road from Southampton to London, stop off at the hospital of St. Cross where, by a ritual that goes back to heaven knows what century, you are expected to ask for your "dole." The dole is now only a token piece of bread and a token nip of beer, and even the beer is brewed by a local brewery instead of on the premises, but it reminds you that there was a time when the custom might have meant the difference between life and death to you.

Now, I may as well confess that I am not by nature a drinker. That is partly because I had a father who was. I have written about him in various disguises, but temperance was never one of them. He drank in what I always think of as a peculiarly Irish way—in bouts. Between the bouts his behavior was admirable, so admirable indeed that he admired it himself, and the more he admired it, the greater grew the poor man's pride till, at last, he had to celebrate it. The result of the celebration was that inside a week he was again a wreck—moral, physical and financial. I remember once, during a slight argument, he opened my uncle's face with a poker. I felt deeply about these bouts, more particularly because I was frequently tagged on to him as a brake, but the only result of this was that I spent the entire day standing outside pubs receiving a lemonade or a penny every few hours to keep me content. Only twice did I manage to act like a brake. Once was very late at night when I was standing in the cold outside a pub miles from home and saw a woolly dog in the window of a shop. The toy dog cost sixpence, and sixpence was exactly what I had collected during the day, so I bought the dog for protection and walked home by myself. That almost cured Father of the drink. The second time was after a funeral when I drank Father's pint when he had his back turned and he, stone-cold sober, had to bring me home, drunk and with a cut over my eye, a sight that steadied him for months.

The result was that till I was thirty I hated the sight of pubs, and I'm still capable of feeling a shudder at the sight of some.

When an Irishman goes to a pub it is usually to get away from women. Drink is his escape from the emotional problems which, according to the best authorities, he now evades more successfully than any male in Europe. He wants nothing suggestive of love, family and home. Anything to do with sex is barred, and the risqué joke which keeps an English barroom happy for an hour is likely to provoke frowns. Conversation is generally serious; it may deal with sports, politics and the likelihood of war. The more intelligent customers may discuss what's wrong with the country, the church, and the government. These are subjects which you cannot discuss with a woman, because she would be bound (a) to disagree and (b) to report the criticisms in quarters where they could do you damage.

At the same time, it must be understood that this Irish way of drinking is schizoid and, as such, leads to rows. Father's behavior with the poker was not exceptional. James Bridie, the Scottish dramatist, enthused endlessly over the fact that F. R. Higgins, the Irish poet, was knocked out in a Dublin bar during an argument about poetry. Except for a few intimate friends, I scarcely know a single Irishman who does not feel compelled at a certain stage of the proceedings to tell me exactly what he thinks of me, and I invariably find it astonishing. It is a tribute partly to the natural sweetness of the Irish character, partly to the repressive power of Irish society that it takes so much drink to bring Irishmen to the aggressive stage.

Mind, I do not resent it. The only type of Irishman I do resent is the kind that tells me what he thinks of me on less than half a bottle, and he is usually paranoic instead of schizoid and may safely be left to the psychiatrists, but all the same it creates problems. I once had a friend, a very gallant soldier with an intelligent and talented wife, and we visited a lot at each other's homes. One evening we were all at my apartment when an amateur musician called, and we played records and discussed music till late in the night. Apparently, my friend the officer was enjoying himself, but a few days later we met in town and went to my favorite pub for a drink. It was only then that I noticed he was slightly "high" and then only because of his unusual frankness.

He wasn't offensive, and I didn't resent it; on the contrary, I am always delighted to see what goes on behind that bland and gentle Irish mask. He merely asked me to admit that, whereas he was a very fine musician and would have had a most distinguished career as a violinist if only he'd continued his lessons, I knew nothing about music and was, in fact, forever chancing my arm by talking about things of which I knew nothing. In fact, he added, with an endearing smile, I was just a phony —pleasant enough, but a phony. I agreed to every single proposition: it may be some unconscious recollection of how Father used that poker, but I always do agree. And sometimes it takes an awful lot of agreeing, because the drinker himself is never so entirely submerged but that he notices something peculiar in his own behavior, so he keeps on reiterating his own propositions, usually in stronger and stronger terms, in the hope that they will begin to sound natural and familiar to himself.

Which they don't, of course, because we met again a few days later and had another drink, and this time he was apologetic, though he didn't know what about. He couldn't remember, and though I said at once that it wasn't worth remembering, he persisted and asked me to tell him frankly what he had said. "I'm quite sure I was offensive," he said, but when I tried to assure him that this was something he couldn't be even if he tried, he remained dissatisfied. He wanted to know his exact words, and I couldn't bring myself to repeat them, because if anybody were to repeat something I had said in that state, I should die of embarrassment. Of course, it did occur to me that he really wished to know because there were so many nasty things he might have said of me. At any rate, since then he has never been at ease with me. Again and again he has reproached me with my closeness; our friendship has lapsed, and it is all because a tiny fraction of his personality has broken loose and is drifting about the world under his name and out of his control. Psychologist friends look grave when I tell the story and imply that I may be causing him a severe trauma. Myself, I wouldn't be surprised if he gave up drink.

On the other hand, this schizoid attitude to drink produces a need for getting drunk that is almost pathological. Dissatisfaction with the climate, with the government, with the church, and above all with the women who fail to appreciate that there is anything to be dissatisfied about, grows in us till it projects itself in a thundering bout. I had an old friend who got his dissatisfaction musically. He was found lecturing a street musician, playing a penny whistle, on the subject of Italian music. "Can't you be joyous, man?" he snarled. "What's the use of playing that mournful stuff? Give us some Italian music with the sun in it! I'm a child of the sun." The child of the sun was one of the most popular men in town.

After all, serious drinking is not a crime; it is a visitation, "a good man's fault." We are not like the English. We do not drink to enjoy ourselves. We drink to forget, and the amount we drink corresponds roughly to the amount we have to forget, so nobody but a completely heartless man could expect us to assume responsibility for what we do under the influence. "Poor chap, poor chap! He had an awful lot of trouble. There was that brother of his, and the wife—you know about the wife, of course?" A drunk is like a blind man or an old person, to be helped across the road.

Accordingly there is no relation between the popular attitude to drink and the licensing laws, which anyhow are an inheritance from the English, who are always trying to regiment people into good behavior. It is true that we have modified them for the worse by the hour's closing in the afternoon, but there's a reason for that too. The hour's closing, known as "Kevin's Hour," is called after its author, Kevin O'Higgins, Minister of Justice. O'Higgins in his youth was, even by Irish standards, a remarkable drinker. After his reformation it dawned on him that if only some kind friend had brought him home each day at 2:30 P.M. he probably would never have had the energy to go back, thereby halving his problems. O'Higgins was later assassinated, but not by the drinkers.

No word of reproach is ever heard against him. "Poor Kevin!" we say. "It was himself he was thinking of." We are a tolerant, gentle race. Why otherwise should we commemorate the Apostle of Temperance himself by naming a Limerick public house after him, and where but in Ireland could you drink yourself stupid in the Father Mathew Bar?

Between Kevin in heaven and the nonconformist English, we have a code of laws relating to licensing that bears as little relation to the facts as did Prohibition in America. But unlike Prohibition, this code has few enemies. It is regarded as something like an act of God rather than an act of Parliament. The last raid I saw was in the town of Clonmel on a Sunday morning. I was cycling through with a Limerick friend and a Harvard professor, and we had to undergo the ordeal of explaining in whispers to half a dozen suspicious townsmen that we were really strangers in search of a drink, not policemen in disguise. We were finally directed up an alleyway into a sort of back yard where a dozen or so unfortunates were waiting in groups of three or four. Significant whispers were passing from group to group, and the faces of the poor victims grew longer. 'Twas unknown if they'd open at all that morning. We were there ten minutes when another townsman whispered us away, then whisked us across the street to a door that opened and closed as if it were operated by an electric eye. No sooner did we start drinking—we were in Murphy's—than the word went round, "a raid," and a few of the customers vanished while Murphy and his wife stood watching the raid at the other pub, the one we had been lured away from. They weren't indignant, just shocked.

There are still things about it I don't understand. Why was Murphy's not raided? Who directed the townsman who directed us? Those raids emanate from young superintendents in faraway towns who do not have to live with the consequences. Older policemen with pensions in view don't like to be mixed up in them; they are usually left to rookies. But even rookies wouldn't like to be caught investigating an American who might after all turn out to be a relation of the brother's boss in Brooklyn. If it had actually been known that he was a Harvard professor, even a District Justice wouldn't like to say a cross word to him, for a thing like that could damage a District Justice to the end of his days. My own view is that before the raid began, our townsman gave information at the barrack, and the guards grew pale and said, "But you couldn't let an American boy see a thing like that. For the love of God get him over the road to Murphy's and we won't raid Murphy's until late tonight!"

When a raid takes place in reality, it is governed by the same civilized attitude, and the legal and moral objections to perjury are politely overlooked by both sides. It always turns out that a funeral or a football match had taken place in the locality, and the policeman had entertained a numerous retinue of relatives and their friends; as to the man found in the outdoor toilet, and the one on the stable roof (one grasping a half empty bottle of whisky and the other using profane language), neither the publican nor his wife had ever seen either of them, or remembered admitting them—and the judge administers a stern warning and only a mild fine.

The Irish publican tends to be a man of charitable views. He can, of course, afford them, because, unlike his English prototype who is merely an agent of the brewery, he usually owns his own premises. Besides, he has probably come through being a grocer's apprentice. The apprentice himself is an unusual type. In provincial towns he comes of an influential family and brings a lot of trade with him. In Dublin he almost invariably comes from Tipperary. He is never the wage slave you find in other countries, but an up-and-coming young businessman. In Tipperary they must, I think, have a lullaby that is sung over every male child who looks like a promising bartender and which warns him forever against the evils of drink. With this temptation forever hanging over them, they plunge with great violence into other activities. When they have saved enough to buy a pub for themselves they have usually mellowed into men of strong judgment and kind hearts.

Yet, though I know that the Irish publican is the real thing, I am a sucker for the English public house. I know all that is to be said against it. It is run by a brewery, a totalitarian organization that wants to leave nothing in the world original and strange, and produces beer that is quite indistinguishable from any other beer. God be with the few remaining small breweries of Ireland that make such wild beer and issue such strange advertisements: "Oh, what can ail thee, knight-at-arms, when one pint of Sweeney's XX will put you right again?" or, "He cometh not," she said, "having no doubt stopped for his usual pint of Sweeney's XX."

The English differ from the Irish in being steady drinkers, like my friend Mr. Franklin, who takes his two pints every Sunday morning regular; and even if the Queen, God bless her, were to come in and order drinks all round, Mr. Franklin would only beam, hold his hand over his glass and say, "No thanks, your Majesty, I've had mine."

Once in an English pub I heard a tragic story of an old regular who had just died, paralyzed, and had been deprived of his daily drinks by his wife and daughter, both teetotalers. The hero of the hour was another customer who had braved the two women the night before the sick man's death, with a quart of bitter hidden under his coat. I can still recall the emotion that spread through the pub as he described the scene in his modest, masculine English way. "When I took out the bottle 'is poor eyes lit up. Couldn't move, couldn't speak, but I shall never forget the way 'e looked. I 'ad to 'old 'is mouth open at the side and let it trickle down 'is throat. Next day 'e was dead, but 'e'd 'ad 'is drink."

The English like to drink in pleasant surroundings, and there is something in the tradition of the English publican that makes him a born museum director with a mania for antiques, pewter, copper and brass. "I don't know 'ow it is," one publican said to me. "I'm as fond of brass as anyone else, but I can't feel the same about it as I do about copper. Copper does something to me inside if you know what I mean." I did. I love to come out of the rain and dark into a low room whose black beams are studded with harness brasses, but it can never make up to me for the fiery glow of copper. Alas, I am a bad Irishman, for what is repressed in me is not the desire to tell my friends what skunks they are but how intelligent, sensitive and truehearted they are, and it is only in an English pub that I find a proper background for such sissified sentiments. "Good God!" said my oldest boozing companion the night I introduced him to an English pub. "Three hours' steady drinking and not one cross word!"

.   .   .

So this Sunday morning when I let my imagination stray, it flies not to any Irish pub but to a little hamlet in Buckinghamshire. My wife is back from church and I slip out quietly so she won't notice the time. The pub is next door, a plain, boxlike, red-brick house with benches outside the front door. Wendy, the cocker spaniel who is standing there, gives me a flick of her tail. She knows me. You enter a hallway, pass two or three tables, and come to a narrow counter—all the bar there is, and a very drafty one, too, in spite of the electric heater. On the right is the room where they play darts, and on the left the parlor, dominated by a colored portrait of Queen Elizabeth, where strangers go when they have women with them. Jack, the proprietor, is not the owner, although his father and grandfather were publicans here before him, and in fact he only runs it not to break the tradition, for he makes his living in a motor works across the county.

Hilda, a Lancashire girl, has no respect for the tradition, though she keeps the pub clean as a battleship and always puts flowers on the counter. Hilda is desperate at arithmetic and has to do everything as a sum, chanting it and writing it out at the same time, but Gordon, one of the regulars, no matter where he may be on the premises, knows the meaning of the chant, and at the end of her list: "Six pints of the best bitter, two Woodbines, two Players, a chocolate bar and a packet of potato crisps," you hear his strong voice chime in, "Eight and tuppence ha'penny."

Hilda dreams of the day when she can have her own home near the motor works and her husband, Reggie, all to herself, evenings and week-days, but Reggie knows the vanity of such dreams, for he, another excel-lent mechanic, has been a publican himself and would still be one if only he could make a living by it. Reggie tells me that the great secret of being a good publican is to "beat 'em at darts," but in his heart he knows that it's an art, just like music, at which he is expert.

"Lummy," he says, "the things you see in a pub. I remember one day a horse and cart drives up, and two men get off the cart with an old dog. The old dog lies on a bench, and they order two bitters. I serve them, and then the old dog lifts his head and yaps. "Oh, sorry, old man,' one of them says. 'I'd quite forgotten about you. Another pint, please, for the dog.' 'For the dog?' I says. 'Yes,' he says, ' 'e likes a drink like the rest of us.' 'Excuse me,' I says, 'but what's his? Bitter or mild?' 'Oh, bitter,' he says, as if he was surprised. So I give the old dog a pint in a pewter and he just laps it up. And believe me, Frank, he drank pint for pint with those two men till they left. I can see it still. Under the cart, he was, between the wheels, rolling from side to side like a sailor. Oh, you do see funny things in a pub!"

And now it is two o'clock—closing time—and my wife has been on the phone to Hilda to tell her the roast is ruined, but anyway we have another, and I remember my Irish friend's cry: "Three hours' steady drinking and not one cross word!"

The Conversion

"The Conversion" draws on a 1950 cycling trip through France with O'Connor's friend Stan Stewart, but it differs noticeably from his more lighthearted travel observations. It seems more a short story with an epiphany, perhaps surprising those who might think O'Connor anticlerical, unaffected by religious mystery.

Géronte and I landed in Dieppe on the afternoon of Holy Thursday. Géronte is the companion of all my cycling trips; we have covered together most of Ireland and a lot of England, but this was our first trip to France, and we were rather scared.

On the whole, we make a good mixture; I, in my late forties, tall, gaunt and seedy; Géronte, in the neighborhood of sixty, a pipe smoker, small and stout, and with the digestion and temper necessary to handle a chronic dyspeptic. He was brought up in an Irish Protestant house where it was a sin to play on Sunday, I, in an Irish Catholic one where I was encouraged to give the Infant Jesus in the Christmas crib a clockwork engine as a present. In our cynical middle age, the difference of upbringing still comes out. I, restive and fiery, can be led a great part of the way by anyone who will talk soothingly to me and pat me on the nose; Géronte, the most good-natured of men, remains the complete individualist, and will submit to dictation from nobody.

There was, for instance, the awful half-hour in Warwick Castle. While the guard showed us the armor, Géronte discovered what he took to be a Breughel; when the guide reached the Breughel, I found Géronte in the castle chapel looking at the ceiling and muttering "Contra-Buhl" between his teeth. In the great hall, when the guide showed the furniture, Géronte affected interest in a gittern presented by Queen Elizabeth to

Leicester, and when the guide, noticing his apparent interest, began to tell us about it, Géronte grabbed me by the arm and hissed, "Tell the damn fellow we're not going to look at any more of his damn rubbish!" Eventually I had to tell the guide that my friend was ill.

Traveling with a man like Géronte has its advantages as well as its embarrassments, for of all men he is the most completely unaffected by propaganda. He can look at the most famous work of art in the world, first through his spectacles and then over them, and finally sum it up without self-consciousness, as though nobody in the world had ever seen it before. It is the story of "The Emperor's New Clothes" eternally renewed.

Only two others on the ship had bicycles; we parted from them with regret on the quay, and, full of suspicions of French traffic, pushed our bicycles up the main street. We were so scared we even left the parish church on our left unvisited. Géronte did buy himself a pair of insoles for his shoes, and that struck me as great boldness, for even in England I had found it hard to make myself understood when I wanted insoles, and it wasn't until afterwards that I realized the natives call them "socks." Instead, I bought a kilo of apples under the mistaken impression that a kilo was a pound, and then wondered what I was to do with them.

Even after we had walked into the open country, Géronte insisted on cycling in single file, a most unsociable practice, and he didn't really relax till after our first meal in a wayside pub, when he, with a French shakier even than mine, had boldly gone out and bought what he called "a yard of bread." That gave him confidence. In the evening light the downland country we cycled through became magical, Sussex with a slight accent. In the village churches there was a mass of baroque and rococo statuary, second-rate work, but wonderful after the bareness of Irish and English parish churches where Géronte's ancestors had smashed everything with a face. But none of the statues were draped in purple. It was Holy Thursday, and I thought it strange to find the statues undraped and the churches empty. It gave me the feeling that something was wrong.

Next day, no longer feeling like foreigners, we cycled on in the direction of Beauvais. It was Good Friday, but the story was the same. We came to a beautiful church and found it locked. Through the plain glass windows we saw that the woodwork and statues inside were excellent. By this time I was becoming really inquisitive, and while Géronte went off with two children from a near-by cottage to locate the key of the church, I remained behind and questioned the children's mother.

"Tell me," I asked, "is there no service here today?"

"No, sir."

"But surely you have Mass here?"

"No. We only hear Mass occasionally. Once in six months, perhaps."

"But why?"

"We have no priest."

So that was it! That was why the statues remained undraped. Here the enemy of the churches was not puritanism, but something more deadly because more logical, something which left them their beauty but removed their significance.

At the next village we found the parish church open because the organist was practicing. He was a young man, good-looking, with a slight mustache, and after a few minutes he got up and joined us. He might have been the expression in the flesh of the logic we had seen at work on the other churches. He proceeded politely to tell us the life stories of the more unfamiliar saints, and by the time he was finished there was little left of the saints. Yet we liked him, as we shouldn't have liked a puritan.

"You're English, I suppose?" he asked as we were leaving.

"No, Irish."

"Ah," he said with a shrug, "of Ireland I know nothing but James Joyce."

"You know quite a lot if you know that," I replied, and again we fell into talk, and he told us how he had read *Ulysses* in the Ste. Geneviève Library in the evenings and given up *Finnegans Wake* as a bad job. He was the sort of young man who makes France worth while, the sort who takes naturally to culture and not because he doesn't feel himself capable of business or games. We parted from him with real regret.

But the parting was not complete. We had cycled some miles farther and found yet another locked church, when he caught up on us. He, too, was riding a bicycle, and he excused himself in terms that were familiar enough to me from having heard them so often in rural Ireland from young country priests and teachers. The poor devil was dying of loneliness; there wasn't a soul in the village he could talk to about books or music except his uncle, the parish priest, a severe, old-fashioned man who still looked on Flaubert and De Maupassant as "immoral writers" and kept their books locked up. How well I knew that old uncle! How often I had argued with him in the days when I was a librarian, trying to get the hospitable, saintly, pigheaded old devil to let me start a library in his godforsaken parish where the unfortunate people were drinking themselves to death for want of something to do! And failed! It isn't the bad priests who break your heart, but the good ones.

"Anyway," said the organist, "as if he couldn't find all the vices of Flaubert and De Maupassant among his own parishioners!"

"Do you think so?" I asked. "I've always wondered if there really were people like De Maupassant's Normans."

"You needn't," said the organist. "Look at me!"

I asked him about the locked churches and our chances of hearing Tenebrae anywhere along the road.

"You won't hear Tenebrae anywhere outside Beauvais," he replied. "You couldn't get a choir together in this whole country. My uncle is having the Stations of the Cross tonight. That was why I was practicing. I'm the one who has to carry the cross."

He tried out his irreverent jokes on us just to see how we responded. He was full of curiosity about us cycling round, looking at statues, wanting to hear Tenebrae—obviously a pious pair and yet laughing at his jokes about religion. It wasn't right.

"You Irish are all Catholics, aren't you?" he asked with mock innocence.

"Not all," I replied. "My friend is a Protestant."

"He has all my sympathy," the organist replied gravely. "That, I suppose, explains his interest in statues?"

"Except modern ones," said Géronte.

"Bah!" said the organist. "Iconoclast!"

Whatever else he may not have shared with De Maupassant's Normans, he certainly had all their inquisitiveness. He wasn't satisfied with my attempts at an explanation. He went on with his probing. As for him, he was an atheist—with an uncle a parish priest, what else could he be? He was a delightful young fellow and excellent company in a strange country.

We cycled on for some miles till we came to a really attractive village green where we halted for tea. It had a wall of trees round it, and behind a hedge at the back rose a great parish church. This was really only the choir of a large church begun by the English during their occupation of Normandy and never completed. There were a few laborers at work on the road. We rested our bicycles against the hedge before the church and got out the coffee and rolls and Irish whisky. Géronte explained to the organist how he must drink the whisky to get the full effect of it, "without hitting his tonsils," and the organist compared it (I thought, without much conviction) to *fine*. We sat on the grass enjoying the meal and the evening sunlight, when suddenly the organist, who seemed to have been following up his own train of thought all the time, began to chuckle.

"I understand it all now," he explained. "*You* are a very bad Catholic; *he* is a very bad Protestant, and so, you can be very good friends."

At last the French intellect had found its formula, and there was sufficient truth in it to make Géronte and myself laugh, too. We were still laughing when one of the laborers hailed us.

"Aren't you fellows going to the flicks?" he shouted.

"Flicks?" the organist shouted back, looking puzzled. "What flicks?"

"In there," said the laborer, jerking his thumb in the direction of the church.

"Flicks," the organist repeated to us.

"The Stations of the Cross," shouted the laborer.

"Ah," said the organist, beginning to laugh apologetically, "the Stations of the Cross."

We listened, but we could hear no organ or anything else from the church.

"Why don't we go in?" I asked, and we packed up our food and went into the church.

It was a huge church, bigger even than it had appeared from outside, and only a bay or two of the nave had been completed before the west wall had been roughly put in to finish it off. It was as bare as it was high, with no ornament but one excellent modern statue of the Blessed Virgin on a crossing pier at the south side of the choir.

I went into the pew farthest from the altar and was followed by Géronte and the organist. It was only then I realized why we had heard no sound from outside. There was no organ. A young priest was celebrating the Stations of the Cross accompanied by two acolytes, and the whole congregation in that great church consisted of three women and two little girls—mothers, aunts and sisters of the acolytes—who had obviously come not to join in the service but to see Jean and Louis perform. I hope they enjoyed them more than I did. There is a frustrated acolyte somewhere in me, and it rose within me like a wave of fury at the incompetence and silliness of those two horrible children. The young priest had to steer them. They didn't know where to go, didn't know what to do, didn't know when to genuflect and when not. Louis was just a plain born idiot; Jean was a show box who knew the music of two whole bars of the canticles, and whenever they turned up joined in in a lusty "la-la-la" and then looked round to his family for approval.

What made the flightiness of the acolytes more striking was the recollection of the young priest. I watched him and found myself falling under a spell. He looked small and lost in that great bare barrack of a church. His voice was weak and toneless. His face wasn't the face of a priest, and it took me some minutes to remember where and when I had seen faces like his before. Then I remembered. It was among young airmen during the war.

But the really extraordinary thing was that he was creating a congregation for himself out of his head. He was not celebrating a service for three reluctant women and two small girls who had merely been dragged in to see members of their family perform in a countryside where God was dead. He was celebrating it in a crowded church in some cathedral town of the Middle Ages. The hypnotic influence he exerted came from the fact that he had hypnotized himself. You saw it in his extraordinary recollection, in the way he managed to push those acolytes about without once letting go the spell. I wondered if I wasn't imagining it all. I looked at Géronte to see how he was taking it. He, whose usual response to a church service is like his response to a conducted tour, was half-kneeling, his eyes fixed on the priest as though he were some work of art which had to be sized up.

"This is one of the most wonderful things I've ever seen," he whispered without looking round.

The organist heard the whisper without understanding it. He was sitting back gloomily, his hand over his face. He bent across Géronte's arched back to whisper to me.

"I must apologize."

"Apologize for what?" I asked.

"This," he said with a wave of the hand. "I'm ashamed. Really, I'm ashamed."

"But of what?" I asked. "The Church of the Catacombs?"

"I beg your pardon?"

"The Church of the Catacombs."

He said nothing to that, and the service went on, disorderly, disconnected, ridiculous, but for the young priest who held it all together by some sort of inner power. What I felt then I have felt on other occasions, but it is hard to describe. I have felt it about a picture of a nun which has been standing before me for some days. I felt it about another picture, which I took in a Fever Hospital when a family whose child had died asked me to photograph the little body for them one summer morning in the mortuary chapel. The photographs I took were beautiful, but I could not live with them. In a peculiar way the positions had been reversed; the object had become the subject; the dead child had photographed the camera. It is the sudden reversal of situation which is familiar in dreams and which sooner or later happens to all of us and to the civilizations to which we belong. Bethlehem itself was merely an interesting object which the Roman Empire had studied with amusement, till suddenly it opened its eyes and the Roman Empire was no more.

The priest finished, went up to the altar, came down again with the cross in his arms and stood there patiently. It was only then that I realized that none of the congregation had attended the Stations of the Cross before, and that the only two people in the church who had were an Irish agnostic and a French atheist. "I can't stand this," I said to Géronte and pushed hastily out past him and the organist. As I went up the nave the priest signaled to the three women. While I stood aside and waited for them to kiss the cross, I suddenly heard the steps behind me. "Iconoclast!" I thought. "Whatever would they say of us in Ireland." But when I turned, I saw that the man behind me was not Géronte but the organist. "So all De Maupassant's people are not like that!" I thought.

After the service we chatted for a while with the young priest. There was nothing remarkable about him; we hadn't expected it. The young organist was the bigger man. To him we said good-by outside the church: it was getting late and we wanted to reach Beauvais before dark.

"You know," he said with sudden emotion as we shook hands, "I thought that service hideous till I suddenly saw it through the eyes of you and your friend. Then I realized how beautiful it was. Perhaps that is conversion."

"Let's be honest," I said. "It's not conversion for me." My French would not rise to an explanation of what it really was.

"I'm younger than you," he replied gravely. "For me, perhaps, it is complete conversion."

"I hope so," I said, and Géronte and I plugged on our way to Beauvais.

Ireland

David Greene spoke of O'Connor's "zeal for Ireland, the real Ireland. Not for pietistic frauds, nor for businessmen with an eye to the main chance, nor for pop-song singers: all those he hated, and they repaid him with their hatred. . . . His love of Ireland began with the land itself, sea and shore, lake and forest: his denunciations of modern despoilers re-echoed the lament for the woods of Cill Chais, which he himself had translated so beautifully.

It was greater still for the works of man in this island, whether the pre-Christian sculptures of the Armagh region, or Ballintubber Abbey, or the Georgian houses of Dublin; nobody knew better than he how little the storms of the centuries have left us, how uncertain our grasp on civilisation" (Michael/Frank, 137). This panoramic 1949 article displays O'Connor's scope—topographical, cultural, archaeological, architectural, historical. His thorough affection for his subject jostles against anger at Irish provincialism, neglect, violence, poverty. His criticism—alerting Holiday's readers to the truth beneath clichés about the Emerald Isle—was at odds with the inviting photographs accompanying the text. This juxtaposition upset some Irish-American readers, who blasted him in letters to the editor as "detrimental to the Irish race," "a well-paid enemy opportunist eager to smear our priceless heritage," writing with a "poison pen." Had they read past his acerbic comments on poverty, dirt, and bureaucracy to his statement, "At any rate I am not tempted to live anywhere else"?

If you could see Ireland from a height at which airplanes don't fly and people don't see, you would notice a shape rather like that of a fat baby sitting with its back to England and its arms outstretched in an attitude of supplication to America: a rather moist baby, visible only between showers. Coming closer, you would see the baby's shape dissolve into that of an irregular-looking plate, flat at the center, with a rim of mountains about it. The plain would be deep green to the east and south, pale gray to the west where the rocks stuck up through it, and brown across the northern midlands where a great portion of the land was bog. You would notice that its only built-up areas were five seaports, and that only one of these was seriously blurred by factory smoke, and that one Belfast, which the British carving up of Ireland has left part of a different state. You would assume that you were looking at a rather poor country, and you would be dead right.

Starting, as you must, at one of these seaport towns, you will find that as well as some handsome 18th-Century buildings, Ireland contains slums you have not seen the like of elsewhere in Europe, with sickly-looking children playing barefoot in the streets. As you travel you will see that the towns are thinly spaced, have little industry or none, and no reason for existence except fair or market days when farmers come in with cattle, or with butter and eggs, our main exports; that the villages are mere hamlets and the old parish churches all in ruin. There will be occasional handsome country houses, but many of these will be gutted, and most of the remainder in various stages of decay. The treeless landscape will be broken up by an extraordinary, and indeed, incomprehensible, network of roads and lanes; and along each of these in a sort of rural ribbon development, a couple of cottages will have sprung up, well apart from their neighbors, without electricity, gas, water, plumbing and probably without a school, church, dance hall or social meeting place within miles of them. In such a landscape public services like transport and telephones will be a nightmare.

There is considerable, and sometimes dreadful poverty. The simplest way of describing the basic poverty is to record that the old-age pension of one dollar weekly introduced during my own boyhood at once turned people like my grandmother, who might otherwise have been destined to die in the workhouse, into independent members of the household who could not only pay for their own modest keep but have a few pence each week for tobacco or snuff. The pension has been doubled, but it still remains an accurate index of living standards.

The standard of life is low. The main food of the poorer classes is bread and tea with potatoes and an occasional egg or sausage. In a country so badly laid out, water—though rain is the most plentiful of commodities—is scarce, and dirt is common and difficult to fight. Two medical reports from Galway and Mayo which I analyzed some time ago show that the medical officers in both counties had to face outbreaks of typhus. Typhus is mainly caused by dirt, and of 535 Galway children examined 289 had dirty heads, 200 dirty bodies. In Mayo, of the same number, 203 had dirty heads and 119 dirty bodies.

The educational system inflicted upon these unfortunate children does little to help them, since it is mainly concerned with the revival of the Irish language. Teachers who did not know the language had been compelled to learn it and teach through it children who did not know it either, and the result has been a scandalous decline in general standards of literacy. In a modified form, the same principle is applied to all public appointments, since Mr. De Valera laid it down that if two doctors apply for a position, the Irish-speaking doctor is to be given preference, even though his qualifications may be inferior—that is to say, human life is less important than the Irish language. But Mr. De Valera was scornful of the merely "real" and "useful" and told us that "spiritual interests are more important than material interests." (In private he was also credited with saying that "the great difference between England and Ireland is that in England you can say what you like provided you do the right thing; in Ireland, you can do what you like provided you say the right thing.")

This "revived" Irish, pumped out by the Abbey Theatre, the radio and civil service, is a very bad joke. Street names and names of institutions all appear in Irish, and as there are no Irish equivalents for many of these, only the poor foreigner is likely to be impressed. In Dublin, for instance, the Irish Sweepstakes advertise themselves as "The Little Sweeping Brushes of the Hospitals of Ireland," while Beresford Place is renamed "The Place of the Ford of the Berries."

Continuous emigration, the feeling that people are fighting a losing battle, induces a feeling of despondency. Over a hundred years, most of the emigration has been to America. The Irish population of America is roughly five times that of the total population of Ireland, and you will discover that people of certain districts still continue to emigrate to the same districts of America where their great-grandfathers settled first, and that the Irish connections will be of the deepest kind. One priest I know in County Clare went to the last Eucharistic Congress in America, where for the first time in its history the whole family assembled. His elder brothers and sisters had settled in America before he was born.

Of the groups which make up the bulk of the middle classes: priests, doctors, solicitors, teachers, shopkeepers and civil servants, the first are all-powerful.

The supremacy of the Catholic priest in Southern Ireland is the result of historical circumstances which for hundreds of years made him the only cultured person in a country parish and the man to whom the people naturally turned for leadership.

When he uses that power wisely he can still achieve miracles, like the late parish priest of Portumna, in County Galway, who cleaned up that squalid little town until it was as bright, clean and enterprising as any in Denmark. Too often, he seems to use it unwisely in the suppression of perfectly innocent social activities like dancing and amateur theatricals, because it is not only poverty and bad social conditions that cause people to emigrate; often it is sheer dullness and unnecessary regimentation.

Once when I was a librarian, organizing village libraries through the country, I tried to start one in a remote town. I had the support of the curate, a splendid young fellow who had graduated from Columbia University, in New York; night after night he went to the carpentry classes in the hope of coaxing the idlers of the town to do the same; but the curate had little hope of my success. The parish priest would forbid it. "You'll find him there," the curate said despondently, "with his dinner gone cold on the table and a volume of Aquinas in front of him, and between you and me and the wall, Mr. O'Connor," he added furiously, "Saint Thomas Aquinas was an ould cod." The curate was right about the dinner, the Aquinas and the library. The old priest, however, was delightful. He was a friend of George Moore's and had at least one presentation volume of Moore's stories; but libraries were a different thing. I was intensely sorry for the curate.

Infanticide in Ireland is appallingly common, though almost from the moment a girl starts walking out with a boy she is kept under observations by the police; if she leaves the neighborhood she is shadowed and if she has a baby in another area, the police return and spread the news throughout her own town. Yet it never seems to have occurred to anybody that there is any other way of stopping the crime.

Southern Ireland is a Catholic state. Protestants are not permitted to divorce one another, to practise or advocate birth control, to become public librarians or to read most modern literature. Northern Ireland, though Britain allows it only a limited self-government, is a Protestant state of an even more intransigent kind, and there Catholics have small hope of *any* public positions. The position was neatly summed up by an American who said that "Southern Ireland contained the finest Catholics in the world; Northern Ireland the finest Protestants in the world— rottenest lot of Christians I've ever met!"

A few months ago I traveled to Belfast with an English businessman who had bought a house here. In some ways he was very pleased with his bargain: there was no trace of hostility to Englishmen; taxation was low, labor and service were cheap. He had a gardener six days a week, without half-holidays, for £2.8. Yet at the same time he found it depressing, cut off by the ignorance of and indifference to, the outside world. "For instance, my gardener," he said, "he's been taught Irish at school, but he's never heard of Czechoslovakia. At home I could go out and talk about the day's news with my gardener." Then he realized what he was saying and grinned. "Of course," he added, "if he hadn't been taught Irish he wouldn't work for £2.8 a week."

Much of this is due to historical circumstances which have already changed or are changing. Unfortunately, the history is largely unreadable, being based on partisan passions. The English myth is that in the 12th Century the Irish were rescued from barbarism by the Norman invasion and have displayed disgraceful ingratitude. The Irish myth was best summarized by a speaker at a political meeting who said that "the greatest civilization the world had ever known was destroyed in the 17th Century by English barbarians."

Nowhere is the racial myth so strong as in Ireland, where you will be solemnly told that all Kerrymen are crafty, all Carlowmen proud, all Leixmen "poor, proud *and* beggarly." I once traveled on the little train between Birr and Roscrea with a thin Roscreaman and a fat Nenaghman. The thin man congratulated the other on living in a really civilized town like Nenagh, but the fat man was not so enthusiastic as you'd expect.

"Ah," sighed the thin man, "the people of Nenagh have one great advantage over the Roscrea people. I can say it because I'm a Roscreaman myself. They're more polite. Roscrea people are very bad-mannered."

"Oh, they are, they are!" exclaimed two girls, also from Roscrea.

"Ah, I dunno is there any difference," the fat man said.

"The Roscrea people are too fond of the money," sighed the other.

"Would you tell me where they aren't?" asked the fat man.

"Ah, well, that might be, too," said the thin man, "but anyway they're more polite. On a fair day in Roscrea a man would have no place to leave his beast, but any shopkeeper in Nenagh would oblige you with the use of his yard."

"He'd oblige you with the use of anything that would bring him custom."

"Even so, even so," said the thin man mournfully, " 'tis more polite."

The highly-civilized Normans, like the highly-civilized Irish, are a historical myth rather like the Roscreamen and the Nenaghmen. Irish and Normans were both Western Europeans, deriving such cultural life as they possessed from the same source. Left to itself Ireland would have developed like any other European country; like Holland or like Denmark. That she did not is due to the fact that the Norman invasion started seven hundred years of intermittent warfare which gave little chance to civilizing on either side.

That is the story behind the monuments which you will see on every hand. If you begin with the Boyne Valley, some thirty miles north of Dublin, you will really begin at the beginning, for this is the High King's country, the country of the early sagas and of the great prehistoric monuments. Along and near it are the early monasteries of Kells (which gave its name to what has been described as "the most beautiful book in the world") and of Monasterboice, which have little to show now but their high carved crosses.

Tara, the seat of the Irish kingship, is now but a lonely grass-covered mound on the road out of Dublin. Its cemetery has fared better. From the charming little village of Slane a winding, hilly road leads to the bank of the Boyne River and the three great tumuli, burial places of the kings of Tara. New Grange, the most sacred spot in Irish mythology, is a vast artificial hill, now covered in grass and bushes, with a long passage of carved stones through its depths, where it opened out into a great vaulted burial chamber, long since rifled.

The sagas of New Grange and the king-gods who were buried there were all written down by monks in places like Kells and Monasterboice. From the remarkable literature of the period, we can form a very clear idea of the lives of hermits and monks. In poem after poem, they describe themselves for us with extraordinary vividness, copying manuscripts in the woods, leaving their huts to see the skylark, "his beak stretched wide against the cloudy, colorless sky."

Another poem, reminding us how people watched the moon rise over London and rejoiced that the German bombers would be grounded, evokes the pirates' roars in this quiet valley during the 9th Century; the little oratories roaring to heaven and the monks screaming with the Viking knives at their throats:

> Tonight at least the wind is high,
> The seas' white mane a fury;
> I need not fear the hordes of hell
> Crossing the Irish Channel.

Here you can trace for yourself the evolution of early Ireland, the early period by the tiny little hermitage oratories, the Viking periods and after, by the cathedral and the round tower with its doorway significantly raised some twelve feet from the ground so that the occupants could drag up their ladder; the growing peace and civilization of the 12th Century by the ornamented quire and north door of the cathedral (what remains of it) and the exquisite little church of the Holy Savior, a half mile down the stream, with the red pine trees shadowing the ruin of its tiny quire.

But to see that civilization at its best, you must go to Cashel, in Tipperary County, and as every visitor must go there anyhow, you may as well go quietly. It is a pleasant little town in the central plain, and Ryan's Hotel is good; it has a small Georgian cathedral and a fine Bishop's Palace, now the Deanery. But the great thing about Cashel is St. Patrick's Rock, which soars far above the roofs of the main street with its 10th Century round tower, 12th Century chapel and 13th Century cathedral, a great gray mass of rock and wall and tower heaped above the colored street and in certain lights more like some great theatrical decor. In 1134, Cormac MacCarthy, king of Munster, and one of the leaders of the Irish reformation, built the exquisite little chapel which bears his name.

The cathedral is still a beautiful church, aisleless, with a raised quire, a soaring chancel arch and lancet windows with beautiful dripstones. But it cannot bear comparison with Cormac's Chapel, probably the most beautiful building in Ireland, a tiny thing with a gemlike perfection of craftsmanship.

This and Mellifont Abbey (now wiped out) were the great monuments of the Irish 12th Century, but between the building of Mellifont in the first half of the century and that of its daughter houses at the very end of it is a gap of fifty years, filled with the clamor of armies. The Irish went down before the great Norman military machine, and the invaders secured a comfortable bridgehead from which they were never afterward dislodged. To understand the mischief they created we must remember that though the Irish would have been glad to accept an English king and English law they were never permitted to, because the Normans intended to conquer every inch of Irish territory and this never became possible until Tudor times. As well as that, the Irish Normans, unlike the English Normans, had no king of their own and were subject to government from London, so that Ireland was forced into a disastrous step-by-step policy in relation to England. Thus, when a complete conquest of Ireland at last became possible, England had itself become Protestant, and this involved a new conquest, not only of the remaining Irish principalities but of the Norman earldoms which had remained Catholic. There was actually no point at which anyone could say, "Now the Conquest is over; now we shall begin to rebuild the country on our own lines."

If Cashel represents Irish Ireland, Kilkenny, for a long time the capital of the English bridgehead, represents Norman Ireland, town and country. With its beautiful river, its well-tended fields where the battlements of some abbey tower rise in the blue mist, the Kilkenny countryside is a still unspoiled 13th Century landscape. You can imagine it as a setting for Canterbury Tales. The city itself must once have been ravishing. There are moments when it still is so, as when you come down the river bank on a Sunday morning, and the pigeon-gray cathedral standing on a rock outside the town sends out its muffled chimes, while ahead of you you see a panorama of towers without realizing how many ruins lie below them.

All through the 14th Century the Irish fought, and architecture of the period is uncommon, but by the 15th Century England was so busy with her own civil wars that she had no time to spare for conquest, and there was a tremendous revival of the arts.

Then came the Reformation, and a new conquest of Irish and Anglo-Irish alike under which the country shuddered for a hundred years. The devastation of this period is almost beyond belief. And no sooner had the people begun to recover a little than came the Cromwellian conquest with its mass massacres and the establishment of a ruling class which was to plague the country until the end of the 19th Century—the Whig Ascendancy, puritanical, bigoted, irresponsible and ruthless.

And at last there was peace, even if it was only the peace of Belsen and Buchenwald. In France, Spain, Austria, even in Russia, the exiled Irish soldiers won fame and titles while at home they were little better than outlaws. They could not inherit property, could not purchase land, lend on mortgage, or take a lease of more than thirty-one years; they could not hold office in the state, the corporations or the army, nor vote, nor sit on juries; nor practice law; nor possess a horse worth more than £5. In Kilcrea churchyard in my native county of Cork there is an epitaph (inconceivable elsewhere, since it so completely expresses the Irish ideal of manhood) on "Art O'Leary, generous, handsome, brave." The story of that grave tells us all we need to know of Ireland in the 18th Century.

In the year 1768, a young woman called Eileen O'Connell, daughter of a great Irish family reduced to smuggling, was staying with her sister, Maire, married to a man named James Baldwin of Kilnamartyr, near Macroom. Visiting in Macroom, Eileen saw a fine-looking man ride in on a brown mare. She asked who it was and her sister told her it was Art O'Leary, the outlaw. "That's the man I'll marry," she said, and in spite of the opposition of her family, she did.

O'Leary was one of the Irish aristocrats, an ex-officer of the Austrian army. One day he was approached by a Cromwellian planter named Abraham Morris, who offered him the legal sum of £5 for his mare. O'Leary responded to the insult with a blow, and was formally out-lawed. When the English troops came for him, O'Leary defended himself in his home, and Eileen loaded his guns. Finally, when one day he was in the town of Millstreet, Morris went for a posse of soldiers, followed him out of town, and attacked and killed him in Carriganimma. O'Leary's mare returned to the house, and Eileen mounted her and was led to the spot where her husband lay dead:

> By a little furze bush
> Without priest or bishop,
> One prayer to whisper,
> But an old, old woman
> And her cloak about you,

> Art O'Leary,
> While your life-blood stiffened
> The white shirt on you.

So she wrote in the mighty lament which she composed and chanted over him as he lay in her sister's house in Kilnamartyr, a poem which has become a classic of modern Irish. We can still imagine her, her arms lifted, as she wept and cursed. James Baldwin, in terror, had surrendered the dead man's mare to Abraham Morris and she cursed both him and Morris:

> Grief on you, Morris!
> Heart's blood and bowels' blood;
> May your eyes go blind
> And your knees be broken!
> You killed my darling,
> And no man in Ireland
> Will fire the shot at you.

Her curse came home. O'Leary's brother, haunting the Cork street where Morris had rooms, at last saw his shadow on the blind and shot at him before he too fled to the Continent.

It is the history of every great Irish family, and it is not mere history, as you will soon discover if you spend any time in the little country cottages, but burned deep into the racial memory of the people. That great poem of Eileen O'Connell, whose nephew, Daniel O'Connell, the Liberator, was to emancipate Catholics in Ireland, is still remembered about Macroom, even to little details of Art O'Leary's gallantries and Eileen O'Connell's jealousy.

One evening I sat in a Longford cottage with a very old man who described the adventures of an ancestor of his own, by the name O'Reilly, in the late 18th Century. That 18th Century O'Reilly, when the Protestants of Ballinya refused to let Catholics buy or sell in the town, gathered a few friends and fought the Protestants to a finish in the streets. "Then he took ship for France. He married a lady of title and property in the Isle of France—the Isle of France, that's what Grandfather used to call it. He beat off Wellington's army on the heights over old Saragossa. When he was old and doddering he disappeared from home. They found him in a seaport town, looking for a ship, and when they brought him back he cried like a child. 'I want to go back to Ballinya,' he said, 'I want to go back to Ballinya.' " God alone knows what echo of a letter from some aristocratic French home is contained in that account of O'Reilly's last days which I picked up in a Midland cabin.

Meanwhile, the Protestant Ascendancy which had driven such men into outlawry and exile was beginning to build. Towns and great country houses grew up. Their greatest monument is Dublin, a perfect 18th Century city, with masterpieces of European architecture like the wonderful little Casino at Clontarf, or the superb Houses of Parliament (now the Bank of Ireland), after Cormac's Chapel probably the finest Irish public building. "Not a bowshot from the College, half the globe from wit and knowledge," growled old Jonathan Swift, who had no love for the Whig Ascendancy.

Swift is the greatest figure of 18th Century Dublin, indeed, of Dublin, *tout court,* the first important figure to face up to the fact that England was attempting to make the Norman Conquest a continuous process. He is buried in his own cathedral of St. Patrick's beside Stella, the English girl who accompanied him to Ireland, under what Yeats has described as "the greatest epitaph in history."

This poker-faced practical joker with the plump, pompous clerical cheeks which never lost their air of gravity, had a secret terror which caused him, in his own revealing phrase, to "fly from the spleen to the world's end." His mother's foolish marriage and his own early misfortunes had left him with an absolute horror of improvident matches, and it is clear that when he invited Stella to Ireland he had no intention of marrying her and told her so, and equally clear that Stella, womanlike, didn't believe a word of it.

The first thing she did was to try to make him jealous. She began a violent flirtation with a clergyman, one Billy Tisdall of Carrickfergus, and when Billy proposed, she artfully referred him to her "guardian," Swift, who promptly refused his consent on the grounds that neither she nor Tisdall had enough to marry on.

Then Tisdall inherited some money and wrote to Swift, again asking his consent, and this time accusing him of being in love with Stella himself. Instead of the thunderbolt he must have expected, he drew from Swift one of the most amazing letters ever written by one man to another. "I think I have said to you before that if my fortunes and humor served me to think of that state I should certainly among all the persons on earth make your choice, because I never saw that person whose conversation I entirely valued but hers; this is the utmost I ever gave way to."

It is addressed to Tisdall, but, of course, intended for Stella, and it called her little bluff. But Swift was now to meet the woman who would call his, and Esther Vanhomrigh, "Vanessa," was not to be fobbed off with his "conversation." She pursued him to Ireland, and faced him at last with the great tragedy of his life, the awakening in a woman of the passions he repressed in himself. "I fly from the spleen to the world's end, you run out of your way to meet it." She took to drink and died.

After her death Swift hurled himself into Irish politics, perhaps goaded by Stella, who had turned into a red-hot little rebel. He had already become involved in the Jacobite plots of Harley and St. John, but now he went far beyond them, and in doing so, fathered the Liberal movement of the generation which succeeded him.

Then Stella died. There are few things in literature so shattering as the memoir of Stella which he began while she lay dead in a Dublin lodging house. From his bedroom window (you can still stand there in the dusk and see what he saw) the lights in the cathedral aisle showed where workmen were opening the grave and he changed his room.

After that he posed as The Man Who Knew Women, the celibate sour grapes with the lavatory complex. But the irony of the last nationalist pamphlets is wonderful; as wonderful as the last quartets of Beethoven, these, too, filled with the utter loneliness of the deaf. It is irony which no longer hopes to achieve anything; irony for its own sake; a voice muttering to itself in an empty house at night. There is the *Modest Proposal* for the export of specially fattened Irish babies for the tables of the English who have already eaten the parents. There is *Certain Abuses,* in which he asks whether the feces about the Dublin streets can possibly be Irish, since the Irish, as everyone knows, have nothing to eat. It is an irony too profound, too searing, to raise a smile; you read, and suddenly find your eyes fill with tears.

Then the great tree died at the top. Now he sleeps by Stella "where savage indignation can lacerate his heart no more." "Timon hath built an everlasting mansion."

·   ·   ·

At the end of the 18th Century the Liberal Protestant movement which Swift had created, inspired by the American War of Independence and the French Revolution, led a rebellion which missed fire, and in which the unfortunate country people were massacred. One small French force landed at Ballina, and, joined by contingents of country people armed with pikes, fought its way to the midlands, where it surrendered and stood aside while its Irish auxiliaries were cut down. That, too, you will find very vivid in the racial memory. The same old Longford man who told me of the exploits of his ancestor in "Old Saragossa" gave me an astonishingly detailed description of it. Some of the Irish auxiliaries he described so vividly that I had to pull myself together and remind myself that it was his grandfather, not he, who had seen them. It was eerie, hearing the names of the traitors who stole the gun chains so that the guns had to be manhandled, and the description of the last stand of the Irish when the French had surrendered but the English had refused to accept surrender from the Irish.

"The Irish gunner was Gunner Magee. In the last stand a shell blew one wheel from under his gun. 'Ah,' he said, 'if only I could lift it—'tis charged—I'd fire it at the English.' Then two big Mayomen threw themselves down and lifted the gun on their backs, and he fired his last shot. The two Mayomen were dead. The explosion broke their backs. Gunner Magee was hanged. When the English put the rope around his neck, he threw back his head and laughed—Grandfather said it."

The first ray of light in modern Irish history came with Daniel O'Connell, Eileen's famous nephew. You can still see that ugly old house of theirs, Derrynane, on the edge of the Atlantic, with its caves where they hid the smuggled goods. He was educated in France, the only place a young Catholic could be educated, and returned to take up practice at the bar (though, as a Catholic, he could not hope to become counsel or judge) and to a long career of political agitation. When each organization he founded was suppressed, he patiently started another. He was the Catholic Irishman as a century of outlawry had fashioned him. His biographers all tell the famous story of the witness who declared that a testator "had life in him" when he signed a will. "You mean he had a fly in his mouth," roared O'Connell. He could tear holes in witnesses like that, because, in fact, that was the sort of mind he had himself, the outlaw's mind. When he later boasted there wasn't an Act of Parliament he couldn't drive a coach and four through, he implied that was what Acts of Parliaments were for.

Like every other virtuoso, O'Connell eventually became his own victim, and there is that sickening moment when he begins to sport with the crowd, to cock his hat at them and wink and roar, "Do yez like me, boys?" and we realize that the piano is now playing the pianist. But he found the Irish people slaves; he taught them the rudiments of political organization and agitation, and though modern historians decry his achievement in Catholic Emancipation, I doubt if the poor countryman of the 40's did.

He was followed by a man every bit as great and much more formidable, the half-Irish, half-American Charles Stewart Parnell. O'Connell had left him a rudimentary organization which he fashioned into an unsurpassable weapon for political agitation, and the British Government, shipping Irish men and women by the hundred thousand to America, obligingly furnished him with an invaluable ally: a public opinion which could neither be bribed nor coerced. Roughly speaking, it is true to say that Irish nationalism has moved step by step with the growing power of America, and that the final achievement of independence was an admission of American supremacy. This is important because, as we shall see, the policy of the present Irish government is based on it.

But without genius, public opinion would have had nothing to focus on, and Parnell, like Swift, is one of our few rockets; a man so great that he throws a brilliant light on ordinary people and invests with all the glamour of romance old feuds and tragedies on which the eye of history would scarcely have lit. While O'Connell had no detachment, Parnell's detachment was inhuman, and what others envied him he must have dreaded, and gone through life searching for a partner who could relieve him of that terrible solitude.

Meanwhile, Nature, preparing great tragedy, had ordained that the woman with that particular gift should be the wife of a brainless, unscrupulous ex-guardsman called O'Shea; and that to further Captain O'Shea's schemes for advancement, she should be obliging any gentleman in a position to help—not of course with the captain's connivance, for gentlemen do not sell their wives, though for a consideration they may overlook the liberties which other gentlemen take with them. So Captain O'Shea was never told in so many words that Parnell and his wife were lovers, and when Parnell was thrown into Kilmainham Gaol during Mrs. O'Shea's pregnancy each man believed the child to be his, and Parnell was distraught by hysterical letters from Mrs. O'Shea, whose husband, believing that she and he were reconciled, was asserting his rights.

No element of melodrama is missing. That the representative of the British Government who interviewed Parnell in prison should be O'Shea would be melodrama enough for any play; but that Parnell on parole should have to visit the O'Sheas while the child was dying and watch the other man receive the condolences of visitors, that to save Mrs. O'Shea from her husband's attentions he should give way to the British in negotiation, and that no sooner had he been released than whatever concessions he had gained should be immediately wiped out by the Phoenix park assassinations which followed like a thunder clap—that is almost beyond recognition.

O'Shea's British masters decided that the time had come for the destruction of Parnell. O'Shea brought proceedings for divorce, and Gladstone refused to negotiate further with an adulterer. Parnell's lieutenants, O'Brien, Dillon and Healy, deserted him. The last fight has the quality of a myth. One old woman I knew hung his portrait over her front door and never entered a church again. Yeats described the comet that appeared at Parnell's funeral; Joyce, in "Ivy Day in the Committee Room," the gloom and awe inspired even by the annual day of mourning for his death; Lennox Robinson the legend which sprang up that "the Chief" had not died at all, and would return one day to confound his enemies. No other Irish leader has ever evoked such passionate devotion.

The first literary effort of James Joyce was entitled *Et tu, Healy,* which shows exactly how the literary movement took up where Parnell left off.

Yeats was the first great native writer, and again, as a mere piece of critical judgment too often overlooked, America made him possible. From Goldsmith to Shaw, young Irishmen had drifted to London and accepted its standards; Yeats was the first to realize that a new English-speaking audience had arisen which made an Irish literature in English a possibility.

The Sligo of which he wrote is the most beautiful of West of Ireland counties; a little pocket of civilization in that great band of wild coast, shut in between the hills. But how much of it is Sligo and how much Yeats it would now be hard to say. A great poet impresses himself on a landscape like a phase of history. You stand on a hill overlooking the town and at once you find yourself murmuring, "The host is riding from Knocknarea" or "When first I saw her on Benbulben's side," and realize that you can never see it now but through Yeats's eyes. He is buried in the little churchyard of Drumcliffe under Benbulben with the epitaph he wrote for himself:

> Cast a cold eye
> On life, on death,
> Horseman, pass by.

Of all the men I have known there was none who cast a more eager eye on both life and death. He was a blazing enthusiast who into his seventies retained all the wonder and spontanaiety of seventeen; you never knew from month to month what the next frenzy would be. In his earlier, revolutionary days, he wanted the secret society he belonged to to steal the Coronation Stone from Westminster Abbey; in his later, Fascist phase, he wanted the Blueshirts to rebuild Tara and transfer the seat of government. His neighbors, who he thought were Blueshirts, kept a dog. Mrs. Yeats, who was a democrat, kept hens. The Fascist dog worried the democratic hens. One day Mrs. Yeats' favorite hen disappeared and she complained to her neighbors of the dog. By return came a polite note to say that the dog had been destroyed. Yeats was delighted. This showed the true Fascist spirit; but Mrs. Yeats, who was fond of animals, was very depressed. Then one evening Yeats came to me bubbling with glee. The democratic hen had turned up safe and sound and Mrs. Yeats was conscience-stricken. Another victory over the democracies!

When I became a director of the Abbey Theatre it was already in decline and within a year or two of his death had sunk to the level of a provincial variety theater. In its early days it had concentrated on plays of poetic quality, and the style of acting had been the old Senecan convention of the university plays: everything sacrificed to the words, nobody moving while an actor spoke, no speaker interrupted by stage "business." The words were delivered in the same simple, almost monotonous way—"Homer's Way," according to Yeats; and when some American lady asked how he knew that, Yeats replied, "The ability of the man justifies the presumption."

The disilllusionment of the Civil War had produced a whole generation of writers—O'Casey, O'Flaherty, O'Faoláin—who were realists rather than poets, and I hoped for a corresponding theatre style. We did a very fine performance of *The Playboy of the Western World* in that style. Yeats was furious, and we agreed to a revival in the traditional style.

The Playboy, you may remember, opens in a country public house after dark, and when the curtain rose, the stage was lit with a battery of amber lights which reduced it to an apparent depth of six feet. A couple of men came on with a lantern and I waited anxiously for the lighting to change. It didn't. Pegeen Mike lit a candle. It didn't change. She quenched the lamp. It had no effect. Finally, Christy blew out the last conceivable source of illumination and the stage continued to look like a fireworks display. Yeats thought it a fine production but I remembered Pascal's remark about tradition: "We think we are shutting in the daylight; we are merely shutting in the dark."

·   ·   ·

The Revolution and Civil War which produced that change might almost be described as an accident. In Elizabethan times the Irish population had been practically expelled from four of the Ulster counties, and their lands settled by people of Scotch Protestant stock. When, in 1914, Britain passed an act granting Ireland a small measure of self-government, the Ulster Unionists revived, formed themselves into an army and imported arms from Germany. The Southern Irish did the same. In 1916 a few hundred of these Southern Irish Volunteers rebelled, seized a few public buildings and within a week were rounded up and their leaders executed.

The executions were fatal. In the Irish, as in the Jews, one injustice wakes the memory of thousands. Overnight the "rebels" became national heroes, and Ireland elected a "rebel" parliament which decided to abstain from attending Westminster and establish itself at home. The British retorted with raids and arrests, and some of the hunted men shot back, no longer caring for flags or uniforms, so that quite accidentally, without anybody's planning it that way, the whole struggle resolved itself into a form of gang warfare, a battle between two secret services fought without mercy in back streets and lodging houses.

The Irish were incredibly fortunate in having an extraordinary leader in Michael Collins, "The Big Fellow," for Collins was simply a businessman of genius. As officer in charge of intelligence, Minister of Finance and anything else which came handy, Collins had offices all over the city, with typists and clerks, who in spite of raids, arrests and murders, worked office hours. Sharp at nine o'clock each morning, whatever sort of escapes he might have had during the night, he stamped down to his own office where his assistant, O'Reilly, had laid out the correspondence, stamped with the day's date and pinned to its envelopes. Collins went through every letter with a red pencil, numbering the paragraphs which had to be dealt with.

Then he dictated the replies, and went off to another office. The presence of those enormous files in which every detail of the revolution was recorded was a constant source of danger; the capture of even one of them might have meant the end of everything. Yet, literally, he may be said to have won the war merely by answering letters.

Collins was the most human of heroes; a tempestuous, blasphemous bully, and at heart the softest creature in the world, who loved old people, children and mothers, and—as his astonished biographer learned —liable on the least provocation to burst into floods of tears. The number of times friends of his put on a coy look when I pressed them as to what Collins did then, and murmured with a look of shame, "Well, he —er—he began to cry!" is known only to God and myself.

Collins signed the Treaty with Great Britain which gave Ireland self-government as a British dominion. This was the maximum Britain would concede and—what was even more important—that American public opinion would stand out for; and, inevitably, it provoked dissension, for by this time all the ghosts of all the centuries were walking. The burnt child had felt the fire again.

The most serious aspect of the Treaty was that it enabled six counties of Ulster to opt out. This partitioning of Ireland was naturally in Britain's interest since it secured bases on Irish soil, bases which during the Second World War proved to be indispensable in preserving the life line from America. In Southern Ireland, the presence of a British garrison on Irish soil fed suspicion; the cutting off of Ireland's one industrial region also made the economy of the country lopsided.

This plunged Ireland into a civil war in which Collins was killed. De Valera, the leader of the Republican opposition, gradually worked his way back by playing skillfully on the hostility to England, while his opponents, the Commonwealth Party, loyally but mistakenly tried to implement the Treaty and even planned to have George V crowned king in Ireland. Mr. De Valera, too, was responsible not for Irish neutrality in the Second World War, but for the form it took, which definitely favored Germany. Hundreds of thousands of young Irish men and women joined the British forces; you saw them every morning on the mailboat to Holyhead throwing open their overcoats as they got aboard and revealing uniform jackets. When they were killed in action their relatives were not allowed to announce the fact, and the *Irish Times* got away with one brilliant report of "a boating accident in the Mediterranean" which passed over the censor's head, but not over the heads of its readers. One lived in a permanent state of claustrophobia and, however bad the bombing elsewhere, it was always a relief to get out of the country. The remoteness induced by this period, combined with a certain feeling of guilt, is still there, and visitors are in danger of having it all explained to them at great length.

When America entered the war the position became fantastic, because America is the only foreign country to which the average Irishman has a feeling of loyalty. This was shown when James Dillon, dropping neutrality, demanded that Ireland should enter the war on America's side and, instead of losing votes, emerged at the end of the war as the biggest single figure in Irish politics. But even then the De Valera group kept their original line; Mr. De Valera condoled with the German ambassador on the death of Hitler and barred all celebration of the Allied victory. I arranged my own private celebration. I wrote a poem entitled *Fiacha and the Louth Men,* which I described as a translation from the Irish and which was supposed to deal with the overthrow of a horrid tyranny in County Louth in the 7th Century. This was submitted to the editor of the *Irish Times* as a poem for his magazine page, passed, and held in storage until Victory Day, when it appeared in place of the banned leader. A sub-editor had the brilliant idea of arranging the photographs of the Allied leaders in the shape of a V. To such shifts were we reduced.

The defeat of De Valera at the elections of 1948 made possible an inter-party government composed of extreme Republicans like Seán MacBride and extreme pro-Britishers like James Dillon. But the inter-party government had learned the lesson of Mr. De Valera's sixteen years of office and were determined that never again should he be allowed to exploit the hostility to England. They decided to go farther than he had dared and declare Ireland a republic. When he retorted by trying to flog up passions about Ulster they again went one better and have endeavored to secure official American support for a United Ireland. As I write, Mr. De Valera's party is talking of making war on Ulster. Britain—wisely I think—has decided that the Irish Republic shall not be treated as a foreign country; and it is highly probable that if suspicion and hatred could be put to sleep, the natural affinities between the two countries would get a chance. As for Ulster, possibly an American guaranty of the bases which Britain needs for safeguarding her food supplies, and of the liberties of the Ulster Protestants, would be the real solution of a problem.

Apart from this, inter-party government seems to have proved an unqualified success: for the first time since the establishment of the state there is real discussion of practical issues, and I, for one, hope I may never again live to see what is known as a "strong" government. It doesn't suit the Irish temperament.

.   .   .

If after that you ask me, "Is it a good country to live in?" I can only reply, "How could it be?" and then, after a moment's reflection, "Anyway, what matter?" It is a mess, and one which will take more than my lifetime to clear up, but it can be cleared up and is a job worth the doing.

At any rate I am not tempted to live anywhere else. Dublin, where I spend my days, is a beautiful city with the mountains behind it and the sea in front, and what more can a man ask? It has no industries to speak of, except beer and biscuits. It has the worst slums in Europe, which is what happens when you build a great aristocratic capital of four-story Georgian mansions without the industry to support it. (Families of six and seven people live in one room, with spindly-legged children dragging water up the great ruined staircases from the yard.)

Dublin has three newspapers, none of which publishes any news. It has one good restaurant and a line of good old Joycean hotels like the Dolphin and the Wicklow where the steaks and beer are excellent and the waiters get to know your life story in two evenings. It has two cathedrals, both Protestant, and two universities, one Protestant and one Catholic, but except that the Protestant one, Trinity, has the Book of Kells, there is little to choose between them. Catholics are debarred by their own archbishop from attending Trinity, but they attend just the same—probably they like looking at the Book of Kells. It has two theaters, one, the Gate, where they produce Continental and English plays; the other, the Abbey, where they produce Irish ones, or variety shows in Gaelic. The pubs are good and the company there is good, for they are filled with distinguished writers you have never heard of, since their works have never reached beyond the pubs.

I was once approached about a play composed by a writer friend, recently dead. Everybody, myself included, knew the play, plot and characters, but the manuscript seemed to be missing, and it was only after months that it dawned on us all that there never had been a manuscript; the masterpiece was purely oral and had died with its author.

It is a pleasant town in the sense that whether you have money or not, or whether you are famous or not, you can know everybody worth knowing, and everybody worth knowing will know you. If an attaché in one of the embassies wants me to meet some visitor and I am not at home, he can ring up my favorite teashop, and if the waitresses don't know where I am, the old man who sells papers at the corner of Grafton Street certainly will.

And except for the waitresses and busmen, they all call me by my Christian name! That is one of the few rigid conventions of a highly unconventional society. Dublin has never forgiven Yeats for not having allowed it to call him "Willie." I have long given up struggling against it, and even defend hotly a member of the new government who insists on his senior officials calling him "Seán." This is a convention that interpenetrates the whole of Irish life. Once in England a priest friend told me of another priest, an old man, who came to him in tears because their English bishop didn't like him and was about to get rid of him. "But why do you say that, Dan?" "Oh," groaned the old man, "he wrote me a terrible letter! A terrible letter!" "But what did he say?" "Oh, it isn't what he said so much as the way he said it—he began *Dear Murphy.*"

I knew exactly what the old priest felt, because in Ireland it is always the personal element that counts, the fact that there are people whom you call by their Christian names who will be prepared to help you in any difficulty. To live comfortably in Dublin you need to know a doctor who knows a specialist or two; a solicitor who knows a counsel; a Catholic priest; a man in each government department and a few men in the principal businesses, and you need to know them all by their Christian names.

As the American scholar Conrad Arensberg points out in the best book ever written on Ireland, *The Irish Countryman,* the whole of Irish life centers about this personal element. You don't buy in the best or cheapest shop. You buy from a shopkeeper with whom your family stands in that particular relationship; he marries a country girl and attracts other customers who stand in the same relationship with his wife's family, and when the relationship is exhausted, the business changes hands. The visible sign of the relationship is your debit balance. You pay money "off" the account, but you never pay off the account itself except as a declaration of war.

In the abstract, of course, it is a terrible system. All abstract considerations like justice, truth and personal integrity melt before it. Year after year the bishops denounce the sin of perjury, but it simply has no effect; the overriding element is always the personal relationship, and people simply do not regard perjury committed on that score as a sin at all. Lawyers tell me that the only place in Ireland where you can expect testimony that is not perjured is Wexford, which has a strong English racial backbone, but my own experience of Wexford was rather different. I was misguided enough to ask an old man the way (a thing you must never do unless you already know the way and are merely in search of copy).

"Are you married?" asked the old man in the way old men in Ireland have of plunging off at a tangent.

"I am not," I said with resignation.

"Don't ever marry a girl without feeling her first," said the old man firmly. "The parish priest will tell you differently, but priests have no experience. There was a man in a house near me that married a girl like that, and the first night they were together, whatever occasion he had of grabbing hold of her, he felt the child jump inside her. I would never marry a girl without feeling her first, and I would never give information about a neighbor."

"You're a man of high principles," said I.

"I am," said he. "There was another man living near me that got into trouble about a man that was shot. The police came and asked me questions about him but I put them astray. I never give information about a neighbor."

As I said, in the abstract it is a terrible system, but in practice it has enormous advantages, for real loneliness is very, very rare, and suicide so exceptional that it is always like a slap in the face for the whole community. An Irishman's friends have been very remiss if he ever achieves suicide.

The farther west you go, the stronger this personal element becomes, the weaker the abstraction of law. Sometimes, sitting in a country cottage, listening to the conversation, noting the stresses and the elaboration of personal implications, I have the feeling of listening to people speaking a foreign language. I know one Englishman who thinks the world begins and ends in a certain parish in Donegal, where, on Christmas Eve, the police politely sent up word to the pub where he was staying that they would have to raid it at eleven, and would the customers mind going across the fields to another pub which they wouldn't be raiding until half past eleven. So at eleven all the customers trooped over the fields in the darkness, and at half past eleven back they came after collecting the customers from the other pub, and at midnight the police solemnly retired to their barracks with the whisky thoughtfully supplied by the two publicans.

I notice it most of all in Donegal. Once, a friend and I walked too far and called at a village post office to inquire if there was a bus back. There was no bus—as you will have gathered, there rarely is—but the postmistress sent out a little girl to inquire if any car was leaving the village that evening. None was, so, in spite of our protests, she rang up the next village; no car was leaving that either. At this she proceeded to give the other postmistress a bit of her mind, and in what must have been an apologetic tone, the other suggested a third village from which MacGinley's car usually set out about that hour. But when, on ringing up, our postmistress discovered that MacGinley's car was broken, there was hell to pay. She immediately rang the police in the nearest town, and ordered them to stop the first car coming in our direction and tell the driver to pick us up. He did, too, and there was no damn nonsense about obliging anyone.

Once in a London hotel during the war, a young Belgian sea captain who sat beside me let his wife cut up his food for him. His hands lay almost dead on the table, like those of a corpse. "Frostbite," he said apologetically to me. When I sympathized he smiled and shrugged his shoulders. "Ah," he said, "I was lucky compared with my crew. We were torpedoed in mid-Atlantic in icy weather. The crew went off in the lifeboat and were picked up after four or five days by a destroyer and rushed to a hospital in England. The mate and I took the small boat; we were ten days at sea and then drifted ashore in a little place you wouldn't know, in the North of Ireland. They took us to the first cottage. The doctor would not let us be shifted to a hospital. He had us wrapped in blankets like mummies, and kept us there; the mate for six months, me for nine. He saved our lives. My crew will never walk again. The kindness of those Donegal people—I could never forget it."

The place he had drifted ashore was close to the spot where the postmistress had ordered the car for me.

There and in Connemara and Kerry, the love of poetry still lingers, and for those who like poetry, the first contact with a community among whom it is the natural and expected thing is overwhelming. "Ah," said one old woman to me of her husband, "he's old, and given to the poetry, and the thing he will say today is not the thing he will say tomorrow"—the most perfect description of the poetic temperament I know. It was nothing unusual when a drunken old tramp in Mayo who asked me if I knew Killeadan, and to whom I replied in the words of Raftery, drew himself erect and finished the quotation:

And if I could but stand in the heart of my people,
Old age would drop from me and youth would come back.

Nor was it unusual when one evening, as I was sitting in a Connemara cabin, writing down a rather tough love song from an adorable little girl of eight or nine, her old grandmother, aged over eighty, should come in and begin another song about a seduced girl, the very first lines of which brought tears to my eyes with their beauty.

Arise and put a fence about the field you spoiled last night;
If the cows get into the meadow, my sorrow on the grass!

I have it on the best authority that the fairies are dying out, but I cannot answer for that, having had no direct experience of them myself. The fairies, I am told, are the souls of those who die without the priest, and since motorcars came in there are few who die like that, so that the fairies are failing for lack of recruits. That is just as well, because they are not at all the sprightly and benevolent figures portrayed in books, and they are only called the "good" people for the same reason that the left hand or a dangerous sea is called "good" by other primitive peoples to avert the evil eye. They can only act vicariously through living people, and that is why, in most of the stories you will be told about them, they will always be trying to steal children or even grownups from their homes. You will be able to gauge for yourself how much belief in them remains by the quality of the stories told, for real Irish fairy stories are bloodcurdling and awe-inspiring. In the west of Ireland they still keep their original thrill.

Oh, yes, life in Ireland has considerable advantages! It has humanity, and poetry, and a sense of the past which is stronger than in any other part of the world I know. In the line of Gaelic poetry that Yeats most loved to quote, the 18th Century poet, O'Rahilly, cried:

"My fathers followed theirs before Christ was crucified."

Let me recount one further incident which haunts my memory, perhaps because I have never solved the mystery behind it. Once some friends and I saw from the road a handsome Georgian house among the trees. A certain lack of symmetry suggested to me that it was only a screen, and that behind it was an older manor house, so we went up the drive to see. Through the open window of a ground-floor room a Tibetan mastiff howled for somebody's blood—preferably ours.

We knocked and the door was opened by a pleasant elderly woman who invited us in. The hall was magnificent. After a while a timid elderly man appeared and agreed to let us look over the house, but first he had to put the mastiff away—"we keep him for protection." We enthusiastically agreed that the mastiff should be put away. There were obviously no servants. The two old people, brother and sister, were alone in this house and as frightened of us as we of the dog.

It was only after they had shown us the splendid paneled interior that it began to dawn on them that we had no intentions on their lives. Really, people were very nice! They had recently had a fire and the neighbors had come and helped to put it out! We introduced ourselves and they did the same. They bore a famous Norman name—let us call it De Courcy.

"You're here a long time then?"

"Oh, yes, since the Twelfth Century. The chapel is Twelfth Century. Perhaps you'd like to see it?"

They led the way across the avenue, and there, under the trees, was a ruined chapel. It made me more certain than ever that the place was a converted manor house. They kept the chapel beautifully; the floor cemented, a modern religious statue inside the door, a beautiful medieval Virgin and Child on the altar.

"You see," said the old man. "Twelfth Century."

"Fifteenth, surely," I said, looking at the details of the windows.

"Oh, I think not," he said, getting very rattled. "Father—said it was Twelfth Century. We found some tiles when we were cementing the floor. Perhaps you could tell from those."

He produced the tiles and they put my nose badly out of joint, because they were undoubtedly 12th Century. It emerged in conversation that the old couple owned no land but the little field behind the house. By this time they had begun to perceive that instead of plotting to murder them we were rapidly falling head and ears in love with them, and, growing more and more reckless, they insisted on our remaining for drinks. They began to think up other things to detain us. The dove house? Were we interested in dove houses?

"Or perhaps you'd like to see our courtyard?"

I nearly replied, "Would we hell!" A man who has made a fool of himself about a little thing like dating a chapel needs something to restore his confidence, and the courtyard proved conclusively that the house was an old manor house.

I could scarcely wait to get home to look it up. There it was in the reference books, all right; old manor house, reconstructed in the early 18th Century by some Cromwellian whose name you could chain a Bible to. But of the De Courcys not a word!

To this day I don't know what the story is; brother and sister with a Norman name, without land or servants, in a reconstructed manor house going back long before Cromwell. Are they the last of the original Norman owners? How on earth did the house come into the possession of these people and why did they want to own it?

I don't know, but I feel that if I did, it would make all this history unnecessary, because all Ireland would be in it. Its romance would be the romance of Irish history. No one who does not love the sense of the past should ever come near us; nobody who does, whatever our faults may be, should give us the hard word.

Works Cited

Works Cited

Blunt, Wilfred Scawen. *The Land War in Ireland*. London: Stephen Swift and Co., 1912.

Breit, Harvey. "Talk With Frank O'Connor." *New York Times Book Review*, 24 June 1951, 14.

———. *The Writer Observed*. Cleveland: World, 1956.

[Contains "Frank O'Connor," an interview-sketch of 24 Aug. 1952, 259–61.]

Cohn, Alan M., and Richard F. Peterson. "Frank O'Connor on Joyce and Lawrence: An Uncollected Text." *Journal of Modern Literature* 12, no. 2 (July 1985): 211–20.

[A 1937 broadcast.]

Cowley, Malcolm, ed. *Writers at Work: The Paris Review Interviews*. New York: Viking, 1959.

[Contains Anthony Whittier's fine interview of O'Connor, 161–82.]

Hildebidle, John. *Five Irish Writers: The Errand of Keeping Alive*. Cambridge, Mass.: Harvard Univ. Press, 1989.

[O'Connor and contemporaries: Liam O'Flaherty, Kate O'Brien, Elizabeth Bowen, Sean O'Faoláin, Mary Lavin.]

Kavanagh, Patrick. "Coloured Balloons: A Study of Frank O'Connor." *The Bell* 15 no. 3 (Dec. 1947) 11–21.

[Kavanagh's attack on O'Connor, "our most exciting writer," for being detached from the Irish "common earth." A vivid example of the enmity O'Connor faced at home, even from his colleagues.]

Kenner, Hugh. *A Colder Eye: The Modern Irish Writers*. New York: Knopf, 1983.

MacShiubhlaigh, Máire [Mary Walker], and Edward Kenny. *The Splendid Years: Recollections of M. Nic Shiubhlaigh*, as told to Edward Kenny. Dublin: James Duffy, 1955.

Matthews, James. *Voices*. New York: Atheneum, 1983.

[The only biography of O'Connor, to be approached with caution: detailed but consistently hostile.]

Mercier, Vivian. *The Irish Comic Tradition*. London: Oxford Univ. Press, 1969.

O'Connor, Frank. "Adventures in Translation." *The Journal of Irish Literature* 4, no. 1 (Jan. 1975): 158–63.

[Text of a Jan. 1962 BBC broadcast.]

———. *Bones of Contention*. New York: Macmillan, 1936.

[Contains "In the Train," "The Majesty of the Law," "Michael's Wife," "Orpheus and His Lute," "What's Wrong with the Country".]

———. "A Boy in Prison." *Life and Letters*, Aug. 1934: 525–35.

———. *Collected Stories*. Introduction by Richard Ellmann. New York: Knopf, 1981.

[More "selected" than "collected," it contains one-third of O'Connor's stories, including "First Confession," "The Little Mother," and "The Luceys."]

———. *Collection Three*. London: Macmillan: 1969.

[Contains "The Face of Evil," "A Minority," "Music When Soft Voices Die," "The Party," "Unapproved Route".]

———. "The Conversion." *Harper's Bazaar*, Mar. 1951, 160 +.

———. *The Cornet Player Who Betrayed Ireland*. Dublin: Poolbeg Press, 1981.

[An intriguing grouping of early and late uncollected stories with a fine introduction by his widow, Harriet Sheehy.]

———. "Darcy I Dtír NA NOG." ("Darcy in Tír na nÓg") In *Nuascealaiocht 1940–1950*, edited by Tomas de Bhaldraithe 24–32. Dublin: Sairseal agus Dill, 1952.

[Irish version.]

———. *Domestic Relations*. New York: Knopf, 1957.

[Contains "The Man of the World," "The Genius".]

———. "For a Two-Hundredth Birthday." *Harper's Bazaar*, Jan. 1956, 94 +.

———. "In Quest of Beer." *Holiday*, Jan. 1957, 72 +.

———. "Interior Voices."

[Thirty-five page typescript of a 1962 television broadcast, from the Harriet Sheehy Collection, now held by the University of Florida Libraries at Gainesville, Fla.]

———. *In the Train*. In *The Genius of the Irish Theater*, edited by Sylvan Barnet, Morton Berman, and William Burto, 248–61. New York: Mentor, 1960.

[O'Connor's dramatized version, in collaboration with Hugh Hunt, from 1937, revised for this volume.]

———. "Introduction." In *A Portrait of the Artist as a Young Man*, James Joyce, xv–xxi. New York: Time Reading Program, 1964.

———. "Ireland." *Holiday*, Dec. 1949, 34 +.

———. "James Joyce: A Post-Mortem." *The Bell* 5, no. 5 (5 Feb. 1943), 363–75.

———. "Joyce—The Third Period." *The Irish Statesman*, 12 Apr. 1930: 114–16.

—————. *Kings, Lords and Commons.* New York: Knopf, 1959.
[Contains "Kilcash," The Midnight Court, "The Lament for Art O'Leary".]
—————. *The Little Monasteries.* Dublin: Dolmen Press, 1963.
[Contains "I Am Stretched on Your Grave".]
—————. *The Lonely Voice: A Study of the Short Story.* Cleveland: World, 1962.
—————. "Meet Frank O'Connor." *The Bell* 16, no. 6 (6 Mar. 1951), 41–46.
[Interview by "The Bellman," Larry Morrow.]
—————. *The Mirror in the Roadway: A Study of the Modern Novel.* New York: Knopf, 1956.
—————. *More Stories by Frank O'Connor.* New York: Knopf, 1954.
[Contains the later text of "Guests of the Nation," and "Lonely Rock".]
—————. *My Father's Son.* New York: Knopf, 1969.
[The second volume of O'Connor's autobiography, assembled posthumously; it takes him to 1939.]
—————. *An Only Child.* New York: Knopf, 1961.
[The first volume of O'Connor's autobiography, ending with his release from the internment camp at twenty.]
—————. "The Rebel."
[Eight-page typescript from the Harriet Sheehy Collection, now held by the University of Florida Libraries at Gainesville, Fla.]
—————. *A Set of Variations.* New York: Knopf, 1969.
[Similar to Collection Three.]
—————. *A Short History of Irish Literature: A Backward Look.* New York: Capricorn Books, 1968.
[Contains "All the Olympians."]
—————. "Some Important Fall Authors Speak for Themselves." *New York Herald Tribune Book Review,* 12 Oct. 1952, 18.
—————. *Stories by Frank O'Connor.* New York: Vintage, 1956.
[Valuable for its foreword.]
—————. *The Stories of Frank O'Connor.* New York: Knopf, 1952.
[Contains "Author! Author!," "Old Fellows," "The Holy Door."]
—————. "Talk With the Author." *Newsweek,* 13 Mar. 1961: 98.
[Interview by William Flynn.]
—————. "A Walk in New York." *Holiday,* Nov. 1958, 60+.
—————. "W. B. Yeats." *Sunday Independent* (Dublin), 12 Sept. 1948, 4.
—————. "Why Don't You Write About America?" *Mademoiselle,* Apr. 1967, 148–49.
[Published as "An Opinion: Frank O'Connor on Writing about America."]
—————. "The Writer and the Welfare State: The Welfare State and I."
[A six-page typescript (with holograph emendations) of a talk given at a Copenhagen literary conference, 8–14 Sept. 1960, courtesy of Harriet Sheehy.]

———. "Writing a Story—One Man's Way." *The Listener*, 23 July 1959, 139–40.
[Text of a BBC broadcast of 24 June. Another version, ("One Man's Way") almost twice as long—perhaps the text not edited for broadcast—appears in The Journal of Irish Literature *special O'Connor issue edited by James Matthews 4, no. 1 (Jan. 1975): 151–57.]*

O'Faoláin, Sean. *The Short Story.* New York: Devin-Adair, 1964.

———. *Vive Moi!* Boston: Little, Brown, 1964.

———. "The Woman Who Married Clark Gable." *The Collected Stories of Sean O'Faoláin*, 423–28. Boston: Little, Brown, 1982.

Sheehy, Harriet. "Listening to Frank O'Connor." *Nation*, 28 Aug. 1967: 150–51.

Sheehy, Maurice, ed. *Michael/Frank: Studies on Frank O'Connor.* New York: Knopf, 1969.
[Essays by Thomas Flanagan, William Maxwell, Wallace Stegner, Eavan Boland, and others.]

Steinman, Michael. *Frank O'Connor at Work.* Syracuse, N.Y.: Syracuse Univ. Press, 1990.
[His creative process, as in "The Genius" and "Orpheus and His Lute" among other stories.]

———, ed. "Frank O'Connor Issue." *Twentieth Century Literature* 35, no. 3 (Fall 1990).
[Contains Richard B. Walsh's translation of "Darcy in Tír na nÓg," "Only Child," recollections and interviews of Harriet Sheehy, Thomas Flanagan, Eric Solomon, early unpublished O'Connor letters, essays, and Michael Longley's 1963 interview of O'Connor.]